A New War Begins

Four Fairgean attacked Isabeau at once and she fought them off with nothing but her fists and feet. She bashed two of their heads together, then twisted aside to avoid the thrust of a sword. Landing on her knees, she held out her hand and her staff of power flew to her across the square. She seized it and used it to hold off the warrior seeking to strike her. With a swift turn of the staff, she knocked him back with a blow to the jaw, and regained her feet. Swiftly she spun and kicked the fourth Fairgean in the stomach, then cracked her staff over his head so that he fell like a stone. She caught her breath and looked about her.

All over the garden the merrymakers were doing their best to fight off the sea-faeries. Some had grasped flaming brands out of the fire, or had seized a chair or candelabra to try and hold the Fairgean off, but the warriors were too well armed and well trained to be stopped for long. Gradually the humans were being overwhelmed. . . .

More praise for the *Witches of Eileanan* series

"An entertaining old-fashioned adventure."—*Locus*

"More depth and imagination than others in this field."
—Australian SF Online

"Kate Forsyth spices up a suitably complex power struggle with vividly depicted imagery and a worthy heroine."—*Romantic Times*

Also by Kate Forsyth

The Fathomless Caves

Book Six of the Witches of Eileanan

KATE FORSYTH

A ROC BOOK

ROC
Published by New American Library, a division of
Penguin Group (USA) Inc., 375 Hudson Street,
New York, New York 10014, USA
Penguin Group (Canada), 10 Alcorn Avenue, Toronto,
Ontario M4V 3B2, Canada (a division of Pearson Penguin Canada Inc.)
Penguin Books Ltd., 80 Strand, London WC2R 0RL, England
Penguin Ireland, 25 St. Stephen's Green, Dublin 2,
Ireland (a division of Penguin Books Ltd.)
Penguin Group (Australia), 250 Camberwell Road, Camberwell, Victoria 3124,
Australia (a division of Pearson Australia Group Pty. Ltd.)
Penguin Books India Pvt. Ltd., 11 Community Centre, Panchsheel Park,
New Delhi - 110 017, India
Penguin Group (NZ), cnr Airborne and Rosedale Roads, Albany,
Auckland 1310, New Zealand (a division of Pearson New Zealand Ltd.)
Penguin Books (South Africa) (Pty.) Ltd., 24 Sturdee Avenue,
Rosebank, Johannesburg 2196, South Africa

Penguin Books Ltd., Registered Offices:
80 Strand, London WC2R 0RL, England

Published by Roc, an imprint of New American Library, a division of Penguin
Group (USA) Inc. Previously published in an Arrow Book edition by Random House Australia Pty. Ltd.

First Roc Printing, November 2002
10 9 8 7 6

R⊙C REGISTERED TRADEMARK—MARCA REGISTRADA

Printed in the United States of America

For all those who died—stripped naked, shaved, shorn,
For all those who screamed in vain to the Great Goddess,
only to have their tongues ripped out by the root,
For all those who were pricked, racked, broken on the
wheel for the sins of their Inquisitors.
For all those whose beauty stirred their torturers to fury;
And for those whose ugliness did the same.
And for all those who were neither ugly nor beautiful, but
only women who would not submit.
For all those quick fingers, broken in the vise.
For all those soft arms, pulled from their sockets.
For all those budding breasts, ripped with hot pincers,
For all those midwives, killed merely for the sin of
delivering man to an imperfect world.
For all those witch-women, my sisters who breathed freer
as the flames took them,
knowing as they shed their female bodies,
the seared flesh falling like fruit in the flames,
that death alone would cleanse them of the sin for which
they died—
the sin of being born a woman who is more than the sum of
her parts

—Anonymous, sixteenth century
(Published in Erica Jong, *Witches*, 1981)

*1. Magic is the mother of eternity, and of the essence of all essences, for it makes itself by itself and is **understood** in the desire.*
2. It is nothing in itself but a will. . . .
5. Magic is spirit and being is its body. . . .
6. Magic is the most secret thing.

—Jakob Böhme, *Base des six points thésophiques*, 1620

CONTENTS

THE WEAVER'S SHUTTLE FLIES

Beltane Fires

T he soaring towers of Rhyssmadill were bright with the light of a thousand lanterns. They blazed from every window and were strung through the palace gardens like garlands of fiery flowers. Beneath their radiance, crowds of gaily dressed people talked and laughed as they watched the spectacular acrobatics of the jongleurs and listened to the minstrels. Many danced around the roaring bonfire in the center of the square, or sat at the long trestle tables, loaded with delicacies of all kinds.

The Merry May ale flowed freely. All were celebrating the victory in Tirsoilleir that had brought an end to the civil war that had troubled Eileanan for so long. No one needed to fear another invasion by the Bright Soldiers of Tirsoilleir, for Elfrida NicHilde had gladly sworn fealty to the Rìgh, Lachlan MacCuinn, after her restoration to the throne. For the first time in hundreds of years, all the lands of Eileanan were united and at peace.

As the two moons sailed higher in the starry sky, the dancing grew wilder, the cheering and stamping grew louder, the minstrels' songs grew bawdier and plates began to get broken. Brun the cluricaun amused the crowd with his antics, swinging from lantern pole to lantern pole, and playing his flute while hanging upside

down from the trees. Dide the Juggler walked on his
hands, juggling a spinning circle of golden balls with his
feet. He left a trail of broken leaves and twigs behind
him, for he had once again been chosen as the Green Man
of the Beltane feast and so wore leafy branches tied to
every limb. With his dark eyes alight with merriment and
his slim muscular body filled with vigor, he was the perfect choice as the embodiment of the life-force that
renewed the world in springtime.

Isabeau took a sip of goldensloe wine. From the corner of her eye she could see Dide dancing a spirited jig
with a pretty blonde girl as the crowd clapped and
laughed and cheered. Resolutely, Isabeau shifted in her
seat so that she could not see him. She had to remind herself quite forcibly that she had no time for dillydallying
with a fickle, volatile, unreliable jongleur, no matter how
handsome. She looked down at her right hand, a gleaming jewel on every finger, then lifted her head proudly,
raising the three fingers of her left hand to clasp the petrified owl talon that hung around her neck on a leather
thong.

The rings on Isabeau's right hand were not for mere
adornment, unlike the jewels at the throats and wrists of
the other women sitting at the high table. Like her tall
staff crowned with a perfect white crystal and her austere
white robe, the rings showed Isabeau to be a powerful
witch. Isabeau was one of the youngest witches in the
history of the Coven to have won all five of her elemental rings, yet she was hungry to go on and sit her Sorceress Test. She needed to focus all her will and desire upon
her studies if she hoped to master the High Magic, and no
black-eyed jongleur with a wicked grin was going to distract her from achieving that goal.

You-whoo gloomy-whoo? the little white owl sitting on the back of Isabeau's chair hooted anxiously.

"No' at all," Isabeau replied firmly and drained her goblet of goldensloe wine.

Despite the noise and merriment of the crowds, the company sitting at the high table did seem rather morose. The Rìgh was slouching on one elbow, a goblet grasped in one hand, his chin resting in the other. His glossy black wings were sunk low, his topaz-golden eyes heavy-lidded, his mouth set sullenly.

In contrast, his wife, Iseult, was sitting very straight, the goblet of wine before her untasted. She was dressed severely in white, her mass of red-gold curls was pulled back from her brow and hidden within a white snood, and she wore only two rings, a moonstone on her right hand, a dragoneye on her left hand. But unlike the plainness of Isabeau's white witch-robes, Iseult's austerity was a matter of choice. As the Banrìgh of Eileanan, Iseult could have been dressed as richly and gaily as any other lady at the Beltane feast. Her only adornment, however, was the clan brooch that clasped her snowy-white plaid about her shoulders.

The brooch was exactly the same as that which pinned together the white folds of Isabeau's plaid, a circle formed by the stylized shape of a dragon, rising from two single-petalled roses surrounded by thorns, for the two women seated side by side at the high table were twins, as alike as mirror images. If it was not for Isabeau's scarred and maimed left hand, and the staff and witch-rings that showed her status as a member of the Coven, a stranger could well have had difficulty in telling them apart.

The chill silence between the Rìgh and Banrìgh had affected the spirits of all the other lords and ladies at the royal table. Most had gone to seek more cheerful company on the dance floor or by the ale barrels. Elfrida NicHilde, who could not overcome her lifelong indoctrination against any kind of merrymaking, had gone to brood over her young son, Neil, sleeping upstairs in the nursery suite with the other children. Her husband, Iain MacFóghnan of Arran, had been drawn into a political argument with some of the other prionnsachan, while the ancient Keybearer of the Coven, Meghan NicCuinn, had sought her bed some time ago. There was only Isabeau, Iseult and Lachlan left, all of them somber and preoccupied.

Connor, the Rìgh's young squire, knelt by Lachlan's side with a crystal decanter of whiskey. "It is near midnight, Your Highness," he said respectfully as he once again refilled the Rìgh's goblet. Lachlan looked at him rather blankly, his eyes bloodshot. "It's time for the crowning o' the May Queen," Connor prompted, rising again and stepping back.

"O' course," Lachlan said, his words rather slurred. "The May Queen. How could I forget?" There was a slight trace of sarcasm in his voice and Isabeau felt her twin stiffen, drawing herself up even further. Isabeau roused herself from her own miserable thoughts to turn and look at her sister, but the Banrìgh's face was averted, her profile as cold and white as if carved from marble.

Lachlan leapt up onto the table, his black wings sweeping out and back so the movement was as swift and graceful as the soaring of an eagle. "My good people," he called, his voice ringing out across the tumult of laughter, chatter and music. Immediately everyone stilled and turned to face him, for Lachlan's voice had a rare magic in it, as compelling as the song of any sea-singer.

"It is Beltane Night, the night we celebrate the coming

o' summer and the passing o' winter. With the burning o' the Beltane fires, we drive away the darkness o' the dead months and beckon the golden gladness o' the growing months. This evening, our Beltane fires have even greater meaning, for we have left the darkness and dreadfulness o' war behind us and celebrate the dawning o' a new season o' peace and fruitfulness."

Cheering erupted everywhere. People clapped their hands, stamped their feet, called out ululations of approval. Lachlan held up his hand for silence and after a long moment, the noise died down again.

"As you know, spring is the time when Eà walks the world in her green mantle, flowers springing up in her footsteps. We like to celebrate May Day by crowning the bonniest lass we can find with a garland of flowers and draping her with a mantle of green, to praise and honor Eà, our mother. I think there can be very little doubt in any of our minds who should be crowned May Queen tonight." He paused once again, to allow the shouts and ribald suggestions to die down. "So I have great pleasure in calling upon . . . Brangaine NicSian to be our May Queen this even!"

Isabeau could not help a little start of surprise. This was not because the NicSian was not a young woman of uncommon beauty. Brangaine NicSian, the Banprionnsa of Siantan, had hair the color and texture of cornsilk, and eyes of clear emerald green. She was without question one of the most beautiful girls Isabeau had ever seen. It was just that Isabeau had expected Lachlan to name his wife as May Queen. Beltane was a night of great significance to Iseult and Lachlan. It was the night of their first loving, the night they had conceived their son, Donncan, now six years old.

There was no change in Iseult's expression, though her

fingers tightened a little on the stem of her goblet. The crowd was cheering and clapping, as a blushing, smiling Brangaine was led up to a flower-bedecked dais. Lachlan draped the green silken cloak about her shoulders and crowned her with a garland of pink roses and white hawthorn, before bending to kiss her cheek.

"I dinna realize Lachlan kent the NicSian so well," Isabeau said rather tentatively.

"Brangaine sailed back on the *Royal Stag* with us," Iseult said. "She can whistle the wind, ye ken. It is because o' her that we were able to get home from Tìrsoilleir so quickly."

As she spoke, a great roar went up from the crowd. Dide had somersaulted right across the bonfire, landing gracefully on one knee before the May Queen and kissing her hand reverently. He then delighted the crowd by pulling her down so he could kiss her hard on the mouth. As everyone cheered and whistled, he leapt to his feet again with a flourish of his green-feathered hat, allowing a flushed and dishevelled Brangaine to regain her seat.

The dancers all came together in great circles of whirling color about the tall maypole, which was decorated with leaves and flowers and long trailing ribbons in all the colors of the rainbow. The inner circle of dancers, all the prettiest girls at the feast, danced under each other's upraised arms, tying up the maypole till it was bound tightly within its cage of ribbons.

"She's very bonny, isn't she?" Isabeau said carefully.

Iseult smiled rather coldly. "Aye, indeed. Are ye worried my feelings are hurt? I could no' be May Queen every year. It would hardly be fair." She rose, Connor leaping to pull out her chair for her. "Would you excuse me? I'll just go up and check the children are sleeping.

Donncan has been having nightmares every night since he and Neil were kidnapped. He likes me to be near."

Although Isabeau nodded and smiled, it was an effort. All around her people were dancing and laughing, rejoicing in the end of a long and bloody war, but Isabeau could not shake off a heavy feeling of misery. She knew she was tired—knew she had gone beyond tiredness to bone-weariness, soul-sickness—but still it seemed she saw portents of trouble everywhere.

The last few months had been hard ones for her. Isabeau had strained her powers to their very limit, confronting and defeating the cruel sorceress Margrit NicFóghnan, who had kidnapped the young heir to the throne, Donncan, and his best friend, Neil, Margrit's own grandson. Margrit had hoped to murder Lachlan and rule Eileanan through Donncan, and it had taken all of Isabeau's wit and courage to rescue the boys and overcome Margrit. She had so overtaxed her strength that she had suffered sorcery sickness as a result, a dangerous illness that could lead to death or madness or the complete loss of one's magical powers. It was the second time she had succumbed to sorcery sickness in as many months. She felt limp as an old lettuce leaf.

Isabeau never enjoyed Beltane Night, anyway, though it was meant to be a celebration of life and love. The Rìgh and Banrìgh never failed to renew their bonds of passion on Beltane Night, the anniversary of their first joyous communion. Isabeau had strong psychic links with her twin sister. On Beltane, the tides of power turned as a new season began, and the psychic current that ran between Isabeau and her twin sister was stronger than ever. She felt pain if Iseult hurt herself, and she felt rapture when Iseult did, particularly if she was asleep and dreaming, all her defenses dissolved. So, every May Eve, Isabeau went to bed knowing she would dream of Lachlan's hands upon her body, Lachlan's silken black wings caressing her, his strong arms enfolding her.

Tonight, though, Isabeau would almost welcome sharing Iseult's joyous release. At least dreaming of Lachlan's mouth upon hers would drive away the nightmarish visions of slimy, webbed hands, curving yellow tusks, and long black hair streaming like seaweed, that every night rose up from the dark well of her unconscious.

Isabeau knew why she was haunted by these dreams. Only a few weeks ago, she had seen the bodies of drowned Fairgean rolling and bobbing about in the waves that curled upon the beach where she stood, their long hair undulating like kelp, their limp arms and legs swaying. The image was scorched upon her inner eye. She tasted the ash of her horror and revulsion upon her tongue every minute of every day.

It was not just the sight of the dead bodies that so troubled her. Isabeau had seen death before. And these corpses had been Fairgean, humankind's most bitter enemy. If those Fairgean warriors had seen her and Donncan and Neil, they would have had no hesitation in gleefully spitting them upon their tridents.

It was the manner of the sea-demons' death which tasted so foul. The Fairgean warriors had been killed by Maya the Ensorcellor and her six-year-old daughter, Bronwen.

Isabeau had helped bring Bronwen into the world. She had struggled to keep the little newborn babe alive, had cared for her and fed her and bathed her when her own mother had refused to even look at her. It was Isabeau who had helped Bronwen take her first unsteady step, Isabeau who had smiled and listened to her childish babbling, Isabeau who had taught Bronwen her letters and numbers. Isabeau loved Bronwen as if she herself had struggled and screamed to bring her, all blue and bloody, into the world. To know Bronwen had been taught to kill sickened her to the very depths of her being.

It had happened during their desperate flight from Margrit's stronghold, after Isabeau had managed to outwit the sorceress by swapping the wine in their goblets so that Margrit herself drank the poison she had meant for Isabeau. Sorely wounded and swooning with the sorcery sickness, Isabeau and the boys had taken refuge on a small island in the Muir Finn. In a coincidence too strange to be mere chance, the island proved to be the refuge of Maya the Ensorcellor, who had fled into exile after her failed attempt to win the throne for her daughter. Bronwen was Lachlan's young niece, the child of his dead brother Jaspar. Named as heir and successor, Bronwen had ruled for just one day before Lachlan had won the throne and the Lodestar for himself.

The Fairgean warriors had swum into the lagoon, seeking only to harvest the kelp that floated in the sea about the island. Although Maya was half Fairge herself, she was in as much danger from the warriors as Isabeau and the boys, for she had failed her father, the Fairgean king, in his plans to eradicate humankind once and for all. She feared the wrath of her father and the Priestesses of Jor as greatly as she feared that of Lachlan and the Coven of Witches. So she had taken up her clàrsach and commanded Bronwen to take up her flute, and together mother and daughter had sung the Fairgean warriors to death.

It did not help that Isabeau had taken Bronwen away from Maya. It did not help that Bronwen now slept peacefully in the royal nursery, as sweet-faced and innocent as the other children. Fairgean warriors still swam

through Isabeau's dreams every night, dragging her down
with their webbed hands, strangling her with their seaweed hair, drowning her.

Isabeau shivered and pulled her plaid up about her
neck, even though the night was balmy and the heat of
the Beltane bonfire had the dancers damp with perspira-
tion. She wished Meghan had not retired to her bed, or
that her old friend Lilanthe was there, to talk and laugh
with and distract her from her troubled thoughts. She
wished that Dide, her oldest friend of all, was not flirting
so outrageously with the newly crowned May Queen, the
prettiest girl Isabeau had ever seen.

Laughing wickedly, Dide was dancing and cavorting
all round the fire, scattering spring-green leaves behind
him. He had not been still since the dawn ceremony but
he showed no sign of weariness, leading the dancing in
an unruly procession that overturned tables and knocked
a tray of goblets flying. With a shout of joyous excitement, he flung himself over in a wild flurry of cartwheels,
flip-flops, lion-leaps, hand-springs, head-springs, sideways leaps and twists of every description that had the
crowd roaring. Brangaine leapt to her feet and clapped
enthusiastically, and Dide bowed and blew her a kiss.
When she blew him a kiss in return, he fell over backwards as if he had been felled by a blow, and lay on the
ground, his arms outstretched, his eyes shut, his chest
heaving.

Isabeau poured herself another goblet of wine.

All the other jongleurs were spurred on to new feats of
acrobatic grace and dexterity. Dide sat up and watched
them, occasionally jeering or applauding a particularly
deft somersault. Another pretty young girl came and tried
to drag him into a dance but he waved her away, pre-
tending he was swooning from exhaustion. Then he spied

Isabeau, sitting alone at the high table, the elf-owl Buba perched on the chair behind.

Isabeau sensed rather than saw Dide get up and make his way towards her. She turned her attention to the musicians, watching them play as if she had no greater desire in the world than to study their fingering. Then she felt him lean over her, his breath warm on her cheek and smelling strongly of ale.

"If it's no' my bonny Beau," he said. "Look at ye, in your witch-robes. And there's your wee owl. If I come too close, will she peck me again?"

"Probably," Isabeau answered, leaning away from him.

"Och, as cruel as ever, my lady," he answered mockingly. He bent and seized her hand and kissed it with an extravagant flourish of his green-feathered hat. "May I have the pleasure o' this dance?"

"No, thank ye," Isabeau replied coolly.

"Och, come and dance, Beau!" he cried. "Come on, ye've been sitting up here for hours like some auld grandam. A bonny lass like ye should be dancing."

"I'm quite comfortable where I am, thank you." Isabeau tried to draw her hand away, but Dide dragged her up to her feet, almost pulling her over in the process. He laughed, grabbing hold of her with both arms as he tried to regain his balance, and almost fell over again.

"Ye're drunk!" Isabeau said.

"I'm the Green Man, it's my job to be drunk," he retorted and tried to kiss her, getting a mouthful of hair in the attempt. "Come on, Beau, why so cold? Will ye no' dance with me?" He whirled her into the dancers, his arm sure about her waist, his hand holding hers firmly.

Isabeau's eyes flashed with angry fire. "I said I dinna want to dance!"

He spun her round. "Did ye?"

"Aye! Let me go!"

"No' likely! I havena seen ye in months! Years! The least ye can do is dance wi' me."

"Ye ken I canna dance," Isabeau protested. "Dide, ye're treading on my feet!"

He laughed. "No' as sure on my feet as I was twelve hours ago," he panted. "Och, what a day!"

"Ye seemed to be enjoying yourself." Despite all her best intentions, Isabeau could not help a note of pique in her voice.

He laughed at her and squeezed her waist. "Och, I have! I'd enjoy it even more if ye'd stop glaring at me and give me a kiss instead. Am I no' your auldest friend? Ye'd think I'd get a warmer greeting than this!"

"I think ye've had quite enough kisses for one day," Isabeau replied primly.

"No such thing as enough kisses," Dide replied. "Especially from ye, my bonny Beau."

He whirled her about so swiftly she had no breath to retort, and smiled down at her with great warmth in his eyes. "So much has happened since I last saw ye," he said. "How long has it been? Three years? I see ye are a witch now, just like ye wanted. Soon to be a sorceress, I hear."

She nodded, finding herself unaccountably tongue-tied.

"Congratulations," he said and bent his head to kiss her, his hand tightening upon her waist. Then the steps of the dance separated them. She was spun about by other arms, went from partner to partner all the way down the line. Isabeau could not help looking back over her shoulder. She met Dide's gaze, blushed hotly and looked away.

They met again at the head of the line. His arm slid

about her waist with great assurance, pulling her closer than the etiquette of the dance truly demanded.

"And I hear ye have been made an earl," Isabeau said lightly. "Who would have thought it, the little boy I played with in the stableyard now an earl with his own coat o' arms and a castle and everything."

He bowed with an extravagant flourish. "Didier Laverock, the earl of Caerlaverock, at your service, my lady." They parted with a bow and a curtsey, danced down the line and met again at the bottom. "I'm no' sure how I feel about it," he admitted. "I'm glad for my grandam's sake, though. She is auld now and badly crippled. I am glad she has somewhere comfortable to bide awhile. And who kens? Happen I'll tire o' the jongleur's life one day."

"Now that I doubt," Isabeau answered. The tune came to an end with a flourish of violins, and they all clapped and bowed to each other. Isabeau gathered up her long robe and stepped away, reminding herself that she was a witch of the Coven and not a silly young lass to be dazzled by a charming smile.

Dide caught her hand and halted her, seizing two cups of Merry May ale from a tray. "Nay, I canna be allowing ye to sit around and mope like a miserable auld maid! It's May Day and I be the Green Man! It is my beholden duty to allow no one to mope, especially a bonny wee lass like yourself. Drink! Drink!"

"Stop it, Dide!" Isabeau protested, almost choking as he poured the ale into her mouth. "I ken what ye're like! Ye're only trying to get me drunk so ye can have your evil way with me." She swallowed, coughing and spluttering.

He laughed at her, his black eyes sparkling. "Och, I do no' have to get ye drunk to do that!" he mocked, kissing her. It was the kiss of a lover, deep, long, ardent. Isabeau was ensnared, unable to break away. For a moment she heard only the beat of his heart against hers, felt only the surge of her own blood in response. Then she broke free, or he let her go, she did not know which. He kissed her again, his hand cupping her chin, and smiled down into her eyes. "See?"

She pulled away, chin raised proudly. He had her plait in his hand, his arm about her waist. He would have drawn her through the dancers to the shadowy garden beyond, but she pulled against his grasp. "I thought ye wanted to dance?" she cried and, laughing, ran back into the throng of dancers. He caught the edge of her robe and pulled her back, and she let him turn her so that his hands were on her waist again and she was laughing up into his very bright black eyes.

Suddenly screams rang out, screams of terror. The throng of dancers milled about, crying, "What's happened?"

There were cries of pain now, and high-pitched whistles and musical warbles. Isabeau froze, her stomach twisting. She had heard that high-pitched trilling before. It was clear Dide had too, for he went white. "Fairgean!" he cried. "But how . . ."

People began to try to struggle free of the crowd, panicking. The screams grew more frenzied, and Isabeau saw a woman run down the steps, blood pouring down the side of her frightened face. Suddenly she fell, and Isabeau saw a long trident protruding from her back. As if in slow motion, fascinated, she lifted her eyes. Tusked warriors stood at the top of the stairs. Their scaly skin glistened in the light of the lanterns, and their long black hair streamed down their backs, dripping wet. One bent and pulled the trident out of the woman's back, casually lifting it and throwing it down into the milling, screaming crowd. A man fell, and the frenzied crowd trampled him underfoot as they struggled to escape.

"I havena even got my daggers!" Dide cried. "Eà curse them! How did they get in? Rhyssmadill is meant to be impregnable . . ."

"They're all wet," Isabeau said. She was surprised at how calm her voice was.

"They must've found the underwater caves," Dide cried. "They've come up the well, curse their black blood!"

Isabeau nodded, sure this was the truth. So that was the explanation of her dreams! Why had she not heeded their warning?

The Fairgean warriors were coming down the stairs, methodically killing one dancer after another. None of the merrymakers had worn weapons so they were defenseless against the sea-faeries, who all carried steel daggers as well as their long tridents of sharpened coral. Body after body fell, blood pooling on the marble.

Dide darted forward and grasped two flaming brands out of the fire, spinning them in his hands. Two of the Fairgean came forward to grapple with him and he beat them off with dexterous thrusts and swipes of the torches.

"Run, ye fool!" he hissed at Isabeau.

She ignored him, conjuring a ball of flame and flinging it at one of the Fairgean warriors, who was about to cut a woman's throat. He fell, screaming and beating at the flames with his webbed hands. Isabeau took a deep breath, swallowed her nausea, and blasted another. She saw Brangaine crouched behind the shelter of an overturned table, her crown of roses askew, methodically knotting and unknotting her sash, while three Fairgean struggled to reach her through a wind that had come from nowhere. It picked them up and threw them across the square, slamming them into another group of Fairgean warriors and knocking them flying.

Brun the cluricaun caught a branch with his long tail and swung up into the trees, just avoiding being spitted on the cruelly sharp prongs of a trident. He crouched in the tree, gibbering with distress, as a woman at the foot of the tree was hacked to death by two of the scaly warriors.

Four Fairgean attacked Isabeau at once and she fought them off with nothing but her fists and feet, the elf-owl Buba raking at their faces with her talons. She bashed two of their heads together, then twisted aside to avoid the thrust of a trident. Landing on her knees, she held out her hand and her staff of power flew to her across the square. She seized it and used it to hold off the warrior seeking to strike her. With a swift turn of the staff, she knocked him back with a blow to the jaw, and regained her feet. Swiftly she spun and kicked the fourth Fairgean in the stomach, then cracked her staff over his head so that he fell like a stone. She caught her breath and looked about her.

All over the garden the merrymakers were doing their best to fight off the sea-faeries. Some had grasped flaming brands out of the fire, or had seized a chair or candelabra to try to hold the Fairgean off, but the warriors were too well armed and well trained to be stopped for long. Gradually the humans were being overwhelmed.

Then the palace guard came running up through the garden, their hauberks still unfastened. The archers knelt and fired a volley of arrows into the ranks of Fairgean, and the swordsmen ran forward to engage. Dide and Isabeau fought beside them, dragging weapons from the hands of the fallen, until at last the company of Fairgean warriors were all dead. No quarter had been offered or asked for.

All the time she had fought Isabeau had been sick with fear at the possible fate of her loved ones elsewhere in the palace. What of Meghan, who had retired to bed, or Lachlan and Iseult and the children? There was so much terror and pain in the atmosphere that Isabeau's witch senses were overwhelmed. She knew Iseult was alive for she felt no physical pain, but the others?

As soon as the last Fairgean had fallen, she set off into the palace. Torn and bloodied bodies lay everywhere, most of them human. Isabeau wept, recognizing many among them. She saw the pretty young girl who had flirted with Dide so boldly earlier in the day, and the scullery maids Doreen and Edda whom she had once scrubbed floors with, and some of her fellow students from the Theurgia, all lying still and lifeless. There was the musician that had so charmed her with his flute-playing; there was the jongleur who had amazed them all by wrapping her legs about her head and walking about on her elbows, and there was Oonagh the White, the city sorceress, her corpse surrounded by eight dead Fairgean, all charred and smoking. Isabeau picked up her robe and ran past, tears choking her.

She came into the great hall of the palace, and saw more bodies lying strewn across the expanse of blue marble and across the stairs, so many bodies it was impossible to count. She had to stop, great sobs tearing at her ribcage. She could not breathe, and bent over, gasping. She felt Dide come up close behind her and take her in his arms. They held each other closely, taking comfort from one another's warmth and strength and the audible pounding of their hearts.

"The bairns," Isabeau choked at last. "I must . . ."

"My master!" Dide cried. "Oh, merciful Eà, let the Rìgh be safe."

As weak-limbed and shivering as if they had been struck down with a fever, they climbed the stairs together, trying to avoid stepping in the pools of blood. The bodies grew scarcer and their step quickened. Up to the royal suite they mounted, past the fallen bodies of the Rìgh's bodyguards. Still they could sense nothing but a fog of black despair which clouded all their extrasensory perceptions.

Then they came to the landing and saw there a great pile of dead Fairgean, sixty or more, their pale scaly skin horribly smeared with blood. Isabeau noticed, with a strange detachment, that their blood was as red as any human's. Then she saw Lachlan kneeling just beyond the dead Fairgean, his dark head bowed, his wings folded in comfort about the still figure of the youngest of his personal guard, Dillon of the Joyous Sword. Dillon was crouched in unnatural stillness, his arms red to the elbow, a bloodied sword in his hand. Across his lap was the lifeless body of his dog, the white fur dark with gore.

Dide scrambled across the piles of dead. "Master, are ye hurt?"

Lachlan lifted his face, twisted with rage and grief. "Nay, no' I, thanks to Dillon and his joyous sword. He saved me and Iseult both. We could no' fight them all off, they came so fast."

"The bairns?" Isabeau whispered.

"Safe," the Rìgh answered, gesturing towards the royal suite.

"Bronwen too?"

He shrugged, his face darkening.

Isabeau ran past him, her heart pounding with dread. The sitting room was empty and undisturbed, but she could hear the sound of childish sobbing from the nursery wing. She hurried that way and came into Donncan's room. She had to step over two sea-warriors who were lying in the doorway, their weapons fallen from their hands. There was no mark of battle on their slim, muscled forms, and although their eyes were closed, the gills at their neck fluttered slightly and their bare chests rose and fell slightly with their breathing.

Iseult was sitting on the floor, comforting her three children who all cowered against her. Bronwen was slumped nearby, her arms huddled about her knees, her silver flute fallen from her hand. On the floor before them lay their nursemaid Elsie, her cap wrenched askew so her blonde curls lay tumbled, her pretty face staring up at the ceiling. Her grey dress and white apron were slashed and stained with blood. Her blue eyes were wide open and rather startled. Across her unmoving chest lay another Fairgean warrior, a long serrated fin curving out of his spine. He was snoring.

Isabeau looked from Elsie's dead startled face to Iseult, then back again. "What happened?" she whispered.

"The Fairgean came to try to kill the children," Iseult replied matter-of-factly. "Elsie held them off as long as she could. Then Bronwen played her flute and they fell asleep. It was too late for Elsie though."

Isabeau knelt and gathered Bronwen in her arms. The little girl gave a great shudder and pressed her face against her, but did not cry or speak. Isabeau smoothed her silky black hair, rocking her gently. She looked down at the nursemaid, lying so still at her feet. "Poor Elsie," she said.

"She saved the bairns' lives," Iseult said, still in that very controlled voice. "If she had not held them off,

Bronwen could no' have reached her flute and they all
would have died."

Suddenly Iseult bent her head over her children and
began to weep, great sobs shaking her slim body. Isabeau
reached for her hand. Her twin's fingers closed hard upon
hers and so they sat, both fighting back their tears, for a
very long time.

THE THREADS DIVIDE

RIDING TO WAR

Now shall ye agree that we must wipe out the Fairgean once and for all?" Linley MacSeinn demanded, striding up and down the great hall so his heavy plaid swung from his shoulders. "Now that they have dared to strike at ye in your own home?"

There was an uproar from the council. Many among them had eyes reddened with grief, for few had not known someone who had died in the Beltane massacre.

Lachlan rose to his feet. He was drawn and tired. He raised one hand but the shouting did not die down until the chancellor had banged his hammer down repeatedly. At last the council quietened down and turned to hear the Rìgh speak.

"The Fairgean have grown so strong and so bold they were able to strike at us here in our very own stronghold," Lachlan said. "Reports from the city and the countryside show that we were no' alone in our duress. All up, we have calculated that up to ten thousand Fairgean warriors attacked Rhyssmadill, Dùn Gorm and many o' the major towns along the Clachan coastline. We foolishly believed that we were safe behind the bulwark. Now many innocent men, women and children have died because o' our—

because o' *my*—foolishness. Their deaths weigh heavily on my conscience."

The court was silent. Lachlan sighed and rubbed his forehead. "Linley is right. We have let the Fairgean rampage unchecked for too long. I hoped that as long as we stayed away from the coast and the rivers, we would no' have to face them until we were strong enough. We concentrated on solving our internal problems before we faced the threat from without. The Fairgean have had time to grow strong, however. They have been breeding up their numbers ever since they wrested Carraig back from the MacSeinn. They are now well armed with swords and spears o' fire-forged steel, and they have had much practice in killing humans."

He paused for a long time, waiting for the groans and exclamations to die down once again. His hands clenched tightly upon his scepter. As if in response to his touch, the Lodestar mounted at the crown glowed with a soft white light. For a moment a chord of exquisite music rang out, though only heard by those who had the gift of clearhearing. The Lodestar was the most potent talisman in the land, and could only be touched by one of MacCuinn blood. Lachlan had only recently begun to master the powers of the magical orb, and its response to his touch obviously comforted and strengthened him.

"We are stronger than we have been since the time o' my ancestor Aedan Whitelock!" His voice rang out proudly. "Eileanan has been united into one land for the first time in its history. Arran and Tìrsoilleir no longer stand against us, and all those o' faery kind, from the mighty dragons to the mysterious nyx, have sworn us their friendship and aid. The Fairgean alone refuse to sign the Pact o' Peace. They alone stand against the might o' a united Eileanan!"

This time there was cheering from the ranks of lairds, merchants, guildmasters and soldiers crowded into the conference hall. Many beat their daggers against their goblets enthusiastically. Again Lachlan waited, though this time his hands were calm on the glowing orb of the Lodestar and his wings were raised proudly. When he spoke again his voice was soft but filled with regal assurance.

"So, yes, Linley, ye are right. It is time for us to strike! It is time for us to win back your land for ye, it is time for us to fulfil the promises we made to ye and your clan. It is time for us to drive the Fairgean back into the sea!"

The room erupted in cheers and shouts of martial joy. Only a few remained somber and quiet—the Banrìgh sitting so still and pale upon her throne; the Keybearer Meghan NicCuinn, her ancient face set in grim lines; Dide and his grandmother Enit Silverthroat; her apprentice Jay the Fiddler, a tall boy with a thin, sensitive face who cradled a viola case in his arms; the young banprionnsa Fionnghal NicRuraich who sat by his side, a dainty black cat curled on her lap. Even Brangaine NicSian, who had lost her entire family to the Fairgean, looked troubled and unsure.

"We must plan the offensive very carefully," Lachlan said. "There must be no chance o' losing this war. Over the past thousand years we have had to take up arms against the Fairgean three times. Three times we have struggled with them, three times we have fought for our lives and our liberty at the cost o' thousands o' lives. There must no' be another time. This must be the last."

A chill fell over the room and many looked at each other sideways, unable even to bear the thought of what would happen if they planned an offensive against the Fairgean and failed.

Lachlan smiled at them all rather grimly. "Do no' fear. We shall no' fail. Have we no' won against far worse odds than these? Did we no' drive the Bright Soldiers from our land and back into the Forbidden Land, and did we no' conquer the Forbidden Land itself? Do we no' have the might o' both witchcraft and arms on our side? Eà shall shine her bright face upon us, never ye fear."

The council broke up with a great hum of conversation as everyone discussed the outcome of the meeting. Lachlan came up to where Iseult and Isabeau sat, leaning his hand wearily on the side of his wife's chair. "Well, it is done. We attack Carraig."

Iseult nodded, not looking at him. Her back was very stiff. "We had best call the war council together," she said. "Once again we plan a war."

He nodded and straightened up, his face grim. Isabeau looked from one to the other, still sensing a coldness and distance between them. Neither looked at her or at each other. When Lachlan moved away to speak to Duncan Ironfist, she said softly to Iseult, "Is all well between ye two?"

She saw color run up under her sister's fine skin but Iseult shrugged and said rather sharply, "O' course, why would it no' be?"

Isabeau said apologetically, "I be sorry, I just wondered . . ."

"We are all just troubled by what lies ahead," Iseult said. "We have just won one war and now we must fight another." Her voice was unhappy.

Isabeau laid her hand on her arm to comfort her, but Iseult shook it off, saying, "We must do what has to be done." She rose and strode off to join her husband and Duncan in front of the maps. Isabeau watched them, her heart still troubled. It had been some time since she had dreamt of Lachlan's hand upon her body, his mouth upon her throat. By the tension in Iseult's shoulders, the smoulder in Lachlan's eyes, she knew it was no coincidence.

The war council convened for three days and three nights. Platters of food and jugs of wine were carried in and out, and when the arguments grew too violent, a break was called and everyone staggered off to bed for a few short hours.

All were driven by a sense of urgency. For the first time in the long, bloody history of Eileanan, a death blow had been struck into the very heart of its people. Rhyssmadill had been breached. The MacCuinn had been attacked in his very home. Blood had been spilt in the throne room and the Rìgh's own bedroom. The Fairgean had declared war in no uncertain terms.

The conference had been called so hastily that not all the prionnsachan were able to attend. Anghus MacRuraich of Rurach was many miles away and deeply immersed in his own problems; but his daughter Fionnghal attended the council, accompanied by Rurach's ambassador to the court, the Duke of Lochslain.

Brangaine NicSian of Siantan was there, pale and quiet, her eyes red-rimmed. She contributed little to the discussion, having no knowledge of war tactics, but listened carefully to everything that was said, her mouth set grimly.

Melisse NicThanach of Blèssem had ridden in only a few days after the Beltane massacre, with a large troop of men and her seanalair, the Duke of Killiegarrie, who had fought at Lachlan's side through many an engagement.

Madelon NicAislin of Aslinn sent her seanalair, the Duke of Gleneagles, while Malcolm MacBrann of Ravenshaw rode in with his son Dughall and a swarm of dogs of all shapes, colors and sizes. The Prionnsa of Raven-shaw was very elderly now, a thin stooped old man with a shock of silver hair and a magnificent full white beard that reached past his sporran. He wore the full regalia of kilt, plaid and badge, with a black velvet doublet, a snowy white cravat, and a *sgian dubh* thrust in his boot. Although he was always the first to hear the step of the servants bringing in the wine, whenever anyone asked him to take the yapping, brawling dogs out to the kennels, he would cup his hand behind his ear and shout, "Heh? Speak up, lad, I canna hear ye."

Of all the people there, Linley MacSeinn was the most vociferous. He had dreamt of marching for Carraig with the whole of Eileanan behind him for so long that now it seemed likely to happen he was in a state of quivering impatience, part exultation, part disbelief.

"Linley, I ken ye are eager to be on the move but indeed we must decide what we are all to do afore we can ride out," Lachlan said with some exasperation. "Please, let us think how we can best overcome the Fairgean. Where and when would be the best place to face them? How should we fight them? Do we spend our money building more ships or do we try to fight them on the land? These are the things that must be decided before we even think about marching forth!"

Argument broke out all round the room. There had been no concerted defense against the Fairgean since they had first driven the MacSeinn clan out of Carraig and begun their attacks against the coast of Eileanan. Every fishing village or harbor town had defended itself as it thought best, or simply packed up and fled at the first sight of a sea-serpent on the horizon. As the years had passed and the Fairgean had grown bolder and stronger, more and more villages had opted for flight until the hinterland was crowded with refugees and the coast virtually deserted.

What little resistance there was had proved to be haphazard and erratic, in stark contrast to the highly organized attacks of the Fairgean. Some villages strung up their fishing nets across the mouth of the bay to try to entangle the sea-faeries, stabbing them through the net with their salmon spears and their gutting knives. This tactic was no longer as effective as it had once been, since the Fairgean now had daggers and swords of their own with which to slash themselves free. Other villages had met the attacks with flaming torches, since all knew the Fairgean were terrified of fire. That had been effective only as long as the number of attackers had been small. Now that the Fairgean were once again many, they had simply overwhelmed the villagers with force of numbers.

"Isabeau, ye ken more about the sea-faeries than anyone," Lachlan said. "What will their movements be?"

"The Fairgean leave the summer seas in mid to late September," Isabeau said. "They then swim around Eileanan, moving slowly up the coast. I believe it usually takes them two months at least to reach their homes in Carraig. They have many newborn babes with them and so can only swim slowly. Besides, they do no' sleep in the water, ye ken. They must come ashore to sleep, and that is why there has always been so much conflict over the few safe harbors and beaches. Where the Fairgean wish to come ashore to rest is where our kind has always settled. So much of the coastline is dangerous and rocky, ye see."

"But canna they breathe underwater like fish?" the Duke of Gleneagles asked. "Do they no' have gills like a fish?"

"They have gills," Isabeau answered slowly, "but no' like a fish. They can breathe underwater for no longer than five or ten minutes. Then they need to surface for air. That is why the Yedda can drown them by singing them to sleep."

"So if we can stop them from coming ashore to sleep, they canna rest," the Duke of Gleneagles said thoughtfully. "They will simply drown?"

"It is no' that simple," the Duke of Lochslain said. "The coast is very long and villages are few and far between. Although it is true that they prefer to come ashore in a safe harbor, we have kent them to climb up very steep cliffs and attack us from the rear."

"That would be the warriors," Isabeau protested, "no' the women and babes. The warriors would've attacked ye so that they could make a safe resting place for the babes, who would have been only wee still."

"Nonetheless," the Duke of Gleneagles said, "if we can try to stop them from coming ashore to rest, we will weaken them considerably and happen that will help us defeat them in battle. Every Fairgean that drowns from exhaustion will be one less to fight later."

"But the babes . . ." Isabeau said in some distress. The soldiers ignored her, taking up the Duke of Gleneagles' idea with some enthusiasm.

"We shall set up coastal watches," Lachlan said decisively after the subject had been discussed exhaustively. "Beacons must be prepared and manned on every headland. At the first sight o' Fairgean in the seas, the beacons must be lit so the villagers have warning. Then when the Fairgean try to come to shore to rest, they must be kept off with sword and flame. The net idea is a good one if they try to swim up a river, as we all ken they do. The idea is no' to waste lives in fighting them to the death, but to wear them out and delay them, to give us more time to get to Carraig. If we can be in Carraig afore them, we shall be able to choose our battlefields. We can secure every harbor against them, and have our men on every clifftop and in every bay."

The MacSeinn gave a hooray of excitement. Lachlan scowled down at his parchment, muttering under his breath as he tried to work out how long it would take to mobilize the army and march upon Carraig. At last he threw down his pencil with a curse and commanded Iain to work it out for him. "Eà kens I was never any good at mathematics!" he cried.

"I can vouch for that," Meghan said with a little smile as Iain began calculating how many months it was likely to take to get their troops mobilized, provisioned and on the march.

"Well, by the time we g-g-gather together our armies here and then m-m-m-m-march to Carraig . . . even if we march at twenty miles a day, we canna be getting there afore Samhain ourselves, and that's no' counting any d-d-d-delays," Iain said at last.

Lachlan scowled. "We need to strike faster than that!" he cried. "There must be some way we can get some men to Carraig by autumn. We want to surprise them if we can."

"Imagine if we can win back the Tower o' Sea-singers, so that when they return we are already in the strongest position possible!" the MacSeinn cried, his sea-green eyes shining.

Isabeau frowned. "The Isle o' the Gods is the most sacred spot o' all the Fairgean," she protested. "Even in the height o' the summer months it would never be left unguarded."

Linley MacSeinn stared at her. "Well, we shall just have to win it back anyway," he said.

"But do ye no' understand the Fairgean will never submit to allowing ye to step foot inside the Fathomless Caves? It is sacrilege o' the highest order. That is one reason why they fight against us so mercilessly, so relentlessly. They believe their gods were all born within the caverns there, that it's the womb o' all that is sacred and divine. As long as ye seek to win back the Isle o' the Gods, they will never submit."

Linley shrugged, his face set hard as granite. "Och, what will they care when they are all dead?"

Isabeau had lost all her color. "Do ye plan to kill them all then? Every single one, women and babes as well?"

She turned on Lachlan. "Is that the plan? To kill them all? To wipe them from the face o' the earth? Did ye no' see that their blood runs as red as your own? They may be faeries o' the sea but they breathe air and make love and bear children and worship the forces o' nature just like any o' us." Her voice broke.

Lachlan gripped his scepter tightly. His face was troubled.

Isabeau rose to her feet, looking from him to Meghan. "Last year ye said we would never gain a lasting peace until we came to some sort o' understanding with the Fairgean, until we learnt to forgive and understand each other. When ye said that, I thought at last ye had become a rìgh, a true rìgh like Aedan Whitelock must have been. I thought how wise ye were, and how brave. Was I wrong?"

Lachlan met her furious gaze straightly, his mouth twisting. "I hope no'," he said. "But it is no' me that sought this war, Isabeau, ye ken that. I have sent messengers seeking to parley, I've offered to come to some sort o' treaty, and no' just me, my father and grandfather afore me. Ye saw how they answered me!"

Isabeau was silent for a moment. "But do ye seek to

kill them all?" she asked at last, her voice a little softer. "The MacSeinn is set on winning back the Isle o' the Gods while I tell ye now the only way humans shall ever set foot in the Fathomless Caves again is over the bodies o' each and every living Fairgean. Is it genocide that ye aim for, or a way o' bringing peace to the land?"

Lachlan stirred uneasily. When he spoke his voice was gentle. "Ye are right, Isabeau. We do no' go to wipe the Fairgean out once and for all, we go because we hope to find some way o' making a lasting peace."

Linley MacSeinn groaned and struck his forehead with his hand. "Are ye all soft in the head?"

Isabeau turned on him. "I hope we are soft in the heart and no' in the head," she cried. "Why are ye so hard? Do ye no' understand the Fairgean feel grief and rage and love, just like we do?"

He laughed harshly. "And what would ye ken, ye bairn? Were ye there when the Fairgean attacked at night, killing all they could reach and driving us out into the bitter snows with naught but a few clothes to our backs? Were ye there when I had to watch my wife and my eldest die with Fairgean tridents in their hearts, or when my daughter died from cold and starvation on the road?"

"Were ye there," Isabeau countered, "when your ancestors first attacked the Fairgean in their sacred sea-caverns, massacring them and driving them out to drown in the icy seas? Were ye there when they took flaming torches into the holy darkness where no light had ever before fallen? Were ye there when the Yedda sang a thousand Fairgean to death, mere babes among them? Ye do no' need to be there to ken."

There was a long moment of silence, fraught with tension. Isabeau faltered a little when she saw many in the council were looking at her with suspicion and condemnation. Then Meghan rose stiffly to her feet.

"Isabeau is right," she said, "and I too am ashamed o' myself. So long we have hated and feared the Fairgean, and never have we thought o' the actions o' our ancestors as anything but right and true. Yet there has been great evil done on both sides. We canna tip the balance so it lies more heavily on our side. We canna go to war planning to annihilate our enemy. It is much easier to destroy than it is to build anew.".

Again there was a long, troubled silence. Then Lachlan sighed. "Yet we canna go to war already deciding the terms o' a peace that may never be possible. Let us take what Isabeau has said into our hearts and our minds and ponder the ramifications but, please, let us now plan a war. For though we may have come to realize that there has been wrong done on both sides, the Fairgean surely have no'! They hate us as much as ever and the Beltane massacre was surely no' their last offensive."

There was much murmuring among the councilors and Isabeau was troubled by the sideways glances many gave her. Everyone knew she had brought Maya's daughter Bronwen back to Lucescere and that she had had some discourse with the Ensorcellor herself. It was clear Isabeau knew more than anybody else about the customs of the Fairgean, and many wondered aloud how that was so. Besides, she was a witch, and despite the restoration of the Coven, many of the people of Eileanan still distrusted witches.

So Isabeau said no more, sitting back in her chair, turning her moonstone ring round and round upon her finger as the arguments went round and round the conference hall. She had so much to perturb her heart, so many doubts and forebodings, regrets and self-recriminations, that it took her some time to notice that her twin Iseult also sat silently, her thin red brows drawn together. Under normal circumstances there would have been nothing in that to remark upon. Khan'cohbans were not given to garrulity. However, this was a war conference. Iseult was a Scarred Warrior, trained from birth in the art of fighting. It was not like Iseult to sit with her hands folded when a war was being planned.

Suddenly Iseult turned and met Isabeau's gaze. Color scorched up her face and she bit her lip and looked away. Isabeau sat very still for a long time, not even hearing the wash of conversation about her. Her hands felt cold, her head hot. All her intuition told her something was wrong and that somehow she was at the heart of it.

That night Isabeau tried once again to approach her sister, though her very anxiety made her awkward. Iseult smiled at her in perfect composure and gave her a brief hug, an uncharacteristic sign of affection. "Nay, o' course there be naught wrong, Beau. No' with us, anyway. I am just tired and irked by all this bickering. They are always the same, these lairds. They talk and talk and naught is ever decided. I canna be bothered arguing with them. If they want my insight, then they can ask me for it."

Although her words seemed fair, there was still enough of a shadow on Iseult's face for Isabeau to seek out Dide in the guardroom. He looked tired, his dark curls tousled, his shirt unlaced at the neck, but he smiled at the sight of Isabeau and sprang to his feet.

"How are ye yourself, my bonny Beau?"

"Och, fine," she answered distractedly. She looked about the guardroom, where all the other officers of the Yeomen of the Guard lounged, playing dice or trictrac, and drinking whiskey. Most regarded her with friendly curiosity and she smiled rather briefly at those she knew. "Dide, is there somewhere we could go to talk?"

"In Rhyssmadill? A hundred places," he replied with a laugh. "This palace was built for intrigue."

She bit her lip at the double entendre, but she allowed him to show her out of the guardroom. They walked upon the battlement, under the silvery-blue light of Gladrielle, the only moon yet to rise. In its clear radiance, Isabeau could clearly see the quizzical look upon Dide's face.

"Much as I would like to think ye have sought me out for some dillydallying in the moonlight, I ken ye must have some other reason," he said. "What be wrong, Beau?"

She took a deep breath and then said hesitantly, "I'm worried about Iseult. She seems so . . . so cold, so . . . distant. I think she is angry, but I dinna ken why . . . or with whom . . ." Her words trailed away.

He twisted his mouth in chagrin and looked away. She stared at him in surprise.

"I would no' worry," he said, still not meeting her eyes. "My master . . . spoke some hasty words one day, in a temper, and I do no' think my lady has yet forgiven him. She holds fast to what she feels, your twin."

Isabeau was puzzled. "What kind o' hasty words?" She laid her hand on his arm. "Something to do with me?"

"Now what makes ye think that?" Dide replied mockingly.

"I dinna ken," she answered seriously. "I just feel it, somehow."

He did not know how to answer her. Watching Dide searching for words, when he was usually so glib of tongue and quick of wit, only confirmed Isabeau's suspicions. "What did he say?" she cried angrily. "Lachlan always thinks the worst o' me. Did he say something against me?"

"He was upset," Dide said. "It was on the *Royal Stag*, after we had heard about the laddies being kidnapped. We did no' yet ken if Donncan was even alive, let alone that ye had rescued him from Margrit. He loves that laddie dearly, ye ken that, and we had come fresh from the war against the Bright Soldiers. We were all tired and over-wrought . . ."

"So he did say something! He blamed me, did he? And Iseult was angry? They argued about me?"

"Dearling, I canna say," Dide answered in some distress. "He is my master. I canna be repeating what he says, no' even to ye. Especially no' to ye."

Isabeau was too angry and upset to notice the endearment. She said furiously, "He is always the same! It does no' matter what I do, he always thinks the very worst o' me. And why? Why?" She held up her crippled hand. "Ye'd think he would feel guilty that I was tortured and maimed in his place. Ye'd think he would speak softly to me and be kind, if only because I am his wife's twin. But no! He is always quick to blame me, to call me traitor and spy, to have me accused of murder and betrayal . . ."

Dide seized both her hands in his. "But Beau, ye do no' understand . . ."

"Nay, I do no'!"

"It is because o' all o' that, do ye no' see? It is because he blames himself for your hand, because ye are as like Iseult as the reflection in her mirror. He said it himself. If he is no' to hate ye, what else is he to do?"

"He hates me . . ." she faltered.

Dide dropped her hands and turned away. "I should no' have said anything," he said stiffly. "It was just I wanted to explain . . . please forget I told ye. Neither

Iseult nor Lachlan would want ye to ken what was said in haste and anger, and under such duress. He does not hate ye, it's just . . ."

"I look too much like Iseult," she said matter-of-factly.

"Aye," he said, not looking at her. "It is enough to drive a man mad, seeing ye side by side, so alike and yet so unalike. Is it any wonder he sometimes questions . . ."

"What?"

"Naught."

"Nay, what? Tell me."

He shook his head. "I have said too much. I wish ye had no' asked me. Ye will take it amiss and indeed, it was no insult to ye that has Iseult so angry." Once again he stopped himself, striding away with his hands clenched beside him, turning suddenly back to seize her arms. "It was no' fair o' ye to seek me out," he said abruptly. "Ye ken I can deny ye naught, it hurts me to see ye upset and so now I have betrayed ye master's confidence. Get ye to your bed, Beau, and do no' be looking at me with those unhappy eyes. There is no need for *ye* to grieve."

"But Dide . . ."

"I shallna say any more, Beau, so there's no point in asking. I wish I had no' said anything at all."

He walked away from her swiftly and did not look back. Isabeau looked after him, her face troubled, gnawing at her fingernail. *If no' to hate me, then what else is he to do?* she thought and, despite herself, gave a little smile.

Lachlan rapped the table and said, "Enough! Let us concentrate on the job at hand. Three days we've been shut up in this room and I do no' ken about all o' ye, but I am heartily sick o' it. Let us put our strategy in place and ride to war!"

Talk broke out on all sides. "We'll just have to kill as many Fairgean as possible afore they get to Carraig," the Duke of Gleneagles cried.

The Duke of Lochslain had fought many times against the Fairgean. He leant forward now, his wrinkled face troubled. "The thing is," he said, "the sea-demons be as slippery as eels. Ye can fight and fight against them, to try to stop them landing, and they'll simply turn and slither back into the sea again and be gone. And if ye try to pursue them by boat, their blaygird sea-serpents are waiting outside the headlands and the boats are crushed and everyone drowned."

"Could ye no' kill the sea-serpents?" Duncan Ironfist said.

"How?" the duke said simply. "Arrows are no good, they just bounce off their hide."

"All the royal fleet are well armed with cannons now, thanks to the Bright Soldiers," Lachlan said, rubbing his tired eyes. "Do ye think they'd be any use against sea-serpents?"

"I do no' rightly ken, Your Highness," the duke said doubtfully. "Their hides be mighty tough. Happen cannonballs would just bounce off."

"And the sea-serpents would have to come within range, and by that time they'd have the ship in their coils anyway," said the captain of the *Royal Stag*, who had been promoted to Lord High Admiral of the Rìgh's fleet.

"The trick is to try to kill the sea-serpents afore they come too close to crush the boat," Duncan Ironfist said, tugging at his beard.

"Och, that be easy enough," the MacBrann said, startling them all, since everyone had thought he was dozing. The old man twinkled at their expressions of astonishment, scrabbled around his huge sporran and drew out a sheaf of crumpled papers. "I brought ye my design for a giant mangonel. We found it most useful against the Bright Soldiers when they tried to storm Ravenscraig. We've thrown a boulder well over four hundred yards!"

There was a little murmur of surprise and the MacBrann beamed round at them. "Aye, I think ye'll find that o' use! Since then I've been working on a balista that can shoot a giant arrow nearly as far. Ye could dip the arrowhead in some sort o' poison so that all ye need do is pierce the sea-serpent's hide, ye do no' need to strike a vital organ to kill it. The poison will do all the work for ye."

"Dragonbane," Meghan cried. "Iain, your mother sold Maya some dragonbane when she was trying to wipe out the dragons. Wouldna dragonbane work on sea-serpents too?"

Iain nodded. "I imagine it probably w-w-w-would, Keybearer. I do no' ken myself how to make it, but there are those who live in the swamps who would k-k-k-k-ken the recipe. I can try to find out."

"My father has another invention which he thinks may be o' some use to ye," Dughall MacBrann said then in his indolent drawl. He was lying back in his chair, his eyes half shut as if he were only just managing to stay awake. "Tell them, Father, for I'm sure I forget what it is."

The MacBrann sat up eagerly, blinking behind his spectacles. "Och, yes, I'd forgotten about that. Thank ye, laddie, for reminding me." He rummaged about in his sporran and drew out a little glass vial which he held up to the light. It held some thick, viscous liquid. "I call it seafire," he said. "Found it quite by accident years ago and scribbled down the formula, which I put in some book for safekeeping. Forgot all about it until last year when I found it again while I was looking for something else. Belle's genealogical chart, I think. Or maybe it was my grandmother's recipe for elderberry wine."

"Who do ye reckon Belle is?" Dide whispered to Isabeau. "His mother?"

"Nay," Isabeau said, stifling a laugh. "I'd wager it's one o' his dogs."

"Anyway, I found it quite by accident and threw it on my desk and when young Dughall here said he was coming along to see ye, my lad, I thought I'd bring it along too and see if ye like it," the MacBrann continued cheerfully. "It took me some time to dig it out again, I must say, but I think ye'll like it. It makes a pretty blaze."

"I'm sure I shall like it, Uncle Malcolm, if ye'll just tell me what it is," Lachlan said with uncharacteristic patience.

"It be seafire, laddie, dinna I tell ye? It ignites on contact with sea water."

"Ye mean, sea water makes it burn?"

"Aye, dinna I say so? Ye could throw it with the mangonel and when it hit the water, bang! It would blow up and all the water about would be one big sheet o' fire. That would give the sea-demons a fright." The old man chuckled and rubbed his hands together in delighted anticipation.

"It makes water burn?"

"Aye, aye. Am I no' making myself clear? Or are ye a bit slow on the uptake, laddie? I suppose it's no' to be wondered at, since ye were a bird all those years. Strange story that one. Very strange. It must have had an effect, your brain being shrunk down to the size o' a pea. We must no' wonder at ye being a few pence short o' a farthing."

Lachlan said with remarkable composure, "Nay, no' at all, uncle. It is just I have never heard o' water being made to burn before. Normally we use water to put out a fire. What in Eà's name is in your 'seafire'?"

The MacBrann tapped his finger to his nose. "Nay, nay," he chortled. "Ye canna trick me so easily, laddie. I do no' give away my secrets so easily."

"How would ye put such a fire out?" Admiral Tobias asked with great interest. "Fire is a dangerous weapon to use on a ship."

"Good question," Dughall answered laconically. "We wondered that ourselves when Father decided to test it out. I'm afraid one wing o' Ravenscraig was rather badly charred before we solved the problem."

"So how do ye put it out?"

"Well, eventually we used sand," Dughall replied with a secret smile, fingering his beard. "Though we found human water had a dampening effect upon it also."

"Human water?" Admiral Tobias asked, puzzled. Then light dawned. His sunburnt face turned even redder as he said, "Oh, I see! Human water."

"Aye," Dughall replied. "Ye can see the problem there."

"Aye, indeed," the admiral replied, trying to hide his embarrassment in the face of Dughall's sophisticated ease.

"Well, then, that means we can use the navy," Lachlan said, his scowl clearing for the first time in days. "That be grand, I'd hate to have wasted our Ship Tax! We'll have to spend some time and money having the ships fitted out and armed. Since we've recovered and repaired most o' the pirate ships, our fleet is now up to sixty-four, including all o' the Tìrsoilleirean ships. That's a good-sized navy!"

"If we sail to Carraig, we'll be able to get there m-m-m-much quicker," Iain said. "Even if the army marches at full speed, the men canna walk m-m-m-much more than fifteen or twenty miles a day. The navy should be able to sail as much as one hundred and sixty m-m-m-miles a day, if we keep the winds blowing fair. And if we can get the army to Bride in time, we'll be able to set sail before the F-F-F-Fairgean have begun their journey north again."

There was a stir of excitement, and Alasdair Garrie of Killiegarrie said, "Besides, if we arm the ships with this seafire and the poisoned ballistas, it will no' matter if there are Fairgean in the sea, we'll just be killing them off sooner."

"And I heard tell ye'd found a Yedda in Tìrsoilleir," the MacSeinn said excitedly. "Och, that be grand news indeed! A Yedda can sing the blaygird sea-demons to death. And she can be teaching the songs o' sorcery to some o' your young witches. I've heard rumors that ye have a few now that have the Yedda Talent, Eà be praised."

There was a long, awkward silence. Dide stilled, his long-fingered hands clenching. Enit Silverthroat turned and looked at Meghan commandingly. The Keybearer gripped her lips together and said nothing. Isabeau looked from one to the other, wondering. There was much about Dide and Enit's journey to Tìrsoilleir that she did not know about. The MacSeinn's words, she thought, obviously touched upon a nerve.

"Well then," the MacSeinn cried, breaking the silence, "is this no' true? Did ye no' rescue a Yedda in Tìrsoilleir?"

"They did," said Meghan. "A Yedda called Nellwyn. She spent eight years incarcerated in the Black Tower. Young Finn rescued her when she rescued the prophet Killian the Listener. She is here now."

"And do ye no' have others that can weave spells with music?" the MacSeinn demanded. "Canna they be taught to sing the Fairgean to death too?"

"Enit Silverthroat can sing the songs o' sorcery and she has taught her grandson Dide, as well as her apprentice Jay the Fiddler," Meghan said quietly. "They were able to sail to Tìrsoilleir safely this time last year, though I ken they encountered Fairgean on the way."

"But ye ken I shallna sing the song o' death," Enit said abruptly. "I have told ye that many times, Meghan. I am no Yedda to use my magic to kill."

"But Enit—"

"Nay, Lachlan. Naught has happened to make me change my mind. Ye ken how I feel about this."

"What foolishness is this?" the MacSeinn cried, staring at the old jongleur in bafflement. "Ye ken how to and yet ye will no'? Why?"

Enit looked at him with pity in her eyes. "I willna use my powers to kill. There are other ways to use the songs o' sorcery."

"Other ways? What other ways? I tell ye, if we could train up a batch o' young witches and put one on every ship, we'll soon win this war! A good Yedda can kill hundreds o' the blaygird sea-demons at once. Hundreds!"

"When we sailed to Tìrsoilleir last year, we were attacked by a group o' Fairgean warriors," Dide explained. "Instead o' singing them to sleep, we sang the song o' love. Jay played the *viola d'amore*, which as ye ken was made by Gwenevyre NicSeinn herself and has great powers indeed—"

"Gwenevyre's viola should never have been given away like that," the MacSeinn cried, trembling with rage. "And to naught but a gypsy lad! The viola is a relic o' the

MacSeinn clan and should have been given back to us. Ye had no right, Your Highness!"

Looking distressed, Jay clutched his precious viola close to his chest. Dide gripped his hands into fists.

"The viola was given to Jay the Fiddler because o' the help he gave me in winning my throne," Lachlan said evenly. "All o' the members o' the League of the Healing Hand were given their choice from the auld relic room and that is what he chose. Linley, the viola had lain there unused for many years. It was pure luck that it was no' lost in the Burning, like so many other precious heirlooms. Or happen it was no' luck, but the invisible workings o' the Spinners. For Jay plays that viola as if it were fashioned purely for his hand. There is none left in your clan who could play it. Do no' begrudge it to Jay, who has done so much to help me."

"Is that so?" the MacSeinn said skeptically. "Let us hear him play it then."

The color burnt hotter than ever in Jay's face, but at Lachlan's nod he rose and tenderly removed the viola from its case. Beautifully carved and polished, the viola had far more strings than was usual, raised over an elaborate wooden bridge. Its graceful neck had been carved into the shape of a woman, her eyes blindfolded.

Jay looked at the MacSeinn with a shy yet direct gaze. "She is blindfolded because they say love is blind."

The MacSeinn nodded brusquely. "Och, no need to be telling me about the *viola d'amore,* my lad. I was taught at the Tower o' Sea-singers. Who taught ye?"

"Myself," Jay answered simply. "And Enit."

Without waiting for a response, he lifted the viola to his chin and ran the bow over the strings. A cascade of notes fell into the room, deep and rich and pure. Then Jay swung into a lilting dance tune that had heads bobbing and toes tapping. He came to the end with a flourish, and a little storm of applause rang out. He blushed and lowered the bow, looking to the MacSeinn.

"Well, there's no doubt ye can play, lad, and play well," the prionnsa answered gruffly. "And it is true what the MacCuinn says, there is none left in my family who could play so beautifully. My daughter might have been able to, but she is dead now." An expression of intense melancholy crossed his bearded face and he sank his chin into his hand. For a moment he was quiet, and then he looked up, the fire back in his brilliant sea-green eyes. "But if you have the Talent, why will ye no' sing the Fairgean to death?"

"She is made for singing o' love, no' death," Jay said quietly. "Canna ye see?"

"I see ye have a relic o' the MacSeinn clan and willna use it to help us!"

"But, my laird, if ye will just listen," Dide said. "I told ye we sang the song o' love when we were attacked by the sea-faeries. My laird, the Fairgean were enchanted! They swam after our ship, crooning and whistling and throwing us fish. And later, when we were attacked by the Tìrsoilleirean navy and our ship sank, the Fairgean rescued us, swam with us to shore. My laird, do ye no' think . . . ?"

"Sang the song o' love," the MacSeinn replied scornfully. "That be a song for courtiers and troubadours, no' a song for war!"

"But we won them over, we forged a connection o' sorts with them," Enit cried. "We could do the same in Carraig."

"Sing the song o' love as an army o' Fairgean warriors charge us with tridents raised?" The MacSeinn's voice was sardonic. "That would be one way to speed up the inevitable end—us all dead and the Fairgean ululating in triumph."

"Ye ken I have said so myself, Enit," Lachlan put in. "Any song o' sorcery only works when the audience listens, and during a battle ye can hear little but the clash o' arms and the screams o' the wounded. And even when the audience does listen, they must hear with the heart and no' just with the ear. Ye yourself taught me that. How should we sing them to peace when they are blinded and deafened by their hatred?"

"But in Tìrsoilleir—"

"Aye, but that was only a small group o' warriors, ye said so yourself. We canna send ye and Dide and Jay out into the midst o' a horde o' ravening Fairgean like a band o' wandering minstrels. It be too dangerous."

Enit said nothing, her crippled fingers gripping the arms of her chair.

The MacSeinn snorted in exasperation. "This is what happens when ye invite *women* into a war council," he said with heavy sarcasm. "Ye get addled with soft notions and foolishness."

"Is that so?" Iseult snapped. "Does that mean ye do no' wish the benefit o' *my* advice, my laird?"

The MacSeinn said nothing, his jaw clenched tight. Iseult said, very softly, "Remember that I am a Scarred Warrior, my laird. It does no' matter whether ye are male or female upon the Spine o' the World. All that matters is whether or no' ye can fight. I did no' earn these scars for nothing."

"O' course, Your Highness," he said after a moment, with obvious difficulty. "No offense meant."

Iseult did not answer, obviously fighting to contain her temper. Lachlan too was angry. He cast an exasperated look around the table and said, "We must no' be arguing amongst ourselves all the time. If we are to defeat the Fairgean we must have a united front. Come, Isabeau says the Fairgean will be back in Carraig by Samhain or soon after. We must be there by then, and if we can, strike them hard and from two sides at once."

Most of the Rìgh's army, called the Greycloaks because of their camouflaging grey attire, were still deployed throughout Tìrsoilleir. It was decided that Lachlan should join them, along with the forces of the southern lairds and prionnsachan, so that they could attack Carraig from the east, sailing the majority of the men up the coast in the royal fleet. Since the troops of the NicThanach and the NicAislin would join them, as well as Iain and Elfrida's men, they should be able to muster over ten thousand men and faeries, a sizable force indeed.

In the meantime, Fionnghal NicRuraich and the Duke of Lochslain would travel back to Rurach to speak with the MacRuraich and enlist his help. On the way, they would speak also with the MacAhern of Tìreich, whose cavalry was famous for its swiftness and bravery. Including the longbowmen of Ravenshaw, an army of three thousand or more could be raised to attack the Fairgean from the west.

"That means a total o' thirteen thousand soldiers, which is a strong force indeed," Duncan Ironfist said with some satisfaction. "Even though we shall have to fight the Fairgean in their own territory, we should have the advantage o' numbers."

"We can swell that even more if your father decides to join us," Lachlan said to Iseult. "He has a few hundred men up there now and he is a Scarred Warrior himself and a bonny fighter. Which reminds me, do ye think he would speak to the Firemaker on our behalf? The Khan'cohbans have signed the Pact o' Peace, which means they have promised to aid us in times o' trouble. They think o' war as some kind o' hobby, do ye think they would join us too?"

"Maybe," Iseult said coolly. "They have no enmity with the Fairgean though, living so far from the sea. And I do no' ken if they would be prepared to leave the snows to fight for a cause in which they have no interest."

At the very slight stress in her words, Lachlan scowled. Duncan Ironfist said, "Besides, it would take months for them to mobilize. By the time a messenger rode into the mountains, persuaded the Khan'cohbans to our cause, and then rode back down to Rionnagan, it would be winter already. By the time they travelled round to join us in Carraig, a year or more would have passed. If only there was some way to cross the mountains into Carraig! Then we could strike from the south as well . . ."

"But there is a way across the mountains," Iseult said.

They all stared at her incredulously.

"Many have tried to cross the mountains and all have failed!" Linley cried. "I myself have tried several times since Carraig was lost to me!"

"Are ye sure, Iseult?" Meghan said. "No' once, in all the thousand years since our kind came to Eileanan, has anyone ever found a way across the mountains. That is why we have always relied so much on the sea routes."

"I imagine none has ever asked the Khan'cohbans," Iseult replied with great composure.

Linley laughed harshly. "The snow-faeries are one o' the major reasons *why* we have never crossed the mountains. No' to mention frost-giants, ogres, goblins, avalanches, sabre-leopards, snow-lions, wolves . . ."

"Well, I have crossed the mountains myself," Iseult answered.

A volley of questions and exclamations followed her

comment. She listened calmly, then said, "Ye can only cross during the summer months, when all the snow has melted in the higher passes. Then the danger o' avalanches is much less too, and the frost-giants are hibernating. If ye were given permission to pass through the dragons' valley, that would cut off almost a month from the travelling. Ye could do it from here in under three months if ye had sleighs."

Everyone looked at each other eagerly. "If we sent a force across the mountains now, we could be there by autumn," Iain said, doing quick calculations in his head.

"And ye could speak to the Khan'cohbans and persuade them to our cause on the way," Linley said eagerly.

Color rose high in Iseult's face, showing the two thin scars across her cheekbones. "But I canna go back to the Spine o' the World!" There was mingled longing and dismay in her voice. "No' unless Lachlan comes too."

Golden eyes met blue eyes in a long charged look, totally unaware of the cries of disappointment and outrage around them.

"A commander must stay with his troops!" the Duke of Gleneagles cried.

"Ye canna leave command o' the army to anyone else, no matter how able! How would the men feel? They all worship ye," the Duke of Killiegarrie said.

"It is too dangerous, master," Dide cried. "Ye canna be risking yourself so!"

"What would we do if ye were lost in an avalanche?" Duncan said, troubled. "Remember how it was when ye were cursed and lay like the dead for months? All the lairds and guilds withdrew their support and we were stalled like a haycart bogged in mud. I fear it would no' be wise, Your Highness."

The Rìgh was clearly troubled. "I canna go through the

mountains," he said. "I must go where the army goes. Alasdair is right, a commander stays with his troops."

"What is the problem?" the MacSeinn demanded. "Her Highness can guide me and my men through the mountains and ye can lead your army around the lowlands. That way we strike from three directions. We canna help but triumph!"

"But I canna leave ye," Iseult whispered to Lachlan. "I am in *geas* to ye."

The MacSeinn leapt to his feet and leant forward on the table, his face hard with anger. "Surely this is no time to be clinging together like a pair o' love-struck doves! No one but the Banrìgh kens the way through the mountains. She must go!"

Other voices joined with his and Lachlan looked from one face to another, and then back to Iseult's. She rose, her face very white and stern. "Do ye release me from my *geas* then?"

Still Lachlan hesitated, as many in the room exchanged mocking glances, thinking he could not bear to be parted from his wife for a scant few months. At last he nodded, holding Iseult's eyes with his own. "Very well, I release ye. Ye shall go to the Spine o' the World."

She gave a low bow and genuflection that only Isabeau recognized as a formal Khan'cohban gesture, then turned and strode away, her back very straight.

Lachlan suddenly shouted after her, "Ye've been longing for the snows, do no' try and say ye have no'!"

Iseult did not reply, closing the door sharply behind her.

Isabeau stared at Lachlan in dismay. "Do ye no' realize what ye have done?" she whispered. By the hot anger and misery in his golden eyes, she thought he came close.

* * *

Jay drew his bow over the strings of the viola, a cascade of music filling the air. The voice of the viola was deep and low, thrilling with tenderness. The song came to an end, and slowly Jay lowered his bow and opened his eyes.

With a start, he realized the heir to the throne of Rurach was sitting on his bed listening to him, stroking the silky black fur of the elven cat that lay sleepily upon her lap. She wore a green velvet riding habit, with a black plaid slung about her shoulders and pinned with a clan badge depicting a black wolf. Her chestnut-brown hair was pinned up under a rather dashing green tricorn hat, embellished with plumy black feathers.

"Finn!" he cried. "I dinna hear ye come in."

"I came to say goodbye, but ye were off in your usual sort o' trance and I thought it might be dangerous to disturb ye," Finn said with a grin. "Like sleepwalkers, ye ken."

Jay grinned rather ruefully. "Well, I'm rather glad ye dinna disturb me. I love that song."

"It's aye bonny," Finn said. "Ye get better every day, Jay. All that time ye've spent practicing is paying off." There was a faint note of pique in her voice.

"Aye, I've been lucky to have had Nellwyn teaching me as well as Enit," Jay said eagerly. "She's a true Yedda, trained at the Tower o' Sea-singers and everything. There is so much she can teach me." Tenderly, he swaddled his viola with a length of silk and laid her back in her case.

"I could find it in me to be jealous o' that lump o' wood," Finn said.

Jay's eyes leapt up to hers, his color deepening.

"Though it is only a lump o' wood," she went on. "Even if it does have a damn fine shape to it." She sighed and looked down at her own lithe, boyish figure. "Och well. Maybe I'd have a shape like that if I dinna spend so much time riding horses and climbing trees. And really, I'd rather be flat as a flounder and get to climb trees than otherwise."

"Well, ye are looking very bonny today," Jay said awkwardly.

She gave a little shrug. "Och, aye, as fine as a goat's turd stuck with cowslips, that's me. The Duke o' Lochslain has high ideas about the manner in which a banprionnsa should present herself. The journey home is no' going to be much fun, I fear."

"Did ye really come to say goodbye?" Jay asked wistfully.

"Aye, I'm afraid so," Finn answered, standing up and draping the elven cat over her shoulder. "So much for escaping my royal duties. Lachlan has promised me he's written to my *dai-dein*, telling him I do no' want to be a banprionnsa anymore, but I hardly think *Dai* will pay much attention, given the rest o' the news we carry. All I can say is he had better take me with him, because if I get stuck back at boring auld Castle Rurach I swear I really will run away! I'd rather eat toasted toads than have to sit around fiddling my thumbs while ye're all off fighting wars and having adventures."

"Well, happen it will be a quick war and we can all come home soon, and go to the Theurgia together, like we planned."

"Happen," Finn replied, without much hope in her voice. "Though I canna see it being a quick war, can ye?"

"Nay," he answered unhappily.

"I must go," she said. "The Duke o' Lochslain already thinks me an undisciplined brat. If I keep him kicking his heels much longer, he'll be giving my *dai-dein* a bad report o' me and I really do want to be in *Dai*'s good books at the moment. Have a care for yourself, won't ye? Dinna go thinking ye can win this war playing that bloody viola o' yours."

"Nay," he said with a sigh. "Though I do think . . ."

"Ye heard what Lachlan said," Finn said firmly. "Remember, if ye wish to be a witch ye must practice humility, modesty and obedience."

"Ye're a fine one to talk!" Jay cried, but she only laughed at him, grabbed him by the ear and kissed him on the side of his mouth. By the time he had recovered his breath, heat scorching his face, she had gone, the elven cat spitting at him from her shoulder.

"So we ride to war once more," Lachlan said, leaning upon his great longbow. Iseult nodded, her face very calm. "But this time no' together," he continued, searching her face with his eyes.

"Nay, this time no' together," she repeated, looking away from him, her mouth set in a firm line.

He put his arm around her shoulders and tried to draw her close. "It will feel peculiar, no' having ye near me," he said softly. Although she did not resist his embrace, she stood stiffly within it and he eased away from her to again search her face for some clue to what she was feeling. But there was nothing. No anger, no sadness, no tenderness. Lachlan's own mouth compressed and he walked away, his back very straight.

Isabeau stroked her twin's arm comfortingly. "He does no' really understand what it is he has done," she whispered. "He does no' ken about *geas*."

Iseult met her eyes in a long, intense gaze and there at last Isabeau saw how her sister was feeling. "He understands. In his heart he understands how important such a debt of honor is to those of Khan'cohban blood. He just did no' want to say so in front o' all those men." There was a faint trace of bitterness in her voice.

"But ye will come back to him?" Isabeau whispered urgently. "Ye are still married to him."

"What do your marriage rites mean to me?" Iseult said, hurt pride in her voice. "Khan'cohbans do no' marry."

"But ye jumped the fire wi' him, ye have borne him three children," Isabeau said anxiously.

"I swore never to leave him, and now he has released me from that *geas*." Iseult's voice was flat with finality. She shrugged Isabeau's hand away and mounted her horse. "Are we ready, my laird?" she asked Linley Mac-Seinn.

"As ready as we shall ever be," he answered gaily, his horse dancing about as the prionnsa's impatience communicated itself.

Isabeau stepped forward, looking up into Iseult's face. "He loves ye, ye ken that."

"Does he?" Iseult replied coolly. "Happen he does." She wheeled her horse away, spurring her elegant mare to the front of the cavalcade. There Lachlan stepped forward and laid his hand on her boot.

"Have a care, *leannan*," he said.

She looked down at him. "I shall. Look after my babes for me."

Lachlan nodded in response, then reached up, grasped her gloved hand and drew her down. For a moment she resisted, her thin red brows drawn together. Then she bent and allowed him to kiss her. Their mouths clung and when at last she straightened, her blue eyes were glittering with tears.

"Eà be with ye," Lachlan said.

"And with ye," she answered gruffly and gave the command to ride out.

Five hundred men rode out in their train, most of them the MacSeinn's, two hundred of them chosen to serve and protect the Banrìgh. They rode their horses hard, rising in the dawn and riding on by the light of torches, changing their mounts at every opportunity. In less than three weeks they had reached the Pass, and were riding up the narrow, winding road beside the tumultuous rush of the Rhyllster.

It was slower riding after that, for the roads in the Sithiche Mountains were not so well tended as those in the lowlands. As she rode, Iseult was unable to help the flood of memories that rose and threatened to engulf her. Here was where she and Meghan and Lachlan had tricked the Red Guards into letting them through the Pass. Up there was where they had made camp one night. Through those woods was the cave where Iseult had first met Lachlan, a surly hunchback with intense golden eyes that had never stopped staring at her. The memory made her stomach twist with longing, and she drove the men on even harder than before.

Then she saw the familiar crooked shape of Dragonclaw rearing up out of the lesser mountains around it and a new longing awoke in her, a yearning for the cool silence of the snows. They rode their horses to the point of exhaustion that day, and camped that night in the meadow below the Great Archway. In less than a week it would be Midsummer's Eve, and then the days would again begin to shorten as the seasons swung towards autumn and the coming confrontation with the Fairgean.

Iseult rose before dawn the next day, and went out into the meadow to gather a great bunch of wild roses from the briars that grew in great profusion all over the rocks at the base of the tall mountain. When her arms were full, she crossed the grass to the wide stone platform that marked the beginning of the Great Stairway.

The sun was just rising when her squire, Carrick One-Eye, came to her, troubled that she had left the protection of the camp without him. He was half human, half corrigan, one of the many faeries to flock to Lachlan's banner during the Bright Wars. Although only short, he was broad and very strong, with a face as rough as granite and one eye set deeply into his head. Carrick had been appointed Iseult's squire and personal bodyguard by the Rìgh, a responsibility he took so seriously that Iseult had not been able to take a step without him. She smiled at him reassuringly.

"Ye must stand back, Carrick," she said. "And no matter what happens, ye must no' approach." He protested. "Nay, I mean it," she said. "Ye do no' understand the way o' the dragons. Many people have died in the past because they have been too foolhardy or bold. Stand back, I say, and let me speak to the dragon alone."

At last Carrick acquiesced, and when the MacSeinn came hurrying up, anxious and concerned, he held him back and would not let him approach.

Iseult looked up at the brightening sky and waited. Despite having lived many years in the shadow of the dragons, her heart still lurched when she saw the great magical creature soar into view above the shoulder of the mountain. It bugled exultantly, and all the horses picketed down the meadow reared and whinnied in panic. Some managed to break the ropes that bound them, though they were so firmly hobbled they could not gallop away. Men everywhere fell to the ground, or cowered back against the frail shelter of a tent, while the men behind Iseult all gasped and fell back a pace or two, sweat springing up on their brows.

The dragon flew down and landed on the platform before Iseult, dwarfing her with his immense size. He coiled his tail about his claws and waited, tiny tendrils of steam escaping from the red caverns of his nostrils. Iseult knelt with her head bowed, the roses laid in a great sheaf before her.

Greetings, Great One, she said in their own silent language.

Greetings, Iseult the Red, the dragon answered, regarding her with slitted topaz eyes. *Thou bringst a sizable force in thy train.* His mind-voice had the symphonic power and resonance of an entire orchestra of musicians.

Iseult nodded. *We come bearing gifts, in the hope that the mighty dragons will allow us to cross through their hallowed ground. As ye ken well, my husband Lachlan MacCuinn and I bear no malice towards the dragons. We revere you and honor you. We have no desire to provoke your anger or to challenge your rule. We shall cross with our eyes lowered and our voices silenced and we shall leave no mark of our passing, if the Great Circle will give us their forbearance and clemency.*

There was a long silence, the dragon regarding Iseult through narrowed eyelids. She took a deep breath and indicated the roses lying before her with a graceful sweep of her hand.

I have also brought the tithe o' roses in the name o' the MacFaghans, as the dragons decreed long ago, and hope that the long friendship between my clan and yours may grow and flourish as the roses do.

The dragon's eyes were mere slits and the tip of the tail was waving back and forth. There was a long silence, then he purred, *Gifts?*

Iseult gestured to Carrick and he came forward carrying a heavy chest, which he laid on the ground before her, his face even stonier than usual in his effort not to show his fear. She gestured him back and stiffly, slowly, he retreated, determined not to scurry back as he would have liked. Iseult unlocked the chest and opened it, and with a swift, menacing grace, the dragon bent his long neck and smelt the jewels within, his cavernous nostrils flaring red.

We also leave ye and your brothers a herd o' five hundred horses to hunt for your pleasure and satisfaction, Iseult said. *We beg pardon that they be so thin and scrawny and hope the number o' them makes up for the lack o' fat.*

The dragon laughed, a sound that chilled all who heard it to the very marrow of their bones. Iseult knelt very still, her head bowed, and after a long tense moment when she did not breathe at all, the dragon moved away, the chest of jewels held in his claws.

We know thee, Iseult the Red. We accept thy gifts, paltry though they are, and give thee and thy men permission to climb our mountain. Remember that we shall brook no impertinence from thy followers. If only one dares look within our palace doors, or leaves a footprint in the mud of our pools, we shall see whether the fat of thy bodies makes up for the lack of fat on those scrawny beasts you call horses.

Iseult inclined her head in acquiescence. The dragon bent his powerful hindquarters and launched off into the sky, the blasting wind from his wing-beats almost knocking her over. She shielded her eyes from the whirlwind of dust and leaves and took her first deep breath in some time.

They reached the dragons' valley on Midsummer's Morn, and slowly filed past the steaming loch, which filled the crater with a writhing mist that smelt unpleasantly of rotten eggs. Although many of the men jumped involuntarily at the slightest sound, all were careful not to stare at the seven great caverns in the side of the hill. No dragon was seen, rather to the disappointment of the bravest among them, and then they were able to begin the long climb back up out of the dragons' valley.

Iseult waited until all the men had filed past her and were out of sight before she crossed the valley floor and laid the great bunch of roses, now rather wilted, on the lowest step. She knelt and said, *I thank ye, Circle o' Seven.*

Deep within her mind, so deep it seemed to reverberate around the hollows of her heart and stomach rather than her brain, she heard the queen-dragon reply, *It is our pleasure.*

Happiness welled up in her, stinging her eyes with tears. She swallowed, nodded her head, and rose to her feet, walking briskly across the valley floor to join her men once more.

DRAGONEYE

I sabeau walked slowly through the forest, looking about her with intent eyes. She had to find the perfect place. She would know it when she saw it, she was sure of that. It would be a place of power, a place where the forces of air and water and earth and fire could connect, a place that strummed some inner chord of meaning within her.

It would have been best if it had been somewhere that already had great meaning to her, like the rock shelf on the edge of the waterfall in Meghan's secret valley, where she had undertaken her Apprentice Test. But the Rìgh's army was riding to war and Isabeau travelled in its train. She did not have the freedom to choose the place and time of her Sorceress Test, as young witches had in days of old. She was lucky that Lachlan had decided to spend a few days at Dùn Eidean with the banprionnsa of Blèssem, celebrating Midsummer's Eve before riding on for Arran, and then to Tìrsoilleir to meet up with their navy. Until now, the Greycloaks had not stayed more than one night in the one place. Isabeau was required to sit in silence, communing with the forces of nature, for three days and three nights before being allowed to sit her Sorceress Test. Such an ordeal was impossible in the noise and bustle of the army camp.

Buba the elf-owl soared from branch to bough ahead of her, hooting in perplexed query. *Why-hooh we-hooh here-hooh? Why-hooh not snooze-hooh?*

I-hooh have-hooh just had-hooh my lunch-hooh, Isabeau hooted back, smiling.

Noon-hooh good-hooh time-hooh for snooze-hooh, Buba hooted.

For-hooh you-hooh, Isabeau replied. *I-hooh not owl-hooh.*

Not-hooh now-hooh, Buba agreed sadly. She had not grown reconciled to Isabeau's reluctance to shape-change ever since her last dreadful bout of sorcery sickness, and was always trying to persuade Isabeau to fly with her once more.

The ground began to tilt under Isabeau's feet. She hung on to the branch of a tree and hauled herself upwards, anxiety tightening her nerves. This small patch of woodland was the only wild spot for many miles, Blèssem being a land of meadows and hedgerows. If she could not find somewhere to sit her Ordeal and take her Sorceress Test, it could be months before she had the opportunity again.

Then she heard the tinkle of running water and her spirits lifted. She followed the sound, coming through a shadowy grove of oak trees into a small clearing lit by the sun. Isabeau knew she had found her place.

A spring of crystal-clear water bubbled up from a cleft in the western face of the rock, cascading down the side of the hill to gather in a small pool in the center of the grove. Waterlilies floated on its surface, white and crimson and blue, while bulrushes stood up straight as spears on either side. Beyond stretched a little meadow where butterflies danced above a tangle of wild herbs and flowers. A hawthorn tree in full blossom stood in a circle of bruised white petals, while an ancient yew leant drunkenly at the far end. The roots of the leaning yew formed a wide seat on the edge of a cliff, where the stream fell down in long, pale tassels. Framed in the overarching branches of the oak trees was a wide view of the valley below, the walls and towers of Dùn Eidean floating above the blue shimmer of a loch.

Suddenly she saw a nixie sitting on a lily pad, regarding her with curious crystal eyes. The little water-faery immediately dived back into the pool but Isabeau's heart had leapt. She stood in the sunshine, smiling, lifting her arms to the sky.

Here-hooh? Buba asked.

Here-hooh, Isabeau agreed.

The sun was just rising when Isabeau came back to the oak grove the next day. She was alone, Buba having reluctantly agreed to wait for her in the forest below, so Isabeau could sit her Ordeal in isolation, as she was meant to.

Everything was very still, the meadow grass heavy with dew, the only sound the carolling of birds. Isabeau carried a large pile of firewood and a heavy satchel upon her back, which she unloaded in the sweet-smelling shade of the hawthorn tree. There were five tall dusk-colored candles, a small bag of salt and another of dried dragon's blood, a bunch of dried herbs and flowers, some pewter bowls, a little bottle of precious oils, a slim book with a blue cover, a loaf of bread, a bottle of goldensloe wine, a bag of little red apples and a wedge of cheese that Isabeau had made herself to be sure it had been curdled with the juice of thistle flowers and not the digestive juices of a lamb.

She arranged everything neatly under the hawthorn, then sat within the yew roots and ate her last meal for three days, washing it down with water from the spring. The water was cold and tasted of earth and darkness. It made her throat ache.

As she ate, Isabeau's gaze kept returning to the blue book which she had laid down beside her knee. Meghan had given it to her the previous afternoon, with a quick, hard hug and a kiss between her brows. "Your acolyte book, Beau," she had said. "Ye are ready to read it now."

Isabeau was not so sure. Meghan had let her read a few pages once before, and it had been a humbling experience. The pages of the blue book recorded Isabeau's growth and progress, and she knew she had been a wilful, disobedient child, more interested in climbing trees, swimming with the otters and playing with the squirrels and donbeags than in concentrating on mathematics, astronomy or history.

Resting upon the book was a ring which flashed with a hot yellow light. It was a rare jewel, the dragoneye, only found in the far distant mountains where the dragons lived, and where Isabeau had grown to womanhood. It had her name engraved upon the inside, and had been a birthing gift from the dragons themselves.

The dragoneye jewel was set between two exquisite single-petalled roses, with the band engraved with the curving spurs of thorns. The same design was repeated in the clan brooch that pinned together her soft white plaid. It was the emblem of the MacFaghan clan, descendants of Faodhagan the Red who had flown with dragons and built many of the great witches' towers, including her own, the Towers of Roses and Thorns, where he had died at the hand of his twin sister, Sorcha the Murderess.

Those who would gather roses must brave the thorns, Isabeau thought and picked up the ring with trembling fingers. She turned it so the stone caught the sunlight and flashed, then slid it on to the middle finger of her left hand. She had not been permitted to wear her dragoneye ring since returning to the folds of the Coven and she had missed it greatly. Soon, Isabeau hoped, she would be able to wear her sorceress-ring openly. If all went well these next three days. She sighed and smiled, and polished the ring with the hem of her tunic, admiring its golden brilliance. Only then did she open the book.

The pages were filled with Meghan's thin, spidery writing, the lines cramped and often crossing each other. Isabeau gave a little impatient sigh but as soon as she began to read, the frown between her brows disappeared and she became absorbed. For the book told the story of her life, from the time Meghan had discovered Isabeau as a newborn babe in the gnarled roots of the tree in which she had made her home, to Isabeau's acceptance into the Coven as a witch the previous year. Often Isabeau laughed aloud as she remembered this misdemeanor or that childish folly, and occasionally her eyes stung with tears. Once, she had to lay the book down while she swallowed a great fist of sorrow and regret, a useless wish that things might have been different.

By the time she had finished, the sun was sliding down behind the hill, the grove of trees filled with long shadows. Isabeau wrapped up the book and tucked it back in her satchel, her head swarming with thoughts and memories like a hive full of bees. It took an effort to wrench her mind back to the present and the task ahead of her. Isabeau had to spend some time with her eyes closed, her hands upturned on her thighs, seeking to control her breathing and with it that elusive life-essence the Khan'-cohbans called the *coh*, the still center of certainty she carried within her.

At last Isabeau felt serene enough to continue. Slowly

she undressed. First Isabeau removed the petrified owl talon she wore hanging around her neck. Like the thin, white scars on her face, the talon was no witch token, but a sign of her Khan'cohban heritage and training. She laid it aside and then unbuckled the long dagger she always wore at her waist. Its hilt was carved into the shape of a dragon, its wings folded along its sides, its eye glowing golden. Isabeau rubbed the tiny dragoneye jewel with her thumb, then laid the knife down carefully. She unwound her hair from its tight braid, so that her bronze-red curls hung freely down her back, coiling and uncoiling in the breeze. Finally she stripped off the long white robe, made without buttons or hooks, and folded it neatly. She was naked, her feet bare.

She walked into the pool of water, parting the waterlilies to reveal green cloudy water. Beneath her feet mud squelched. Her toes curled involuntarily, but she felt her way forward, feeling the shock of the cold water upon her skin. For long moments she floated, her hair drifting behind her, watching the sky fade to a clear greenish-blue, and then darken to violet. Gladrielle began to rise above the horizon, then Magnysson, the sooty marks on his flank very clear. The light of the two moons turned the surface of the pool to rippling quicksilver, and Isabeau spread wide her arms and legs, gazing straight up into the starry expanse arching so far above her.

At last she stood up and waded out, shivering a little. She beat herself all over with branches of juniper and rosemary, then rubbed herself dry with a rough towel, her flesh stinging. She then, with great ceremony, anointed herself with the precious oils, a blend of murkwoad, hawthorn, angelica and rose, for clear-seeing, far-seeing, far-travelling and protection from evil.

Isabeau sat in the embrace of the yew tree's roots. She

felt very clean, very confident. Staring out into the night, she emptied her mind of all thought, all emotion. Under her breath she chanted: "In the name o' Eà, our mother and father, thee who is Spinner and Weaver and Cutter o' the Thread; thee who sows the seed, nurtures the life and reaps the harvest; feel in me the tides o' seas and blood, feel in me the endless darkness and the blaze of light; feel in me the swing o' the moons and the planets, the path o' the stars and the sun; draw aside the veil, open my eyes, by the virtue o' the four elements, wind, stone, flame and rain; draw aside the veil, open my eyes, by virtue o' clear skies and storm; rainbows and hailstones; flowers and falling leaves; flames and ashes; draw aside the veil, open my eyes, in the name o' Eà, our mother and father, thee who is Spinner and Weaver and Cutter o' the Thread . . ."

Slowly Isabeau felt herself drawn ever higher and thinner, as if someone were tugging at a rope through the top of her skull, through the base of her spine. She was rooted into the earth, rooted into the sky. Her spinal cord was a sapling, her branches entwined with stars, her tap-root submerged deep into the soil. She could feel the almost imperceptible pulse of the planet beneath her, felt herself grow smaller and smaller within the immensity of the night, until she was a mere pinprick of light in a roaring darkness.

She fell into this abyss of night, at first in sudden jerks that she had to struggle not to resist, then smoothly, quickly, spiralling down in an ever widening corkscrew.

In that stillness that was not sleep, that quietness that was not death, she travelled back down the path of her life. It seemed to her she was hurrying down a great spiral staircase. It was night-time still and the stone steps glimmered with an unearthly light. With each turn of the staircase, she was deeper into her trance and deeper into her past. Old sorrows rose up to haunt her. She saw the purple face and protruding tongue of Margrit the Thistle, who had drunk the poison meant for Isabeau. Margrit reached out her hands, begging forgiveness, but could not speak, her throat strangled.

Isabeau would have stopped and tried to calm her pulse, seeking her *coh,* but the staircase kept twisting round, and she kept sliding down, down.

Once again she skimmed down a pure sweep of snow and, turning, saw behind her a frost-giant with his ice spear poised to throw. Her heart thundered. Desperately she tried to flee. The ice spear was flung towards her. She saw the great wave of avalanche rising to swallow her. Once again she soared away into the sky with the wings of an owl. Exquisite relief flashed through her, the joy of abandoning her maimed, cumbersome body for the swift, free, clear-sighted body of an owl, a snow-lion, a golden eagle, or any creature she chose. At the time Isabeau had felt only bewilderment. Now she wept and laughed together.

Down she fell, through whirling snow and leaping fire, through hunger and loneliness and cold, loss and heartache. She saw Maya casting a black poppet upon a fire, she saw Bronwen playing a tune upon her flute while all her toys danced and cavorted about her. Isabeau saw her father transform from a wild, incoherent man back to a wild, incoherent horse, rearing and bucking with rage. She saw her mother sleeping within a cocoon of hair and herself shaking her, pleading with her to wake. For some reason, this memory stabbed her with greater sorrow than all those that had come before. Isabeau felt tears falling down her cheeks, felt as if they were tears of quicksilver, scorching her soul. *Maman . . .*

In that instant, Isabeau realized how much her mother's

absence had bothered her all her life, like an aching tooth that one probes and probes with one's tongue, flaring with quick agony if probed too hard, subsiding into a dull throb if left alone. Both Isabeau and Iseult had always chosen not to confront Ishbel, to leave the aching doubt alone, but now Isabeau realized how deeply it had hurt, knowing her mother had taken refuge in her strange enchanted sleep in preference to caring for her twin daughters herself.

She saw Ishbel awaken, and look for her, but this time her mother smiled at her and embraced her, calling her by name. To Isabeau's surprise and pleasure, she saw Ishbel now lay in a bed all hung with curtains, rather than in the nest of her own hair. Her husband and Isabeau's father, Khan'gharad, slept peacefully by her side. Somehow the coil of the staircase had taken Isabeau across space as well as time, and it was the Ishbel of now, not of the past, who had responded to her inarticulate cry. *Is all well?* her mother asked anxiously, and Isabeau nodded, wiping away tears of sudden relief. She clung to her mother but the staircase was turning, and Isabeau was turning with it.

She saw Lachlan lift the baby Bronwen from her bath, her fins streaming with water, her scales shimmering like mother-of-pearl. He shook her, hissing through clenched teeth, "Keep her away from me. By the Centaur's Beard, keep this *uile-bheist* away from me and my son!" And Isabeau took Bronwen in her arms, sick and shaking with fear.

The little girl dissolved away into nothing in her arms. Isabeau was hurtling down the stairs now, back through all the grief and fire of the Samhain rebellion, back through the sick confusion of her feverish journey to Rhyssmadill. Each vision came so fast she barely had time to cope with the tumult of emotion, yet she knew she was swiftly approaching the time of her torture. She struggled to break the trance, to leave the stairway, to fly back up to the present. It was no use. Inexorably she was led back to that time, the moment when her world was cracked apart and remade, marred and spoiled forever. She saw Baron Yutta's smile as he bent over her and in a paroxysm of terror and shame, she plunged down, deeper into the abyss, free-falling.

The world spun around her, stars and night whirling past in dizzying spirals of white fire. She was falling so fast she could not breathe, her lungs squeezed in the grip of some cruel giant. Visions whirled with her as if seen from the corner of her eye, all blurred and distorted with tears. The shadow of a dragon crossing the moon. Meghan spinning wool and telling her stories. Holding Meghan's hand and watching a young boy with laughing dark eyes turn cartwheels faster than she could run. Then she saw herself, a newborn babe, lying in the embrace of a great tree's roots, a dragoneye ring clutched in her hand.

Deeper she fell. A red confusion, filled with screaming and sobbing and the shadow of dragons' wings. An unbearable pressure all around her. Then some sort of peace. Darkness. Floating. She curled in upon herself, resting, unsure where she was. The only sound was a great, distant booming, like the organ of the ocean deep. She rested there for a long time, grateful to be still, lulled by the boom of the ocean and the gentle rocking waves. Once again she felt herself dropping, though so slowly, so gently, it was almost imperceptible. She gave a little cry, reluctant to go.

White radiance. Light filling her ears and eyes like water. Falling faster, the world spinning. A sudden disconnection, a high echoing scream as she fell immeasurable distances. Then she saw other lives, other times, though distantly, as if gazing through a clouded glass, and all twisted together into a vast helix that stretched both ways into the great infinity, like finely spun thread.

The insight lasted only a moment. Isabeau drifted back down into her body and opened her eyes, wonderingly. It was dawn. She had two more nights to endure.

She bathed again, trying without success to wash away the sweat and terror of the night. She read her acolyte book once more, crying more often than she smiled, and caressed the dragoneye ring with her thumb, trying to recapture her easy insouciance of the day before. She kept her mind resolutely turned away from the bread and cheese growing stale and hard in her satchel, and her warm, soft plaid, which she longed to wrap about her.

Night came and passed, and turned into day, and then again to night. Where Isabeau had been cold, she was now as hot as if she had a fever, and all her limbs trembled. Dawn broke again, birds shrieking. The day dragged itself along on its elbows. She was filled with self-loathing and self-pity, one moment weeping for all her mistakes, which she seemed condemned to repeat over and over again as if she were a spit-dog running in a wheel, the next moment filled with rage and resentment at everyone she knew and loved, for all the times they had failed to save her.

She dreamt of sticky, frantic, reckless love but dreaded to see the face of the man she desired so desperately, afraid it would be Lachlan, or the beautiful inhuman face of a Mesmerd kissing her to death, or worst of all, Baron Yutta, caressing her with one hand while he inflicted agonizing pain with the other. So she thrust the vision away with all her strength, chanting to Eà and the Spinners as if the ancient, well-worn words had the power to banish all evil, all harm. There was no respite, though, for it was dreams of war and death and drowning that filled the void, and she had no strength left to cast the dreams away.

The last night passed in a sick blur. It seemed strangely short, as if the three days had telescoped upon themselves. Once again she had strange dreams, of coiled snakes, whorled seashells and ammonites, the staircase twisting round and round, a black spinning whirlwind, ripples of water over her eyes, swirling into a maelstrom to suck her down, down, down . . . then she saw Meghan's spinning wheel whirring round and round, and the flash, flash of light upon the blade of a giant pair of scissors that cut, cut, cut the thread, snip, snap, snip, snap, cutting the thread, severing life . . .

Isabeau came back to herself in the dawn of the third day, trembling with cold and fatigue, her eyes still sticky with tears. She would have liked to have stayed where she was, curled into the knotty embrace of the yew tree, until the last shreds of the nightmares were gone, but she stood and stretched, and splashed herself with cold water. She had gone through too much to lose everything now.

When the sorcerer and three sorceresses came solemnly through the oak grove, in the first spill of light, Isabeau was as ready as she could be.

A circle and pentagram had been scratched into the soil of the meadow, the weeds all cleared away so the shape was stark against the green riot. Five purple-blue candles, smelling sweetly of murkwood, hawthorn, angelica and rose, stood tall at the five points of the star. A bonfire had been built at the center of the circle and Isabeau sat, naked, at the southern point, her staff thrust into the soil behind her, the candle and a bowl of water before her.

Slowly the sorcerers entered the circle. The Keybearer, Meghan of the Beasts, came first, wearing naught but her eight rings and the shining disc of the Key. Behind her limped Gwilym the Ugly, leaning heavily on his staff, then Arkening Dreamwalker, a very frail old woman with a vague, dreamy smile on her withered face. Last came Nellwyn the Sea-singer, the sorceress that had been rescued in Tìrsoilleir. Still gaunt after her years spent as a prisoner in the Black Tower, Nellwyn had a very long plait of ash-blonde hair and watchful green-grey eyes. Eight years as a prisoner had given her a tense, wary air, but over the past few months her unnatural alertness had begun to dissipate, revealing her as a woman of great strength and commonsense.

Isabeau closed the circle behind them, then sprinkled the deeply scored lines with water, ashes and salt, chanting: "I consecrate and conjure thee, o circle o' magic, ring o' power, symbol o' perfection and constant renewal. Keep us safe from harm, keep us safe in your eyes, Eà o' the moons. I consecrate and conjure thee, o star o' spirit, pentacle o' power, symbol o' fire and darkness, o' light in the depths o' space. Fill us with your dark fire, your fiery darkness, make o' us your vessels, fill us with light."

As Gwilym and the sorceresses bent their heads, making the sign of Eà's blessing with their hands, Isabeau lit the candles and the bonfire with a thought. Sweet-smelling smoke began to climb into the sky.

"I have drawn today a five-pointed star within the circle, for the five elements, the five senses, and the head and four limbs, the circle being the sixth sense and Eà, mother and father o' us all," Isabeau said a little nervously. "I have laid the fire with the seven sacred woods, and the candles are colored blue for wisdom and the hidden powers, and purple for clear-seeing and far-seeing and the higher realms of consciousness. I have anointed myself and the candles with murkwoad, hawthorn, angelica and rose. May Eà keep us safe and protect us from evil."

Meghan nodded, driving her staff, all carved with flowers and vines, into the earth at the northern point of the star. She eased her ancient body down to the ground, crossing her legs and allowing her mass of snowy white hair to veil her. The others sat too, their faces all stern and rather forbidding. Isabeau could not help wondering anxiously what she had forgotten.

"Isabeau Shapechanger, ye come to the junction o' earth, air, water and fire, do ye bring the spirit?"

"May my heart be kind, my mind fierce, my spirit brave." Isabeau spoke the ritual words with a quaver in her voice. Indeed, she had thought she was ready for her Sorceress Test but all her confidence was shaken now.

"Ye have sat your Ordeal?"

Isabeau nodded, unable to speak. She saw they regarded her closely and did her best to hide how disturbed and shaken she was. It was hard, for Isabeau had not eaten or slept in three days and she was sick and weak.

"Isabeau, ye come to the pentagram and circle with a request. What is your request?"

"To learn the secrets o' the High Magic, to learn to wield the One Power in wisdom and in strength, with cunning and with craft. To be worthy of my sorceress-ring. May my heart be kind enough, my mind fierce enough, my spirit brave enough."

She made a circle with the three remaining fingers of her left hand and crossed it with one finger of her right. The other four witches mimicked her.

The Sorceress Test of Fire began. Isabeau should have found it easy. She had undertaken all these challenges many times before. She could summon fire and dismiss it, she could use fire as a tool, forging herself a silver chalice set with moonstones and opals, and engraving it with runes of power. She could scry through the embers, she could handle flame without pain, she could walk upon hot coals or juggle balls of flame, she could step into a roaring bonfire and stand as cool and composed as if standing in the rain. She could wield a sword of fire, she could write her name in stone with a thin, blue quill of flame.

Finally she could do what no other sorceress had ever been able to do. As the old cook Latifa had once told her, fire was the element of change and metamorphosis. It transformed living wood to ashes, it consumed air, evaporated water, charred the earth and all its fruits, turned coal to diamonds. It gave Isabeau the power to change shape. For this, her Sorceress Test, Isabeau had chosen to transform herself into *salamandra salamandra*, a fire salamander, in mythology and witch-lore the elemental being of fire. In this guise she crept within her roaring bonfire and sat there, watching the witches with fire-glazed eyes.

Isabeau should have found the Sorceress Test of Fire easy. She had prepared herself carefully, had practiced all her Skills and planned her Ordeal meticulously. Nothing, however, had prepared her for the harrowing of her spirit. She had not expected to sit her Sorceress Test trembling in every limb, sick with fear and envy and self-doubt. She had not expected the flames to turn in her hand and lash her with sparks, or for the inner spark within her to flicker and sink, as it had done after her torture and fever, so that for many long months she had worried she had lost her powers. Isabeau had to struggle all the long day to do as she had planned, in the face of her examiners' unwavering silence and severity.

At last, though, it was over. Isabeau had at her knee her sorceress's cauldron, the silver chalice in which to

mix her potions, scry through water, and burn incense.
She had demonstrated every known Skill of Fire, and dis-
played her rare and mysterious Talent, without doubt of
sorceress level. She knew everyone there wished her well
and desperately wanted a new sorceress to add to their
meager ranks. There was no doubt she would gain her
sorceress-ring and be permitted to begin studying the
High Magic. Isabeau had just not expected the cost to be
so high.

"It is always thus," Meghan said softly, drawing Isabeau's head down into her lap so she could stroke the
mass of fiery red ringlets that snapped and snarled down
her back. "The Third Ordeal was a shock to all o' us. Yet
we canna warn ye or shield ye. Ye must just endure it as
best ye can, and hope ye are no' broken in the enduring."

"Many are," Nellwyn said, her rich contralto voice
quavering with sympathy. "Ye are young indeed to sit
your Sorceress Test. I must admit I was afraid . . ."

Isabeau's shoulders were shaking. In the fiery refuge
of her hair, she rubbed at her face furiously, angry with
herself for her weakness, but unable to control her shuddering sobs.

"Come, it is over. Ye have passed indeed. Let me put
your dragoneye ring upon your finger. Wear it with pride,
for indeed ye have earned it this day. It is the rewards
most hardly won that mean the most, ye ken that, my
Beau."

Isabeau sat up, shook back her heavy hair, wiped her
nose with her fingers. They all smiled at her mistily, and
Meghan slid the glittering topaz-yellow jewel onto the
middle finger of her left hand. It made the white pits of
her scars more obvious than ever, and she clenched her
hand shut.

"Come, my bairn, breathe deeply o' the good air, and

goodwish the winds o' the world, for without air we should die," Arkening said tremulously. Isabeau nodded, and took several great, sobbing breaths, feeling herself begin to calm.

"Drink deeply o' the good water, and goodwish the rivers and seas o' the world, for without water we should die," Nellwyn said. Isabeau filled her silver chalice with water and lifted it to her lips, admiring the glow of the moonstones and opals about its brim. Excitement suddenly quickened in her veins.

"Eat deeply o' the good earth, my bairn, and goodwish the fruits and beasts o' the world, for without them we should die," Meghan said. Isabeau toasted her stale bread and cheese with the palm of her hand till they bubbled golden, and ate with enjoyment. She then made herself a restorative herbal tea and heated it with her finger, more to see the quick smile that flashed across Meghan's face than because she did not have the patience to wait for the water in her cauldron to boil.

"Come close to the good fire, warm yourself and bask in its light. Goodwish the fire o' the world, for without warmth and light in the darkness we should die," Gwilym said. Solemnly Isabeau obeyed, making the sign of Eà's blessing and bowing her head very low. Indeed, she was so heady with relief and gladness that it seemed her very veins ran with wildfire.

Together the witches all chanted, "Feel the blood pumping through your veins, feel the forces o' life animate ye. Give thanks to Eà, mother and father o' us all, for the eternal spark, and goodwish the forces o' spirit which guide and teach us, and give us life."

Isabeau looked down at her golden sorceress-ring and said, with heartfelt gratitude, "I thank ye, Eà, for shining your bright face upon me this day."

Suddenly an elf-owl hooted sleepily from the branches of the oak tree. *Now-hooh can we-hooh snooze-hooh?*

"Aye, thank Eà!" Isabeau laughed. "I'll *snooze-hooh* for a week, I think."

I sabeau gazed expectantly out the window of the carriage as they wound their way deeper into the swamplands of Arran. Contrary to her expectations, the marshes were not bleak and grey and eerie. Swamp-lilies bloomed in gaudy clusters of scarlet and gold and pink, bulrushes thrust their blood-red velvety swords into a clear blue sky, and pale yellow drifts of flowering sedge waved in a gentle breeze. Huge trees raised strong green branches into the sky, their feet soaking in water. Insects chirruped everywhere, and the sound of bird-song filled the air.

Beside her the two-year-old twins, Owein and Olwynne, squirmed and wriggled, one minute squabbling over a toy, the next trying to climb on to Isabeau's lap so they too could see out of the window. Both had dark brown eyes and bronze-red curls, and already their fair skin was liberally splattered with freckles. Like his elder brother, Donncan, Owein had inherited his father's wings, though his feathers were not black like Lachlan's but as red-bright as his hair. Since Owein was likely to launch off into the air at any given moment, Isabeau tended to keep a tight hold on the back of his overalls.

Donncan and their cousin Bronwen hung together out of the other window, talking excitedly, pointing as they saw the strange marvels of the swamps—a bogfaery peering shyly through the rushes, a giant frog sunning itself on a log, a pair of bulbous eyes floating in a stretch of swamp. All four children had the striking white lock at their brow that showed they had bonded with the Lodestar.

Isabeau glanced over at Meghan, who sat with her hands folded on her lap, her eyes shut. As she was wont to do of late, Meghan had dropped off into a light doze, despite the noise of the excited children. The Keybearer looked very old and very tired, her face falling into deep wrinkles about the mouth and eyes and brow, her eyelids as crinkled as crepe paper. The braid that hung down to pool upon the floor was as white as snow, and the veins on her thin, age-spotted hands stood up very blue and knotted. Isabeau felt a little constriction of her heart. It worried her to see the Keybearer looking so frail. Meghan had been such a force in her life it was impossible to imagine an existence without her, yet Isabeau knew the day was fast approaching when she would have to manage alone. This journey to Arran had reminded her forcibly of the bargain Meghan had made with the Mesmerdean, the strange, enigmatic faeries of the marshes.

Isabeau did not need to hang out the window like the children did to know that twenty-one Mesmerdean elders flew behind their carriage in a uncanny guard of honor. The marsh-faeries had risen up out of the swamp-grasses the moment Meghan's carriage had crossed the border into Arran, their shining translucent wings held proudly erect, their glittering clusters of eyes fixed upon Meghan's thin form. Meghan had returned their gaze as enigmatically, her dark lined face revealing nothing. After that she had ignored them.

For Isabeau, just the dank swampy smell of the Mesmerdean was enough to make her feel sick and dizzy. She had fought the marsh-faeries before and knew them to be a formidable enemy. The whirring of their wings, the unswerving stare of their green metallic eyes, the well-remembered shape of their claws, were all enough to keep her on edge. She wondered at Meghan's calmness, when the old sorceress knew the Mesmerdean only waited for the day when they could take her in their arms and kiss her life away.

The carriage jolted to a stop. Donncan opened the door and flew out, Bronwen close on his heels, both shouting with excitement. Isabeau helped the twins down and then gently shook the old sorceress awake.

"Wake up, we're here, Meghan," she said.

No snooze-hooh anymore-hooh, Buba hooted sleepily, her feathers rather ruffled.

The Keybearer came awake with a little start and a snort. "What? What was that?"

"Time to wake up, Meghan, we're here."

"Nonsense, I was no' asleep. What, are we here already?" Meghan straightened her plaid irritably and hauled herself to her feet, gripping her flower-carved staff tightly. Her familiar, the little donbeag Gitâ, grumbled a little and crept into her pocket to resume his nap. Isabeau repressed a smile and helped the old sorceress out of the carriage.

They had drawn up in front of a series of wooden wharves which jutted out into a wide, tranquil loch. Men and bogfaeries were busy everywhere, loading and unloading boats and wagons with sacks and crates and huge ceramic jars, all marked with the sign of a flowering thistle. Water-oaks dipped and nodded at their reflections in the water, their leaves fresh and green, while crimson-winged swans glided about on the water, some followed by a family of fluffy pink cygnets.

In the center of the loch was a long, low-lying island. Built upon it was a great palace that soared up into the sky in a cluster of tall, twisted towers, all painted in soft colors like the first flush of dawn. Smoky-white, pale pink, apple-green and cloud-blue, the towers were ornately decorated with intricate carvings around the arched windows and balconies.

"Legend has it that Fóghnan raised *Tùr de Ceò* out o' the mists with a spell, but the truth is, the Tower of Mists took a century o' hard labor by the faeries o' the swamp," Gwilym the Ugly said, his voice harsher than ever.

Isabeau smiled at him. "Glad to be home?"

He snorted. "Glad to be back in this dank-smelling mud-hole? By my beard and the Centaur's, I'll be gladder when I can shake its stinking mud off my stump and feel solid ground beneath me again."

"Liar," Isabeau said.

He smiled back at her reluctantly. "Och, well, I canna deny I miss the marshes when I'm away from them. Eà kens why, it's a miserable land, fit only for frogs and swamp-rats."

"I was surprised by how bonny the marshes were," Isabeau replied. "I thought it would be all grey and drear."

"Och, the swamp has put on her feasting clothes in honor o' your visit," Gwilym answered with a low bow. As always it was difficult to tell if he was being serious or sarcastic, but Isabeau thanked him nonetheless. She had spent much time studying the secrets of the High Magic with the one-legged sorcerer since undertaking her Sorceress Test and had grown to like him very much, sharing with him a rather mordant humor and a liking for the ridiculous, and admiring his quick intelligence and wit.

The Sorceress Test had been a shock to Isabeau, breaking down some walls within her, walls that had perhaps also been props. Certainly Isabeau had since become aware of an acute heightening of sensitivity along with the heightening of her powers. An unexpected glimpse of beauty, the sight of Bronwen's eyelashes resting on her sleep-flushed cheek, a strain of exquisite music, the heady scent of summer roses, all filled her with a joy akin to pain. It was as if she had been peeled like an onion, layers of hard skin torn away to reveal a pure white core. She was terribly aware of the fragility of being. It was as if she could see the shadow of death pressing up close to the brightness of life, sharply underlining every moment. She felt as if her whole body was brimming over with tenderness and gladness yet, paradoxically, she was filled with fear and sorrow and a new uncertainty. This confusion of emotion often troubled her, and only the hot rush of pride and gladness she felt every time she saw the dragoneye ring on the middle finger of her left hand persuaded her that it had all been worthwhile.

Brun the cluricaun, sensing her vulnerability, had kept close to her side, bringing her little clusters of flowers or a handful of eggs, polishing her boots and playing strange little tunes on his flute for her. His concern touched her greatly, and she accepted his little gifts and services with real gratitude. He stood beside her now, his furry ears pricked forward with eager curiosity, his necklace of found objects chiming gently.

Suddenly he whimpered, laying his ears right back, his long tail twisting about anxiously. Isabeau looked up at once. A swarm of Mesmerdean nymphs had risen silently out of the marsh and now hovered all round the clearing, their bulging multifaceted eyes fixed upon Meghan. She did not seem to notice, but Gitâ was wrapped tightly around her throat, his paw on her ear. Gwilym indicated the silver-winged faeries with a subtle gesture of the hand.

"They are like ravens hovering about a corpse, but their prey is no' yet dead," he said with a shudder. "Havers, I hate Mesmerdean!"

"When I saw they no longer followed Meghan everywhere she went, I had hoped they had forgotten," Isabeau said.

"Mesmerdean never forget," Gwilym said somberly.

Isabeau's throat muscles tightened and she had to breathe in deeply and calmly through her nose before the constriction passed. "So there is no chance?"

He looked at her sardonically. "No' while a Mesmerd lives."

"Will they wait?" Isabeau laid her hand on his arm and felt his muscles clench.

"To the very hour o' the agreement and no' a second longer," he answered, his dark ugly face very grim. "Strange as it may seem, the Mesmerdean are an honorable race, more honorable than most men. They are immovable, however. Nothing that could cause a man to change his mind, love or gold or power, would change a Mesmerd's."

Isabeau stared at the swarm of nymphs, fascinated. Unlike the dry, shrivelled-up faces of the elders, the nymphs possessed an unearthly beauty that somehow made them seem even more sinister. For long moments they hovered, motionless, wings whirring, then suddenly darted sideways, causing her heart to jolt and her breath to quicken. All round them a miasma seemed to hang like the effluvium of a freshly dug grave. It brought back many terrifying memories and she shuddered and stepped a little closer to Gwilym.

"Will they remember that *I* have killed Mesmerdean?"

"Mesmerdean never forget," he repeated, looking down at her with an unreadable expression on his face.

"Never forget," Brun echoed. "Never forget, never forgive, forever and for-never, never ever forgive."

She bit her lip, frowning, unable to take her eyes off the hovering marsh-faeries with their strange, beautiful faces, their huge glittering eyes and gauzy wings.

Gwilym gave a harsh laugh. "Never fear, Beau," he said. "I have killed many more than ye. Meghan has taken all o' our sins upon herself. Mesmerdean do no' forget and do no' forgive, but they shall no' exact vengeance upon us all as long as Meghan fulfills her pledge and gives herself to them. As long as Meghan dies in their arms we shall be safe."

Isabeau said a little huskily, "I hate to think that she must go to them, they are such horrible ghoulish creatures. I wish—"

"If wishes were pots and pans, we'd have no need for tinkers," Meghan said gruffly, so that Isabeau jumped and gave a little cry of surprise. She could think of nothing to say, but Meghan required no words, just patted her on the arm and said, "Come, it is our turn to cross the loch. Ugly, will ye ride with us?"

"It would be my honor," Gwilym replied and handed Meghan down into the long pinnace, which had been carved into the shape of a swan with proudly raised head and folded wings. Isabeau jumped down beside her, then reached up her arms to the twins. Owein almost fell into the water in his eagerness to jump off the wharf and only Isabeau's quick reflexes saved him. She

hugged him close, not wanting to scold him when she
knew how much he must miss his mother.

"Snuggle up close, my bairns, else we'll no' all fit,"
she said and cuddled Bronwen and Olwynne close under
her arms as the one-legged sorcerer clambered stiffly
down beside them, almost overbalancing when his
wooden stump slipped on the damp wood. Isabeau had to
restrain herself from offering him her hand, knowing how
much Gwilym hated to be reminded of his disability.
Brun the cluricaun jumped in last, causing the boat to
rock wildly.

The pinnace glided across the still waters of the Murkmyre with no need for anyone to raise the sail or lift an
oar. Isabeau let her hand trail in the water, admiring the
beautiful reflection of the palace in the loch. The swan-
boat's white breast cut through the reflection, swirling it
into a shimmer of pearly colors. Then the pinnace
bumped up against a wide marble platform where Iain
and Elfrida were waiting, Neil jumping about eagerly by
their side.

"Welcome to my h-h-h-home, Isabeau," Iain said with
a smile, reaching his hand down to her. She took it and let
him pull her up, staring wide-eyed at the immense palace
soaring above them.

"It's huge," she cried.

Huge-hooh haunt-hooh! Buba said, her head tilted
right back, her golden eyes round with amazement.

Iain smiled ruefully. "Aye, and m-m-m-most o' it lies
empty. Once we have won peace, we shall have to see
what we c-c-can do to fill it wi' life again. Ye ken our libraries here are the b-b-best in all the land? Happen ye
should come and stay with us and study here for a while."

"I'd like that," Isabeau replied rather shyly.

Iain helped Meghan and the twins out. Bronwen

scrambled out to join Donncan, who had flown out as soon as the pinnace had touched land and was now scrapping good-humoredly with Neil.

"Come and I'll show ye my rooms, Bronwen," Neil said. "I have the best rocking horse ye've ever seen."

"I bet it's no' as big as mine," Donncan immediately cried, bristling up.

"Is too!"

"Is no'!"

"That's enough, laddies!" Isabeau said. "Donncan, ye are Cuckoo's guest here, please mind your manners."

"But that's no' fair!" Donncan cried. "When Cuckoo was at Lucescere, ye said I had to mind my manners because he was *my* guest. When do I get to *no'* mind my manners?"

"Never," Lachlan said, giving Isabeau a rueful smile as he came out of the palace. "Ye are a MacCuinn, Donncan, and heir to the throne. Ye can never forget your manners."

"It doesna seem fair," Donncan said sulkily, following Neil as he proudly showed Bronwen up the steps and into the palace.

"We must do something about finding the bairns a new nursemaid," Lachlan said apologetically to Isabeau. "Ye seem to be doing naught else but minding them for me."

"Och, that be no trouble," Isabeau replied, rather disconcerted. "I fain do it, and besides—"

"Ye be a sorceress now," Lachlan said. "Ye canna be wasting your time running after a passel o' bairns."

"I fain do it," Isabeau replied shyly, taking Olwynne's hand and helping her up the steps. "Ye ken I love them dearly."

"Aye, I ken," Lachlan said softly, taking Owein's hand and walking up the steps beside her, his night-black wings brushing against her legs. The little boy fluttered his own wings so that he hopped and bounded up the stairs rather than climbed. He was still too young to have worked out how to use his wings fully, but he nonetheless found them a great help in reaching things the adults would much rather he left alone.

Isabeau found it hard to look at Lachlan or to say anything that sounded natural, so she kept silent, concentrating on helping Olwynne, who was still rather prone to tripping over her own feet.

After a moment, Lachlan said, "Besides, I do no' think Meghan will thank me if I allow ye to spend all your time looking after the bairns. I ken she is looking forward to having ye near on this journey, for she says your studies have already been too hurly-burly."

"Well, that's true!" Isabeau laughed at him. "What wi' being on the Spine o' the World and then chasing your laddiekin all over the Muir Finn, it's a wonder I've won any rings at all."

"I ken and I'm sorry," Lachlan said rather awkwardly.

Isabeau regarded him skeptically. "Sorry for what? That my studies have been a wee bit haphazard? Och, that was no' your fault, though o' course I'm glad to blame ye if ye want!"

Lachlan flushed, opening his mouth angrily, then shut it with an exasperated glance at her. "Here I am trying to be nice to ye and all ye do is provoke me!"

"Och, I'm sorry," Isabeau said sweetly. "It's just I'm no' used to ye trying to be nice."

Lachlan swung round, his wings opening a little, his flush deepening. "Isabeau!"

"Aye?"

He glared at her for a moment, then reluctantly laughed.

"True enough, I suppose, and for that I'm sorry too. I'll try harder."

"It must be hard," Isabeau said sympathetically. He looked at her suspiciously and she grinned at him, saying, "Being nice, I mean. It's so alien to your nature."

As he struggled between anger and laughter, she skipped away down the hall, Olwynne and Owein both hanging off her hands, Buba fluttering from chair back to balustrade. Halfway up the stairs she turned back and called, "And o' course, I'm such a difficult person to be nice to."

He laughed despite himself, and she smiled at him, before turning away to help the twins once more.

Elfrida was waiting for her on the landing above, saying, "I thought I'd give ye a room close to the babes, Isabeau, for I ken they would fain have ye near."

"Thank ye, that was thoughtful," Isabeau answered, looking about her with great interest as Elfrida led the way up the stairs. The palace was very richly furnished with finely woven carpets and tapestries, many very large paintings in ornate frames, and bowls and vases of the finest porcelain. The device of the flowering thistle was everywhere—engraved on doors, set in mosaic on the floor, embroidered on velvet cushions, and worn on the breast of every one of the hundreds of servants that moved soundlessly through the corridors. It was even set at regular intervals in the gilded balustrade of the grand staircase.

"It is very nice to be home again," Elfrida said. "It is odd, even though I lived in Tìrsoilleir all my life and am now its banprionnsa, I still think o' Arran as being home." She smiled at Isabeau shyly. "It was the first place I was happy, I suppose."

"Ye were raised in the Black Tower, though, were ye

no'?" Isabeau asked. "I imagine that was no' a happy place."

"Nay, no' a happy place at all. Happiness was no' an objective o' the Tìrsoillerean. I was whipped across the hand if I was ever caught smiling, and dare no' think what punishment I would have been given for laughing."

"How horrible!"

"It was no' pleasant, particularly when I was naught but a bairn myself."

They came into a big sunny playroom that was filled with every imaginable toy a six-year-old boy could want. There was a miniature castle complete with a moving drawbridge and tin soldiers dressed in the Arran livery; there were balls and building blocks and a chest of clothes for dress-ups and a rocking horse as large as Cuckoo's own pony. The children all ran forward with cries of delight and were soon busy playing, as Elfrida showed Isabeau where they would all sleep. Cots had been set up for the twins in an antechamber to the room that Donncan would share with Neil, while Bronwen had been given a room across the hall, right next to Isabeau.

An old bogfaery was sitting in a rocking chair, sewing. She had heavily wrinkled skin of a purplish-black color, with black ripples of fur over her head and arms. As Isabeau and Elfrida came in she smiled, showing two sharp little fangs.

"This is Aya," Elfrida said. "She was Iain's nanny when he was a lad and now she has come back to help look after our own laddiekin."

"How lovely for ye," Isabeau said warmly to the bogfaery. "It must make ye very happy to see wee Cuckoo growing up so bright and happy."

The bogfaery nodded. "Ee-an big man, no need Aya no

more, Aya sad, Aya go 'way. Now Ee-an have wee man, Aya come back, Aya glad."

"When Iain was a bairn, Aya was the only one to be kind to him and look out for him," Elfrida said, showing Isabeau through into the corridor again. "He loves her very much. Bogfaeries make wonderful nannies, for they're so gentle and loving."

"Happen I shall have to borrow one," Isabeau sighed. "I must admit I'm finding it rather hard looking after four bairns as well as studying with Gwilym and directing the healers. We've had rather bad luck with our nursemaids recently."

Elfrida nodded, appreciating the bitter irony. "Well, why do ye no' take young Maura, Aya's grand-daughter? She is a sweet wee thing, and very strong, despite her size. She can cook and sew and has worked here with Aya and her mother Faya for some years now, so she's had experience with bairns."

As she spoke she opened the door into a small but charming bedroom, its wall hung with a tapestry of a boating party on the loch, with a wedge of crimson-winged swans flying above. It had a wide window overlooking the water.

"Och, this is lovely!" Isabeau exclaimed, following Elfrida in.

Isabeau's luggage had already been brought up from the boat and another bogfaery was padding about quietly, packing away her few clothes and pouring her out some honey-scented water in which to wash. Isabeau thanked her and then stood at the window, admiring the view. At the sound of peals of childish laughter from across the corridor, the two women turned and smiled at each other.

"That is why I do so want Cuckoo to have a happy childhood," Elfrida said impetuously. "And I ken Iain feels the same. In some ways his was worse than mine because I at least kent my parents had loved me. My tormentors were my prison guards, no' my own mother."

Isabeau hesitated, then found the courage to raise something that had been troubling her greatly. "Elfrida, Iain does ken, does he no'? That it was me that killed his mother?"

Elfrida looked at her in some surprise. "We have heard the story o' how the Thistle died. I had thought it was more by her own hand than yours."

"But I was the one who swapped the wine," Isabeau said, a knot of anxiety in her chest.

Elfrida smiled at her. "But Margrit who put the poison in the wine. Aye, Iain kens. It seems a fitting way for her to die, and I must say we are all relieved. We do no' need to fear she shall try to steal Cuckoo away from us again, and this way she did no' die by Iain's hand, which would have been a terrible thing, regardless o' how evil she was. She has been a shadow on our happiness from the very beginning and now that shadow is gone, and for that both o' us are grateful to ye, truly."

"Och, I'm glad," Isabeau cried. "I would have been so unhappy if Iain had hated me!"

Elfrida laid a cool hand on Isabeau's arm. "He would never hate ye, Isabeau. The only person Iain has ever hated was Margrit, and believe me, she deserved it. So do no' think on it anymore. We wish ye to enjoy your stay in Arran. Tomorrow we have organized a boating expedition up the river so ye can see the golden goddess in flower, and tonight we shall have a feast to celebrate the Rìgh's visit." She moved away, her pale face coloring a little. "I hope ye do no' mind, Isabeau, but I can no' help noticing that ye do no' have any feasting clothes. Ye are here tonight as our honored guest, no' as a witch o' the

Coven, and so I have brought ye some dresses to choose from. If ye prefer to wear your witch's robes, well, o' course ye may, but I just thought . . ."

Isabeau's face lit up with pleasure. "Och really?" she asked eagerly. "Nay, I'd love to wear something festive! I do have some other clothes back in Lucescere, but since we ride to war, I did no' pack them."

Elfrida was pleased at Isabeau's delight and clapped her hands imperiously. Within a few minutes a procession of bogfaeries came in with piles of silks and satins in all colors of the rainbow, spreading them out on the bed or hanging them up from the curtain rail. "They all belonged to Margrit," Elfrida said, "but most o' them have never been worn. Ye must no' mind that they were hers. The seamstresses will take them in for ye."

Isabeau could not help exclaiming in delight. Even though she was a fully fledged member of the Coven of Witches, and so used to a life of austerity, she had not lost her love of finery. Somehow this sensuous side of her nature had never been given a chance for full expression, and the sight of all those luxurious fabrics and gorgeous colors went to her head like a draught of goldensloe wine.

After twirling about in front of the long mirrors in one gown after another, Isabeau at last decided what she would wear to the feast that night. It was a gown of pale ivory satin printed all over with tiny crimson roses, golden lilies and delicate sprigs of forget-me-not. The skirt was trimmed and embellished in velvet ribbon of the same forget-me-not blue, with a blue velvet bodice and long, tightly fitting sleeves slashed to allow wisps of ivory gauze to billow out. The gold-embroidered cuffs came to a long tapering point over the hands, hiding Isabeau's maimed fingers, while the bodice was cut low over her breasts, the embroidered neckline softened with pleated gauze of the same pale ivory.

That evening Elfrida's maid dressed Isabeau and drew her hair from her face with a simple fillet of blue velvet and pearls, allowing the mass of fiery curls to hang free down her back. When the maid had at last expressed her satisfaction, Isabeau stood and stared at herself in the mirror. For the first time she looked like a banprionnsa. More important, in Isabeau's mind, she looked beautiful. She smiled at herself, thanked Elfrida's maid, gathered up the little gold-embroidered reticule that went with the gown, and squared her shoulders. For some reason she felt much more nervous having to face Lachlan and his court now that she was dressed like any of the other ladies.

Snooze-hooh? she asked Buba, who had settled on the back of a chair, her ear tufts lowered sleepily.

Snooze-hooh, the little owl agreed, her round eyes already closing.

Meghan was waiting for her in her own room just next door. She too had changed her clothes and was dressed in a severe gown of dark green velvet, relieved only by her plaid and the great emerald that fastened it about her shoulders. As usual Gitâ was perched on her shoulder, his black eyes bright as pools of ink, his plumy tail carefully groomed. Meghan looked Isabeau over rather caustically, saying, "Och, ye're gaudy tonight, my Beau."

Isabeau flushed, but said laughingly, "Well, I do no' often get a chance to dress up!"

She helped the old sorceress to her feet and offered her arm for Meghan to lean upon. They made their way slowly down the corridor, often stopping to admire a particularly fine piece of porcelain or cunningly carved box, thereby covertly allowing Meghan to catch her breath.

As they made their way down the sweeping staircase they heard a hum of conversation, and then, as they turned the corner to the last flight, saw the grand hall below packed with people. There was the blue-clad Yeomen of the Guard, Lachlan's personal guard, captained by Duncan Ironfist, who was also seanalair of the Rìgh's army.

Then there were the lairds, all dressed in their family tartans, and their officers and courtiers. Most important of the lairds were Alasdair Garrie of Killiegarrie, uncle to Melisse NicThanach and seanalair of her army, and Cameron Guthrie of Gleneagles, the NicAislin's seanalair. Neither the NicThanah nor the NicAislin rode to war, like most women of Eileanan bowing to tradition and leaving the fighting to the men. As a result the majority of the crowd gathered in the grand entrance hall were men, the only women being witches or healers. Isabeau knew the witches and healers well, but their faces were lost in the crowd so that it seemed she was entering a sea of strangers.

As Meghan and Isabeau made their way down the steps, a lull fell over the crowd and many turned to stare, even though they had seen both the witches many times before. Isabeau hesitated in sudden shyness. Then Dide came forward to offer her his hand and lead her down the last few steps.

Like all of the Rìgh's officers, he wore a long blue cloak, pinned back at the shoulder with a badge depicting a charging stag, the ensign of the Yeomen of the Guard. His dark curls were tied back neatly under a cockaded blue tam o'shanter, and his blue kilt swung with every step. There was no sign of the shabby jongleur Isabeau had always known and she felt a sudden surge of shyness.

Then he grinned at her, and all her awkwardness dissolved.

"Flaming dragon balls, ye're fine tonight," he said. "If Finn were here, she'd say ye were as fine as a goat's turd stuck with buttercups."

Isabeau laughed at him. "Such a courtier," she mocked. "Now I understand why Lachlan usually insists on ye travelling around like a gypsy."

"Och, that be because he's afraid o' the havoc I'd cause among the ladies if I stayed wi' the court," he answered, his black eyes glinting with laughter.

"If that is the sort o' compliment ye normally pay, I can just imagine the sort o' havoc ye'd cause," she replied. "It's a wonder that guitar o' yours has no' been broken over your head afore now."

"A few people have tried," he admitted, "but never a lady. Always their husbands, I fear."

Isabeau screwed up her face at him. "To hear ye speak, anyone would think ye were a libertine o' the worst sort, but I ken it be all talk and no truth."

"Is that so?" he asked. "And how do ye be kenning?"

Isabeau looked him over consideringly. "I be a sorceress now and can see into the hearts o' men," she said with great solemnity.

Color rushed into Dide's cheeks. "Is that so? What am I thinking now then?" he challenged.

Isabeau let a small smile grow on her lips. "I may be a sorceress, but I am also a banprionnsa and far too finely bred to give such thoughts expression," she said piously.

He was startled into a shout of laughter. "Wha' a drayload o' dragon dung!"

This time it was Isabeau who was startled. "What did you say?"

"That's another o' our young Finn's sayings. Believe

me, a few months in her company and we have all extended our vocabulary remarkably. She be a banprionnsa too, and the foulest-mouthed lass I've ever kent. If ye take her as your model, ye need have no hesitation in saying what's on *my* mind."

At that moment he brought Isabeau to where Lachlan stood waiting with his courtiers. The laughter still lingering in her eyes, Isabeau swept the Rìgh a graceful curtsey. He acknowledged her with a rather curt nod of the head, then came forward to offer Meghan his arm. The old sorceress had been talking with her old friend Enit Silverthroat, who was sitting on a padded chair with long poles that enabled her to be carried about. At Lachlan's gesture, though, the sorceress allowed her great-great-great-grand-nephew to lead her forward and into the feasting hall. Iain and Elfrida followed, then the Duke of Killiegarrie offered Isabeau his arm. Isabeau accepted, unable to help feeling snubbed by Lachlan's curtness.

Isabeau's moment of pique soon faded. Lachlan's men competed avidly for her attentions, flattering her shamelessly and being quick to fill up her goblet and offer her the tastiest tidbits of roast swan. Since Isabeau ate no meat, this gambit failed to win her approval, but she blushed and laughed at all their compliments, her eyes shining brilliantly blue with excitement.

All of the soldiers were filled with high spirits. They boasted of their victories in Tìrsoilleir, recounting this battle or that charge, describing with many gestures and explanations how the heroes of that campaign had fought and won the day. Even though Lachlan figured strongly in their stories, he alone did not join in the laughter and storytelling, his dark face remaining somber. Isabeau was uncomfortably aware of how often his regard turned to rest upon her face. His brooding gaze reminded her of the first time they had met, when he had sat by her fire and eaten her porridge and stared at her with that exact same intense, inscrutable awareness. It made her restive, bringing blood to pound at her temples and tingle in her fingertips. She did her best to ignore him, though it seemed to her a current of awareness ran between them, palpable as a flash of lightning.

Certainly Dide noticed, for he often glanced from one to the other. He leaned a little closer to Isabeau as a consequence, often laying his hand on her arm or touching her shoulder to gain her attention.

As usual the young earl kept the table in a stir of merriment, bringing the characters of his tales to life with such deft mimicry that it seemed they thronged at his shoulder, speaking and acting for themselves. Dide was a gifted storyteller. Every tale he told, no matter how exciting or amusing, had a prick of pathos and a twist of terror, so that everyone gathered at the high table was torn between horror, sympathy, amusement and anticipation, breathlessly awaiting his next word. As riveted as anyone else there, Isabeau nonetheless could not help but notice how deliberately Dide played upon his audience's emotions, and how ready the lairds were to be diverted. It was clear much of the cheerful confidence about the upcoming confrontation with the Fairgean was mere bravado.

When the plates had all been cleared away and platters of fruits and sweetmeats brought out, Enit's chair was carried to the center of the room. Dide was brought his guitar and Jay the Fiddler his viola by the dark-skinned bogfaeries who had served the meal. Brun bounded forward excitedly, his little silver flute in his hands. Isabeau leant forward eagerly. She had heard Jay and Dide play together at the May Day feast and was eager indeed to hear them again. She had never heard Enit sing, but knew she had a rare power. It was a privilege indeed to hear her for the old woman was now so badly crippled that she rarely performed.

Music spilled across the grand hall and the loud hum of conversation slowly died. It was a most haunting tune, plaintive and sweet. Then Enit leant forward a little in her chair, opening her mouth to sing. Her voice soared up towards the vaulted ceiling, as silvery pure and melodious as a nightingale's.

"I wish, I wish, I wish in vain,
I wish I were a maid again;
A maid again I never will be,
Till apples grow on an orange tree,
Aye, till apples grow on an orange tree.
Now there's a tavern in the town
Where my love sits himself down;
He calls another lassie to his knee
And tells her the tale he once told me,
Aye, tells her the tale he once told me.
I wish, I wish my babe was born
An' smiling on yon nurse's knee;
An' I myself were dead and gone,
Wi' green, green grass growing over me,
Aye, wi' green, green grass growing over me."

Enit's voice quavered and broke. Isabeau found tears were stinging her eyes, a shiver running all over her skin. Enit sang with such pathos quivering in every note, it was impossible to believe she was not a young girl, abandoned by her lover, longing for death.

There was a long silence when she had finished and then riotous applause. Isabeau pressed her fingers against her wet eyes, not wanting anyone to know how much the song had stirred her. She looked up and met Lachlan's intense golden gaze and felt the color surge up under her fair skin.

Enit sang another song, this time a merry lilting tune, and then retired, while Dide sang a stirring war song, Brun the cluricaun exchanging his flute for a little round drum. The table began to break up, people moving around to speak to others or withdrawing to the terrace to drink whisky, smoke their pipes and talk.

Meghan rose to speak with Enit before she was carried back up to her room, and Elfrida went to give her compliments to her chef. For a moment Isabeau was left alone at the high table with Lachlan.

There was a long silence. Isabeau said rather shyly, "I have never heard Enit sing before. Is she no' wonderful?"

Lachlan nodded. "Aye, I have never heard her equal."

Isabeau tried to think of something else to say. It occurred to her that she had never really been alone with Lachlan since that first meeting so many years ago. When they had met again, he had been Iseult's husband, and crowned Rìgh soon after. She looked up at him through her lashes. He was staring moodily into his wine goblet. Obviously the silence did not bother him at all.

Suddenly he looked up, staring at her again. Hot and uncomfortable, Isabeau dropped her gaze, staring at her lily- and rose-strewn lap. "Do ye like my dress?" she asked, rather at random. "Elfrida gave it to me. Is it no' bonny?"

"Very bonny," he answered with an odd inflection in his voice.

Conscious of that fierce unwavering gaze, she glanced up again, then away. With the fingers of her good hand she twisted her napkin about.

"Ye look like ye did when we first met," Lachlan suddenly said, very low. "Your hair has grown long again. It was very long that first time, in the woods."

Isabeau put a hand up to her hair self-consciously. "Aye, it was down to my knees back then. They cut it all off when I had the fever, after . . ." She faltered.

"After ye lost your fingers?"

Isabeau's cheeks burnt. Unconsciously she tugged at the tapering cuff of her dress, pulling it lower so that her maimed hand was hidden. Lachlan held out his hand.

"May I see?"

Isabeau hesitated, then slowly, reluctantly, held out her left hand. He took it in his, turned it over so the light of the candles fell full upon it. Where the two smallest fingers should have been were two deep, ugly pits of white scar tissue. The other two fingers and the thumb were bent and misshapen, though since Isabeau had swum in the Pool of Two Moons, she had regained the use of them.

Lachlan rubbed his thumb over the scars. "I am very sorry," he said with difficulty. "That is the fate ye saved me from, when ye rescued me that time. It should have been me that was tortured."

Isabeau pulled her hand away. "I canna say that I'm glad to have taken your place," she said frankly, "but I am glad that ye were spared. Ye had already suffered enough."

Lachlan nodded a little. "I am sorry though. I do no' think I ever told ye so."

"Ye said ye'd never asked me to rescue ye." Remembered indignation brought the sparkle back to Isabeau's eyes and she looked at him fully for the first time.

He smiled at her ruefully. "I was full o' bitter rage at everyone and everything in those days," he said. "All I kent was that I had to escape the Awl, find Meghan, try to overthrow the Ensorcellor. It did no' matter who was crushed on the way."

"But what about later?" Isabeau said hotly. "Ye've always been very quick to fraitch wi' me!"

Lachlan scowled and dropped his eyes. "I suppose I was angry wi' ye for putting me in the wrong." Then he looked up, saying with an ironical smile, "Besides, ye must realize it was very confusing for me. Ye look just like Iseult. When I first met her, I thought it was ye, and when I met ye again, ye could have been her."

"I can imagine that must have been a wee bit confusing," Isabeau said, her laugh rather forced, her cheeks hot. "Hopefully ye can tell us apart by now though."

His smile died. "Aye, o' course."

Isabeau looked at him hesitantly. Even as she was searching for the right words or gesture, she became aware of Dide coming up to the table, his guitar hanging from his hand, his black eyes turning from one to the other. She sat back, suddenly aware that she and Lachlan had leant close together in their conversation. Her cheeks heated again.

Frowning a little, Dide said to Lachlan, "Any requests for me, master?"

Lachlan's expression was very somber. "Play for me the song ye wrote about my brothers."

Dide hesitated. "Master—"

"Play it for me, Dide."

The young earl nodded and went back to his seat, his face troubled. The melancholy tune crept out and filled the room, then Dide began to sing. His face dark with remembered grief, Lachlan signaled for the servants to fill his goblet once more.

"Once there were four brothers true
Four brothers who together grew
Jesting and laughing together the four

In summer's brightness and winter's hoar.
O where have ye gone, where have ye gone, my
    brothers,
Leaving me all alone?
O where have ye gone, where have ye gone, my
    brothers,
Where have ye gone, my brothers?
One day a fair maiden rode by,
Whither she came none knew, or why.
As pale as seafoam was that maiden fair,
And black as night her silken hair.
O where have ye flown, where have ye flown, my
    brothers,
Turning my heart to stone?
O where have ye flown, where have ye flown, my
    brothers,
Where have ye flown, my brothers?
On the oldest brother she cast a spell,
Madly in love with her he fell,
That very week they were together wed,
Though the hearts of his three brothers bled.
O where have ye gone, where have ye gone, my
    brothers,
Leaving me all alone?
O where have ye gone, where have ye gone, my
    brothers,
Where have ye gone, my brothers?
For she held a mirror to their eyes,
laughing as in terror they cried,
first one, then another, and then the third,
were transformed into three blackbirds.
O where have ye flown, my black-winged birds,
Turning my heart to stone?
O where have ye flown, my black-winged brothers?

Where have ye flown, my brothers?
Flung into the dark lonely night,
Three blackbirds took desperate flight,
Upon their trail her cruel hawk flew,
First one, then another, to their deaths pursued.
O where have ye gone, where have ye gone, my
*   brothers,*
Your joyous life all turned to bone?
O where have ye gone, where have ye gone, my
*   brothers,*
Where have ye gone, my brothers?
Only the youngest, he flew free,
Hid in the branches of an old oak tree,
Five years he was trapped in the shape of a bird,
Though he sang and sang, none understood a word.
O where have ye flown, my black-winged birds,
Leaving me all alone?
O where have ye flown, my black-winged brothers?
Where have ye flown, my brothers?

Isabeau listened in silence, little shivers running down
her spine. The song was so very beautiful and so very
sad, and she could not help an upwelling of sympathy and
compassion for the young Rìgh, who had had his life destroyed by Maya and her sorcerous schemes. No wonder
Lachlan hated the Fairgean, when they had killed his father and all three of his brothers.

When the song had finished, she rose and said, without looking at Lachlan, "It grows late, Your Highness. I
think I shall go to bed."

Lachlan nodded, glancing up from the dregs of his
wine to say very softly, "Sleep well, Isabeau."

"Thank you," she answered and went swiftly out of the
room, once again feeling as if tears would choke her. She

did not know what it was that had moved her so powerfully, whether it was just because she had been so emotionally wrought up since her Sorceress Test, or whether this new warmth of Lachlan's pierced all the armor she had constructed against him. All she knew was that her emotions were in turmoil.

Though Isabeau found it hard to calm her thoughts she did at last sleep. In the clear radiance of the morning she could not help but wonder if all the undercurrents the previous evening had been purely her imagination. She dressed again in her austere white robes and witch's dagger, bound her hair back tightly and hung the owl-talon necklace around her neck. With Buba riding on her shoulder she went downstairs and was directed by one of the soft-footed servants out to the terrace.

There a long table had been set up, loaded with fruits and cereals and silver pots of piping hot tea. Gravely Isabeau greeted those already seated at the table. Though most smiled at her and returned her greeting, Lachlan merely shot her a searching glance before returning his attention to his plate. Despite his brusqueness, Isabeau was immediately aware of the tension simmering away under the surface.

Dide leapt up and pulled out a chair for her, saying teasingly, "I see we have lost Beau the belle o' the ball and have back our stern sorceress. How are ye yourself, my bonny?"

She sat down, cursing her fair skin which showed the rush of blood to her face so clearly. "I am well, thank ye," she replied and served herself some of the rather odd-looking marsh fruits, which were enclosed within a thick prickly skin that stung her fingers as she peeled it. The flesh within was tender and white, however, and spurted into her mouth with a piquant sweetness.

Iain said warmly, "It be a lovely day, Isabeau. Elfrida and I thought we'd get together a party to sail up the river to see the golden goddess, who is in full bloom right now. Have ye heard o' our golden goddess? It is a flower, ye ken, as tall as ye and, unlike ye, always hungry for meat. They are carnivorous, did ye ken? My ancestors were wont to throw unwelcome intruders to her, which may explain some at least o' Arran's fearsome reputation. She is bonny indeed, though, and well worth seeing."

He cast a sly glance at the young earl, saying, "Happen ye'd fain taste Arran's famous mulled wine, Isabeau, made from the golden goddess honey. I am sure Dide for one would fain drink a toast with ye."

Both Lachlan and Dide looked up, one frowning, the other laughing.

"Thank you but I've tasted o' the honeyed wine," Isabeau replied gravely.

"Is that so?" Dide demanded. "And wi' whom, may I ask?"

"None o' your business," Isabeau replied, smiling.

There was much laughter and teasing comments from those gathered around the table. Dide pretended to be mortally wounded, holding his heart and rolling his eyes back in his head. "Och, ye are cruel," he protested. "Never mind, if ye've drunk it once, ye'll be eager to taste it again and I am here, at your service as always, my lady."

"I'll order the punts then," Elfrida said through the laughter. "Meghan, will ye come too?"

Lachlan stood up abruptly. "We have no time for dillydallying," he said harshly. "I'll thank ye to order our guides instead. I am grateful for your hospitality but we all must be on our way."

Elfrida's face fell. "Oh, but Your Highness, I was hoping . . ."

"Will ye no' bide a wee?" Iain said gently. "We have all been on the march for months now, Lachlan. We were hoping we could take the time to rest."

"I have no time for feasts and picnics," Lachlan said harshly. "If we are to have all our men in position by autumn, we must make haste. Who kens how long it will take? Nay, we must be on the road again just as soon as we can reprovision and mobilize." He threw the end of his plaid over his shoulder, thrust the Lodestar deeper into its sheath and walked away, his black wings held stiffly behind him. His gyrfalcon gave a melancholy cry and flew after him. Without looking up, Lachlan held out his gauntleted wrist for the great white bird to drop down upon.

There was a momentary silence. Elfrida clung to Iain's arm, her grey eyes brimming with tears, her lip trembling. "Oh, Iain, I had hoped we could bide a wee . . ."

Iain was clearly disappointed that he could spend only the one night in Arran but he comforted his wife, saying, "Do no' greet, sweetling. Ye ken ye spent too little time in Bride as it is. Ye are Banprionnsa there now, ye must make yourself kent to your people. And I must go to war, that is the way o' it."

"But what if . . . ?" she wept. Iain drew her close and kissed her, smoothing back her fair hair.

"Do no' even think it, Elf, let alone say it," he warned. "Eà will turn her bright face upon us, I am sure o' it. We canna have come so far and against such odds to fail at the last ditch. Besides, do ye no' remember how Lachlan drew upon the Lodestar and cast all the pirate ships to the winds? Such a man canna lose, I promise ye."

The Duke of Killiegarrie had stood up and was giving

terse orders to his lieutenants, his thick dark brows meeting over his nose. The NicAislin's men were grumbling under their breath as they hurriedly drank down their tea and crammed in the last morsel of toast. It was clear none were happy at the directive to mobilize again immediately.

"I hope that cursehag o' yours has made the dragonbane for us already," Duncan said gruffly, "for the mood his Highness is in, I do no' think he'll be happy if he has to bide much longer."

"I'll send a messenger to Shannagh o' the Swamp now," Iain replied, frowning. "We're going to need that dragonbane."

Dide stood up also, smiling at Isabeau ruefully. "Well, my Beau, we shall just have to drink that honeyed wine together another time. No rest for the wicked, as they say."

"But he is such a strange moody man," Elfrida said unhappily. "I do no' understand him at all. What would another day or two matter? Why could ye no' stay here where ye are all comfortable, instead o' riding out to camp in the marshes tonight?"

Iain said rather tightly, "He is right, sweetling. Midsummer has been and gone and we have a long way to go and much to do. Please try to understand."

Meghan had been standing at the low stone balustrade, staring out at the serene blue loch. Isabeau realized she was watching a group of Mesmerdean nymphs who were hovering a short distance away, their many-faceted eyes flashing a metallic hue in the sun. The old sorceress turned at Elfrida's words and said now, with much the same harsh arrogance as the Rìgh: "Lachlan is right, Elfrida NicHilde, and ye should ken it, being the descendant of the Bright Warrior-maid herself. Many a war has been lost because an army was too slow to mobilize." She turned back and stared at the watching marsh-faeries. Isabeau thought she heard her say, very low: "Besides, we canna leave too soon for my liking."

Isabeau went up to her and slid her hand under her elbow. Meghan pressed her hand closer. "Happen I am growing auld," she said softly, "but I dread this coming war. I have fought the Fairgean before, a long time ago. They are no' easy to defeat."

"But ye triumphed over them," Isabeau said reassuringly. "Ye helped Jaspar raise the Lodestar and together ye swept them back to the sea. Ye and Lachlan shall do so again."

"But Jaspar had been properly trained, and still he could no' fully master the Lodestar," Meghan said, a hot ache of misery in her voice. "Lachlan spent the years he should have been studying trapped in the shape o' a blackbird. And he is so quick to lose his temper, so prone to melancholy. It is no' enough to have strength o' will and desire to control the powers o' the Lodestar, no' nearly enough. One needs mastery o' oneself."

"But ye—"

Meghan turned a fierce black gaze upon her. "I will no' be here, Isabeau. Do ye no' realize that? The red comet shall rise in only a few more months and then I shall be dead."

Isabeau was too shaken with grief and misery to speak. Meghan stared at her. "I will be dead," she said softly, "and Lachlan shall have to raise the Lodestar alone. Do ye wonder that I fear for ye all?"

After a moment Isabeau was able to say fiercely, "Do no' speak that way, Meghan. Happen we can do something . . ."

Meghan shook her head. "There is naught ye can do.

Have I no' given the Mesmerdean my word? Come the rising o' the red comet I shall be dead."

Isabeau had to swallow hard before she could speak. "By then we shall have defeated the Fairgean," she said with a confidence she did not feel.

Meghan shook her head. "Defeat them so easily? I think no'. Besides, there is something I have no' told ye. Jorge foretold the rising o' the Fairgean with the rising o' the red comet. He saw the sea itself rear up and flood the land . . ."

I saw the scaly sea rise and flood the land, the Red Wanderer like a bloody gash in the sky. That is when they will come, with the rising o' the red comet the Fairgean shall come . . . Jorge's words echoed in the space between them as if the old seer himself spoke.

Memory suddenly rose up in Isabeau like a great dark wave itself, flooding her so that for a moment she trembled and almost fainted. Meghan seized her arm and supported her, while Buba hooted in dismay. Isabeau came back to full consciousness to hear Meghan saying sharply, "What is it? Isabeau . . ."

"I have had the same vision," she said shakily. "In the eyes o' the queen-dragon. I saw the Red Wanderer burning in the sky, its tail a streak of fire. The sea reared up into a gigantic black wave, taller than any tower I've seen, and came crashing down upon a forest, drowning it. It was horrible . . ."

Meghan regarded her gravely. "It seems ye have a Talent for future-seeing, my Beau. Why did ye no' tell me this?"

Involuntarily Isabeau glanced at the sacred Key of the Coven, hanging on Meghan's chest. Clearly she remembered the star within the circle, which had hung upon her own chest. That had been the last of the visions she had seen in the queen-dragon's eyes and the one that had stayed with her.

Meghan's hand rose swiftly to cover the Key, and Isabeau raised her eyes and met the fierce gaze of the Keybearer. There was no need to speak.

"So," Meghan said at last, "ye too have had visions o' the conjuring o' a tidal wave to drown the land. I wonder how the Fairgean plan to enact such a spell. They are creatures o' the sea, they have no affinity with things o' fire magic like the comet."

"Maya drew upon the comet magic," Isabeau reminded her.

"Aye, but Maya was half human . . ." Again Meghan paused, lost in thought. At last she sighed, looking very drawn in the bright sunshine. "I fear the vision is a true telling, now that I ken ye saw it in the dragon's eye. Dragons can see both ways along the thread o' time."

"But ye ken even better than I that all visions o' the future are naught but a vision o' what *may* happen. It is a future *possibility,* nothing more," Isabeau said swiftly. "Jorge told me so many times. We can change the future, we can strike hard and swift at the Fairgean before they suspect a thing. Ye have six months to teach Lachlan how to control the Lodestar and me to use my powers. And Iseult shall convince the Khan'cohbans to come to our aid. Ye ken she has a genius for warfare, she shall win the day for us . . ."

Meghan sighed even more heavily than before.

"What is it?" Isabeau asked, though she was afraid she knew what it was that troubled the Keybearer so much.

"Ye think I do no' ken the meaning o' the broken *geas?*" Meghan replied. "I may no' have lived among the Kahn'cohbans like ye, but I have listened and tried to understand as much as I can about their ways. A *geas* is more than just a debt o' honor, it is a sacred oath, as binding as the Creed o' the Coven is to the witches. A Khan'-cohban would rather die than break a *geas*, that I ken. Iseult kent what it was she did when she swore that sacred oath to Lachlan—she swore never to leave him, to always serve and obey him. That oath has been dissolved now. Iseult is free to stay upon the Spine o' the World if she so wishes, and do no' think she does no' wish to. She is, and always will be, a Khan'cohban."

"But the bairns . . . and Lachlan. She loves him, I ken she does. Iseult will no' stay on the Spine o' the World. She'll come back and help us win the war."

Meghan stroked Gitâ's fur, her eyes hooded. "Will she?"

The Gathering

Iseult stood on the ridge, breathing in great lungfuls of the sharp cold air. For as far as she could see tiers of tall pointed mountains rose into the sky, glistening with ice. Enormous voluptuous clouds enveloped the higher peaks, their deep folds shadowed blue by the brilliant sunshine, so that it seemed as if the mountains climbed into the very heavens.

Linley MacSeinn stood beside her, his face shadowed with awe and fear. "Ye mean to say ye ken a way through there?"

She nodded. He cursed under his breath and pulled his blue-checked plaid closer about him. His breath clouded the air and his face was mottled with cold. A tall man with a strong nose, piercing sea-green eyes and a neatly trimmed black beard, he had two deeply scored lines between his brows, marks of grief and anger. He wore a great two-handled sword strapped to his back, with a slim dagger at his belt and another thrust into his boot. Beside him stood his son Douglas, as tall and pale-skinned, with the same brightly colored eyes and dark hair. Both had their plaids pinned over their shoulders with a badge forged in the shape of a crowned harp.

Behind them wound a long train of men, all well

wrapped up against the cold. On their backs they carried light packs, and each had a coil of rope and an icepick dangling from his belt. At the rear of the convoy were sleighs drawn by huge woolly creatures with spreading horns and enormous flat feet. The sleighs were all piled high with weapons and provisions provided by Iseult's father. They had spent a week with Iseult's parents at the Towers of Roses and Thorns, while Khan'gharad had prepared both his men and Iseult's for the crossing of the mountains. Iseult had spent the week playing with her new brother and sister and talking with her mother, whom she had not seen since the signing of the Pact of Peace.

It had been a bittersweet time for Iseult. The round curve of the babies' cheeks and their sweet, milky smell had brought a rush of longing for her own children. Iseult had very much wanted to bring them with her to the Spine of the World, but Lachlan had forbidden it angrily. It was too dangerous, he had said. The Rìgh's heir should stay with the Rìgh. The twins were still babes, too young for such a journey.

Iseult knew that he simply could not bear to let Donncan out of his sight after the shock of the little boy's kidnapping, but Lachlan's veto had hurt and angered her nonetheless. She too felt the need to keep Donncan and the twins close and safe. Being apart from her children was a cold ache that grew unbearable at times. She longed to hold them close again, to feel their chubby arms about her neck and to kiss the soft nape of their necks, softer than the most luxurious silk, softer than the petal of a rose. Sternly she repressed her longing, immersing herself in the logistics of moving such a large body of men through the harsh, inhospitable mountain heights. She was the first to wake each morning and among the last to roll herself in her furs and sleep, and only her silence and the gravity of her expression told those who knew her best how troubled and unhappy she was.

The clean smell of the snow and the grandeur of the landscape had brought color to her cheeks and a sparkle to her blue eyes, however. It gave her new resolve and the comfort of knowing that she was at last coming home. Seven years she had been away, seven long years. Iseult took one more deep breath, then strode forward once again, her long steps bringing her to the side of her father.

Khan'gharad was dressed all in white furs like Iseult herself, his shaggy mane of red-grey hair tied back with a leather thong. Two thick curling horns sprang out from either side of his lean, hard face, which was slashed with seven white scars.

"If we move swiftly, the prides shall still be together for the Summer Gathering," he said in his native language. "You shall be able to address them as one and try to win them to your cause. Otherwise your task will be much more difficult."

Iseult made the swift Khan'cohban gesture of assent. She was frowning. She knew the Summer Gathering would be breaking up tomorrow. No matter how hard she had tried, she had simply not been able to push the men along any faster. They were not used to the high altitude or the cold, and the weather had been unseasonably stormy, so that their progress had been much slower than Iseult had expected.

"The snow on the far side of this ridge is firm enough for skimming," Khan'gharad said.

Iseult glanced at him quickly then looked back at the long line of men, which stretched as far as the eye could see. Not for the first time, she wished that the MacSeinn's men knew how to skim. How swift their progress would be if they could fly over the surface of the snow instead of this painfully slow slog. She saw her father's glance linger on the sleighs and his meaning came to her. She gave a sudden quick smile.

"Far better that we do no' come to the Summer Gathering with a show o' force," she answered. "We should leave most o' the men behind and take only our personal guard when we approach the prides."

For the first time in their quick conversation she spoke in the common dialect so that the MacSeinn could understand her also. He had been watching with narrowed suspicious eyes the rapid exchange of grunt and gesture, and at Iseult's words, his expression darkened even further.

He said gruffly, "If we arrive without a proper guard, they will think us weak, and we shall be vulnerable to attack."

"There can be no blood shed during the week o' the Summer Gathering," Iseult said tersely. She found it hard to remember how little most people knew about the prides. Their ignorance angered her, though she rarely allowed her feelings to show. The suspicion in the MacSeinn's eyes, however, brought her simmering resentment to the boil and so the anger was clear in her voice.

"There may be a truce amongst your people but we are no' o' your kind and there is no love lost between us," the MacSeinn said. "Last time we tried to cross the mountains I lost many good men to the snow-faeries, who crept upon us without any warning. I will no' risk that happening again."

Iseult waited a moment before answering. When she spoke her voice was calm and low. "The prides are very territorial. Ye may no' cross their lands without first seeking and being granted permission. It is a procedure o' great ceremony. Ye would have been given warning before attack."

He stared at her. Color slowly ran up his pale cheeks. "Some fellow did come and wave a spear at us and grunt at us a day or two before, but it was gibberish, there was no sense in it at all." His voice was sharp and defensive.

Iseult said softly, "Believe me when I say there are right and wrong ways o' approaching the prides. Ye have no way o' knowing but I was brought up with them, I ken their ways. Please trust me when I say that to approach with an army o' this size will be foolishly aggressive. A small group will be able to utilize one or two o' the sleds and travel down to the Gathering with great speed. If ye wish me to address the prides on your behalf and win their support, this is what we must do. Otherwise I must spend weeks and even months traveling from one haven to another, speaking with the Auld Mother o' each pride separately."

Despite all her attempts to keep her voice conciliatory, all Iseult could manage was the kind of slow deliberateness one uses when speaking to a young child or a simpleton. The MacSeinn's color darkened and he stared at her with great anger and suspicion. The sense of what she said struck him, however, and so he nodded, though with obvious reluctance.

An early dusk was dropping over the mountains and it was colder than ever. Iseult gave the order for the men to make camp, an operation that took some time, then ordered two of the sleighs to be unloaded, their baggage redistributed among the other sleighs. She was conscious of a rising excitement. The smell of the snow sang in her veins. Tomorrow she would see the Firemaker and all her old comrades. Tomorrow she would be among her own kind once more, among those who understood the meaning of honor. Tomorrow she would at last attend the Summer Gathering.

This was a spectacle Iseult had always longed to see. In her youth the prides had gathered only every eight years, in the spring of the Dragon-Star, when the comet had flared red in the night skies. When Iseult had decided to leave and marry Lachlan, the Firemaker had declared a truce between the prides and proposed that they meet each year instead, in the midsummer. At the Gathering, all enmities were set aside. There was much feasting and dancing, trade and bartering, and competitions of strength and skill. Many new relationships were forged, both political and personal. Although Khan'cohbans did not marry in the same way that the islanders did, it was common for young Khan'cohban girls to see a man whose vigor they admired and to agree to accompany him back to his pride. In this way, the blood-lines were kept pure and the possibility of inbreeding avoided. The woman was free to move her furs to the fire of anyone else she admired, or to return home to her family at any time, though she must leave behind any child of the union.

Iseult woke early the next morning and in the bustle of preparing to leave did not think about Lachlan or her children at all. It was a clear day, the white points of the mountains very sharp against the blue sky, the air zinging with the smell of the pine forests. Iseult was filled with energy and good humor, much to her maid Gayna's relief, and it was not long before they were on their way.

Iseult, Gayna and Carrick One-Eye rode in one sleigh with Khan'gharad and his squire, a thoughtful young man called Jamie the Silent due to his ability to go for hours and even days without uttering a word. It was this quality which had caused Khan'gharad to choose him as his squire. Like Iseult, Khan'gharad sometimes found the humans' need to talk incessantly very wearing. Gayna was a sturdy girl with more cheerful commonsense than style, who had been chosen to accompany Iseult as much to maintain the proprieties as to have a care for her person.

In the second sleigh rode Linley MacSeinn and his son Douglas; the MacSeinn's gillie, a tall, grey-haired man named Cavan; and his chamberlain Mattmias, an elderly man with a shock of white hair. In the two sleds behind traveled the MacSeinn's piper, his standard-bearer, his purse-bearer, his seanalair the Duke of Dunkeld and six of his personal bodyguard, called the *luchd-tighe*. If the MacSeinn had had his way, many more among his retinue would have accompanied them. Iseult had been rather bemused to find that the MacSeinn was accompanied everywhere by a whole crowd of aides and courtiers. Most of the posts were hereditary and had been passed down from father to son for a thousand years. Lachlan himself did not have so many personal servants, though Mattmias had very diplomatically explained to Iseult that he should have.

The MacSeinn, Mattmias said, was a clan chief of the old school, a man who ruled over his clan and his country with absolute authority. He was very proud and Iseult knew that he had found the thirteen years of exile from his own country very difficult to bear. Most of his retinue now served him without pay, for the MacSeinn had lost his wealth along with his throne and was totally dependent upon Lachlan's largesse. The desire to regain his independence and his homeland were all that permitted the proud laird to submit to Iseult's ruling that most of his retinue be left behind with the soldiers. To her amazement Iseult found she had a sneaking sympathy for the prionnsa, despite his haughtiness, and so she had not insisted he limit his retinue to two, like herself or her father.

The four sleighs sped down the smooth white slope as the teams of woolly-coated *ulez* galloped ahead at a quite amazing speed given their ponderous build and huge hooves. Iseult leant forward eagerly, drinking in the pine-scented wind that burnt her lungs with cold. Soon the forest had closed about them but still the *ulez* galloped on, the lead pair obeying Khan'gharad's slightest touch on the reins. Khan'gharad's experienced eye recognized every rock or fallen log hidden below soft mounds of snow and so, although the men behind sometimes shouted in alarm at their breakneck speed, he brought them to the floor of the valley without a single spill.

It was high summer and the valley floor was free of snow, sunlit glades stretching in vivid spreads of alpine flowers and lush grass. The *ulez* were tethered and allowed to graze while the party proceeded through the forest on foot. Khan'gharad led the way, his scarred face turning from side to side as he drank in the scents and sights of the forest. He often had to stop and wait for the older men, who flushed with vexation as they paused to catch their breath. Iseult could see Khan'gharad's silent ways, his air of arrogance, his somber scarred face and curling horns all alienated the MacSeinn and his men, who found him intimidating and disliked him for it. It gave Iseult an odd feeling, for suddenly she understood why so many people seemed wary of her too. She did what she could to ease the gulf between them and was rewarded by a new sense of closeness with Douglas and the old seneschal Mattmias. Even the MacSeinn smiled at her once as she held back a prickly branch for him, thanking her gruffly and warning her to mind her soft skin.

Khan'gharad was waiting for them at the top of a low

ridge. Iseult came up eagerly beside him and looked down into a deep green bowl circled by stands of dark forest and bordered on one side by a narrow river that ran swiftly over stones.

In the very center of the meadow was a large circle, marked out by ropes hung with clusters of feathers dyed in the various colors of the prides. At regular intervals around the circle stood tall, ornate poles, all carved with faces, wings and claws in symbolic representation of the prides' totems. Behind each totem pole burnt bonfires, with the members of that pride standing before it, wearing their ceremonial cloaks, their faces painted with charcoal and ocher. The Pride of the Fire-Dragon was the largest, with nearly a hundred members all wearing red feathers and tassels. They were gathered close around an old woman with a high-boned face, snowy white hair and eyes the same vivid blue as Iseult's own. Despite the warmth of the summer sun, she wore a heavy cloak of thick white fur with the snarling, white-maned head of its original owner hanging down her back. Iseult drew in her breath at the sight of her, anticipation quickening her pulse.

In the center of the fighting circle were two men with long poles, their bare torsos grey with mud. One vaulted high over the other, tucking his body into a neat somersault and landing nimbly on his feet, and a few in the crowd made a silent gesture of approval. There were no shouts or catcalls, no applause, no hissing or booing, as there would have been if the audience had been human, for such noises were considered extremely impolite.

Khan'gharad led the small party to the edge of the clearing, choosing to position himself in the empty area between the Pride of the Grey Wolf and the Pride of the Fire-Dragon so as to make clear their neutrality. No one

in the crowd took the slightest notice of them, which
made the MacSeinn draw himself up to his tallest height,
his hands clenched on his sword hilt. The young men of
the *luchd-tighe* muttered angrily amongst themselves.
Iseult would have liked to tell them that the Khan'cohbans were only being polite in paying them no attention
but she dared not speak while the Scarred Warriors
fought.

The pyrotechnic display of feints, ducks and somer-
saults brought a wary respect into the soldiers' eyes.
Again Iseult would have liked to tell them that all this
was merely a sign of the Scarred Warriors' arrogant youth
and inexperience. When Scarred Warriors of seven scars
clashed, there was very little movement, and when a
move was made, it came with the suddenness and venom
of a viper's strike. Iseult watched with a critical eye,
knowing already who would be the victor. A pole lashed
out with sudden ferocity; there was a thud and a groan,
and one of the combatants fell heavily.

After the Scarred Warriors had bowed to each other
and to the Firemaker and quit the circle, Khan'gharad
motioned the others to follow him. He walked slowly and
with great ceremony around the outside of the circle until
he came to the bonfire of the Firemaker.

"Ye must do as he does," Iseult murmured under her
breath, angry with her father for his failure to explain
some of the Khan'cohbans' customs. As Khan'gharad
knelt in the mud before the old woman, his head lowered
and his hands folded, the MacSeinn halted for a moment,
his heavy brows drawn together. Eventually he too knelt,
and the rest of the retinue followed suit, though with obvious reluctance.

The Firemaker swept two fingers to her brow, then to
her heart, then out to the ring of white mountains.

Khan'gharad crossed his hands over his breast and bowed his head. Iseult mimicked his response and the others did the same.

"Greetings, son of my daughter," the Firemaker said. There was a sheen of moisture in her eyes, though her gestures were made with ritualistic slowness. "Welcome to our Gathering."

"Greetings, Old Mother," Khan'gharad said with great respect. "May I have your blessing?" When she made the gesture of assent, he rose and knelt at her feet, his horned head bent very low. The Firemaker raised her thin, vein-knotted hand and made the mark of the Gods of White on Khan'gharad's brow. He thanked her and rose, retreating back to where the others still knelt, gazing with amazement. Only Iseult kept her eyes lowered as one should, wishing she dared whisper to the others not to stare so rudely.

"Greetings, daughter of my daughter's son," the Firemaker said. Iseult returned the greeting and received the blessing from her great-grandmother, seizing the old woman's hand and kissing it before retreating back to her position. The Firemaker allowed the indiscretion with an austere smile before regarding the others coldly.

"Who are these mannerless strangers?" she asked then, indicating the kneeling men. "Who are they that they dare raise eyes to the Firemaker?"

"Please forgive them their ignorance, Old Mother," Iseult said softly. "They mean you no disrespect. In their own land they are men of honor. For them to kneel to you at all is a sign of their great respect and courtesy towards you. They are strangers among us, and know little of the ways of the People of the Spine of the World."

"Tell them to lower their eyes or we shall need to teach them respect," the Firemaker said with cold anger.

"Yes, Old Mother," Iseult responded and turned to the others. "Ye must no' gaze upon the Firemaker. Lower your eyes until she has given ye leave to address her."

The MacSeinn opened his mouth angrily but Iseult said with smiling calm, "My great-grandmother can speak our language, my laird, and will understand all that ye choose to say to her, when it is time. For now, please lower your gaze."

He fingered his beard and then nodded, moving his gaze down to the ground before him.

The Firemaker stared haughtily until she was sure no one's eyes were still raised. Then she said, "Why have you brought strangers to the gathering of the prides, Khan'derin?"

The sound of her Khan'cohban name brought a hot rush of emotion to Iseult but she explained their mission with great formality, using all the appropriate ceremonial gestures and keeping her face and voice free of any expression.

Although none of the many Khan'cohbans listening made any sound or interjection, she was aware of a little involuntary stir as she asked permission to cross the mountains.

"This is something that must be discussed by the Old Mothers and the councils," the Firemaker said with a chill finality in her voice. "Such a thing has never been asked before. You ask us to allow a force of overwhelming strength to enter our lands, with the only surety your word."

Iseult was incredulous. "You doubt my word of honor?"

"Many years you have been away from us, daughter of my daughter's son. You have lived among the white-skinned barbarians for seven of the long darknesses. Who is to say whether you have not been deceived by them or even corrupted into dishonor?"

Color flamed in Iseult's face. She rose, drew her dagger and flung it with one sure, swift motion. The men behind her gasped and leapt to their feet, but neither the Firemaker nor any of the Khan'cohbans moved so much as a muscle in their faces. The dagger struck the ground just before the Firemaker's feet and drove in to its hilt, quivering with the force of the impact.

"I shall prove my honor and the honor of those with me with blood, should it be so desired," Iseult said with great formality.

The Firemaker stared at the dagger and the smallest of smiles softened her stern mouth. "So be it," she said.

Iseult bowed her head in acceptance.

"These are matters of great importance," the Firemaker said. "They should not be discussed in the open like this. Tonight is the time for the meeting of the Old Mothers and their councils. Then shall we have the telling of the story in fullness and in truth. Till then, be welcome at our Gathering."

"Thank you, Old Mother," Iseult said, and at her prompting the men repeated her formal gestures and then withdrew.

Iseult spent the rest of the day watching the athletic contests with the MacSeinn and his men, doing her best to explain the customs of the Khan'cohbans. Her father had gone to greet many of his old friends and was eventually persuaded to take his place in the fighting circle, where he showed that he had lost little of his skill in his years away from the prides. As the sun set the Scarred Warriors retired and the storytellers took their place. Iseult was given permission to translate to the humans and had the gratification of seeing the haughty prionnsa weep at the culmination of a tale of particular tragedy.

"The stories o' the Khan'cohbans are nearly always very sad," she said as the MacSeinn surreptitiously blew his nose. "The only ones that are no' are the hero-tales, which usually involve a battle o' some sort, or the naming-quests. If ye are lucky, they will tell the tale o' my father's naming-quest. It is very famous. He is called the dragon-laird for, on his naming-quest, he rescued a baby dragon who proved to be the only daughter o' the dragon-queen. If she had died, the whole race o' dragons may well have died out, for she was the last female young enough still to breed. As a reward, the queen-dragon gave him the right to call her name, a gesture o' immense honor and power."

It was not long before this tale was told to celebrate Khan'gharad's return to the prides.

Then, after a silent exchange with the Firemaker, Iseult quietly made a request of the storyteller in the center of the circle. As a result, he told next the story of how she herself had won her name. Although not as dramatic as Khan'gharad's, it was still a story of great courage and daring and Iseult was glad to see a new respect and understanding in the eyes of the MacSeinn and his men.

Then he spoke of Isabeau's journey, the tale of She of Many Shapes. Iseult had a particular reason for wanting this story and watched the faces of those in the Pride of the Fighting Cat closely.

The Pride of the Fighting Cat had always been bitter enemies of the Pride of the Fire-Dragon. An uneasy peace had been settled between them, after Iseult had relinquished her claim as heir to the Firemaker, allowing her second cousin Khan'katrin to replace her. Khan'katrin, as redheaded and blue-eyed as the twins, had always claimed she was the true heir since she was descended from a straight line of daughters. Iseult and Isabeau were the daughters of the Firemaker's grandson, and for Iseult to have inherited would have meant the breaking of a tradition that had seen the powers and duties of a Firemaker passed from mother to daughter for a thousand years. By naming Khan'katrin her successor, the Firemaker had brought peace between the warring prides and allowed Iseult to marry Lachlan and pursue her destiny away from the Spine of the World.

Khan'katrin had already found it hard to conceal her anger and suspicion at Iseult's return, and now, as the storyteller told the story of Isabeau's naming-quest, her cheeks burnt and her eyes glittered like blue ice. Isabeau had ignominiously defeated the young redheaded warrior in a duel of honor, which Khan'katrin had forced upon her in the hope of killing one of her rivals. Now everyone knew the young heir to the godhead was in *geas* to Isabeau. Perhaps as important, Iseult had made a gift of her name and her twin's name to the entire race of Khan'cohbans. Such displays of trust and confidence carried with them their own invisible *geas*.

They feasted that night and more stories were told. Then when the fires were beginning to die down low, and the children all slept curled up in their furs, the Old Mothers of the seven prides rose and led the way into the forest, followed by the Scarred Warriors, the storytellers and the soul-sages. All wore their cloaks of animal furs, and their faces had been freshly painted with fearsome masks of red and white and black. Behind them strode Khan'gharad, silent as ever, Iseult, and a rather grim-faced Linley MacSeinn. Everyone else had stayed with the warmth and comfort of the fires.

High on a rock suspended above the river, under the

icy stars, the true Gathering occurred. The Old Mothers sat in a circle, with their First Warrior, First Storyteller and Soul-Sage clustered close behind. Here the Fire-maker was just one more Old Mother, given no greater precedence than any other. Iseult stood with the others while the long business of the council was undertaken—discussions over trade and hunting rights, concerns over falling birth rates and the turmoil in the weather, the comparison of the visions of the soul-sages and the resolution of many slights and insults.

At last they invited Iseult to speak. She stood and bowed to all the Old Mothers and thanked them for allowing her to address them. Then she sat with her legs crossed, her spine very straight, her hands upturned on her lap.

"We seek permission to cross the Spine of the World on a matter of great urgency," she said. "The people of the sea have declared war upon the people of the land and have attacked them many times, inflicting much hurt and damage. As you know, the leader of those of humankind, he who is my husband, wishes to live in peace and amity with people of all kinds. He has extended the hand of friendship to the people of the sea, only to be spurned with grievous insult."

She described how the Rìgh's messenger had been returned to them, horribly maimed. A stir ran over the listening Khan'cohbans, for the snow-faeries took the etiquette of war very seriously indeed. Iseult explained how they planned to strike against the stronghold of the Fairgean from three directions at once, a strategy that met with polite gestures of approval, and then, very carefully, she requested the prides' assistance.

At once there was a stir of excitement and consternation. Many of the younger warriors were pleased at the idea. There had been few skirmishes between the prides in recent years, most of their differences being settled in the annual Gathering. They were trained rigorously as warriors but now had no one but goblins and ogres to fight. Many of the older warriors vetoed the suggestion, however. "Who would hunt?" they asked. "Our people would starve."

When a natural pause occurred in the discussion Iseult, subtly and with great respect, reminded the Pride of the Grey Wolf how Isabeau had helped one of their children survive his naming-quest. She then reminded the Fighting Cats of Khan'katrin's *geas* to Isabeau and how they had challenged her while she was under the protection of the White Gods. The Fighting Cats were ashamed of that memory and shifted uneasily. Khan'katrin herself sat bolt upright, her hands clenched upon her weapons belt. Iseult met her gaze and bowed her head respectfully.

"I know that the sister of my womb has not claimed the debt of honor owed her. It is very important to her to acknowledge the ties of blood between us, which have made foes of us in the past and shall, we all hope, knot us close together in the future."

Iseult had difficulty in saying this. She had been raised to consider her second cousin the bitterest of foes. They had always looked for each other on the battlefield and had done their best to kill one another. Sometimes their clashes had reached such a pitch of ferocity that the other warriors had drawn apart to watch, understanding that here was a conflict of honor and so never interfering.

Such things were hard to forget. Behind it all was Iseult's knowledge that she was now released from her *geas* to Lachlan. She had given up her right to the god-head to be with him. All her life she had thought herself destined to be the Firemaker, the sacred gift of the Gods of White to the people of the Spine of the World. She had never truly adjusted to having lost that, even though she had accepted her *geas* with fortitude, as a Scarred Warrior should. To be free of that *geas* was a sudden draught of heady liberty. It confused her to have committed her life and her being to one destiny and suddenly to have choices open up for her again.

In the clean sweeping air of the mountains, their every shape and shadow so dear and familiar to her, her other life seemed unbearably restricting. Iseult had been bound by court etiquette, frowned upon for fighting like a man, for refusing to dress in corsets and petticoats, for keeping her hair bound back and closely covered like a scullery maid. She had found the staid conventionality of Lachlan's court so exasperating that she had wanted to scream, yet she had bitten down her aggravation and spoken softly and with such good sense that they had had to listen to her. All the time, though, she had longed for the free uncomplicated life of a Scarred Warrior, where one's gender mattered less than one's ability. She had missed the bite of icy air, the thrill of skimming down a sheer immaculate slope, the camaraderie that came of winning food for one's pride when all would have starved without you. She missed the awe and respect that came of being the Firemaker's heir, the descendant of the Red. She missed being the chosen one of cruel gods.

Yet Iseult had gone gladly into Lachlan's embrace. She had recognized and accepted the *geas* with knowledge of its cost. She had grieved bitterly when he had been cursed and prayed to all gods and any gods for his release. She loved her three children with the low, heavy, passionate intensity of all mothers and felt their absence like the loss of a vital organ, like a slow dying.

She had been angry when she had ridden away from

Lachlan but that anger had grown cold with time and distance. She felt as if she was poised on the brink of a dangerous slope, having to choose which way to skim. If she wished, she could stay in the mountains, resume her life with her own kind, regain the liberty she had lost. She could wrest back the godhead from her second cousin, and be once more the heir to the Firemaker, the gift of the Gods of White. It was clear Khan'katrin read these thoughts in her mind, for her face was stiff with suspicion.

Iseult was not yet ready to turn her back on Lachlan, however, despite the cold pain of her anger. To leave her children was a wrench almost impossible to imagine, and Iseult had grown to love Meghan and her twin sister Isabeau, and Duncan Ironfist too, the huge captain with the broken nose and tender heart. To leave them would be a betrayal, and so she tried hard to banish thoughts of freedom from her mind, concentrating on the task she had been given. She had given the MacSeinn her word of honor that she would lead him through the mountains and so that is what she must do.

So she spoke fairly to her second cousin, and used all her skills of diplomacy to persuade the Old Mothers to support her in their cause. She allowed the MacSeinn to speak, translating for him. A proud people with a strong, almost mystical attachment to their land and territory, the Khan'cohbans understood his urge to win back his domain. Many among them made the gesture of sympathy as he struggled to express his feelings, and Iseult saw they had warmed to the idea of helping him.

At last she obliquely circled back to Khan'katrin, for she saw her as the key in winning the prides' support. Iseult reminded the council that the Firemaker herself came from a long line of humans and that she had served the people of the snow faithfully for many centuries. She reminded them without speaking of it that both she and Isabeau had given up their claim to the godhead to return to the human world. There was a debt to be paid, she intimated, and saw in Khan'katrin's eyes that the point had been made.

Khan'katrin rose to her feet proudly, her red head held high. "Whatever the Old Mothers decree, know that I shall travel with you and fight at your side, in payment of my debt to your sister, She of Many Shapes."

"I thank you," Iseult replied. As if Khan'katrin's words had broken a dike, many more young warriors leapt to their feet and swore the same, led by the young warrior of the Grey Wolf Pride whom Isabeau had once helped.

The Old Mothers nodded their white heads together, their lined faces troubled. It was then that the soul-sages were asked to cast the bones and augur the future.

Iseult had known that no official decision would be made without the soul-sages' soothsaying. She had both dreaded and longed for their casting. All her clever words would count for nothing if the soul-sages spoke against her. Yet Iseult also longed to know what lay ahead. She was so troubled in her own heart that any insight into the future would be welcome. So she watched with anxious eyes as the soul-sages spun an ogre's knucklebone to decide who would be the one favored to receive the words of the Gods of White this night.

The Soul-Sage of the Pride of the Snow-Lions was chosen. Iseult felt a measure of relief. He did not have the emotional involvement of the soul-sage of her pride or of their enemies, the Fighting Cats. She sat back a little, as the Soul-Sage slowly and with great ceremony purified his soothsaying bones in the smoke of the fire.

He was a young man, no more than thirty of the long darknesses, with a gaunt face all angles and bony slopes. The fitful light flickered over his intent features, making his eyes cavernous hollows. His white mane was bound back tightly from his prominent brow, so his horns looked too heavy for his long, slender neck. He was dressed in *ulez* furs like a child or a servant, but his face was slashed with five arrow-shaped scars and around his neck hung a raven's claw. Iseult knew he was a man of power.

For a long time there was silence. A wind was rising, making the trees sing eerily. Overhead the stars burnt in a cold bright vastness, the mountains a ring of blackness below. Their fire seemed very small in all that blowing, sighing darkness. The Soul-Sage cupped his bones in his hand, his head bent, his eyes closed. Iseult wondered if his spirit still dwelt in his body or if he was skimming the night sky above, part of the stately dance of suns and planets and space. Suddenly he threw his hands outwards, the bones and stones within flying out and then falling down into the circle he had scratched in the earth. A little sigh went up from those watching. The Soul-Sage opened his eyes, stared down at the pattern with inscrutable eyes.

"Much darkness lies ahead," he said after a long, tense moment. "The circle is full of the darkness of death. Fire shall bring water. Water shall bring death. And out of the drowning wave shall rise fire once more and it shall bring life." He paused, frowning, pointing at first one pattern of stones and then another. "Then shall dreams and waking life collide. Death lies before and death lies after, but in that moment will destinies be broken and remade."

He looked down at the pattern for a very long time, then slowly swept up the bones and purified them once more. One stone he cradled in his hand thoughtfully. It was a moss agate with the fossilized shape of a bird's skull delicately etched upon its smooth green surface. He weighed it in his hand and suddenly pointed at the Mac-Seinn.

"He says that ye will fail in your endeavor," Iseult translated, "but that if ye accept that the world has turned, ye will find peace and plenty. If ye struggle to put together a broken stone it will crumble in your hand, but if ye sharpen the broken edges ye will make an arrowhead."

"What does that mean?" the MacSeinn said blankly.

"It is a riddle," Iseult said. "It means accept what ye are given and make something o' it. Otherwise ye will lose all."

A sort of despair settled down over the MacSeinn's face. Iseult said gently, "He sees peace and plenty ahead for ye, remember. It may just mean that ye shall no' find things as ye remember, that ye must settle for a broken stone, no' a whole one. Do no' despair."

The MacSeinn gripped the crowned harp badge in his hand, saying nothing.

There was much low muttering among the gathered Khan'cohbans as the Soul-Sage finished purifying his bones, pouring them back into his pouch and tying the drawstrings tight. Iseult felt her body tense. The words of the soothsayer had not been as positive as she had hoped, but there was always death ahead, the council knew that. She waited patiently. The Old Mothers muttered together, the First Warriors leaning over to make their points with emphatic gestures. At last the Firemaker turned to her and said, "It is done. The people of the Gods of White have heard the gods' message. You may cross our lands on your way, and any warriors who so choose may accompany you with our blessing."

Iseult sighed in relief. She translated for the MacSeinn and watched the fire come back into his eyes. He struck one fist into the other and cried, "Now we shall surely win! Death to the Fairgean!"

Waves reared up all around, frothing with white. The pod of Fairgean warriors swam strongly through the green swell, occasionally leaping out of the water with a great thwack of their muscular tails. Prince Nila sat astride the neck of his sea-serpent, watching without pleasure. Although the sun glittered in the spray like sea-diamonds, he felt as if he was sunk in the black depths of the octopus pit, slimy tentacles dragging him ever deeper.

He had lost Fand, the half-human slave girl who had been his childhood playmate and was now the true love of his heart. To save him, she had revealed her telepathic powers to his father the king and had been given to the cruel and enigmatic Priestesses of Jor. They had done terrible things to her, had washed her mind and soul away and turned her into a vessel for dreadful powers. There was nothing left of the girl he loved. Now every breathing moment was black with despair.

It was not just losing Fand. It was not just the bitter shame of having failed to save her. As dark as the sorrow and guilt, and far far colder, was the ominous shadow of fear that hung over him everywhere he went. His dreams were filled with the echo of the priestesses chanting. Every night he woke in a sweat of terror and then lay there, dreading sleep, dreading daybreak, haunted by what he had seen and heard. The past month had been the most difficult of his entire life, even though the death of four more of his brothers had seen him promoted to leader of his own pod, with his own sea-serpent. Once he would have been overjoyed. Now he felt only leaden misery.

His brothers had been killed during the attack on the human stronghold on the shore of the southern sea. Nila had fought at his father's command during that attack, had fought with fierce desperation even though he knew the assault was doomed to failure. Nila had been sickened to the depths of his being by that assault. It was one thing to kill in defense of oneself, or to drive people away from a stretch of soft sand so exhausted children could sleep in safety for a night. It was quite another to attack without warning, to kill without mercy, to murder children and young women and men without weapons, people who a moment before had been laughing and dancing. Nila knew that such an evil act could only bring bitter reprisals.

Yet if he had refused to fight he would have been executed for cowardice and insubordination. Nila wanted to die. He had no wish to live a life without joy or love or tenderness. Yet he did not want to die without honor, branded a coward. So he had sought death on the battlefield. Four of his brothers had died that night, and yet somehow Nila had lived. And for his reckless disregard for life, Nila had at last won his father's regard, and had been made a *jaka,* rider of the sea-serpent. There was no higher honor for a Fairge warrior.

Under his command were forty warriors. Ten were *ralisen,* or riders of the *ralis,* a creature of sea, loch and river that had the ability to swell to almost twice its normal size when threatened. With skin of glistening dark green, the *ralis* had a long, looping tail split at the end, and broad flippers tipped with two hard claws. A crested mane surrounded its long snout, lying flat upon its strong curving neck when at rest. When the *ralis* was swollen to its largest size, this crest stood up all round its face, a vivid blood-red color fading to orange at the black spiked edge. These spikes were poisonous. A mere scratch from a *ralis*'s crest was enough to kill a sea-serpent. As a result the *ralisen* were formidable warriors when fighting at sea, for their mounts fought with them with claw and teeth and crest.

The remaining thirty warriors swam alongside in their full sea-shape, able to dive under an enemy and come up on the other side. Called the *zasha*, they had to be very strong swimmers to keep up with the sea-serpent and *ralis*, who could swim very fast indeed. The *zasha* were the first ones to change into their land-shape and set foot upon the shore, to search for food for their *jaka* and find a safe place for him to rest. They had to be ferocious fighters to survive long enough to be promoted to *ralisen*, for they were the first rank of any pod to meet attack. Few could ever hope to become a *jaka*.

From his vantage point high on the sea-serpent's neck Nila could see for many miles. Far to the north he saw a flash of silver. He shaded his tired eyes and stared to the horizon. The flash came again. A curve of a silvery body. The flip of a frilled tail. It was a Fairge that swam there alone. Nila frowned. Fairgean never swam alone. The seas were far too dangerous. There were wild sea-serpents and deep-sea monsters of much greater ferocity, sharks and doom-eels, riptides and reefs. The Fairgean always swam in well-organized pods; everyone had their place and all must serve it.

He gave a high-pitched whistle and raised his arm. Two of the *ralisen* answered his call and set off in swift pursuit, the snouts of their steeds held high above the waves. The rest of the pod wheeled and followed at a more sedate pace.

Nila could clearly see the convulsion of anxiety that passed over the lone Fairge's body when she heard his whistle. She was pushing along one of the long narrow canoes the slave women used to carry supplies on the long sea journey. At the sound of the whistles, she abandoned the canoe and began to undulate through the water at a tremendous pace. Her wake creamed long and white behind her, her tail thrashing the waves into spume. Nila's frown deepened. He whistled again, long and high. Two more of the *ralisen* broke away from the pod to pursue and capture her. It was clear this lone Fairge was not someone who had been swept away from her pod by a freakish rip. She sought to escape him, which meant she could be a runaway slave or concubine. Although all his sympathies were aroused, Nila could not let her escape.

The *ralis* were powerful swimmers, their broad flippers and long looping tail pushing them through the waves at a far swifter pace than the Fairge woman could manage. They closed upon her swiftly. Suddenly she turned upon them, floating upright in the water. Nila could see her white face and the long flowing black hair. The *ralisen* surrounded her. To Nila's surprise they seemed to be listening to her. They swayed upon their steeds' backs, and then slowly toppled over and sank beneath the waves. The *ralis* sank also, the waves closing over their glistening backs, their orange frilled crests.

For a moment Nila was frozen in surprise. The Fairge woman plunged on through the waves, increasing the distance between them. Then Nila gave a sequence of furious whistles. The Fairge had *sung* his men below the waves! This was no ordinary slave. She had to be captured. It was not sufficient to just surround her and seize her, however. This woman had the power of enchantment in her voice. She could kill them all.

He sent some of his remaining warriors to dive under the waves in search of their drowning comrades, and instructed the others to muffle their ears with their fur cloaks. He only hoped it would be sufficient to stop the sound of the enchanted singing. A few more men were sent to retrieve the canoe, now bobbing about erratically on the waves. When they brought it to him his sense of wonder increased. Within was a large, iron-bound chest, a small lap-harp fashioned in the human way, tools and weapons made of iron, a red velvet dress. These were the sort of wrack washed up on the shore after a sea-serpent had wrecked one of the humans' ships. It was not what one expected to find within a slave's canoe.

The Fairge woman fought her capture desperately. She managed to drown a few more of Nila's warriors by dragging away their cloaks as she sang, or by stabbing them with a knife she wore at her belt. At last the warriors overpowered her, however, and she was dragged, her mouth tightly gagged, to where Nila waited on his sea-serpent.

The first thing that struck him was her enduring beauty, even though she was past forty and there was grey in her silky black hair. She was thin to the point of gauntness but if anything this only emphasized the strength of the bones beneath the delicately lined skin. One cheek was marred by a fine spiderweb of scars but her ice-blue eyes had lost none of their brilliance. She stared at him defiantly, her webbed hands clenched into fists.

"Leave us!" he said sharply to the warriors. They protested, and he drew his dagger and laid it against her throat. "If she sings, I shall cut her a new mouth," he said indifferently. Reluctantly they drew away, working to revive the unconscious warriors dragged from the sea. Nila wheeled the sea-serpent about, the Fairge held hard against his knee. The great beast undulated away until none could overhear their conversation. Then he released the iron-hard grip on her and let drop the knife.

"Maya," he said.

She stiffened all over, staring at him with frightened eyes.

"It is me, your brother," he said. "Nila."

"Nila? Little Nila?"

"Not so little now."

She stared at him closely, noting the newly grown tusks, the black pearl on his breast, the jewels in his hair and on his belt, the rich fur of his cloak. "No, not so little anymore. You are a man now."

He was scowling at her. "What do you do here? Where have you been for so long?"

"Trying to stay alive," she answered.

His scowl deepened. "Then what do you do here, swimming in these seas? We swim north again, home for the winter. Do you not realize our father the King is enraged at your failure to break the power of the human witches? He has pronounced the death sentence upon you."

"I thought he would."

"Then why do you swim here?"

"I am following my daughter."

"Your daughter?" Unconsciously Nila's voice held all the scorn for women that every male of his race felt.

Maya's face hardened. "Yes, my daughter," she snapped.

"But why?"

There was silence for a moment. "I love her," Maya said at last. "I did not think I would but I do, more than I would have thought possible." She shifted a little uneasily and then said, with her head raised proudly, "Besides, in her rests my only chance for survival."

"So you swim north now, when all the pods are on the move? That is no way to survive. Do you not know what he would do to you if he caught you?"

"Has he not caught me now?" she said huskily. "Are you not your father's son?"

Nila's eyes fell. One hand came up to cup the black pearl hanging on his breast.

"I hate him," she whispered. "I hate him so very much. I warn you now, I would kill him if ever I fell into his power again."

Nila was silent for a moment and then he said, very low, "I hate him too." Never before had he allowed the dark passion in the pit of his belly to take shape and be uttered. He felt at once a great release, and then, sharper than ever, the fear that rode with him always.

They were silent for a moment, rising and dropping with the natural swell and fall of the waves. The sea-serpent grazed calmly on a dark tangle of kelp.

Nila said swiftly, incoherently, "You must take care, Maya. He plans—the priestesses plan—something dreadful. Everything that lives upon the ground shall die, not just humans but all creatures. He plans to raise a tidal wave and drown the land . . ."

"When?" Maya was paler than ever, lines graven deep into her brow.

"They said something about harnessing the power of the fire comet. Fand . . ."

"Fand, the little slave girl?"

"She is a Priestess of Jor now. They have turned her into something horrible. She speaks . . . She speaks with the voice of . . ." He hesitated, then said with a voice stifled with dread, "She speaks with the voice of Kani. They have called upon the powers of Kani!"

Maya looked white and sick. "The poor child," she

said involuntarily, remembering her own years upon the
Isle of Divine Dread.

"Our father grows confident now. We struck a cruel
blow against the humans in their very stronghold. Many
were killed. Four of our brothers, but many hundreds of
them. They will strike back at us now but we are ready,
more ready than we have ever been. We lure the humans
into a trap."

"Four of our brothers killed?"

"Just recently. Seven in this past year. I am now the
tenth son." Nila gave a cruel grin and lifted the black
pearl upon his breast. "Jor sent this to me, and it has
saved my life more than once. Even my father respects
me now, and seeks to win my favor with sea-serpents and
jewels. But it is too late. I hate him!" This time the words
burst out of him. "I hate them all! I hope they all die."

For a moment his hand closed so tightly about the
black pearl it seemed he would crush it to powder. Then
he released it and glanced quickly back at the pod of warriors, floating only a small distance away and watching
curiously.

"So you see, you must go far, far away from here, else
you will be drowned too," he said rapidly. "Forget your
daughter, she is more parts human than Fairgean anyway.
She will drown with the others. Swim south and you shall
be safe. Now you must sing. Open your mouth and sing
me to sleep like you did the others. They will not let the
tenth son of the king drown."

She hesitated and he said harshly, "Do you not remember I was born with a caul over my head? I shall not
die by drowning, I promise you. Sing!"

She nodded, her eyes fixed on his, as pale as moonlit
water. Then she took a deep breath and sang.

For a moment he listened, entranced. As deep as the

voice of the ocean, as hypnotic, her voice lulled him into warmth, into darkness. He felt himself fall, felt the waves close over his head, felt himself sink. For a long moment there was only the black abyss of sleep. Then suddenly light was surging all around him, he was gasping and coughing for air, he was retching up water.

"My prince, my prince, are ye alive?" One of his *ralisen* leant over him, cradling Nila in his strong arms, his tusked face anxious.

Nila nodded, coughing. *For now . . .*

THE FORBIDDEN LAND

She be a Fairge! Look, a blaygird sea-faery!"

Isabeau spun around, her hand tightening on Bronwen's. A man stood pointing at them, his face suffused with anger. At his words cries of shock and outrage rose from the villagers crowded around the market stalls.

"Ye can see her gills. How disgusting!"

"What does a slimy frog like her be doing here? How dare they bring her?"

"Look, that be a witch wi' her! See her rings and staff."

"She got an owl riding on her shoulder! Mam, look at the wee white owl."

"And look at that hairy wee demon!"

"They be *uile-bheistean*, all o' them!"

Brun's ears flickered unhappily and he clutched the little jangle of rings and spoons hanging around his neck. Isabeau pulled the little girl back against her as the mood of the crowd grew uglier. A few of the men hefted tools in their hands as if they were weapons. One or two bent and picked up stones from the ground, and all pressed closer, muttering ominously. Isabeau was suddenly very glad of the guards who stepped close around them, hands on their sword hilts.

Suddenly someone threw a sharp-pointed stone. Isabeau deflected it so that it fell harmlessly to the ground. There was a hiss of outrage. "She works sorcery!"

Quietly Isabeau said to the sergeant in charge, "We had best go back to the camp, I think."

"Aye, my lady," he said with a swift salute and gestured to his men.

With the villagers glowering angrily from every side, the small party moved quickly through the crowded marketplace. A few apples were flung, and then an old cabbage. Isabeau caught the apples deftly and bit into one with a friendly grin, tossing the stall owner a copper coin in payment. The mouldy cabbage she sent back to the stall from which it came, settling it back gently among the other vegetables. A few in the crowd grinned. Most just stared suspiciously, holding their children close or pulling them from the path.

"Do no' let her lay her evil eye on ye," they whispered. "She be a witch!"

Isabeau looked down at her empty basket ruefully. "Och well, at least we got some apples," she said to Bronwen. The little girl did not smile. Her cheeks were crimson, her pale eyes glittering with tears. Isabeau smoothed back her silky hair with a gentle hand.

"Never mind, dearling," Isabeau said. "Just ignore them. They do no' ken any better."

"Why are they so mean?" the little girl whispered. "That woman called me a slimy frog? I'm no' a frog!"

"Ye must no' mind what they say, dearling. People are afraid o' what they do no' ken, and when they are afraid they strike out, to try to make themselves feel bigger and braver. It does no' work, but for a wee while they feel better. But then the feeling fades and all they feel is smaller and more afraid than before. That is why ye must no' say anything back. It willna do any good, and afterwards ye will just feel small and mean yourself."

"But why are they afraid? Why do they hate me?"

Isabeau chose her words with care. "Ye are one quarter Fairgean, Bronwen, and you bear your ancestry in your face. Your mother's people are the enemies o' your father's people. They have fought many, many wars over the years and there is much mistrust and hatred between them. It is easier to fight someone if ye can hate them, and to hate them, ye must make them seem different to you, lesser. That's why they call ye a frog, or a fish, because it makes ye less like them. What ye need to do is show them that ye are really just like them underneath, even though ye have fins and gills and can change shape and swim underwater."

Bronwen was silent, though her full bottom lip jutted out and her eyes were swimming with angry tears. Isabeau pulled her close but the little girl shrugged her away. Unhappily Isabeau let her go. Isabeau had not given any thought to what it would be like for Bronwen, part-Fairge in a land where the Fairgean were hated. When she had decided to bring Bronwen back to Eileanan, she had thought only of the positive results of her actions. She had imagined Lachlan coming to love his niece, as surely as he must once he knew her. Even deeper had been the hope that Bronwen would in some way be instrumental in bringing about a true peace in the land, standing as she did between two worlds, two cultures.

Isabeau had barely acknowledged her deeper, more personal reasons. The fact was she had missed Bronwen with an empty ache in the hollow of her shoulder where the little girl's head used to lie. She had only ever given Bronwen back to her mother so Maya would break the curse she had laid on Lachlan. Isabeau had not found it hard to find reasons to take the little girl back again.

Yet Bronwen was unhappy. The little girl was very sensitive to the thoughts and emotions of others, and all about her were only suspicion and dislike. Her uncle Lachlan had said little about her presence, but he regarded her coldly whenever he saw her and Isabeau was careful to keep Bronwen out of his way. Lachlan's court whispered behind their hands and stared at Bronwen's gills. Even Meghan thought Isabeau had been unwise in bringing her. She shook her straggly white head when Isabeau insisted that Maya had had a change of heart, saying merely that the Fairge had always had a great deal of charm.

Only Donncan persisted in his warm admiration for his part-Fairge cousin. Now that Neil travelled in his parents' retinue, Donncan had no other competitors for her attention. They played together happily in the evenings while the servants set up the tents and prepared their dinner, and whiled away the long wearisome hours of traveling with word games, cards or trictrac. Only rarely did they squabble, even though they were cooped up in a stuffy carriage all day, soldiers riding close all around.

The Greycloaks had been marching through Tìrsoilleir for several weeks now, able to make good time once the swamps of Arran were left behind. Isabeau was most excited about traveling through Tìrsoilleir, having often wondered about the land beyond the Great Divide. The Forbidden Land looked much like anywhere else, however. Softly rounded hills slid down into valleys where slow wide rivers wound their way towards the sea. Villages were small, cottages clustered close together about a green square where chickens pecked and goats were tethered to graze. In the larger towns the rattle-watch called out the hours, the mill ground grain into flour, and people went about their daily business with the same sure routine as country folk anywhere. The only difference between Tìrsoilleir and Blèssem that Isabeau could see was that here, in the Forbidden Land, every village and town had its kirk.

Built of stone, the kirks were constructed in a cruciform shape, crowned with tall spires that pierced the sky like a sword. From the hilltops one could locate every village for miles about by their spires which towered above tree and rooftop, competing with each other for height. Used as she was to the round domes of the Coven, Isabeau found the sharp-pointed spires strange and a little frightening. Elfrida said that the builders of the kirks were all trying to get closer to their god, who lived in the heavens. Isabeau thought it looked like they were trying to stab him.

At least twice a day the villagers put down their work and filed into the dim interior of the kirk, which was plain and white and cold, with uncomfortable pews of dark wood. Meghan, Isabeau and Gwilym had covered their witch gowns with heavy cloaks and gone in secret to one kirk meeting, curious about this religion that was so different from their own.

Dressed in a black cassock as austere as their gowns, the pastor had shouted out his sermon from a high wooden pulpit, his eyes alight with fervor. He had spoken of justice and retribution, of terrible punishment in a pit of everlasting fire, of torture that would never end. Isabeau had been sickened and frightened, and Meghan angry. Gwilym had had to seize the old witch's arm to stop her from leaping up and arguing with the pastor. The Keybearer's eyes had been flashing as they hurried away from the meeting, her voice cracking with emotion.

"I canna believe they sit there and listen to that every day!" she cried. "No wonder they are so ready to die on the battlefield when their lives are so full o' fear and misery. Isabeau, we need to teach them that they do no' need to suffer in order to achieve some unreal vision o' happiness in some unreal paradise when they die!"

Talking all the way back to the camp, Meghan had been the most animated that Isabeau had seen in months. Every town the army passed thereafter, the old sorceress insisted on going in and climbing upon a box in the village green to explain the ways and beliefs of the Coven. Isabeau and the other witches accompanied her, along with those faeries in Lachlan's retinue, including Brun, Sann the corrigan, the wild-eyed satyricorns who had formed their own company in the army, and a handful of bogfaeries serving Iain of Arran and his friends.

For the first time in many years the Rìgh's army was accompanied by thirteen witches and sorcerers, creating a full circle of power. Apart from Meghan, Isabeau, Arkening and Gwilym, the ring of power included Nellwyn Sea-singer, who had a wonderful mezzo-soprano voice, full of emotion and candor. When she and Enit sang together, silver and golden voices weaving together, they could bring a room of hard-bitten soldiers to tears.

A deep friendship had sprung up between Nellwyn and Enit, much to everyone's surprise. All knew Enit had a deep aversion to using the songs of sorcery, having been sickened by the Yedda's use of their powers in the past. The two women had traveled together for some months, however, and had much in common. Even though Enit remained adamant that she would not use her powers to murder, she had been convinced to lend her considerable natural powers to the Coven once again.

Brangaine NicSian had also lent them her powers, as

had Iain of Arran. It had been decided that Iain's magical Talents far exceeded his fighting ability and so he no longer rode into battle beside the Rìgh if his powers were needed by the witches. Isabeau knew this decision had greatly relieved Elfrida's fears.

The other witches were Toireasa the Seamstress; Riordan Bowlegs; a fat, merry witch called Stout John; and a newly fledged witch from Siantan called Stormy Briant, who had a strong Talent with weather, a most useful power. His younger brother, Cailean o' Shadowswathe, had been taken on by Meghan as her new apprentice and so accompanied the old sorceress everywhere, an enormous black shadow-hound slinking along at his heels. Since he was much the same age as Jay the Fiddler, the two young apprentices had struck up a close friendship and were often to be seen together.

The last witch to make up the circle was Didier Laverock, the earl of Caerlaverock, who had once been only Dide the Juggler. Although Dide, like Enit, had never formally joined the Coven, he had been persuaded to join Isabeau in her studies with the older sorcerers. He proved to be a very clever and capable witch, strong enough to have sat his Sorcerer Test if only he would accept the strict discipline of the Coven.

Isabeau found herself growing closer than ever to the black-eyed young earl, walking with him in the evenings as they argued about some point of philosophy, or listening to him play and sing. Of all her companions Dide was the closest to her in age and shared her love of music and stories, the forest and its creatures, her sense of adventure and her love of the ridiculous. Sometimes Isabeau felt the easy camaraderie between them warming into something deeper but she always withdrew, though she would have been unable to explain why. Now that she was a sorceress and ripening towards her full powers, there was no reason for her not to explore a deeper intimacy. Something held her back, though, some imprecise fear that troubled her. "Let's no' spoil our friendship," she said to Dide when his teasing turned too warm, his gaze too intent. Once she said, slipping from his grasp, "It's no' the time, Dide, ye ken that. We ride to war, have ye forgotten?"

"How could I forget?" he had retorted, anger springing into his eyes. "I have done naught else but fight, all my life. Sometimes I think we shall never have peace. We should seize what we can now, for we could be dead tomorrow."

Isabeau had been unable to reply, choked with hot, unexpected tears. She had shaken her head and pushed him away, and he had sprung up and gone, angrier than she had ever seen him. When she had seen him next, though, he had been as easy with her as if nothing had happened, but he had not again tried to kiss her or teased her with that devilish intentness in his eyes. Isabeau told herself it was better that way, and tried not to feel a little sting of disappointment.

Since the General Assembly had been overthrown and Elfrida NicHilde had been crowned, most of Tìrsoilleir had accepted the new order peaceably. Many had welcomed it. Lachlan was received everywhere with awe and joy, for he was seen as the living messenger of the Tìrsoilleirean sky god. People fell to their knees when he rode by and children were held up for him to bless. Elfrida too was welcomed with cheers and bouquets of flowers and the waving of her red and gold banner.

Despite their acceptance of the restoration of the monarchy, few Tìrsoilleirean approved of Lachlan's Decree against the Persecution of Faeries, nor the Restoration of the Coven. There was also much fear that the new order would oppress those who had worshipped in the kirks, despite all Lachlan's proclamations to the contrary.

So no matter how enthusiastic the response to Lachlan, it always turned chill when the crowd saw Meghan, Isabeau and the other witches with their long white robes and tall staffs. Often the reaction was violent. Isabeau was rather shocked by how much disgust and loathing were evident in the faces and thoughts of those Tìrsoillerean she met. She had expected fear and mistrust, but not revulsion. She knew long-held prejudices were difficult to overcome and so she tried not to blame the Tìrsoilleirean too much. She did blame herself, however, for bringing Bronwen into contact with it. And the closer they came to the coast, the more violent the antipathy would be, especially towards the Fairgean, and so the greater the danger of harm to Bronwen.

The Greycloaks forded the Alainn River early the next day and pressed on towards Bride, the capital of Tìrsoilleir. The villages grew larger and closer together, until the breaks of fields and orchards were rare among the houses and shops and kirks. Isabeau noticed that there were no taverns on the corners, as there would have been in any other land in Eileanan. Instead, there was now a kirk every few blocks, some with steeples so tall it looked as if they must topple over and crush the smaller buildings all around. The lazy curves of the river were built close with jetties, wharves and warehouses, and boats and barges of all kinds were rowed or poled about on its smooth waters.

They came over a hill and saw a great city laid out on the shores of a wide harbor. It was crowded with spires and towers, many gilded so that they gleamed in the fitful sunshine. Isabeau leant out of the window of their carriage, fascinated. The twins hung out beside her, clamoring with excitement, and Donncan and Bronwen hung out the other side. Even Meghan leant forward to see the fabled city of Bride more clearly. The cavaliers rode close on either side and she waved them away irritably. "Move over, man! I've seen enough o' your horse's rump this past month, let me see the view, for Eà's sake!"

The cavalier spurred his horse away with a grin and Meghan stared out for a long time, unable to help showing her amazement and wonder. Bride had been hidden beyond the Great Divide for most of her supernaturally long life. She had never thought to see it. At last she sat back with a sigh and said to Isabeau, "Well, the Mesmerdean could take me now and I wouldna mind a bit. To think I'd live to see Bride!"

Isabeau smiled and nodded, even though the old sorceress's words cut deep. Meghan read her thoughts as always and smiled grimly. "Och, ye have a few more months o' me yet, my bairn. Make the most o' it!"

The long cavalcade of infantrymen, cavaliers, supply wagons and carriages clattered in through the city gates and through a long, heavily guarded tunnel. Beyond the high, grim walls, houses crowded onto the streets, which were filled with garbage, sewage running down the gutters. Although the main thoroughfare was wide, a tangle of dark, mean-looking streets twisted away on either side, all overshadowed by the immense spire of the High Kirk which crouched on a hill in the center of the city surrounded by yet another high, heavily guarded wall.

Many curious, anxious faces stared at them from windows and doors. At first the mood was one of trepidation but as the soldiers waved and smiled, the bagpipes skirled and the drums boomed, the people of the city began to come out to look and marvel. Quite a few waved their

aprons and cheered, and children ran alongside, shouting
with excitement. All were dressed very plainly, in black
or grey, with their hair dragged back and rough wooden
sabots on their feet.

Lachlan's piper led the procession, playing a martial
tune, followed by a small marching band of drummers
and fiddlers, Dide and Jay among them. Lachlan's squire
Connor proudly carried Rìgh's standard, a crowned white
stag on a green background, while the Rìgh rode slowly
forward on his great black stallion, his magnificent wings
folded, the white gyrfalcon riding on his gauntleted wrist.
Iain and Elfrida rode beside him, waving to the crowd
and accepting their accolades with smiles and nods. Elfrida looked very young and beautiful upon her dainty
white palfrey, and the cheers grew loudest as she passed.
Her standard-bearer was a local boy and he was swollen
with pride as he held high the flag of the MacHildes, a
golden sword held aloft by a gauntleted fist on a scarlet
background.

The deeper into the city they marched, the more joyous grew the reception. Hundreds of people thronged the
highway, making the army's progress very slow indeed.
Dusk pressed down upon them. Lanterns were kindled
along the road and on the sides of the carriages. The roofs
of the houses pressed so close over the street that no
moon or stars could be seen. The air was fetid, causing
Donncan and Bronwen to choke and cover their noses as
they peered out the windows. The twins fell asleep with
their heads on Isabeau's lap, and at last even the older
children drooped and rested their heads against each
other's shoulders.

At last they came to another high wall, as strongly protected as those encircling the city. Beyond that wall were
many parks and fine mansions, their windows all blazing

with lights. Although crowds lined the avenue or leant out of the windows, throwing streamers and flowers, the road was much wider here and so the cavalcade was at last able to pick up speed. They came to the last of the city's three walls and passed through yet another dark tunnel, the horses' hooves booming. By now Isabeau was yawning so widely her jaws cracked, but still she peered out the carriage window, eager to see everything. They passed the High Kirk, its hundreds of spires all lit up against the night sky and then, some time later, drove through a magnificent set of gates, with the shield of the MacHilde clan set upon them. Beyond stretched only darkness, though in the flickering light of the torches carried by their outriders, Isabeau could see they were driving down a long straight avenue lined with blossoming trees.

At last they came to the palace. Isabeau received a confused impression of many tall turrets, all topped with cone-shaped roofs, before the weary horses dragged the carriage in through the castle gates and into the gatehouse. Here they were asked to step down out of the carriage. Rather hesitantly they did so. The buildings towering about were so grim and militant-looking, the guards in their white surcoats so stern, that even Isabeau could not help feeling a little apprehensive. Meghan stepped down willingly enough, though, scorning the hand offering to help her, and so Isabeau clambered down too.

She had first to wake the children, the twins beginning to wail from tiredness. Maura Nursemaid, the bogfaery hired to attend them, tried without success to quieten them. She was only young, born and bred in the marshes of Arran, and she had never before left her home. As shy and timid as most bogfaeries, she found her new role very intimidating indeed. Isabeau took Olwynne into her arms and patted her back to sleep against her shoulder. Maura tried to imitate her, but Owein's wails turned into angry roars.

The cavaliers were milling about on one side of the courtyard. Isabeau saw Lachlan among them, his dusty cloak flung back, his sweaty curls hanging on his forehead. He turned at the sound of Owein's angry cries and started towards them, Isabeau's heart lifting at the sight of him. He took Owein in his arms, rocking him gently, and the little boy at last stopped crying, though he clung very tightly to his father's neck.

"How are ye yourselves?" the Rìgh asked tersely.

"Stiff, tired and very, very hungry," Meghan replied, just as curtly. "Could we no' have stopped for some tea at least?"

"Bride was so close, I wanted to get here afore dark," he answered. "I did no' expect it to take so long coming through the city. We're here now though. Come on in. Hopefully they'll be ready for us."

"Where are we?" Isabeau asked, stumbling a little in her weariness.

He cast her an oblique look from his falcon-yellow eyes. "This is Gerwalt, the palace o' the MacHildes. It was until recent times the home o' the Fealde and the berhtildes, but the new Fealde, Killian the Listener, prefers to live and work among the people."

"It's no' very welcoming," Isabeau said.

"Nay, I suppose no'. Still, it is Elfrida's home now and the only place large enough to house most o' our men. The others shall be lodged in the city. Come in, there'll at least be hot food and a bed o' sorts."

He strode off, giving his instructions to the tower guards, handing over his white gyrfalcon to the falconer and giving his big black stallion one last caress on his velvety nose. Then he led the weary travelers through the gatehouse into the outer bailey, through another stout barbican, and then into the inner bailey, Owein asleep on his neck.

The palace soared above him. Within its formidable walls it was a building of great elegance and beauty. Isabeau found its many round towers very restful to her eyes, after all the square corners and sharp-pointed spires of the city. They climbed the stairs and entered through an enormous fortified door of ancient oak.

The luxury within astounded her. She had been amazed at the magnificence of Iain's palace but Gerwalt's entrance hall far overshadowed it. The floor was fully carpeted in an intricately woven rug of blue, pale green and crimson, while huge tapestries depicting scenes of battle hung on the walls which rose over a hundred feet high. An enormous crystal chandelier hung down from the domed ceiling far above, dazzling Isabeau's tired eyes. Shields and swords and axes hung on the walls, and suits of silver armor stood on the landing of the grand staircase, which swept up from the far end of the hall, dividing in two to lead up to galleries on either side.

Above the galleries were tall lancet windows filled with stained-glass pictures. Isabeau saw a man in armor receive a sword from an angel with wings of gold and crimson. She saw roses and black crouching devils, books inscribed with strange letters, a child floating in a halo of golden light, white doves carrying twigs, a woman in a blue dress weeping by a grave, and men fighting while angels sang above. Her mind could not take it all in.

"Gracious alive!" she said.

"Look at that one!" Donncan cried. "It looks just like *Dai-dein*."

She stared where he pointed. In the round window above the staircase was a black-winged angel kneeling before a throne, holding aloft a golden sword. On the throne sat an old man, robed all in white, with a stern bearded face and one finger raised above a huge book. The angel's hair curled blackly, his face was clean-shaven, and his eyes were as gold as the halo of light about his head.

"No wonder they fall to their knees when he rides by," Meghan said crossly. She looked about her irritably then picked up a solid gold bowl, set with gems. "I thought the Tìrsoillerean believed luxury and comfort the work o' their Arch-Fiend?"

"The former Fealde was rather too interested in luxury," Lachlan said with a grin. "That was why the people were persuaded to rise up against her. Luckily Elfrida finds all this rather daunting."

Meghan limped forward, saying caustically, "I'm as dry as a Clachan salt basin. Is there no one to offer us some tea?"

Elfrida had been busy talking with some servants at the foot of the stairwell. She hurried over, looking tired and harried. "I am so sorry, Keybearer. All is still in disarray. We left here so suddenly when we heard o' the bairns' kidnapping, and there was no time to get things into order. Will ye no' come through to the red drawing room, and I'll try to have some tea sent up? Ye must all be tired, we've all been on the road since dawn."

Meghan allowed herself to be led to a large but comfortable room where a fire had been lit and the dustcovers shaken out and thrown into a heap in the corner. The old sorceress looked very drawn indeed and Isabeau made her sit down and drink some *mithuan* and warm herself by the fire, while she calmed the fractious children and set them to playing spillikins on the hearth. The sleeping twins were laid down on the red brocaded couch and covered with a plaid.

The team of healers came in rather hesitantly, all looking tired and rather overwhelmed by the grandeur of the palace. Johanna the Mild, who had once been part of the League of the Healing Hand and was now the head healer, was among them. Isabeau spoke to her swiftly and Johanna took one look at Meghan's grey face and busied herself making up a restorative tea of skullcap, valerian and rue for the old sorceress. Tòmas the Healer clung close to Johanna's side, a thin little boy with arms and legs like sticks below his gaudy blue-and-gold surcoat, and deep shadows under his eyes. Johanna gave his fair head an affectionate rub, saying, "Why do ye no' go and play wi' the other bairns, dearling?"

He shook his head and pressed even closer, greatly hampering her movements. She did not protest, however, bending over Meghan with the cup in her hand. From the shelter of her long green robe he stared round the room with enormous blue eyes, ducking his head back when Donncan smiled at him. With his small stature and shy ways, Tòmas seemed much younger than his thirteen years, making the power he carried in his two small hands seem even more incredible.

It was not until Johanna's younger brother Connor came, the Rìgh's hat and cloak in his hand, that Tòmas grew more animated. The two boys were the same age and had been friends for many years. Connor greeted him affectionately and, after a curt jerk of the head from Meghan, tenderly laid down his burden and drew the other boy into conversation. Soon they were both sitting by the fire with Donncan and Bronwen, playing at spillikins with great enthusiasm.

Lachlan came striding in, followed as usual by his retinue, all talking and laughing, shaking out their dusty cloaks and calling loudly for whisky and food. Dide set himself to amuse them, saying in an undertone to Isabeau, "Ye willna find whiskey here, but the quartermaster will have some wine somewhere and some food too, if there's none in the house. I'd be quick about it though, we've all been riding hard since dawn and everyone's tired and a wee cantankerous."

Isabeau nodded and went in search of the kitchens. Here all was confusion. The cook was in hysterics, the oven unlit, and the servants all milled about, gossiping and exclaiming. Isabeau was tired and very hungry. With a few sharp well-chosen words she sent the servants running to turn out bedrooms, air all the sheets, light the fires and carry up the baggage, which was still piled about in the entrance hall. She lit the oven with a snap of her fingers and rummaged through the cupboards, emerging hot, dirty, empty-handed and very angry.

"Why is all in such disorder?" she demanded. "Did ye no' receive the message that we were coming?"

"But we were only given a day's notice and none kent how many would be coming," the chamberlain protested. "And no money was sent and we had none here to buy supplies with, for the Fealde cleaned out the treasury when she fled . . ." The old man was almost in tears.

"How like a man!" Isabeau snapped. "So bloody impractical."

The chamberlain stepped back a little and she said, "No' ye! I meant the Rìgh. Never mind. Send one o' the potboys down to the quartermaster and tell him we need potatoes and leeks, some flour, butter, milk and eggs, if he has them. Oh, and wine. Do no' forget the wine!"

"Wha' about some meat?" the chamberlain asked nervously.

"If I have to cook them all a meal, they must eat what I choose to cook and I shallna cook them meat!" Isabeau exclaimed.

In too much of a hurry to worry about what the servants thought of her, Isabeau brought pots and spoons whizzing out from the cupboard. She started chopping vegetables furiously with six large knives all working away at once, while a cauldron waltzed itself out to the well to be filled with water. Salt rose up from its sack in a tiny tornado, and threw itself into the water as the cauldron swung itself onto the fire which had leapt into life on the hearth. Isabeau did not wait for the water to boil by itself but stuck her finger into the water, which bubbled up, hissing and steaming.

"God's teeth!" the cook cried, startled out of her hysterics. "No wonder the blaygird witches won the war!"

"We won the war because we were quicker and smarter than ye!" Isabeau cried. "Why do ye sit there, weeping and wringing your hands? Come help me, in the name o' Eà's green blood!"

For a moment the cook stared, open-mouthed, color surging. Then she gave a belly laugh that set all her double chins shaking, heaved her great bulk to her feet, and seized a knife.

The potboys came running in with sacks of potatoes, carrots and leeks, and great sheaves of spinach they had dragged from the kitchen garden.

"Make yourself useful and get peeling," Isabeau ordered. Obediently they sat down and began peeling potatoes at a great pace, their eyes round with amazement as they watched the wooden spoon whisk round and round in the cauldron, the knives chopping away, and the lids of herb jars float up by themselves, as pinches of that herb and this floated down into the boiling water. As each vegetable was peeled it flew by itself to the knives and was duly chopped and then flung by an invisible hand into the soup. Meanwhile, Isabeau was kneading dough while the bread pans greased and floured themselves. The oven door flew open and the dough settled itself into the pans as they flew into the oven, the door shutting itself behind them.

"Now," Isabeau said, looking about her with floury hands on her hips, "is there any cheese?"

In little more than half an hour the chamberlain was able to show the Rìgh and his retinue into a long dining room sparkling with crystal and silver and decorated with bunches of flowering herbs which the cook herself had helped to pick.

The servants brought in steaming tureens filled with a thick, delicious-smelling white soup, platters of hot bread sprinkled with poppy seeds, wedges of roasted vegetables and a tray of little cheese and spinach pies. The mood in the room brightened immediately. The servants poured out wine that Isabeau had chilled between her hands, and served the food with a flourish. For quite a time there was no sound but chomping jaws, sighs of appreciation and the occasional mumbled request for more.

At last Alasdair Garrie of Killiegarrie leant back in his chair and said, "My word, that's the best meal we've had in months. My compliments to your chef, my lady."

As hearty endorsements were heard all round the table, Elfrida said her thanks in a rather puzzled voice. She had seen the cook in the full flight of her hysterics and could not think how such a feast had materialized so quickly. Isabeau grinned at her, rubbing away a smear of flour on her cheek, and Elfrida gave her a heartfelt look of gratitude.

"I do no' ken how ye did it," she whispered as they left the dining room, "but och, thank ye!"

"I was a cook's apprentice once," Isabeau answered, smiling in remembrance. "I dread to think what Latifa would have said if she'd seen the state o' those kitchens. Och, so dirty! And rats in the grain bins and the kitchen garden all neglected. Ye have work ahead o' ye here."

Elfrida sighed as she showed them back into the drawing room, where the children all slept, curled on couch and chair. "But I do no' ken a thing. I wish ye could stay and help me get things in order."

"And no' just the kitchen," Meghan said, her voice still rather sharp, though her manner had mellowed a great deal since she had eaten. "The whole country is in disarray, Elfrida. The filth in the city streets! And all those crows spouting hellfire! The people have no lift in their step, no spirit in their eyes. There is much to be done!"

Elfrida sighed. "I ken! And ye all marching off to war again and taking my husband wi' ye. I do no' ken how I shall cope."

"Ye will find the strength. *Bo Neart Gu Neart*," Meghan said sternly. Isabeau recognized the quotation as the MacHildes' family motto, *From Strength To Strength*. "Have ye forgotten ye are a NicHilde?"

Elfrida said dispiritedly, "Nay, I have no' forgotten. How could I? Ye keep reminding me o' it all the time."

"Come, we are all tired," Isabeau said, slipping one hand under Elfrida's elbow and giving it a little squeeze. "Let us go to bed and all shall look better in the morn.

Happen we shall no' be moving on again so quickly and we shall all have time to help ye a wee."

Elfrida nodded, though the heaviness of her expression did not lighten. She picked up an elaborate golden candlestick and gave it into Isabeau's hand, saying, "At least there is plenty for me to sell to try to raise some money! I have never seen such a wicked waste as all this gold and velvet. And everything so gaudy! When I remember how I was whipped for wanting a little ribbon to trim my cap."

Isabeau lit the candles with a thought. "Well, ye are banprionnsa now and can wear as much ribbon as ye like. And I would, Elfrida. I bet the people o' this country are starved for a little color and finery, just as they are for festivity. When I remember that crowd this afternoon, all grey and black and not a touch o' color among them—it made me want to drag them out into the country and show them all the colors o' the fields and forest. How can they think it wrong to wear color when the whole world is clothed in brightness?"

"Charm is deceitful and beauty is vain," Elfrida protested. "We are taught it is wrong to flaunt ourselves and wear bright colors or jewels or big buttons, or to surround ourselves with luxury."

Isabeau lifted the golden candlestick. "The Fealde dinna seem to mind."

"Aye, but the people o' Tìrsoilleir rose up against her and helped us overthrow her," Elfrida reminded her. "They hated the fact that she clothed herself richly and hung jeweled crosses in the High Kirk and dined from plates o' gold."

"Aye, but surely it was the hypocrisy?" Isabeau asked. "They all preached denial and self-sacrifice but dinna practice it. That would make me angry too, particularly if

I was punished for it. I do no' think a wee bit o' ribbon would hurt, or wearing some other color except grey. It does no' have to be scarlet, in the name o' the Spinners! Though ye'd look lovely in red, wi' all that fair hair."

"I couldna wear red!" Elfrida was scandalized.

"Why do ye no' try blue then? Or some bonny flowery print. Though red be a lovely color, the color of roses and sunsets and elderberry wine. It's the color o' your family plaid, after all." Elfrida said nothing, her lips thinned, and Isabeau said cajolingly, "Come, ye must be tired o' grey!"

"Well, I am," Elfrida admitted. "But what about ye? Ye wear white most o' the time, like all the witches."

"Now I am a sorceress I'm allowed a little silver trimming. So daring!" Isabeau said with a laugh. "Nay, ye saw how I leapt at the gorgeous dress ye gave me in Arran. Witches really only have to wear the witchrobe during rituals or when performing our duties. It is just that I am always on duty at the moment, Meghan being my mentor and us all riding to war. Besides, I do no' really have very many clothes, having never spent much time at court."

"Well then, I'll make ye a deal. We'll each have ourselves a new dress made up and be really daring and choose something colorful. Like pink or yellow!"

"No' wi' my hair," Isabeau said ruefully. "But either o' those would suit ye. I'll have green, to remind me o' the forests."

"Grand!" Elfrida said, excited. "Let us shake hands on it then."

They spat their palms and shook hands like children, and then Elfrida went back to the dining room, a smile on her lips and a spring in her step, to direct the lairds to their rooms and make sure all were comfortable.

Meghan had sat silently through all their conversation,

her eyes closed. She opened them now and smiled at Isabeau, saying rather gruffly. "Ye did good work tonight, my Beau, and I do no' just mean cooking for all those people."

"Thank ye," Isabeau said. "Come, ye must be exhausted. Let us get these bairns to bed and find one ourselves. Havers, I be tired!"

As she bent to pull the old sorceress to her feet, Meghan surprised her by kissing her cheek and patting it with her trembling hand. "Ye're a good bairn, my Beau," she said. "Though no' a bairn anymore, are ye? A woman and a sorceress." She sighed and smiled a little, and went very slowly out of the room, Gitâ a little round bulge in her pocket.

Nila stood before his father, his cloak of seal fur hanging down his back, his tusked face raised proudly. His shadow stretched long and thin across the sand.

The King was sitting on a high rock, water ebbing and flowing around his webbed feet. Even in the diminishing light it was clear that he was very angry. The sound of his roars echoed all round the cove, and his skin was flushed the color of seagrapes. Behind him stood his own personal pod of warriors, many looking troubled, while on either side stood Nila's ten brothers, all grinning like tiger sharks.

"So what do you have to say for yourself, you jelly-spined fool!" the King roared.

"I have told you what happened," Nila said quietly. "My pod has given their evidence also. She has the power to sing as the human witches do. Many, many of our kind have drowned as the result of their enchanted singing. We were lucky to have survived."

"I had thought you had grown some sense with your

tusks. I thought that being given your own pod and your own sea-serpent would see you begin to show some respect for your king and your people," his father roared. His face was purple with rage, his tusks gleaming yellow in the long rays of the setting sun. "Yet you capture my misbegotten daughter, my sly sneaking treacherous daughter, the double-dealing snake-eel that betrayed me and failed me! You had her in your fingers and you let her slip through."

"You're shark bait," one brother said.

"Burrowing barnacle," said another contemptuously.

"Thought yourself so proud, flaunting a black pearl upon your breast," Lonan, his eldest brother, hissed.

"You let yourself be tricked and ensorcelled!" the King raged. "As soon as you knew she could sing the foul songs of human sorcery you should have torn out her tongue! You should have slit her throat and fed her to the sharks!"

Nila could feel anger building inside him but he said nothing, knowing no excuse or explanation would be acceptable. His silence only enraged the King further.

"Impudent beardworm! What did you and your misbegotten sister talk about so long? What slippery treachery do you plan?"

Nila could keep silent no longer. "I plan no treachery!" he cried. "I have always been loyal!"

"You and your taste for filthy human flesh," Lonan jeered. "Always cuddling and canoodling with halfbreed dugongs. You lost your little slave, so seek now to replace her with another filthy halfbreed—"

Disgusted, Nila launched himself at his eldest brother. "How can you say such things?" he shouted. "Maya is our sister, you loathsome seaslug!"

"You think I claim kinship with that treacherous

snake-eel?" Lonan said contemptuously, knocking Nila to the ground. "Daughter of a human slave? I'd rather claim kinship with an elephant seal!" He kicked him in the head.

Nila rolled free and staggered to his feet, only to be tripped over by another brother. Lonan laughed, bending down to rip the black pearl from Nila's throat. "Think yourself chosen by Jor? I am the Anointed One, jellyfish! I am the heir to He Who Is Anointed by Jor!" Viciously he kicked Nila in the ribs. As Nila rolled in pain, clutching his ribs, Lonan hung the black pearl about his own neck, already laden with necklaces of sea-diamonds, carved coral and white pearls.

Nila managed to get to his knees, but all nine of his brothers circled him, jeering, kicking and punching him mercilessly until he was unable to stand or fight back any more. Dazed, panting, bruised and covered in sand, he was dragged before the King once more.

"So you feel sympathy for your traitorous *sister*?" the King asked, his pale eyes glittering. "You let her escape our justice out of pity? She is nothing but a halfbreed slave, worth less than a blob of spawn jelly. Do you not realize we could have defeated the humans by now if not for her, we could have wiped them off the face of the earth! They would be mere bones picked white by crabs and fish, dissolving at last to sand. We would be once more the rulers of the sea and shore, the mightiest warriors in the world!"

There was a ragged cheer.

Knowing his case was hopeless, Nila drew himself upright, spitting out a mouthful of blood and sand. "Do you not understand that you condemn us all to doom?" he said. "For a thousand years we have thrown ourselves against the humans and been dashed to pieces. It is our people who are picked clean by the crabs, it is our people who suffer hunger and cold and exile because of this stupid feud. When are we going to stop? When are we going to find some way to live in peace, forever and happy? When are we going to realize that the humans are here to stay?"

He was cut short by a vicious elbow in the face. He fell down to one knee, holding his jaw, involuntary tears welling in his eyes. He dashed them away with one hand and looked up at his father, who was roaring with rage.

"You have lost seven sons already," Nila said. "How many more will you lose? How many more sons will your people lose?"

"Only one more," his father roared. "Take him and kill him, the traitorous snake-eel!"

Nila's brothers seized him and dragged him back, but Nila kept on shouting. "You have summoned the powers of Kani, you seek to raise the powers of the earth to drown all the land, but do you not realize you will kill us all as well? Do you think you can control Kani? Do you think you can subject *her* to your will? You condemn us all to death and destructiveness. How will the whales survive being flung upon the land? How will the fishes survive? How will we?"

Then there was only the roaring red of blows and kicks and taunts, and then the roaring black of unconsciousness.

Isabeau rolled over once again, bunching up the pillow under her head and sighing with frustration. Although she was so tired her very bones ached, she found herself unable to sleep. Her mind traveled round and round in well-worn paths, despite all her attempts to break free, and at last she sat up with a sigh of exasperation.

No-hooh snooze-hooh? Buba hooted softly from her perch on Isabeau's bed-rail.

No-hooh snooze-hooh, Isabeau answered ruefully.

You-hooh troubled-hooh?

Isabeau shrugged and got up, wrapping her white woolly plaid about her shoulders. "I feel . . . Aye, I suppose I feel troubled. I do no' ken why exactly," she said, more to herself than the owl.

Owl soar-swoop through moon cool-hooh? Buba said hopefully. Although the elf-owl had grown used to Isabeau wanting to be awake during the day and sleep at night, Buba was always eager for the sorceress to change shape and be an owl with her again.

Isabeau smiled and shook her head, opening her door quietly and stepping out into the corridor. *No-hooh, sorry-hooh.* "I thought some hot milk might help. I'm going down to the kitchen. Want to come?"

Hooh-hooh, Buba answered, swooping out the door eagerly.

The castle was very quiet. With her white plaid wrapped around her shoulders, her bright hair flowing down her back in thick waves and rivulets of curls, Isabeau went quietly through the dark corridors. She needed no candle, seeing her way clearly despite the lateness of the hour. Buba floated ahead of her, silent as smoke. They came down the grand staircase and into the front hall.

There Isabeau paused. She could hear the soft murmur of voices and see the golden flicker of light. For a moment she stood, undecided, then very quietly she made her way down the hall. One of the double doors into the dining room stood ajar. Isabeau touched it so it swung open a little more, allowing her to see into the room.

Lachlan sat at one end of the table, his wings drooping, his head laid on his arms. At his elbow was an empty glass. An almost empty decanter of whisky stood on a silver tray nearby.

Dide sat by the fireplace, strumming his guitar softly. He was singing, in a low plaintive tone, the song of the Three Blackbirds. He looked up at the sway of the door and saw Isabeau standing just outside. He frowned at her and shook his head slightly, but it was too late, the draught of the swinging door had caused the candles to gutter in their sconces and Lachlan had glanced up blearily. His eyes were red-rimmed, his face haggard.

He saw Isabeau, a tall figure all in white, the candlelight wavering over her face and the red-gold river of her hair. He leapt up, his chair falling backwards, and lurched towards her.

"Iseult!" he cried hoarsely.

Isabeau just stared at him, the words of denial in her throat but her mouth not moving to make the sound. He seized her arms in his big rough hands and pulled her against him, his mouth seeking hers. Isabeau lifted her eyes to look at him, not really knowing what she was doing. He kissed her. It was like a shock of lightning. For a moment she simply stood there, her heart hammering, one hand clasping his forearm, drawing him closer. Then she stepped back, her senses reeling. He fell back also, staring at her, eyes wide.

"I am Isabeau," she said, her voice hoarse, just as he cried her name.

For a moment longer they gazed at each other, then a shadow came down over Lachlan's face; he stepped back, half staggering, and sat down heavily in a chair. He was very drunk.

Isabeau looked up and met Dide's eyes. He cradled his battered old guitar, the smooth wood of its face painted

with faded tendrils of leaves and flowers and birds
singing. His hands were very still, his face closed. She
gazed at him a moment and then stepped forward, laying
her hand on Lachlan's shoulder. "Ye should be in bed,"
she said. "Do ye forget we ride out with the dawn? What
do ye do here, drinking in the darkness by yourself?"

His shoulder had tensed at her touch. He leant back,
saying with a bitter twist of his mouth, "My bed is cold
and lonely, I canna sleep in it, why should I seek it?"

"Ye shall make yourself ill," Isabeau said tersely. "Is
this what ye've been doing, night after night, drinking
alone? No wonder ye look like a death's head."

"I havena been alone," Lachlan replied. "Dide has
been with me."

"Dide should ken better," Isabeau said acidly. She
looked up and met his black eyes. For once they were not
merry with laughter, but shadowed and unhappy. One
corner of his mouth lifted and he began to strum the guitar again, as gently as if he stroked a lover's body. Isabeau recognized the poignant chords of the Three
Blackbirds.

"Canna ye play something else?" she snapped.

Lachlan shook his head. "Nay. I want him to play that.
I am the Rìgh. I command him to play it. Play, Dide!" He
had difficulty in speaking, his words slurring into each
other. Dide played on, his head bent. The music crept
through the dark room, exquisite, full of loss and sorrow.
Isabeau felt a little prickling of her skin. From the far corner of the room Buba hooted sadly. *Rue-hooh.*

"Ye must no' grieve so much, Lachlan," Isabeau said
very gently.

He flung out one hand. His eyes glinting with tears, he
sang:

"O where have ye flown, my black-winged birds,

Leaving me all alone?

O where have ye flown, my black-winged brothers?

Where have ye flown, my brothers?"

His voice was so beautiful, so deep and pure and full of magic, that Isabeau shuddered.

She wrapped her arms about her body. "Come, will ye no' go to bed? Ye must no' wear yourself out like this."

"Is that an invitation?" Lachlan leered at her. One hand shot out and grasped her wrist. Although Isabeau stood stiff and unyielding, he was too strong for her and she was forced to step closer. She could smell the whisky on his breath, see the fire in his golden eyes as he lifted his face to look up at her. The candlelight played over the hard, strong planes of his face, the unruly jet-black curls, the powerful line of jaw and neck and shoulder, the soft sweep of black feathers. She leant back against the cruel grip of his hand, unable to help the tightening nerve and muscle, the acceleration of her heart.

He felt the leap in her pulse and smiled at her, heart-breakingly sweet. "What do ye say, Isabeau? Will ye warm my bed for me? Iseult is gone, she has left me like my brothers, like everyone I have ever loved." Again he sang, under his breath, "O where have ye flown, my brothers, leaving me all alone?"

"Iseult has no' left ye," Isabeau said. "Ye were the one who sent her away. Ye released her from her *geas*."

"Why does she need a *geas* to stay with me?" Lachlan cried. "Why canna she just love me for myself?"

"She does love ye," Isabeau said, trying to draw her wrist free. He tightened his fingers, drew her down so they were face to face, only inches apart.

"She does no' love me," he said with great solemnity. "She does no' love me at all. She loves her snows. She left me."

Isabeau lifted her hand and smoothed back the curls from his brow. "She does love ye," she said very quietly. "She will return to ye. Ye must trust her."

His breath was ragged. He stared at her intently. Isabeau knew that if she leant forward just a little, if she kissed the pulse that beat so rapidly in his throat, if she pressed her mouth against his, Lachlan would be hers, at least for the night. She knew it was in his mind, that all she had to do was let herself flow towards him, let herself close that small distance between them. She could not breathe with the certainty of it. Her mind flew towards Iseult, her womb-sister, her twin. Slowly Isabeau drew herself away. "Ye must trust her," she repeated, her voice wavering.

He let her go. "Yes," he said. He leant his head back, stared up at the ceiling.

Isabeau took a deep breath, stepped back, became aware again of the melancholy spill of music. She looked across the table at Dide. "Come, will ye no' help me?" she said, angry at herself for the weakness of her voice. "We must get him to bed. Ye must no' let him brood like this. He needs to rest, he needs to be strong. He has a war to fight."

"Often the hardest wars are the ones we fight within ourselves," Dide answered softly. "It is no' enough to say ye must no' grieve. Grief and love are no' commanded by the mind and the will, they are driven by the heart."

After a moment she nodded. "Ye're right," she said with difficulty, pierced by his words as if they were a sword. "I'm sorry."

His long fingers stilled on the strings of the guitar, the last quivering chord dying away into silence. He laid the guitar down and got to his feet, coming round the table to kneel by Lachlan's feet. He took one of the Rìgh's hands in both of his. "Come, master, ye must go to bed. Ye will sleep now, I promise."

Lachlan looked at him, barely able to control the movement of his head. There was the shine of tears on his face. "Promise?"

"Aye, I promise. Ye will sleep like a babe, like your wee Olwynne, deep and sweet and free o' dreams. Come, master, let me help ye up."

Together Isabeau and Dide helped Lachlan to his feet. He was heavy, the broad line of shoulders and the great sweep of his wings weighing them down so they could barely support him between them. Together they helped him up the stairs to his room, Buba flying along behind them, the ghostly sweep of her wings ruffling their hair. Isabeau and Dide led Lachlan to his bed, where he sat silently watching as they unbuckled his belt and laid it on a chair. Kneeling, they took off his boots and then helped each other unwind his plaid. When he wore nothing but his shirt, Dide gently pushed Lachlan back down upon his bed, saying, "Sleep now, master. I will watch over ye."

Obediently Lachlan rolled over so he lay upon his stomach, his wings folded along his back, his head resting on his crossed arms. He nestled his cheek into his pillow, saying, "I'm so tired . . ."

Snooze-hooh, Buba hooted softly from her perch on top of the mirror.

"Ye'll feel better in the morning," Isabeau said gently, unable to help tucking the sheet about him more securely. He opened his eyes at the touch of her hands, saying, "Isabeau . . ."

"Aye?"

"Thank ye. I'm sorry."

"That's all right. Go to sleep."

He closed his eyes again, murmuring, "Sleep. I think I'd like to."

He was asleep in a moment, his breath rising in a little snore. Dide and Isabeau watched him in silence for a moment, then Isabeau rose to her feet, drawing her own plaid about her. Buba fluttered down to perch on her shoulder, moving her feathered claws uneasily and swivelling her head.

"Ye could have had him tonight," Dide said, very softly. Isabeau nodded, unable to look at him.

"Why did ye no'? Ye wanted him."

"He was no' mine to have," Isabeau answered.

"But ye wanted him." He drew closer to her, bending his head to try to see her face.

"Aye," she answered. "He has been in my dreams for many years." Somehow it was easy to tell Dide this, words she never thought she could utter, standing close to him in the darkness with the soft sound of Lachlan breathing behind them. "We are linked, ye see, Iseult and me. In my dreams I see through her eyes, and feel what she feels. It is no' always a good thing."

"Does she ken? That ye dream o' him, I mean."

"I do no' think so," Isabeau answered with a little shiver. "I hope no'."

"Does Iseult see through your eyes too?" he asked, tucking his hands into the warmth of her plaid and bringing it closer about her throat. Tears prickled Isabeau's eyes.

"I do no' think Iseult's Talents lie that way. I do no' think she walks in her dreams," she answered, her voice again failing her.

Dide shook his head. "It is hard, to be dreaming o' someone ye can never have."

Isabeau nodded, looking up at him. He bent his head

and kissed her, and then kissed her wet eyes, and she bent her head into his shoulder and let it rest there. He held her for a moment, his arm strong about her back, and then he drew away.

"Come, ye must be off to bed yourself," he said. "Dawn is close and we have a long way to travel today. Ye must try to get some sleep."

She nodded, scrubbing her face, moving away a little. "What about ye?"

"I shall watch over my master," Dide answered.

She nodded again and moved quietly to the door. As she opened it, Dide said with a little quiver of laughter in his voice, "Isabeau?"

"Aye?"

"Your wee owl dinna peck me this time."

"Nay, she did no', did she?"

"Happen she likes me a wee better now."

"Happen she does."

Time for you-hooh to mate-hooh, Buba hooted. *Time for you-hooh to build-hooh nest-hooh, lay-hooh eggs-hooh.*

Sudden heat scorched Isabeau's cheeks. She hoped Dide could not speak Owl.

A CRIMSON THREAD IS STRUNG

SKIMMING THE STARS

seult opened her eyes. Above her arched the night sky, the stars beginning to fade between heavy slabs of low cloud. She rolled over, sat up, tucked her arms about her knees, staring at the silhouette of the mountains beginning to rise up against a grey dawn. She was frowning. The dark remnants of a dream hung over her. She tried to shake her mind free but, although the details were already dissolving away, the sense of misery and betrayal lingered.

"My lady?" Carrick One-Eye whispered, sitting up in his furs on the far side of the embers. "Is all well?"

She nodded, rubbing her eyes with her hands. "Aye, all is well. Get ye back to sleep, Carrick, it is no' quite dawn."

He climbed out of his furs, shivering as the cold struck through his clothes. "Nay, my lady. Let me blow up the fire and make ye some tea. Ye look cold."

"I am cold," she answered, surprised.

The corrigan blew upon the embers, which gleamed red in the darkness, and fed in a handful of leaves and twigs. He scooped up some of the snow in the battered black pot and hung it over the fire, saying, "That's one good thing about snow, ye do no' need to travel far in search o' water."

Iseult said nothing, content to sit and watch her squire as he dropped fragrant leaves and flowers into the melting snow and got out a cup for her. In the dimness he looked more like a great hunched boulder than ever, his blunt features crusted all over with silvery lichen, his one eye like a crack in a stone.

He brought her the steaming cup and, as she drank, busied himself making porridge and gathering more wood for the fire. By the time she had eaten and was warm again, most of the dream had faded away. The rest of the camp began to stir and Iseult rose and shook off her foreboding like a wolf shaking snow from his coat.

"Looks like we're in for another storm," Khan'gharad said, leaning on his pole and staring off at the clouds pouring in over the edge of the ridge. The wind was shaking the boughs of the pine trees and sending snow skirling about in little white devil-dances. The men all had their hoods up and were bent against the wind as they struggled to pack up the camp. The silvery light of the dawn had faded into a dusk almost as deep as the darkness of night.

"I hope no'," Iseult answered. "We're behind schedule. We canna waste any more time sitting out a storm."

"Ye dinna want to be caught in a blizzard while crossing the heights," he answered.

"Aye, I ken, I ken," she said. "Happen we can climb above it though? It looks low."

"We can try," her father answered. "What a shame we do no' have that hawk o' your husband's. It'd be able to fly above the clouds and see if it be fair sky above."

At the mention of Lachlan the shadow came back to Iseult's face. Khan'gharad did not notice, busying himself packing up his knapsack.

Iseult was very conscious of time trickling away. Lammas had been and gone, and the green months were almost over. Soon the days would begin to grow shorter and Iseult knew, better than anyone, how swiftly winter descended upon the mountains. She wanted to be through the passes and down the other side before the snow began to fall too thickly.

"I can fly up and see," she said.

Khan'gharad looked at her quickly. "It be too dangerous."

"It is more dangerous for us all to be trapped here on this side of the pass," she answered. "I will no' fly too high, I promise. I ken I am no gyrfalcon!"

He nodded and she took off her coat and let it drop to the ground, bouncing slightly on the balls of her feet. Iseult's ability to fly was not as profound as her mother's, who flew as swiftly and powerfully as a snow goose. Iseult could only fly with short bursts of speed. She could not hover in the air for more than a few moments, nor fly as high as an eagle. She mainly used her Talent to get downstairs quickly or jump over high walls. Anything more taxed her strength to the utmost.

She bent her knees and soared up into the air. The wind buffeted her. She had to fight to keep from being thrown back down to the ground. Ice needles drove into the exposed flesh of her face. For a while all was grey and rough and freezing cold, her sight wrapped in mist, then she burst through the canopy of clouds.

Below her were white billows of cloud stretching as far as the eye could see, dazzling in the sun which poured down from above. All round stood a ring of high mountains, their steep sides grey and bare, their heads crowned with ice. Spindrifts of snow floated from every peak, like an exhalation of warm breath into the radiant blue sky.

Iseult hung motionless for a moment, gazing about

with pleasure, then she felt the weight of the earth dragging her back down. She slid back into the clouds, flailed by hail and sleet, the wind dragging at her strength. She came down faster than she wished, landing with a great splash of snow and an ungraceful "Humph!" as all her breath was knocked out of her body.

"My lady!" Carrick cried, bending over her and offering her his huge, clumsy hand. "Be ye all right?"

"Aye, I be fine," she answered breathlessly and let him pull her up. "It be clear above the clouds, we should be able to climb out o' this gale. Let us get moving!"

All morning they slogged through the storm, hoods pulled close about their faces, the snow soon reaching past their knees. Iseult ordered the men to lash themselves together, for nothing could be seen but white blowing snow and the occasional black thrashing of a tree. The ground began to tilt steeply. Men fell and slid helplessly, and were dragged up to their feet again. Rocky walls rose up all around them, the wind screaming down a long tunnel of ice. They had to cut steps with their axes and hammer in picks to lash their ropes to. Higher and higher they climbed, the *ulez* straining to drag up the heavy sleds, their broad feet somehow finding purchase on the slippery ice.

Suddenly Khan'gharad called down, "I'm above the storm! Ye were right, Iseult, I can see blue sky."

Galvanized with fresh energy, the men scrambled up the steep pathway, one by one climbing out onto the shoulder of the mountain. Below them was a tossing sea of white cloud. All around rose the jagged peaks, sharply etched against a crystal clear sky. Immaculate sweeps of snow, unmarked by a single footstep, fell down in graceful folds to their feet, shadowed a deep indigo blue. Iseult took a deep breath, feeling the last phantom of her dream drop away.

The MacSeinn exclaimed with pleasure. Iseult pointed up to the mountain directly ahead of them, sheer cliffs of snow soaring up on either side. "This is the last o' the mountains," she said. "When ye step over that peak, my laird, ye will step into Carraig. See that path? We o' the Khan'cohbans call it the Bridge To Beyond The Known. It marks the end o' the land of the Gods o' White."

At her words the exhausted men gave a ragged cheer. Khan'gharad turned on them savagely. "Ye must be quiet. Do ye no' see how the snow overhangs us here? Do ye wish to set off an avalanche?"

They sobered immediately, looking up at the sheer white cliffs in some trepidation. "I ken ye are all eager to see the last o' my homeland," Khan'gharad said with the faintest inflection of humor in his voice. "But nonetheless, be very careful how ye climb. Try no' to make any noise, for if ye set the snow to moving, the whole mass o' it shall come tumbling down."

They nodded and he gestured to the Scarred Warriors to lead the way. He and Iseult stood in silence for a time, watching the long procession snaking up the hill.

"Once we have crossed the Bridge To Beyond The Known, ye have fulfilled your promise to show the Mac-Seinn the way into Carraig," Khan'gharad said at last. "What shall ye do then, Khan'derin my daughter?"

Iseult did not reply. She knew what he asked. Khan'gharad, more than anyone, knew what the breaking of her *geas* to Lachlan meant.

After a long moment she turned a wretched face towards him and said, "I dinna ken, I dinna ken."

He nodded his head brusquely. "I see. Well, in a few hours more we shall have crossed the Bridge To Beyond

The Known. Happen your path will lie clear before ye then."

Iseult nodded unhappily. He unstrapped his skimmer from his back, tied it to his boots, and went flying across the snow towards the final ascent, as swift and graceful as a bird. Iseult watched, torn with grief and longing. This was her home, this world of white snow and black shadows, this world of cold purity, cold absolutes. All she had to do was stay here, bid goodbye to the MacSeinn on the threshold of his land, and skim back to her own people. She would have fulfilled her last promise to Lachlan, she would be free.

Tears stung her eyes. Despite all her best efforts she could not help being haunted by fragments of her dream. Iseult had seen Lachlan and Isabeau, mouth to mouth, body to body, yearning together. She had heard Lachlan ask Isabeau into his bed. She told herself once again that the dream was just a phantom of her mind, an extrusion of her deeply buried jealousy and fear. Lachlan had met Isabeau first, Iseult's sister who looked as much like her as a reflection in a mirror. He had met Isabeau first, and who was to say he had not fallen in love with her first? Certainly Lachlan had not said so, but he had *meant* so. Even Duncan Ironfist had seen it, and he was naught but a rough soldier with little knowledge of the ways of the heart.

And Iseult had ridden away and left Lachlan alone, all her anger and resentment unresolved, their bodies frustrated from weeks of coldness. She had left him there with Isabeau, her womb-sister, who would travel close beside him for months, with her face like Iseult's face and her body like Iseult's body and her straight fearless gaze just like Iseult's. Lachlan had called Isabeau the most

beautiful, bright thing he had ever seen. He had said he
tried to hate her, for otherwise he could only love.

And though Iseult would trust Isabeau with her life,
and Lachlan with more, the dream gnawed away at her
like an insect at a leaf. Round and round her thoughts
went, reassuring herself that Lachlan loved her and only
her, that it was not enough for Isabeau to look like her, Isabeau was *not* her, telling herself it was only a dream,
only a silly dream. The last of the Scarred Warriors
passed her, and Iseult began to climb in their tracks,
hardly aware of the darkening of the indigo shadows, the
rise of the bitter wind, too caught up in the tumult of her
mind.

Up the slope she toiled, not noticing that she was far
behind the others, not noticing the creeping of cloud upon
her footsteps. The sun dropped down behind the peak, its
light blotted out. Darkness closed in upon the valley,
upon the small figure alone on the steep fall of snow.
There was a low mutter of thunder. Again it came, louder,
more insistent.

Iseult looked up. All at once she realized she had been
left far behind. The light was gone, there was a strange
purple dusk lying heavy on the valley. She began to climb
more swiftly. Again came that low, angry growl of thunder. It rolled around the valley. Suddenly, a livid slash of
lightning. Iseult's heart constricted. The snow beneath
her feet was trembling. There was a strange dull roar that
rose up to meet the thunder, engulfed it. She looked up
and saw the cliff of snow rearing above her like an enormous wave. The ground beneath her feet shuddered and
heaved. Iseult was flung down. With a gasp she scrambled to her feet, launched herself into the air. Iseult had
already flown high that day, however, and climbed a
mountain and fought a nightmare. She did not have the

strength to soar above the avalanche. With a boom like the clash of a god's cymbals, the mountain fell down upon her and swept her away into darkness.

After leaving Dide in the darkness, watching over his sleeping master, Isabeau made her way back to her own bed but still she could not settle. No matter how hard she tried to disengage her mind, it rattled round and round on the same rutted road. At last, in the chill of the dawn, she got up, straightened her tangled bedclothes and finished her packing. When the castle began to stir, she went downstairs and made herself some hot tea, which helped warm and revive her, then took up some breakfast for Meghan. The old sorceress exclaimed over the shadows under her eyes,

"Could ye no' sleep?" she asked. "Silly lass, your last night in a real bed for weeks! Why could ye no' sleep?"

Isabeau shrugged. "Who kens?" she answered. The old sorceress scanned her face with keen eyes but said no more, and Isabeau busied herself packing up her belongings and checking over the medicinal supplies with Johanna the Mild.

Isabeau saw both Lachlan and Dide in the outer bailey as they mounted up, ready for the ride through the city. Both were pale and tired-looking, the Rìgh obviously nursing a bad headache and an ever worse temper. Isabeau ducked back inside the corridor before they saw her, her heart lurching uncomfortably. Even though she knew she would have to see them eventually, she found herself quite unable to go out and greet them and pretend nothing had happened. Isabeau waited for the Blue Guards to trot out through the long tunnel before stepping out herself. Finding the bustle and noise of the courtyard almost too much to bear, she climbed up into the carriage and buried herself in a book in the hope no one would speak to her until she had regained her composure.

Brun hopped up beside her, the collection of rings and spoons about his neck jingling. He had put off his green velvet doublet and wore the same rough clothes of most of the other soldiers in the Rìgh's army, covered with one of the grey cloaks that gave the troops their nickname. The cloaks had all been woven through with spells of concealment and camouflage, making it difficult to see the wearer when they crept through long grasses or hid behind rocks.

The cluricaun observed Isabeau with bright brown eyes, his ears pricked forward. "Though o' many faces, it is no revealer o' secrets," he said. "The two-faced one is the one to show the secret. The secrets o' its face shall confide in ye, and ye will hear it wi' the eye as long as ye are looking."

"What on earth?"

Grinning, the cluricaun repeated his words, touching her book with one hairy paw. Isabeau stared at him blankly for a moment before she caught his meaning. "Och, it's a riddle," she said. "I see, ye mean my book. The two-faced one is the open page, the secrets o' its face are the words. That's very clever, Brun, I've no' heard that one afore."

She tried to push away the flash of guilt and self-recrimination his words had given her, knowing the cluricaun delighted in riddles and conundrums. It did not mean he knew she had a guilty secret, or that he thought her two-faced. It was nothing but a riddle.

Determinedly Isabeau turned her attention back to her book, but the children were scrambling in, laughing and shouting and knocking the book flying. Then Gwilym was helping Meghan up and Isabeau had to help settle the old sorceress. As she sat back in her seat she felt the cluricaun's inquisitive gaze upon her and flushed a little. The sun glinted off his jangling necklet and Isabeau suddenly leant forward.

"Brun, where did ye get that spoon? I have no' seen it afore."

The cluricaun closed one hairy paw about the cluster of silver oddments. "Nowhere," he said guiltily.

"Brun, let me see."

Reluctantly the cluricaun opened his paw and Isabeau examined the trinkets hanging from his chain. There were silver keys, bells and buttons, a silver coin with a hole drilled through it, and two small spoons, all brightly polished. Upon the handle of one of the spoons was a crest she recognized immediately, a sword held up in a gauntleted fist. "Brun, ye wicked cluricaun! This be a MacHilde spoon."

"But it be so marvelous bonny," Brun said weakly. "I have never seen one like that, all curly. It be so wee I dinna think anyone would mind."

"Ye canna be stealing spoons!" Isabeau scolded. She leant out the window of the coach. Elfrida was standing within the circle of Iain's arms, her face pressed against his shoulder. His brown head was bent over her fair one and he was talking earnestly. Neil was clinging to his father's leg, his face screwed up with the effort of holding back his tears.

"Elf!" Isabeau called. Elfrida looked up, her face wet with tears, and came closer, holding Iain's hand with one of her own, the other mopping her eyes dry with a handkerchief.

"I'm sorry to disturb ye, Elf, but . . . did I ever tell ye to count the spoons when ye've had a cluricaun visiting?" Ruefully Isabeau held up the spoon.

Brun peeked a look at Elfrida and ducked his face down again. "I found it in the garden, all dirty. I dinna think anyone would miss it. I polished it till it was all sparkly again." He peeked up at Elfrida hopefully.

"A MacHilde spoon!" Elfrida exclaimed. "I wonder how long it had been lying in the dirt? It must have been years, I swear the Fealde would never have used a spoon with the MacHilde crest on it. After all, it is only silver, no' gold." There was bitter sarcasm in her voice. She turned it over in her fingers, hesitated, then gave it back to the cluricaun. "Ye can have it, Brun. He may keep that finds."

The cluricaun grinned happily and hung the spoon back on his chain.

"I am glad to have a chance to say farewell," Elfrida said. "Thank ye for all your help and support, Beau, I do no' ken how I would've managed without ye."

"My pleasure," Isabeau answered, smiling. They kissed warmly, then Elfrida leant through the window to bid the children goodbye. "Ye must come back and visit my Cuckoo soon," she said.

"We'll have beaten the Fairgean by winter," Donncan said exuberantly. "We'll come back and have my birthday party here."

"That would be grand," Elfrida answered. "I ken Cuckoo had a very happy birthday wi' ye at Lucescere."

"They gave me a pony," Neil said importantly.

"Well, if Donncan is back here at Bride for his birthday, we'll have to try to think o' something just as good for his present," Elfrida said with a smile, though her eyes were shadowed.

"Ye have a care for yourself, Elfrida," Meghan said. "May Eà be with ye!"

"And wi' ye," Elfrida answered, her voice choked, and

stepped back as the coachman cracked the whip. With a lurch the carriage started forward, rattling over the cobblestones as the horses trotted down the long tunnel and out into the city streets.

Once again it took a long time to make their way out of the city, for the streets were crowded with well-wishers. The children all hung out the windows, waving and smiling. Many recognized the golden-winged boy as the young heir to the throne and cheered him lustily. Bronwen had taken to wearing high-necked, long-sleeved dresses so her gills and fins were hidden, and so none recognized her as a Fairge. They waved to her too, and threw her flowers, and she laughed and waved back. They had just clattered out through the city gate when suddenly Bronwen's face blanched and she shrank back into the carriage.

"What is it, darling?" Isabeau asked.

"Naught, naught," Bronwen stammered, sitting back against the cushions.

Isabeau leant forward to look where the girl had been looking. Suddenly her breath caught. Maya was standing right at the front of the crowd, staring straight into Isabeau's eyes. She was dressed in a rough grey gown and had a black shawl held close about her face. "Tonight," she mouthed. "Meet me tonight, by the shore."

And then she stepped back into the crowd and vanished. Isabeau sank back against the cushions, astonished and frightened. No one had seen, however. Meghan had been dozing, Gitâ curled on her lap; Donncan and the twins had still been hanging out the other window, waving and smiling; and the bogfaery Maura had been sewing up a rent in a pair of Owein's breeches. Bronwen had been fiddling with a button on the sleeve of her dress. She looked up as she felt Isabeau's gaze, then looked away, color rising in her cheeks. Isabeau almost believed she had imagined Maya's face, Maya's silvery gaze. But she knew she had not.

So now Isabeau was making her way through the army camp to the shore, her thin red brows drawn together in a frown. Twilight was enfolding the harbor in a warm violet light and all the men were busy settling in for the evening. The army encampment filled most of the valley with rows of twinkling campfires and low, grey tents. Raising a forest of masts against the darkening sky was the royal fleet of ships, anchored in the wide sweep of the bay. Tomorrow the army would set sail for Carraig, but tonight the soldiers enjoyed their last night on solid ground. Barrels of whisky had been rolled out and shared around, and a herd of sheep had been slaughtered and roasted slowly over the fires. The sweet smell of burning flesh made Isabeau sick to the stomach.

There was a burst of laughter from one circle of men, and Isabeau glanced their way before hurrying on. She had to use every trick she had ever been taught to pass through that bustling, rowdy camp unnoticed. Isabeau had been taught by Meghan of the Beasts, though, and so was as silent and unobtrusive as a shadow.

Somewhere someone was playing a guitar and singing, rough voices joining in the sentimental chorus. Beyond the camp the forest pressed close upon the brow of the hill, the foliage black against the twilight sky. In her dark green dress, her bright hair covered with a dark shawl, Isabeau passed silently through the line of sentries and disappeared into the shadows.

Down on the shore the last of the light lingered. Waves rushed and flowed, leaving scallops of foam like lace on the sand. The camp was hidden from view by low sand dunes where tall silvery grasses bent in the wind. Buba swooped first this way, then the other, catching the grasshoppers that leapt about in the undergrowth. It was almost dark.

Isabeau walked along the edge of the water, her bare feet sinking into the damp sand, listening for any step other than her own, for the slither of sand or the rustle of grass. All was quiet. Despite the peace of the seashore, Isabeau was tense and unhappy. She felt a deep foreboding. Why was the Fairge taking such a dreadful risk? Had she come for Bronwen? What would happen if Isabeau was caught talking to her? Isabeau knew something dire was going to happen.

There was the faintest disturbance behind her. She turned. A shadow stepped out of the deeper shadows in a cleft of the dunes. It was Maya.

"What are ye doing here?" Isabeau whispered. "How can ye take such a risk?"

"I have come to warn ye," Maya said softly. Her husky voice was as full of charm as ever. She drew close to Isabeau, her face very white in the dim violet light.

"Warn me? Warn me o' what?"

Maya hesitated. "The Priestesses o' Jor plan a trap for ye all. They ken ye shall plan a strike against them in reprisal for the attack on Rhyssmadill. I do no' ken all that they plan but they have drawn upon dreadful powers. They have a new acolyte. Like me, she is a halfbreed. She has recourse to both Fairgean and human power. I kent her as a child. Her mother was stolen in a raid on Siantan. She was a witch o' some sort . . ."

"Happen a weather witch if she came from Siantan," Isabeau said.

"I do no' ken. Happen she was. This lass must have strong powers though. She managed to stay alive." There was an ironic inflection in Maya's voice. "Nila says—"

"Nila?"

"My brother. Half-brother, rather. He captured me as I was swimming along the coast, and told me all this, and then let me go. I do no' ken why. He is either very brave or very foolish, or both, to dare the wrath o' our father so."

"Happen it was part o' the trap."

"I do no' think so. He hates our father as much as I do, that I will swear to. Besides, he did no' ken that I would come and tell ye. He told me so that I could flee."

"What did he tell ye?" Isabeau was white. The feeling of foreboding was heavy upon her now, pressing her down like a giant hand.

"That the Priestesses o' Jor plan to raise a tidal wave and drown the land, using the magic o' the comet, as I did when I conceived Bronwen. They will be able to do it, Red. They have drawn upon the power o' Kani. She is the mother o' all gods, the goddess o' fire and earth. It is Kani that brings volcanoes and earthquakes and lightning and the evil glow o' the viperfish . . ."

The world was spinning around Isabeau. She put out a hand, but there was nothing to grasp. "I ken," she managed to say. "I ken . . ."

Then she felt a dark roaring, felt the world crash down all around her. She fell to her knees. Very faintly she heard Maya cry, "Red, what is it? What is it?"

"Iseult . . ." she said. "Iseult!"

She felt pain like daggers piercing her all over, felt a bitter cold like death. *Iseult!* For a moment she hovered over the clearing. She could see Maya's dark form bending over her own, collapsed on the white sand. Then her spirit turned and fled. *Iseult . . .*

Over the dark undulating landscape she flew, effortless as an eagle. She could see the tangled knots of rivers shining green and blue as they writhed and tumbled to-wards the sea. She could see the glowing clusters of town and village like throngs of fireflies, the light of people's souls rather than the light of their lanterns. As she passed she felt shivers of their lives run over her, grief and joy, hope and despair, small contentments, small spites. Above her the stars wheeled and sang, a cruel terrible music like a death requiem. She soared among them, felt their temptation tug at her. *Iseult . . .*

Below her the landscape upsurged and downfolded, creasing into sharp peaks and deep valleys. Isabeau felt herself growing weak. She glanced back for the first time, afraid. Behind trailed her spirit-body, as frail as candle smoke. From her heart spun a long thread, as silvery and delicate as a spider's cobweb. It stretched behind her, throbbing slightly. It looked as if it might break at any moment.

Isabeau flew on. Below her were shining sheets of ice, a sweep of glacier. Isabeau was having to fight now. Wind seemed to throw her up, suck her down. The music was clamoring in her ears. *Iseult,* she called. *Iseult . . .*

She saw a great mass of broken snow and rocks below her. Very faintly she could feel her sister's heartbeat, feel a great mass of cold and grief pressing her down towards death. *Do no' sleep!* she called. *I am here.*

Then, drowsy, faltering, she heard, *Isabeau . . . ?*

Isabeau flew down towards the mass of broken snow. She could see lights bobbing about. People were search-ing, digging, weeping. She could feel their horror and dismay more strongly than she could feel Iseult's heart-beat. *No,* she cried. *No' there . . .*

No one heard her. She was a ghost, wailing in the darkness. She was the wind, voiceless, faceless, without hands to dig, without words to warn. For long futile minutes she flung herself against their deaf unheeding ears, and then she swung away, searching, searching.

Her mind brushed against someone she knew. Desperate, Isabeau flew down. She was at the end of her strength, the cord that bound her to her physical body was stretched thin, far too thin. Isabeau knew she would die if it should break. Isabeau knew both she and Iseult would die.

On a ledge overlooking the valley lay a snow-lion. He was a magnificent creature, his paws huge and strong, his snowy mane tipped with black. Isabeau hung before him, pleading. In the proud golden eyes she saw her own reflection, frail and silver as the reflection of moonlight. She spoke in a tumble, her disembodied powerless hands stretching out, pleading. *I saved ye when ye were but a cub, do ye remember? Ye are in* geas *to me, help me now . . .*

The snow-lion stood, shook his noble mane, began to lope down the hill. Exhausted, Isabeau drifted after him.

Almost dissolved into the ether, she watched him as he ran across the snow. A longing came over her. How well she remembered the deadly grace, the sure power of a snow-lioness's body. How much she longed to be running there, leaping over concealed rocks, stretching into full speed. How much she longed to be able to dig for Iseult, her sure sense of smell knowing where she lay buried under mounds of snow. But she was feeble as candle smoke in a wind, she was dissolving away.

Iseult, help comes, she whispered. *Hold on . . .*

Then she turned, followed the disintegrating trail of smoke, flew with desperate haste back the way she had come. In her mind she heard her Soul-Sage teacher warning, *Never skim too far . . .*

Hurricanes buffeted her, dragged at her strength, confused her. *Up, down, in, out, where am I, where am I?*

Somewhere, a long way away, she heard Meghan's voice. *Isabeau, Isabeau . . .*

She followed the sound.

Isabeau came back to consciousness only slowly. She was aware first of angry voices. She recognized Meghan's, sharper than she had ever heard, then Lachlan's deep baritone, and then, surprisingly, Maya's voice, raised in angry denial. Isabeau lay in a sort of stupor, wondering why they all sounded so angry. Then the oddness of it struck her. Lachlan and Maya?

She opened her eyes. She lay curled on her side in sand. It was dark, but a group of men stood nearby with lanterns in their hands, casting wavering orange light over pale sand and the dark shapes of people. The orange light seemed to throb, making her feel sick. She turned onto her hands and knees, and retched into the grass. The ground seemed to tilt under her body. She clutched it, trying to reorientate herself, but the sand slithered away under her fingers. Then Meghan knelt beside her, holding her, asking her how she was. Isabeau had to concentrate hard to understand the meaning of the sounds. Then she said shakily, "In a minute. I'll be fine in just a minute."

Meghan cradled her, soothing her as she would a sick child. Then Lachlan was kneeling beside her, gripping one of her hands. "What did she do to ye?" he asked fiercely. "Did she try to enchant ye?"

Isabeau did not understand. "Iseult . . ." she whispered, then as agony suddenly lanced through her arm, she screamed. "Oh, Eà, Iseult!"

Lachlan let go of her hand. "Iseult?" he asked. There was an odd intonation in his voice. "What about Iseult?"

Isabeau turned her head restlessly. "She was hurt, injured. She was near death. I could feel her slipping away. The pain ... the cold ... I had to go. I have never skimmed so far. I kent it was dangerous but I had to go."

"Iseult is hurt?" Lachlan's voice, his whole manner, had changed. He leant forward, seizing Isabeau roughly by the shoulders. "Where? What happened? Is she ...? What happened, tell me, in Eà's name, tell me!"

"She's alive." Isabeau found herself weeping. "I could no' make them understand me, the soldiers searching for her under the snow, I could no' make them hear me. I could feel her slipping away, it was so cold, it was so cold! At first it was like knives and then ..." She could not go on. She wiped her eyes with her hands, tried to catch her breath.

"But she's alive?" Meghan said. "Are ye sure? Ye can feel her?"

"Aye, I can feel her. The pain, I can feel it here and here and here." Isabeau pointed to her ribs, her arm, her knee. "They have set her broken arm. I could feel it, damn it. Why, oh, why do I have to feel everything she does?"

"Oh, ye do, do ye?" Lachlan said, raising an eyebrow.

Isabeau could not look at him. She was grateful for the darkness. "How did ye ken?" she said to Meghan. "I could never have found my way back if ye had no' been here."

"Your wee owl came and got me," the sorceress said. "Luckily I speak Owl quite well, for she was very distressed indeed. She told me ye'd been speaking to someone on the seashore when ye'd suddenly fallen and then flown out o' yourself. She told me ye were lost. I dinna understand at all, o' course, but I came where she led me and Lachlan and the Blue Guards too. That was when we found Maya."

Isabeau sat up with a jerk. "Maya!" Her gaze flew across the beach. She saw the former banrìgh standing proud and tall within the grasp of two burly soldiers, a dagger held to her throat. "Och no!" she cried.

"Naturally we thought the blaygird Fairge had tried to ensorcel ye," Lachlan said angrily, "though she swore she had no'."

"I told ye I had done naught to Red but stand guard over her when she fainted," Maya said silkily. "Ye always think the worst o' me, MacCuinn."

The soldiers jerked her arms, crying, "Silence!"

"Maya, why did ye stay?" Isabeau said in distress. "Ye could have swum away and no one would've kent. Oh, why did ye no' flee?"

"Ye mean ye kent she was here?" Lachlan said incredulously. "We thought ye must have stumbled upon her and tried to detain her." His voice sharpened. "Ye met her here on purpose?"

"Aye, I did," Isabeau said angrily, "and do no' start thinking the worst, Lachlan MacCuinn, for if ye do, I swear I'll slap ye! Why canna ye ever trust anyone, for Eà's sake?"

"Why?" Lachlan began angrily. "Ye can ask me that?"

"Aye, I can," Isabeau blazed. "We all ken ye suffered greatly, Lachlan, but ye are no' the only man in the world to be betrayed and hurt. Do ye really think I'd betray ye? Do ye? Do ye think I'm a spy for the Fairgean?"

"Well, no," Lachlan admitted.

Isabeau's temper suddenly drained out of her, leaving her deflated. "Well then," she said, suddenly at rather a loss.

"Ye have got to admit I've a right to be angry," Lachlan said reasonably. "My own wife's sister, sneaking out at night to meet with Maya the Ensorcellor. What am I meant to think?"

"That I had a damn good reason," Isabeau said, her anger sparking again.

"Well, I would fain hear it," Lachlan said.

Isabeau eyed him resentfully. "I've been trying to tell ye."

"So, tell me."

Isabeau took a deep breath. "Maya came to give me news," she said. "At considerable risk to herself, I might add! She came to tell us we're heading into some sort o' trap. The Fairgean are expecting us to make a strike against them, they're prepared for it."

"Well, that is no' altogether news," Lachlan said slowly. "I did no' really expect to find Carraig empty and undefended, in spite o' all your assurances that the Fairgean all swim south for the summer."

"*My* assurances!" Isabeau cried. "Ye asked me to tell ye what I kent, I only—"

"Aye, aye, I ken. No need to get your drawers in a tangle. Is that the only news she has, for if so—"

"Nay," Isabeau cried, thoroughly exasperated. "She has more, much more. But if ye are no' interested . . ."

"Come, my bairns, that's enough fraitching!" Meghan said. "Ye are as bad as Owein and Olwynne, I swear ye are. Is this the place for a discussion such as this? We are all tired and overwrought and talking in circles. Let us go back to the safety o' the camp and talk about all this in private. And since the Ensorcellor has so kindly traveled all this way, and at such a risk to herself, to give us this news, happen she can do it herself. And explain *why* she would take such a risk. Forgive me, Maya, if I'm skeptical but I, like Lachlan, find it hard to believe ye would warn us out o' the goodness o' your heart."

"I did no'," Maya said huskily. "Why would I? Nay, I came to warn Red because she has my daughter. I do no' want my wee Bronny to be drowned."

"Drowned?" Lachlan said cynically. "She has fins and gills, remember. I doubt she'll die o' drowning."

"Ye will all die o' drowning if the Priestesses o' Jor have their way," Maya replied indifferently. "As far as ye or your nasty auld aunt there are concerned, I do no' care. But I do care about my Bronny, and oddly enough, about Red. I came to warn *her*, No' ye."

"Oddly enough, I believe ye," Meghan said. "Please, this damp sea air makes me ache all over and that makes me very irritable. Let us retire to somewhere where we can all sit down and talk things over in a civilized manner."

Lachlan gave a snort of incredulous laughter. "I suppose ye'll want me to offer the Ensorcellor some wine and a wee bite o' supper."

"Thank ye," Maya said suavely. "That would be most pleasant."

Lachlan laughed, though with a razor-sharp edge. He gave a courtly bow and offered Maya his arm. "Madam, may I escort ye to the royal pavilion?"

"Thank ye, kind sir," Maya replied, the same bitter sarcasm making the words a mockery.

Together they strolled away from the beach, the soldiers lighting their way with lanterns. Dide came and pulled Isabeau to her feet. "Whoever would have thought we'd live to see that?" he said. "It just goes to show, all things are possible."

Isabeau did not reply, too tired and troubled at heart to think of a witty response. He squeezed her arm. "Do no' look so worried, Beau. I can feel the Spinners' hand in this. Can ye no' feel it? A new thread has been strung and who kens where it shall take us."

Snow flew up from the sleigh's runners in a perfect parabola.

The *ulez* cantered down the slope, their ugly heads held high with eagerness. Lying in the sleigh, one arm in a sling, her ribs tightly bound, Iseult watched the green forest come closer and closer. The Spine of the World was behind her, the ugly chaotic world of wars and politics and courtly intrigue before her once again. She sank her chin down into her furs with a little smile.

Her father had known without needing to be told. He had merely said, "So ye travel wi' us to Carraig?" and she had answered merely, "Aye."

So, tucked up in one of the sleighs, the Scarred Warriors swooping and skimming all around her, she had left the Spine of the World for the last time. Soon they would be among the trees, and the sleighs would have to be abandoned. She would have to get out and walk like the other soldiers. Iseult could hardly wait. She hated being treated like an invalid, hated to be reminded that she had been foolish enough to be caught in an avalanche. The MacSeinn and his men had thought they were being kind, fussing about her and forbidding her to exert herself, but Iseult was a Scarred Warrior. She wanted to be invincible.

Of them all, only Khan'gharad understood. He made no mention of her injuries and treated her as if she was whole and well. Not once did he offer to help as she limped about the camp, doing her duties as usual, nor did he ever enquire how she had slept.

Slowly Iseult's strength was returning. It would be some time before she had the use of her broken arm again, but the healers said her fractured rib was knitting well, and already the swelling and discoloration 'round her knee were fading. It was the injury to her pride that would take longer to heal; and all the fussing over her health, and constant exclamations over the strangeness of her rescue, only exacerbated her feelings.

For some reason Iseult's rescue by a snow-lion appealed to the superstitious imaginations of humans and Khan'cohbans alike. Iseult was rather perturbed to find that the story was already reaching mythic proportions, with many a new rich detail embroidered to the plain fabric of the truth. No matter how many times Iseult told them that it was her twin sister Isabeau who had sent the snow-lion, they all thought she had been merely hallucinating due to the cold and the shock. The snow-lion was a manifestation of the Gods of White, said the Khan'cohbans. Maybe, agreed the human soldiers. "It's certainly no' natural, a great wild creature like that coming down out o' the storm to dig out the Banrìgh. It must mean she has a great destiny to fulfil. It must be a sign." Iseult could only hope they would find something new to talk about soon.

At last the procession reached the edge of the forest. Tall trunks rose high all about them. The *ulez* came to a panting halt, nudging their noses through the thin snow to find the grass beneath. Iseult threw off her furs and clambered out of the sleigh, refusing Carrick's eager offer of help.

"We shall leave the sleighs here," Iseult said. "We are below the snowline now. The *ulez* can carry most o' the luggage on their backs, but from now on all the men must carry their own weapons and their own supplies. We shall see some good hunting, I think. The land is lush and, by the looks o' it, there is plenty o' game."

Douglas MacSeinn was looking about him with undisguised pleasure. Sunlight struck down through the columns of trees in long, slanting lines. Small, brightly colored birds darted about, twittering and chirping. The grass was thick and green and wound about with bright flowers, gold and crimson and blue. Hovering above the flowers were huge butterflies, their wings an iridescent blue. Iseult had never seen butterflies so big. They were larger than both her hands clasped together. They dipped their wings lazily, sipping at the flowers' honey, their black velvety antennae quivering.

"It be aye bonny," Douglas said eagerly. He had been only a child when he had left Carraig and this homecoming filled him with joy and excitement.

"Aye, that it is," his father said, looking about with satisfaction. "I have never actually been up here. I had no idea it was so pretty, or for that matter that the land was so rich. The MacSeinn clan have always been tied to the sea. No one ever came up this way except the furriers and fossickers."

"What were they fossicking for?" Douglas asked, settling down on the grass to eat his rations in two huge bites.

The MacSeinn shrugged, chewing his portion with rather more circumspection. "Gold, jewels? What do fossickers usually look for?"

"Havers, imagine if we found gold," Douglas said excitedly. "Then we'd have the money to pay back the Rìgh and to pay all our men, and to build a new castle . . ."

His father frowned at him. "That's enough, Douglas! As far as I ken, none o' them ever found more than a handful o' gold dust. Nay, when we have won the war we shall have to reopen the saltpetre mines and start manufacturing gunpowder again. Eà kens we've been using enough these past few years!"

"Though once we've won the war, who'll be needing gunpowder again?" Douglas said, lying back in the grass and staring up at the green-golden-blue interlock of leaves and sky, as bright as any enamelled glaze.

The MacSeinn looked unhappy. "Aye, would that no' be my luck? I own the richest saltpetre mines in all the land and canna access them when we need the stuff, and as soon as I win back my lands, the need is gone."

"We shall need fireworks to celebrate," Douglas said. "It'll be the biggest explosion o' fireworks ever, won't it, Your Highness?"

Iseult opened her eyes. "Aye, indeed it will," she said, trying not to show how much her ribs were paining her. "Come, we have rested long enough. Let us be on our way."

The MacSeinn looked at her shrewdly. "Why do we no' make camp here?" he said. "We have traveled far today and indeed I am feeling weary."

She smiled at him. "And ye so keen to be striking the first blow against your enemy," she replied, gently mocking. "Nay, my laird. I can hear water. Let us push on till we reach the river. It is no' too much further, and once there I can busy the men to start felling trees to build us some rafts. Why should the river no' carry us to the sea?"

"What a grand idea," Douglas replied, leaping to his feet. He helped his father rise and then turned to offer Iseult his hand but she had taken advantage of his distraction to clamber to her feet herself, her hand clamped to her side. With her face wiped clean of all expression, she was rather gingerly shouldering her very heavy pack.

"Your Highness," Douglas cried in dismay, just as

Carrick One-Eye leapt forward, saying, "My lady, please, let me carry it for ye!"

"Ye are already carrying your pack and Gayna's," Iseult said reprovingly, sliding her splinted arm back inside her sling. "I ken your shoulders are broad, my lad, but then so are mine. I canna order the men to all carry such a load and then no' carry it myself."

"But my lady . . ."

"Come, stop fussing!" she said sharply. "Let us be on our way."

Reluctantly Douglas and Carrick fell into step behind her, as she called to Khan'gharad and the other Scarred Warriors to lead the way.

By sunset Iseult was white, the weight of the knapsack on her shoulders obviously bothering her. She would allow none to help her, though, and only the MacSeinn's repeated requests that she slow down and wait for a poor old man who could not step as sprightly as she could gave her the excuse to stop occasionally and recover her strength.

"Ye are no' so auld," she said on one such occasion, when he insisted on her sitting beside him on a fallen log and sharing a wee dram of whisky with him. Through the trees they could see a blue winding ribbon of water that led to a wide stretch of sparkling loch.

"No' so young any more either," he replied. "And definitely no' used to all this clambering over rocks. It's grand for ye young things, bounding around like puppies, but I find it does no' suit my dignity to have my men seeing me pant like an auld dog. So humor me, lassie, and let me bide a wee and catch my breath."

In the soft twilight they finally reached the banks of the river. Iseult was able to drop her load and sit quietly for a while, keeping the MacSeinn company while the men set up camp. The river murmured quietly to itself, running deep and swift over fine gravel between banks crowded with slender birch trees, their leaves blowing grey.

The loch glimmered beyond, reflecting in serene perfection the tall peaks of the mountains behind them, radiant in the last bright burst of light from the sun. Douglas came and sat next to his father, breathing out a sigh of pure happiness. "This must be the loveliest spot on earth," he said. "I would fain live here always. Canna we build a castle here, *Dai-dein?*"

His father frowned. "The MacSeinn clan has always lived on the coast," he said slowly.

"Och, well, happen the coast is bonny too," Douglas said, not wanting to disturb the tranquillity of the evening.

His father smiled rather grimly. "Actually, it be a wild, rugged sort o' place," he admitted. "The cliffs are very high for much o' the way and there are only a few safe harbors, which we've always had to fight hard to keep, the sea-demons wanting them too. There are no beaches like the ones ye have seen in Clachan, with soft sand where the waves creep in as gentle as a kitten. It's all rocks and wild waves and steep cliffs, and in winter icebergs as big as castles drift past, and the water is so cold a man will die in minutes if he falls in."

"Oh," Douglas said, daunted.

"It has its own beauty," the MacSeinn said, a faraway expression in his eyes. "But the wind in the winter! It never seems to stop, blowing the very soul out o' ye."

He looked down at his son and smiled suddenly, though the deep lines between his brows did not soften. "I had forgotten the wind," he said. "Happen we can build a house here for the winter and come here to fish and hunt and climb in the mountains. Happen ye can learn to skim like the Khan'cohbans."

The sparkle came back into Douglas's brilliant sea-green eyes. "Och, I'd like that!"

In the morning the valley rang with the sound of axes against tree trunks. Iseult walked with her father on the gravelly river bank, discussing the safest method of rafting the river. Suddenly Khan'gharad squatted down, turning over the stones in his big hand.

"What is it?" Iseult asked.

He turned his dark, scarred face towards her, holding up a pile of large, opaque pebbles. "These be diamonds."

Iseult's breath suddenly caught. "Diamonds?"

"Aye."

She took the pebbles from his hand. "But they're so dull."

"All gems look like that in the rough. They are like weapons, they need to be honed and sharpened and polished." He straightened in a single fluid movement. "Like Scarred Warriors."

Iseult nodded, testing the weight of the pebbles in her hand. "Let us go and tell the MacSeinn," she said with a little rush of happiness. "If there are diamonds in this river, he need no' worry about being poor ever again."

"If he survives," Khan'gharad replied.

Nila woke. All his body ached. He felt cool wetness on his brow. He opened his eyes with difficulty, light stabbing into his brain. He moaned and tried to cover his eyes with his hand, but his arm would not move. A shadow fell upon him. He flinched back, but a gentle hand held him still. One of his *ralisen* was leaning over him, his face creased with concern.

"How do you feel, my prince?" he asked.

"Like shark bait," Nila answered hoarsely, coughing. He tried to sit up and the warrior helped him, passing him a shell full of cool rainwater. Nila drank thankfully, looking about him. They were on a narrow stretch of sand between high rocky headlands. Nila recognized it. It was the same beach where he had woken before. There was the rock where his father had sat and ordered his brothers to beat him to death.

"Why am I alive?" he asked.

The warrior gave an ironic laugh. "I do not know, my prince. We thought you were dead when we found you. Almighty Jor must have his hand upon you, for you still breathed despite the beating they gave you."

There was anger and condemnation in his voice. Nila squinted up at him. "We?" he asked.

"The warriors of your pod, my prince."

Nila looked about and saw the faces of all his men leaning over him. Involuntary tears sprang up in his eyes. He swallowed, determined not to show how deeply touched he was.

"They bade us follow them but when they had beached for the night, we left the others and came back," another warrior said. "We did not expect to find you alive, my prince. We thought only to give you the honors due a prince and send you into Jor's embrace as one of your courage deserved. You may have trusted the sea-singer foolishly but you did not deserve such a death, nor to be left stranded on a beach like a jellyfish. We thought to chant the rites and send you out to sea, with your pearl upon your breast and gifts for the gods at your feet."

Nila put up his fingers and feebly touched the black pearl upon his breast. "But my brother . . ."

"Your brother Lonan was stung by a sand scorpion,"

the warrior said softly. "Somehow one crept into his furs."

"They gave *him* all honor due a prince," another said. "The proper rites were spoken and he was put to sea with many fine gifts for the gods."

"But *not* the black pearl," the first said. "Jor gave the pearl to you, we thought you should be the one to give it back to him."

"Except you were not dead. So we washed you and bound your broken ribs and arm, and hung the black pearl around your neck once more."

"Why?" Nila asked. "Do you not realize what they will do to you if they find out?"

There was an uneasy movement. The warriors looked at each other.

"It would not be honorable for us to do anything else," one of the warriors said at last. "You are our *jaka*."

"You spoke against the King with wisdom and great courage," another said. "It was wrong for a wise and brave man to die with such dishonor. Our king may choose to act so and command his sons to act so, but we are beholden only to our own consciences. That is not the way of a warrior, to beat a good man to death because he speaks what he sees to be true."

Nila could not speak for a moment. At last he was able to say, "I thank you."

They nodded their heads. One gave him some more water to drink and another brought him some fish, tender, white and salty. He ate gratefully, although the salt stung his bloodied mouth.

"Is it true what you said?" one said at last. "That the Priestesses of Jor seek to raise the sea into a tidal wave?"

Nila nodded.

"And that tidal wave shall fall upon the land and drown it?"

Nila nodded again. With one eye sealed shut with puffy bruises and the other still wincing from the light, it was hard for him to read the expression of the *ralisen*, and his voice was carefully free of intonation. Nila wondered where these questions were leading.

"And all life on the land shall be drowned?"

"All life near the sea," Nila answered.

"And is it true that the Priestesses of Jor have called upon Kani, Mother of the Gods, for the power to raise this tidal wave?" Despite all his best intentions, the warrior could not keep the fear and dismay from his voice.

"Yes, it is true," Nila answered. "I was there, I heard Kani speak through one of the priestesses."

"It cannot be a good thing, to raise the goddess of earthquake and volcanoes," the warrior said, his voice shaking a little.

"No," Nila said.

"How will we survive?" another said anxiously. "How will any of us survive?"

"I do not know," Nila answered, feeling the shadow of despair falling upon him again.

"What can we do?" the warriors all asked. "How can we stop it? How can we save ourselves? And our soul-brothers the whales? What can we do?"

"Nothing," Nila said, closing his eyes again. "There is nothing we can do."

CASTLE FORLORN

ar is an unpredictable beast. Once unleashed, it runs like a rabid dog, ravening friend or foe alike. It can drag on for years, a slow attrition of nerve and fortitude, or be over in one brilliant flash, an extravagant conflagration of flame and blood and waste.

At first it seemed as if the war against the Fairgean would be won in just such a blaze, a holocaust of burning ocean in which flaming sea-serpents writhed and shrieked, and a hundred Fairgean warriors were incinerated in an instant. Black, oily smoke rolled up, choking those that watched in stunned horror from the royal fleet. The waves themselves burnt with a strange green fire. No matter how frantically the sea-serpents thrashed, no matter how deep the warriors dived, still they burned and burned until all that was left was a crust of ash and cinders that clogged the roll of the waves. The sides of all the ships were smeared with it, black and oily.

"Eà's green blood!" Lachlan coughed, wiping his streaming eyes. "That seafire o' my uncle works as well as he promised!"

"It does no' seem honorable, to spray them with that stuff and then simply watch them burn," Duncan Ironfist said, his bearded face very grim.

"Was it honorable for them to attack us in the midst o' our Beltane feast?" the Duke of Killiegarrie retorted. He was holding his plaid over his mouth, his eyes red-rimmed from the acridity of the smoke. "We are at war, and any strategy that brings us victory must be honorable."

Duncan Ironfist shook his head. "Eà save us from such a war," he answered. His golden eyes troubled, Lachlan watched him walk away down the forecastle.

"They shall no' attack our fleet so quickly next time," Admiral Tobias said with satisfaction. "And the wind blows unusually fair, thanks to the wind-whistling o' your witches. We shall round Cape Providence in just four days if we have no more trouble."

"There'll be no more trouble," the Duke of Killiegarrie said confidently. "With this seafire o' the MacBrann's we shall simply incinerate any Fairge that pops his head out o' the water."

"Pride goeth before destruction and a haughty spirit before a fall," Arvin the Just, the first mate of the *Royal Stag*, intoned solemnly. Like many Tìrsoilleirean, he had a proverb for every occasion, most of them very depressing. In this case, though, he was proved right. As the royal fleet rounded Cape Providence three days later, they were taken by surprise by a storm of such ferocity that seven of the royal fleet were sunk, and the remaining ships much damaged. Nearly every boat had one or two broken masts, their sails torn into shreds and holes ripped in the hulls. Supplies were ruined by saltwater, men were swept overboard, and many of their goats and sheep were drowned.

Isabeau and the other witches wrought a circle of power and sought to calm the storm, but they were hampered by the pitching and rolling of the ship, the drag of the gale-force winds and the lashing of the icy sleet. All they were able to do was swing the calm eye of the storm over the fleet long enough for the navy to limp to safety in one of the few deep harbors along the wild and rocky coastline.

There the royal fleet was stuck for almost a week, struggling in the gusty aftermath of the gale to repair the ships. And there they were ambushed by the Fairgean. The sea-faeries slipped up to the damaged ships under the cover of darkness, so silently and so swiftly that they were swarming over the railings before a single alarm could be sounded. Savage hand-to-hand fighting resulted. In such close quarters the seafire could not be used, nor the giant ballistas and cannons lined up along every deck. It was sword against trident, dagger against dagger, webbed fist against fist. When the fighting grew too fierce, the Fairgean dived back into the water and swam back out to sea.

Plagued by foul weather and constant ambushes, the fleet took twenty-two days to reach the Firth of Forlorn, a journey they had expected to take ten. Another four ships were lost, one being incinerated by its own load of seafire after a capricious wind changed just at the wrong moment.

By the time the Firth of Forlorn was reached, the mood upon the *Royal Stag* was grim. All had hoped they would be able to sail up the coast without even sighting a Fairgean. Isabeau grew defensive since it had been on her knowledge of the Fairgean migratory habits that the plan had been based.

"It is no' my fault," she protested one evening. "The Fairgean have obviously swum north earlier than usual. They were expecting a strike against them, ye ken that . . ."

"Och, aye, so our Fairge spy has told us," the Rìgh replied acidly, glancing at Maya, who was sitting placidly at the far end of the cabin, playing trictrac with Bronwen.

The former Banrìgh had been kept under close custody ever since her capture at Bride Harbor. Isabeau had been afraid Lachlan would lose his judgment in his hot desire for revenge against his brother's wife but she had misjudged him. Much as Lachlan hated Maya, he knew she could prove useful indeed in the war against the Fairgean. Maya knew more about the customs and beliefs of the sea-faeries than anyone and she swore that she wished only to ensure her and Bronwen's safety. Besides, Lachlan knew he had more to gain by putting Maya on trial for her crimes and showing the people of the land that he was a fair and just rìgh than there was in killing her out of hand.

So Maya sailed with them and had been of some use in explaining the military formation of the pods and what their likely strategies would be. The Fairge had remained composed the entire journey. Despite the iron cuff and chain she wore on one wrist, she acted as if she was an honored guest rather than a prisoner-of-war. Bronwen was overjoyed to have her mother back again, though she was humiliated by the chain and angry at Lachlan for insisting upon it. She would have unlocked Maya if she could have. Isabeau had to warn her to be careful not to arouse Lachlan's anger.

"The Rìgh could have your mother locked down in the bilges if he so chose," she had admonished. "And remember, she is safer here than out there in the open sea, for if the Fairgean caught her they'd put her to death straightaway. Ye ken your family motto is 'Wisely and Boldly'? Well, now is the time to be wise, no' bold."

Now, biting back angry words, Isabeau looked across

at the two sleek dark heads bent over the trictrac board. "We always kent this would be a bitterly fought campaign," she said softly. "I ken it is a hard blow to have lost eleven ships afore we even reach the Firth o' Forlorn, but we could've lost more wi' all these gales. Indeed, I think this priestess-witch o' the Fairgean must be descended from weather witches, for indeed these storms canna be natural."

"She must be aye powerful," Lachlan said gloomily. "I am meant to have a Talent with weather too, but even with the Lodestar and the circle o' witches, it is all I can do no' to lose the entire fleet!"

Maya looked up. "Do no' forget the Fairgean have their own magic," she said coolly. "Nila told me that he saw Fand using the Nightglobe o' Naia. That is the most powerful talisman o' the Priestesses o' Jor, and far more ancient than your wee orb."

Isabeau and Lachlan just stared at her, then the Rìgh's brows knotted together. "It is eavesdropping ye are now?" he demanded angrily.

"No' at all," Maya replied sweetly. "Did ye no' ken the Fairgean have very acute hearing? We can find our way safely by listening to the echoes o' our whistles bouncing back from rock or iceberg or whale. If ye wish me no' to hear what ye say, ye should no' talk anywhere near me."

Lachlan's color deepened. "Thank ye so much for telling me," he said with dangerous calm.

"No' at all," she answered and turned back to her game.

Lachlan glared at her, seething, then rose and caught up his plaid. "Come and walk on the deck with me then, Beau," he said through his teeth. "We dinna want the Fairge listening to all that we say."

"Do no' be walking just overhead then," Maya said without looking up.

Isabeau followed Lachlan out onto the deck. It was grey and blustery, spray slapping them in the face as the *Royal Stag* pitched forward in the wild seas. To the port side, high cliffs soared out of the sea, waves smashing violently upon the rocks at their base. Many spectacular crags reared up out of the waves, some forming archways with the mainland. To the starboard side the grey ocean stretched as far as the eye could see, broken only by the tall, triangular peaks of many small islands. They looked like giant shark fins.

Lachlan stared out at the horizon, his black brows drawn close over his eyes, his mouth grim. "I wish I had no' brought the bairns," he burst out.

"Why did ye?" Isabeau asked. "A war campaign is no' the place for bairns."

"I wanted to keep them close," Lachlan answered. "I kent we could be away for many months. It seems I've spent all o' Donncan's childhood away fighting one battle or another. I never really kent my father. He was killed by the Fairgean king at the Battle o' the Strand when I was only three. I did no' want that to happen to my bairns."

Isabeau was silent. She thought of Owein and Olwynne, in the midst of their second year, fighting constant seasickness down in their cabin. She thought of Donncan, not yet seven, who had seen one dreadful sea battle after another. Isabeau herself had been sickened by the conflagrations of seafire, and she was no innocent child.

"Donncan has been waking with nightmares," she said. "Every creak o' the ship has him starting awake in terror."

Lachlan nodded. "He wants his mother," he said. "I want her too. Oh, Beau, will she come back? She was so angry . . ."

"She'll come back," Isabeau said. "Wait until we reach Castle Forlorn. Iseult will be waiting for ye there, I'm sure o' it."

Lachlan gave a little shiver, his wings rustling. "What a name," he whispered. "Indeed the MacSeinns are a strange, melancholy clan. Who would call their castle such a thing?"

They saw Castle Forlorn the next morning at dawn. It was a bleak, cold morning, the waves running high below the prows of the ships, seagulls crying plaintively. They all clustered at the port side, staring up at the small fortress built at the very height of the headland guarding the entrance into the Firth of Forlorn. Once it had been a tall, proud tower, guarded by high walls and thick flying buttresses. Now it seemed no more than a tumbled pile of stones, dwarfed by the immense height of the cliff.

"It's naught but a ruin," Dide said in disbelief. "We canna take shelter there. We shall have to rebuild the whole damn thing!"

"Nay, look!" Isabeau cried, her keen eyesight seeing what the others had not. "It flies a blue and gold flag. The MacSeinn must be there!"

The fleet of ships came round the headland, the *Royal Stag* leading with a billow of white sails. The green flag of the MacCuinn clan flew proudly from every mast. The Firth of Forlorn stretched before them, guarded on each side by a great headland surmounted by a ruined fortress. The one on the far side was called Castle Forsaken. If everything had gone according to plan, Anghus MacRuraich would already be there with his men. It was too far across the firth to see if the wolf ensign of the MacRuraich clan flew there, but they could see a thin column of smoke rising from the ruins.

"The Fairgean canna make fire so it must be the MacRuraich," Isabeau reassured them.

"Do ye really think so?" Jay asked wistfully, leaning against the rail and staring across at the trail of smoke.

"I certainly hope so," Lachlan said. "That is the worst o' being at sea, we canna scry over water and so we have no way o' communicating with each other. Just as soon as we have landed I shall send Stormwing across with a message. We shall soon ken if it is the MacRuraich."

"I wonder if Finn is wi' him?" Jay murmured. "She was determined she would no' be left behind this time."

"Och, then I'd say she's there," Lachlan replied with a wry grin. "Even if she had to conceal herself in the baggage train to get there!"

The fleet of ships tacked against the wind and sailed in through the headlands. Rising out of the grey water was an island that rose high into a pointed peak, its apex concealed by a wreath of hazy cloud. Faintly through the dark smudge of smoke they could see the shape of a wall and a broken arch. It was all that remained of the Tower of Sea-singers.

"The Isle o' the Gods," Maya said, triumph ringing out in her voice. She hugged Bronwen close to her side, the chain above her wrist jangling. "See, Bronny? That is the divine home o' the Fairgean. Within its Fathomless Caves all the gods o' the world were born—Jor the God of the Shoreless Seas, Mika the thunder god, Tahsha the ice god, Muki the god of our soul-brothers the whales, Ryza the god of dreams . . . All were born there and spat into the world in the fiery breath of the Mother of all Gods, Kani, the goddess of earthquakes and volcanoes."

Maya hugged Bronwen closer, giving a strange little

shiver that could have been fear or joy. She then raised herself proudly, looking across at Lachlan defiantly. "Do ye ken I have never afore seen the Isle o' the Gods, the most sacred place for all Fairgean? When I was born, the Fairgean lived on rafts or clung to auld bits o' driftwood or whatever rocks the humans did no' bother to guard. If we tried to swim ashore we were beaten to death or sung into oblivion by the evil Yedda. When I was about the same age as Bronny, or happen a wee younger, I was taken to the Isle o' Divine Dread." She pointed back at another island peak that rose black and forbidding behind them. "That is the island o' the Priestesses o' Jor. I did no' see daylight again for many, many years."

She laughed. It was a terrible laugh, full of a ferocious glee that had them all staring at her. Even Bronwen shrank back. "Ye are in the heart o' the Fairgean waters now, MacCuinn," Maya said. "Indeed I always kent ye were a fool."

Lachlan stared at the smoking island, his hands nervously gripping and releasing the shaft of the Lodestar, his face drained of color. A few of the other men made mocking replies, full of bravado, but the Rìgh said nothing. He could not take his eyes off the Isle of the Gods.

From high above the deck they heard a shrill, frightened cry. "Sea-serpents, Cap'n, hundreds o' them! Coming this way."

The lookout's cry broke the spell that seemed to have fallen upon Lachlan. He raised his hand to his eyes and stared out across the waves. Isabeau could clearly see the long, undulating shapes of sea-serpents swimming towards them. In a tight wedge shape behind each sea-serpent were the smaller shapes of horse-eels, swollen to immense size, each ridden by a Fairgean warrior. The swift, sleek forms of more warriors leapt through the waves on either side.

"All hands on deck!" Admiral Tobias cried.

The bosun blew his whistle shrilly. "All hands on deck!" he shouted.

"We just need to make it to the harbor below Castle Forlorn," called Lachlan. "If the MacSeinn is there already, they will have remade the fortifications."

"Get the seafire ready," the admiral ordered. "Load the cannons and the ballista!"

"Load the cannons!" the bosun shouted. "Ready the ballista, starboard side!"

Amidst the flurry of activity, Lachlan said coldly, "Take the prisoner below deck, chain her to her bunk. Her daughter too. We want no treachery now."

Maya laughed again. Her long black hair whipped about her scarred face, her strange pale eyes shone. "We rely on ye, MacCuinn, to keep us safe. Ye think I want to be fodder for a sea-serpent this morn?"

"Take her away," he ordered.

Bronwen cried out as two sailors clamped their hands on her arms. "But Lachlan, if ye chain them they will drown should we be sunk!" Isabeau protested.

"If we are sunk we all drown," he replied tersely. "I think the Fairge and her get have a better chance o' no' drowning than any o' us. They at least have gills."

Donncan shrank back against Isabeau, his face pale and frightened. As Bronwen called out again, the sailors half carrying, half dragging her struggling towards the hatch, he protested, close to tears. Lachlan went down on one knee and hugged him, his great black wings cupping the frightened little boy. "Do no' be afraid," he said. "None o' us shall drown. Our ship is swift and strong. All we need do is race those sea-serpents to safe harbor. Now ye go down below as well, and look after your wee brother and sister. Brun shall go with ye."

"Nay, I want Aunty Beau!" Donncan cried.

Isabeau knelt beside Lachlan, his wing brushing her arm. Donncan huddled against her, tears streaking his face. "Go with Brun," she said gently. "I must stay on deck to help Aunty Meghan and the other witches. We need the wind to blow us sure if we are to make it past the sea-serpents. Do no' be afraid, dearling."

He clung to her but she stood up, unhooking his hands and pushing him into the arms of his frightened nurse-maid. Brun stood nearby, his ears twitching nervously, his tail drooping. Donncan began to cry in earnest.

"Donncan," Lachlan said sternly. "I need ye to be brave now. I canna stay with ye and neither can Aunty Beau. Ye must go below deck and stay there till I call ye. Do ye understand?"

"Aye, *Dai-dein,*" he answered, lip trembling, then took Brun's hairy little paw. "Come on, Brun," he said. "Do no' be afraid. We'll go down together."

Hand in paw, the little boy and the cluricaun climbed down the ladder together, followed closely by the bog-faery Maura, her black wrinkled face scrunched up in fear.

Isabeau pressed her hands against her chest as if she thought that would calm the hammering of her heart. Quickly she joined the other witches upon the forecastle deck in the now familiar joining of the circle. Holding hands with Dide and Gwilym, she chanted the rites and called upon the winds of the world to do their bidding. They all felt the ship leap forward as her sails filled to breaking point.

Ahead of them was the cliff, the sea torn into turmoil as its base by wicked rocks. Isabeau could see how it curved round into a small natural harbor, surrounded on all three sides by cliffs, its mouth protected by a high wall and a massive gate of enmeshed steel. The fleet of fifty-three ships had to pass through that gate in time for it to clang shut behind them, locking the Fairgean out. It was slowly groaning open now, the gap between gate and wall growing wider and wider. Isabeau stared from the gate to the sea-serpents, who raced towards them at an incredible speed.

Long, slim, sinuous as a snake, the sea-serpents were emerald green, with small heads rising high out of the water. A golden crest ran down the length of their necks, while spectacular flowing fins surrounded their gaping jaws and sprouted from their shoulders like wings. The warriors rode astride the neck, between the two sets of fins. Although the sea-serpents rose and plunged at enormous speeds, they never lowered their heads into the water and so the warriors were only ever immersed in water to their waist.

Closer and closer they came, until Isabeau could see the tusked faces of the warriors, their necks heavy with necklaces, their long black hair flowing down their backs. The gate of the harbor was wide open now, but it looked as if the sea-serpents must cut them off before they could reach it. Isabeau gripped Dide's hand.

"Fire!" cried the admiral.

The bosun blew his whistle. "Aim and fire!"

The ballista had been wheeled across to the port side and secured to the deck. Designed like an enormous crossbow, the two arms of the bow were held in tension, with the string operated by a windlass. When this windlass was released, a poison-tipped arrow was projected forward at immense speed. Isabeau watched it fly across the waves and embed itself in the glossy scales of one of

the sea-serpents. The sinuous creature reared up, screaming in pain, lunged forward once more, then suddenly
began to thrash about in agony. Its rider was thrown into
the water. They could see him desperately trying to keep
afloat as the sea was whipped into chaos, then he was
crushed beneath the writhing coils.

It took a long time for the sea-serpent to die. Isabeau
hid her face against Dide's shoulder as Meghan said
somberly, "Dragonbane is an evil concoction. To think I
saved the dragon-prince from this fate, sickened by
Maya's use o' it, only to inflict it now upon the sea-
serpents. Indeed, war makes all o' us evil."

Again and again the ballistas whined from every ship
in the royal fleet. Although sea-serpent after sea-serpent
succumbed to the baleful poison, still the Fairgean warriors raced towards them, shouting and brandishing their
tridents. Once the enemy was within bombardment distance, the cannons began to fire their heavy bronze balls
and the air was filled with foul-smelling black smoke.

"We willna make it!" Isabeau cried in despair, watching as cannonball after cannonball splashed into the water
and sank without hitting their mark. Cannons were noto-
riously unreliable and were not really designed to be used
against a target as swift and agile as sea-serpents and
horse-eels.

"They'll have to bring out the seafire now," Dide said
grimly. Sure enough, the bosun was shouting his orders
and the barrels of seafire were being gingerly rolled out.
Very carefully the viscous liquid within was siphoned
into glass jars, which were then corked firmly and loaded
into the mangonels. The seafire was so very volatile that
no one felt comfortable using it, and it was always kept
as a very last measure.

The mangonel was a large catapult that, like the ballista, could be wheeled about the deck. The jars of seafire were loaded into the cup, and the arm was released from its tension, flinging the jars four hundred feet away from the ship. The jars smashed upon contact with the waves and ignited immediately. Everything within a hundred feet was incinerated. Not even diving under the surface of the water would avoid the flames, for the saltwater was the seafire's fuel. There was no escape.

The air was filled with the agonizing screaming of beast and Fairge alike. Smoke billowed everywhere, the very air orange with it, and the lurid light of the burning sea played over sail and mast and carved poop, making the faces of the gargoyles and angels smirk and grimace.

"Come about, come about!" the bosun screamed as the seafire raged back towards them. The sailors heaved on the ropes and the helmsman leaned hard on the tiller. The *Royal Stag* swung about, her sails slackening and then filling once more. Isabeau glanced over the port rail and saw the cliffs rising over them, dwarfing the tall masts. Then the ship was racing through the immense mesh gates which were topped with cruel curving spikes and reinforced with thick steel bars.

Buckets on long ropes were flung overboard to slow the galleon's speed, and all the anchors were dropped. The sails were dragged down, everyone shouting and scrambling as they fought to halt the ship's headlong advance. The harbor cliff loomed over them. Instinctively Isabeau flung her arms about her head, expecting to hear the crash as the ship leapt upon the rocks. Instead she was flung to her knees as the ship came about once more. Then the anchors settled down into the seabed and the *Royal Stag* rocked into stillness.

*   *   *

It was a long climb up the cliff to Castle Forlorn. Donn-can and Bronwen counted five hundred and eighty-six steps, all of them steep and slick with moisture. At first they counted loudly and enthusiastically, then haltingly between pants of breath, and finally sullenly, even tear-fully. Isabeau had no breath to reply, since Olwynne had given up trying to climb after about ten and had refused to be carried by any of the soldiers. Lachlan was carrying Owein but he was much stronger and had wings to help him. He often flew from one landing to another, the little boy clinging to him and shrieking, half in excitement, half in terror.

Most of the heavy weapons were left on the ships or down in the harbor guardhouse, but innumerable sacks and barrels had to be swung up with ropes and pulleys. Enit and Meghan were lifted up in the same way, much to Meghan's chagrin. She had to admit the climb would be too much for her, though, and so she sat in the canvas sling, her back very straight, her black eyes flashing.

From the steps Isabeau could see straight down the Firth of Forlorn, where the broken wrecks of four ships floated among a black stain of oily residue, thick with the charred bodies of dead sea-serpents, horse-eels and Fairgean warriors. Smoke drifted everywhere. Isabeau was too tired to feel anything more than numb, but the weight of her niece in her arms dragged her down until she thought she might weep from sheer exhaustion. Then Dide came and lifted Olwynne from her arms, settling the sleeping child against his shoulder, and lending her the strength of his hand. He smiled at her and said, "Almost there. Chin up, my bonny!" so that Isabeau found a well-spring of fresh energy to climb the last flight.

They came out into a wide bailey, surrounded on all sides by immense walls and watchtowers. From every

broken tower fluttered the MacSeinn flag, a golden harp
on a pale blue background.

Castle Forlorn had been discarded thirteen years before when the Fairgean had driven the MacSeinn and his
clan out into the storm. The sea-faeries had done their
best to eradicate the fortress but they had no fire or ma-
chines of destruction. Time and the weather had done
more to destroy the castle than anything the Fairgean
could do.

Most of the castle itself lay in ruins, a mere pile of
mossy stones and the occasional half arch of broken
stone. The central tower was open to the sky, the great
hall filled with grass and thistles, its staircase collapsed
and scattered. Some of the smaller wings still had some
roof and it was here that the MacSeinn and his men had
set up camp, stretching tarpaulins across the holes and
clearing out the worst of the thistles. Most of the labor
had been devoted to repairing the outer walls, which once
again stood tall and stout against possible attack.

The bailey was crowded with people, all greeting the
new arrivals and helping unload the weapons and supplies. Isabeau sat abruptly on a barrel to one side. "Eà's
green blood, what a climb!" she panted. "My legs are
aching."

Lachlan thrust Owein into her arms, snapping, "Mind
him a second, Beau?" Before she had a chance to agree,
he strode off through the crowd, accepting each shout of
greeting brusquely, looking about him with a scowl. Suddenly his expression cleared. "Iseult!" he cried.

Iseult had just appeared at the head of the stairs leading into the ruined castle. She was wearing her battered
leather armor, her hair concealed beneath a leather cap,
one arm in a sling. She saw Lachlan and her whole face

kindled. She leapt from the top step and swooped down, straight into his arms.

Lachlan had spread his wings and flown to meet her, so Rìgh and Banrìgh met midair, breast to breast, mouth to mouth. She freed her arm from her sling so she could fling both arms about his neck, pulling his dark head closer. For a long moment they hung there, oblivious to the cheers of the crowd, then slowly, slowly they slid down to the ground. Lachlan's wings cupped around her, hiding her from view. Their mouths met, clung, dragged apart to speak, met again. He dragged her cap from her head so all her long red curls hung down over his arm. Her fingers cradled the back of his head, slipped down to caress his broad, strong shoulder, slid down his back. Then Donncan was there, squirming through his father's wings to clutch Iseult's leg.

"Mama!" he cried.

Iseult's eyes were wet with tears. She dropped to her knees to hug him close, rocking back and forth. Lachlan bent and embraced them both, then Iseult was looking about for the twins. "My babes?" she called huskily.

Isabeau rose, lifting Owein in her arms, and carried him through the crowd. Dide was at her shoulder, carrying Olwynne, who looked about her sleepily. They saw Iseult and both lunged for her, their plump cherubic faces lighting up with joy. "Mama, Mama!"

For an instant Isabeau and Iseult's eyes met. They smiled at each other, then Isabeau passed over the eager little boy and stepped back.

"I was afraid . . ." she heard Lachlan mutter. "Oh, Iseult, I was so afraid ye would no' come back. I'm sorry!"

"I'm sorry too," she whispered and they kissed again lingeringly.

"What made ye come back?" he asked. "Ye were so cold when we parted, I was sure ye meant to stay in the snows."

Iseult nodded. "I meant to, if only to punish ye. For breaking the *geas,* ye ken. But when I lay beneath that avalanche, thinking I would never see ye again . . . or my bonny bairns . . ."

Once again Isabeau's and Iseult's eyes met. Everything that needed to be said was said in that one glance. Isabeau turned and hurried away, her joy and her grief choking her. She reached the wall and stood in its shelter, her back turned to the crowd, scrubbing her wet eyes furiously and telling herself not to be a fool. Then Dide was beside her, his hand slipping inside her elbow. She turned and smiled up at him, knowing her face was blotchy with tears.

"Does it hurt that much to see them together so?" he asked, his voice low and intense.

She nodded. "Aye, hurts with happiness. I'm a fool, I ken, but I am so glad . . . I was so afraid . . ."

His tension slackened. "Afraid o' what?".

She shook her head, laughing and crying at the same time. "I hardly ken. That one or the other would be too proud, or too tongue-tied. Both find it hard to say what is in their hearts."

He gazed down at her, then suddenly took her by surprise by bending his head and kissing her. She could not help her mouth responding, did not want to help it. He lifted his head and said huskily, "Well."

Isabeau laughed at him, and wiped away the last of her tears. "Did ye think I was greeting for grief or for envy? Well, I was too, but no' for the reasons ye thought."

"I'm glad," he said with difficulty.

"So am I," she said with heartfelt sincerity. She saw he

wanted to kiss her again and held him off with both hands. "Come, now is no' the time or the place. We have much to do."

"So when shall be the time and place?" he asked, some of his usual sparkle returning.

Isabeau hardly knew how to answer. It was her impulse to answer him lightly but she saw that beneath his insouciance was a true intensity of feeling. She took his hand, looked down at it, spreading his long, calloused fingers and winding her own through it. "I dinna ken," she answered simply.

He was silent for a time, looking down at their hands, fingers entwined. "Is it . . . ? Do ye no' feel . . . ?"

"I dinna ken," she said again. "I'm afraid . . ." She could not finish the sentence. Something rose in her and choked her throat, filled her eyes with heat again.

"Isabeau, when they took ye prisoner . . . when ye were tortured, did they . . . ?" He could not finish either. The heat in her eyes turned to a rush of tears but she did not answer. She pulled her hand free.

"I'd best go and help Meghan," she said, pushing past him.

He caught her arm. "Isabeau . . ."

She pulled her arm free, moved past him in a rush. There was a great deal to do and Isabeau busied herself in doing it. Occasionally that hot rush of emotion threatened to undo her and she had to stand still and breathe deeply and find her *coh* before she could again be calm. She felt again that dangerous vulnerability that had overtaken her in the weeks after her Sorceress Test, her sense that barriers were being broken down which she would rather stayed intact. Brun the cluricaun hovered near her, sensing her distress, and Buba hooted an occasional worried question. She fobbed them both off with distracted smiles and assurances. To Meghan's sharp query, she merely said, "It's the war, the seafire. All that horrible death."

The Keybearer nodded. "Aye, it's even harder for witches to shut out when we hear the psychic distress as well as the physical agony. I find it hard myself and I've grown used to it after four hundred and thirty-five years."

Isabeau had never really seen a war before. She had fled Lachlan's court with Bronwen before the true conflict against the Bright Soldiers had begun, and she had been away during all the long years spent overcoming them. She found Meghan's observation to be true indeed.

For this war, called now the Fourth Fairgean War, was to be the slow attrition of nerve and fortitude that all had dreaded. All winter it dragged on. The Fairgean defended the Isle of the Gods with the desperate valor of fanatics. The Rìgh's fleet was never able to come within spitting distance of the old volcano, despite all their cannons and ballistas and barrels of seafire. There were conflagrations in plenty, an abundance of flame and blood and waste and grief. Isabeau worked with the healers to bind up the wounds and send the soldiers out to be wounded again. Tòmas the Healer grew as thin as a twig as he poured all his energies for living and growing and being a child into healing one shattered body after another.

The Greycloaks concentrated on holding the shore. Their men occupied the old forts built on every major headland, and most of the key walled towns protecting the safe harbors. Although the towns had been deserted for many years, the news that the MacSeinn had returned slowly spread back into the hinterland where many people had fled. Gradually people began to return, fired by old hatreds, to help in the casting out of the Fairgean. Those sea-faeries that had settled in the old towns were driven back into the sea, and parties were sent with flaming torches into every cave and burrow in the cliffs. Each small victory was won hard, though, and there were many small defeats.

Lachlan spent most of his time on the *Royal Stag,* in constant attacks against the Fairgean, and Dide sailed with him. On the few occasions when Isabeau saw them, both were tired, anxious and preoccupied.

Bronwen's seventh birthday came and went, and then Samhain, the darkest night of the year. No one remembered what it was like to be warm, to be replete with food, to be free of sick anxiety. Sunshine was like a vague dream of childhood. Despite all the efforts of the witches, storms constantly lashed the coast. Lachlan's Ship Tax was slowly wrecked upon the rocks; sacks of grain were ruined with mold, and it was impossible to keep the babies clean and dry. Illness wracked them all, and their medicinal supplies ran out. For days Owein's temperature soared so high that Isabeau thought they must lose him. Tòmas was rushed home to touch him and heal him, and meanwhile seventeen soldiers died of dysentery in Castle Forsaken, the fort built on the headland on the far side of the firth, where the MacRuraich was camped with his men and his disobedient daughter.

Often the gales raged for so long that none of the soldiers even bothered to leave Castle Forlorn. It was too dangerous to set sail in those winds, too cold to walk outside, too difficult to raise the energy or enthusiasm for another useless assault. The Fairgean had retreated into their Fathomless Caves and Maya taunted them with descriptions of their warm caves, hot steaming pools and thick seal furs. The Fairge was unaffected by the bitter cold. She could swim in seas where the very surface was frozen over and still survive.

By midwinter the witches had given up trying to con-

trol the weather. A brewing storm had whipped itself into
a high gale. The continual roaring wind brought waves so
high they would have towered over the *Royal Stag's*
mast, if Lachlan had been foolish enough to take her out
of the meager shelter of the harbor. Lightning glared continually, thick throbbing veins of incandescence plunging
through the white sheets of electricity. Thunder rolled
around Castle Forlorn, an orchestra of crashes and
booms. Snow built new walls over the old. No messengers had got through in almost a week and no one could
scry to those with witch senses in any of the other forts
because of the static disturbances in the heavens. They
were besieged, marooned, trapped, by the force of the
storm.

Midwinter's Eve was spent huddling together and trying to stay warm. Then it was Hogmanay and the stark,
fateful dividing of one year and another. It was impossible for them all not to reflect on the past year and fret
about the next. It was impossible not to feel bitter regrets.

It was shockingly cold. The wind shrieked like a ban-
shee. Snow whirled out of the darkness, beating against
the stones of the ruined castle. Despite all Isabeau's efforts, the fire shrank and winced, sending out more
smoke than warmth. The twins cried miserably. Isabeau
rocked Olwynne against her shoulder, patting her with
numb, frozen hands, murmuring, "Ssshhh, honey-bee,
ssshhh, honey-bee." The words no longer had any meaning.

"So much for being back in Bride for my birthday,"
Donncan muttered.

"Never mind, laddie," Isabeau said. "Would ye rather
no' be here with your *Dai-dein* and *maither* than in Bride
by yourself?"

"No," Donncan said rebelliously. "Who would ever

want to be here? Why are we fighting to win back this horrible place? Let's beg the Fairgean to take it off our hands and go home."

Isabeau said nothing. She could not have agreed more. From the looks on the faces of everyone clustered together in the freezing little room, she thought she was not the only one.

"Besides," Donncan said angrily, "Mama and *Daidein* are no' here. They're stuck over in that other awful castle and there's no way they can get back in this storm. And they promised they'd come back for my birthday!"

"They'll get here if they can, dearling," Isabeau said, but Donncan had thrown himself down on his makeshift bed, his face turned to the wall. Bronwen burrowed into the blankets beside him, throwing one finned arm over his shoulder. Isabeau sighed heavily. Lachlan and his retinue had been at Castle Forsaken for two weeks now. She did not really believe they could make it back. The snowstorm was too ferocious.

"Well, there canna be any doubt that this priestess-witch o' theirs has a Talent wi' the weather," Meghan said, sitting as close to the fire as she could get. "Two months this blaygird wind has howled and no' one day o' peace have we had."

"The MacSeinn says the wind can blow like this in winter anyway," Isabeau said.

"Aye, happen that is so," Meghan answered irritably. "But he canna tell me that it blows like this all day and all night, every single day. It's no' natural, and if it was, well, no one in their right mind would ever settle here, no' even a MacSeinn."

"Canna ye do anything?" Isabeau said, her voice sharp with irritation.

"If I could, do ye think I wouldna?" Meghan snapped back. "I'm no weather witch!"

"But the Lodestar? Canna ye help Lachlan raise the Lodestar and stop the storm?" Isabeau was almost in tears. The constant whine of the wind was enough to wear anyone's patience down, particularly when accompanied by the grizzling of two cold and hungry three-year-olds.

Meghan sighed. "The Lodestar is Lachlan's now, only he can raise it, Beau. Ye should ken that. Besides, weather is always difficult to control. It is the interaction o' air and water and fire and earth, and a witch needs to be strong in all these elements if they wish to manipulate the weather, and strong in spirit too. And a storm like this is virtually impossible to control. Once it has reached this pitch o' intensity, the best thing ye can do is let it run its course." She huddled her plaid closer about her shoulders, holding her gnarled hands to the sullen flames. "At least we have the satisfaction o' knowing the Fairgean are suffering the foul weather just as much as we are."

Maya looked up with a malicious smile and Meghan said, "One word, Ensorcellor, and I'll blast ye to ashes where ye sit. I do no' lie!" Maya held up her hands placatingly, then mimed locking her mouth and throwing away the key. Bronwen giggled.

Driven to breaking point, Isabeau stood up abruptly and went out of the room, huddling her plaid close against the shock of the icy wind.

In the courtyard a herd of goats and sheep huddled together under the makeshift lean-to the soldiers had built against the wall. The snow banks were up to their withers and each sheep was so heavily encrusted with snow it was as if they wore another coat, heavier and whiter than their own.

Isabeau stroked their stoic, miserable faces and looked

out into the stinging wind. Winter in Carraig was like winter on the Spine of the World. It had no mercy. "I just want to go home," she said to Buba. *Home-hooh* . . .

There was a sudden flash of brilliance. The castle was silhouetted black and broken against the silver light. Isabeau heard the clamor of music, the shiver of electricity that was like lightning but was instead the work of great magic being wrought. She sprang upright, all her hairs standing on end. *And radiance shall flood the land* . . .

It was not lightning that had lit up the sky from end to end. It was the kindling of the Lodestar. She heard the sudden cessation of the wind, heard the silence like the bang of a gong. Soft flurries of snow drifted down and then fell no more. Horses were whinnying from their stables, the sheep were milling about, bleating. Isabeau's heart was pounding, her cold cheeks stretched in an unaccustomed smile. After all this time, after all the fighting and death and horror, Lachlan had at last kindled the Lodestar—and not to win a battle, not to defeat their enemy, but to fulfil his promise to his son.

Isabeau's tears froze on her cheek. She struggled across the courtyard, climbed the stairs and clambered over mounds of snow to the front gate of the castle. She was not the only one. Everyone in the castle had heard that triumphant ring of music, had seen the surge of radiance. They hurried to the castle gates, all animated by new hope. Meghan came, leaning heavily on her flower-carved staff, Gitâ perched on her shoulder. Donncan and Bronwen were hopping about, full of questions, while Maura Nursemaid clung tightly to Owein's and Olwynne's hands. Tòmas was leaning against the wall, color in his face for the first time in weeks, while Johanna the Mild fussed about him with a warm cloak and a mug of hot milk. All the soldiers, wounded or whole, crowded close behind with the healers and the servants and the witches. "Himself will be here soon," they told each other. "And the storm blown over. What an omen for the new year!"

The guards flung open the door cut into the massive wood of the castle gates. Moonlight cast its pale radiance all over the snowy landscape, and bright stars were scattered across the sky like daisies in a meadow. A deep hush hung over everything. Far away they could see clouds still ringing the horizon but over the Castle Forlorn all was tranquil.

A bonfire was kindled in the courtyard for everyone to crowd close about as they waited, no one wishing to go back into the dark, stuffy rooms. They huddled into their coats, plaids wrapped close about their throats, stamping their feet to keep warm as they kept watch for any sign of the Rìgh and his retinue.

"I kent they'd come," Donncan said happily. "*Daidein* promised!"

One of the guards suddenly shouted, "Look! They come."

Bobbing along the clifftop was a chain of orange lights. The crowd cheered. Closer the bobbing lights came, then at last they saw the procession clambering up the steep road to the castle. Lachlan was in the lead, riding upon his black stallion, with Iseult on his right side upon her grey mare. Dide and Duncan Ironfist rode close behind, with the officers streaming out beyond them. In the rear were packhorses, struggling under heavy loads, the snow up to their hocks.

Lachlan dismounted in the courtyard before the castle gates. He held up one hand, preventing those within from surging out. His raven-black wings and hair were all silvered with snow. "Is it midnight yet?" he demanded.

"No' yet," Meghan called out. "Almost."

"We must wait until the hour strikes," he answered, smiling broadly. "No crossing the threshold until after midnight!"

Laughter broke out. Everyone appreciated the point. The first person to cross the threshold after midnight on New Year's Eve determined what sort of year the household would have. It was considered bad luck for someone old or ugly or disadvantaged in some way to be the First Foot, and very good luck for someone strong and hale and handsome. So superstitious were most people about this tradition that the First Foot was usually appointed, just to make sure. He would move from house to house in the village, carrying gifts to ensure a year of prosperity, health and happiness.

"So are ye to be the First Foot then, Your Highness?" someone in the crowd called.

Lachlan held up a green branch, torn from one of the pine trees along their way. "Who better?"

Cheers rang out. A festive mood animated the crowd, in stark contrast to the gloom of only a few hours earlier. Then Meghan said, "I feel the tides turning. It be midnight now!"

Lachlan's chamberlain solemnly consulted his timepiece, which he carried about in his waistcoat pocket. "Midnight it is."

"Then let us get in out o' this cold!" Lachlan cried. With great ceremony he dismounted, took an armful of bundles from Dillon, and then advanced up to the castle gates, his boots sinking deep in the snow. Quiet fell over the crowd. He passed through the door and flung his evergreen branch upon the fire. Sharp-scented flames sprang up, the pine needles shriveling in writhing threads of white fire.

Lachlan smiled, his tired face filled with exultation. "Well, we made it," he said, "though to be sure I dinna think we could! How are ye all yourselves?"

As Donncan ran and embraced him joyfully, Iseult and the rest of the weary travelers came through the gates, Dillon leading the Rìgh's black stallion. They dismounted heavily and came to warm themselves by the fire, as Lachlan gave over his bundles to the chamberlain.

"See, bread for wealth, rather stale, I'm afraid, but better than none, and salt for luck, and whisky to warm our blood. And would ye believe it, eggs and honey! We can be making ourselves some Het Pint for Hogmanay."

"Ye kindled the Lodestar and stilled the storm," Meghan said, clasping his arm with both her hands. "Och, Lachlan, I am so pleased and proud! That was powerful sorcery you wrought."

Lachlan nodded, unable to restrain his grin of joy and pride. "Aye, and all by myself this time. I was determined that we would make it back here for Hogmanay and Donncan's birthday. Everyone thought we were mad setting out in such weather and indeed we were, crazy as loons. The snow was up to my chin and the wind was strong enough to lift the horses and throw them down the cliff. We were all sure we could hear death's bells.

"But the more wildly the wind blew, the angrier and more determined I got, and so at last I seized the Lodestar and commanded the storm to be still. No one was more surprised than I was when the Lodestar leapt into life! It was like being struck by lightning, I swear all my hair stood up on end and my fingertips were smoking!" Lachlan laughed. His golden-topaz eyes were brilliant with excitement, his dark face alight. "After that we just slogged on through the snow and so here we are, as promised." He cuddled Donncan close, the curly golden head nestling down into his shoulder, golden and black feathers mingling. "I tell ye what, though, I be in need o' a wee dram! I feel like I've climbed the Spine o' the World."

Smiling, Isabeau poured him some whisky and he tossed it back, then held out his cup for another. She poured him some more and then moved through the chattering crowd, pouring out cup after cup for the tired, chilled travelers. Someone had swung a cauldron onto the fire and the spicy smell of Het Pint began to drift through the courtyard. She saw Dide leaning over the fire, stirring the cauldron, and felt a sudden, unexpected lurch of her heart. He turned his head and saw her, and gave a weary smile. Isabeau went up to him, the pot of whisky hanging from her hand.

Silently she offered him a cup but he shook his head. "Nay, Het Pint for me. That's the stuff to warm a frozen heart."

She felt her color rise. He ladled out some of the hot, spiced ale and offered her a cup. She took it in her gloved hand and he served himself some, then lightly touched his cup to hers.

"Happy Hogmanay! Love and peace to ye."

"Happy Hogmanay," she repeated and drank a mouthful. Their eyes met. The cold air between them seemed to crackle. His expression changed and he drew closer to her.

"How are ye yourself, my bonny Beau?"

"Cold, hungry, homesick," she answered, trying to smile. "Sick o' this war."

He gave a little nod, then smiled at her, his black eyes glinting in the dancing firelight. "Well, I canna do much about the homesickness, but hungry I can help . . ." He brought out a rather squashed package from his pocket and handed it to her with a ceremonial flourish of his crimson cap. "Bread and the finest goat's cheese Carraig can offer and spread o' quince jam, courtesy o' Castle Forsaken. The MacSeinn is much better provisioned than us, having Siantan just across the bay."

Isabeau opened the package eagerly. The bread was stale but the goat's cheese was soft and tart and the quince jam sweet. She ate hungrily, washing down the dry bread with her spiced ale.

Dide watched her, sipping her own Het Pint. When she had finished, Isabeau gave him a radiant smile. "Thank ye. Amazing how much better I feel with some food in my stomach."

He took her cup and set it down, seizing both her hands in his and chafing them between his own. "I can do something about ye being cold too," he murmured and drew her closer. She went to him willingly as he enfolded her within the warmth of his heavy coat, wrapping it and his arms about her. Through the layers of his clothes she could feel the thud of his heart and smell the tang of his sweat. She rested her head on his chest and closed her eyes.

Slowly Dide's hands slid under her plaid, holding her waist lightly. "Did ye miss me?"

Isabeau nodded, not opening her eyes. He kissed her forehead. "I missed ye too, my Beau."

She looked up at him, saying with concern, "Ye look tired. How have ye been yourself?"

"Busy as a body louse," he said sardonically. "We've had bitter fighting this past few weeks. They attacked Kinnaird through the storm, did ye ken?"

Isabeau cried aloud in dismay. Kinnaird was the largest town on the shore of the firth, built halfway between the Castle Forlorn and the Castle Forsaken. Geographically, it was the closest to the Isle of the Gods, only a narrow stretch of water separating the island from the mainland at that point. It had once been one of the richest towns in Eileanan but it had been abandoned after the invasions of the Fairgean. Lachlan had established it as one of the primary strongholds of the Greycloaks, basing many of his men and ships there.

Dide answered the unasked question in her eyes. "No' good, Beau. We lost close on three hundred men and the fortifications were smashed to pieces by their blaygird sea-serpents. We had to call the retreat. They've split our forces now. We may hold the headlands still, but we no longer hold the shore."

Isabeau slumped against him, tears rushing to her eyes. "This war will no' be over soon, will it?"

"Nay. And if Jorge's prophecy be true, we shall have to retreat into the hinterland before the rising o' the comet. We have only a few weeks left to strike a death blow to them, else we'll be lucky to escape with our lives."

"And so many dead already," Isabeau murmured. "And for what? For what?"

Dide cradled her face with both hands, so that she had to look up at him. With his thumbs he wiped away the tears from her cheeks. "Do no' forget, my master this night kindled the Lodestar and stilled the storm. We are no' beaten yet, my Beau."

Her breath caught. The firelight was playing over his face, glinting from his night-deep eyes. All the devilish merriment was gone from his face. It was set grimly and somberly yet with a vulnerability that struck deep into her heart. For a moment they stared at each other, his hands still cupping her face, then he bent his dark head and kissed her.

Their mouths fitted together perfectly. His hand slid

under her plaid again, smoothing the muscles of her back, caressing the curve of her waist. His hand slid lower, but found nothing but the heavy fall of her dress. He pressed his hand flat against her, bringing the lower half of her body up hard against him. His other hand slid back up to grip her arm, just grazing the side of her breast. Despite the layers of clothes between them, his touch was like the brush of fire. Isabeau was unable to help a little murmur in her throat. She rose a little on her toes, trying to get closer to him. At once the kiss deepened, intensified. She could feel his heart hammering against her. When he lifted his mouth away from hers, Isabeau followed it instinctively, straining to reach higher. He put both hands on her waist, holding her body away from his. His eyes were heavy-lidded, his breath hurried. "Beau . . ." he said. "My bonny Beau."

Her breath steadied. She stepped back from him a little, her legs unsteady. For those few moments she had lost all sense of the world around them, there had been only sensation. Now it all rushed back upon her, the bitter cold of the night air, the sinking flames of the fire, the lack of feeling in her feet. Only a few people still stood about, talking and drinking. Most had gone back inside. No one seemed to notice Dide and Isabeau together in the shadow of the archway, but Isabeau was flushed with embarrassment nonetheless. She stepped back, feeling a little sense of loss as the cold darkness struck between them.

"Ye're cold," Dide said. "Come, let us get in out o' the snow, for Eà's sake!"

Isabeau nodded, feeling a familiar surge of uncertainty. He bent and picked up their cups and ladled the last of the Het Pint into them. "This will warm ye," he said, smiling. He slid one arm about her waist. "Come on, let's go in."

Together they went in from the courtyard. The Grey-cloaks had taken over most of one wing of the ruined castle, most of the soldiers camping out in one small hall. The women had set up camp in two or three smaller rooms to one side, with the Rìgh and his retinue sleeping in a smaller hall at the far end. Isabeau normally slept in small antechamber to their room, sharing her bed with Maya and Bronwen and sometimes Olwynne too.

The long hall where the soldiers slept was now quiet, most rolled in their blankets to sleep. A low fire burnt in the center of the room, blue smoke filling the air. Dide steered Isabeau through the long rows of sleeping soldiers, holding her hand firmly. He took her through into one of the small antechambers, where the Rìgh's officers slept. This room had a fireplace so that the smoke did not sting Isabeau's eyes so much. She saw the dark forms of sleeping soldiers and pulled against Dide's hand. He smiled at her in reassurance, his teeth flashing white in the semidarkness. "Come sit wi' me a while, and drink your Het Pint and get warm," he whispered. "We canna be talking in your room, with the Ensorcellor there and the bairns."

She let Dide pull her forward. He stumbled over one sleeping form, hissed an apology with a sparkling glance at Isabeau, then led her to a pile of furs and blankets in one corner. She sat down, hugging her knees, and he wrapped one of the blankets around her shoulders then sat down beside her, leaning his back against the wall. Isabeau sipped at the warm ale and felt herself relax.

"Where's your wee owl tonight?" he asked, laughter in his voice.

"Out hunting," she answered, caught as usual between

laughter and embarrassment. "She's eaten every spider in this Eà-forsaken castle, and since the storm has passed has flown down to the forest to search for some grubs."

"So I do no' need to fear being pecked if I try and kiss ye again?"

"No' this time," she answered, her heart beginning to beat faster again. In the darkness she could see little of his face, but she could feel his closeness and smell the warm, male scent of him.

He shifted a little towards her. "That be grand," he said and kissed her, so suddenly and swiftly that she was taken by surprise. Her pulse leapt. Deep within her she felt an abrupt twist of desire. She melted back beneath him, unable to keep any sense of direction with all her senses reeling. His arm was behind her head, supporting her, the other sliding down from her throat to her breast. Through all the thick layers of wool, her nipple felt the brush of his thumb and hardened. She pulled away from him, her breath harsh in her throat.

Somehow she and Dide were lying side by side on the blankets, his arm pillowing her head, his body half covering hers. It was very dark. She could not see his face, but she could feel the quick rise and fall of his chest, the tension in his limbs.

He sighed and rested his head beside hers, inches away. One hand played with her hair, but otherwise he did not touch her. After a moment she relaxed, turning her face towards him. "I'm sorry," she whispered. "I just canna . . ."

"Ye ken it's always been ye for me, Beau," Dide said at last. He did not look at her, speaking with some difficulty. "Ever since . . . I suppose it's really been since we were bairns, that time we met in Caeryla."

Isabeau shook her head, surprised. "How was I to

ken?" she asked in some indignation. "And ye flirting with every pretty lass ye saw!"

She saw him smile. "Did it make ye jealous?"

"Was it meant to?"

"O' course." His voice was warm with laughter. "Most o' the time anyway."

She smiled too, though she felt a little prick of jealousy. He wriggled a little closer. "What was I meant to do?" he asked in mock despair. "Ye ignored me most o' the time. What was a poor young jongleur to do?"

"I do no' ignore ye!"

"Och, that ye did," he said. "I did everything I could to gain your attention and all ye did was scold me and order me around, or disappear on me. I canna count the times ye disappeared."

"It was only once or twice," Isabeau said, "and each time I had to do it."

He nodded. "Aye, I ken," he answered, all laughter gone from his voice. "I told myself the time was no' yet right. When it was time, I thought, the Spinners would bring our threads together."

They lay silently in the darkness, their faces only a few inches apart. Isabeau felt a familiar tightening of her chest muscles, the roiling of confusion. He coiled one of her ringlets round and round his fingers, but said nothing.

After a moment she said, with great difficulty, "But I . . . I do no' ken . . ."

There was a long silence and then he said calmly, still playing with her hair, "What, Beau?"

"I do no' ken if I . . ." She paused, trying to sort out her tangle of thoughts. Then she said in a rush, surprising herself with the words, "Ye ken I canna have babes?" His fingers kept on with their coiling. "Jorge said so, he did a sighting for me. He said:

'I see ye with many faces and many disguises;
Ye will be one who can hide in a crowd.
Though ye shall have no home and no rest,
All valleys and pinnacles will be your home;
Though ye shall never give birth,
Ye shall rear a child who shall one day rule the land.' "

Her voice had changed, grown deeper, more tremulous. "Do ye see? I shall never have a home or rest, I shall never have babes. When have any o' Jorge's sightings been wrong? Meghan says witches often prove sterile. It has something to do with the use o' the One Power." Her words tumbled over themselves. "And because witches rarely marry . . ."

Dide said nothing, though his fingers slipped down from her hair and lightly drew circles on the side of her neck.

"And ye see, I am a witch now, a sorceress. I've sworn myself to the Coven."

"So?" he said. "Ye have sworn yourself to one master, I've sworn myself to another. What has that got to do with us loving?"

The slow circling touch of his fingers was calming her jumping pulse. She put up one hand and seized his wrist. "It means I'm no' like a normal lass that ye can be jumping the fire with, or making a life with."

He turned his hand so their fingers clasped. "I do no' want a normal lass, or even a normal life. Ye've said all this afore, Beau, it does no' change how I feel about ye."

There was a moment's silence and then he shifted towards her. Immediately her pulse leapt again. He very gently kissed the side of her mouth, and then her lips, and then her chin. "The question is . . . how do ye feel about me?"

His mouth moved down to the pulse jumping in the

hollow between her collarbones. One hand was swiftly, expertly, unravelling the laces of her bodice. His mouth followed his hand. Isabeau felt again that sharp stab of desire, and with it, sharper still, fear. He felt her movement and drew away from her a little, though his hand was still pressed to the junction of her ribs, the place where *coh* was meant to be centered.

"I would no' hurt ye, Beau," he said gently. "Why do ye fear me?"

She said nothing. Her whole body was very still, very tense.

"Have ye been hurt before, my Beau?" he asked gently. Stiffly she nodded. "The Awl?" She nodded again. He kissed her ear, his other hand tangling in her hair. She could feel the hand against her sternum trembling. "How badly . . . ? What did they . . . ?" He could not finish. She gave a little twist away, feeling again a spurt of shame and revulsion. He held her steady, stroking her hair away from her forehead. Slowly the gentleness of his touch soothed her. "Did they . . . ?"

She shook her head. "Nay. Worse has been done to others." Her voice was very low, and bitter. "They just touched me. He liked it, Baron Yutta, the Grand-Questioner, he said he liked to hear me scream. So they touched me a lot, all over my body, and up inside me, very hard . . ." Her voice trailed away. "Then Baron Yutta, he did it too, while I was on the rack. He . . ." Her voice broke and she said no more, amazed that she had been able to say so much. It was the warmth, the closeness, the darkness, Dide's hand so gentle on her brow. "I bit him," she said then, more strongly. "He laughed. And then he put the . . . the thing on my hand. That was when I killed him." She said it very matter-of-factly.

Dide's hand stilled. She twisted a little, wanting to see

his face now. The fire had almost gone out but Isabeau had always been able to see in the dark like an elven cat. She could see how grim his mouth was, how tense the line of his jaw, and felt again the cold wind blowing between them.

Then he caught her to him, so hard she lost the breath in her lungs. "I wish I could've killed him for ye," he said. His voice was very rough. He pressed his face against hers and she was surprised to find his eyes were wet. She put up one finger and laid it against his damp lashes. He caught it and kissed it, and then kissed the scars where her fingers used to be. Something dissolved in Isabeau's chest. She found she too was near tears. It was not the dreadful hot choking that had so often overwhelmed her in recent months, but something much softer, like an autumn rain.

Dide felt the little heave of her chest, the catch of her breath. He stroked her back, and she buried her head in his shoulder, allowing herself the luxury of crying. "Sssh, *leannan*, ssshhh," he whispered, stroking and patting her as she did the twins. The little storm of tears was soon over, but Isabeau was so tired, so drained, she could not lift her head from his shoulder. He shifted a little, drawing her down beside him. "Go to sleep, little one," he whispered. "Go to sleep."

Irresistibly Isabeau's lashes fell. She sighed, crept a little closer, and fell fast asleep.

She woke just before dawn, her arm prickling with pins and needles. Dide slept beside her. She propped her head up on her arm and watched him. His dark, tousled curls hung onto his forehead, his swarthy skin flushed with sleep. One hand was resting beneath his cheek like a child.

She eased herself away from him, flushing a little as she realized her bodice was half undone. Quickly she laced it up again. When she lifted her eyes, she realized his eyes were open and he was watching her. The devil-may-care glint was back in his slumberous black eyes.

"Must ye?" he asked.

She flushed. Dide put out a lazy hand and very gently ran his finger along the curve of her breast. They both watched the nipple harden.

"I suppose ye must," he said regretfully. He glanced back at the sleeping forms of his fellow officers. "As ye've said to me before, this really is no' the time or the place."

"So when shall be the time and place?" she asked roguishly. Quick as a flash Dide reached out and gently grasped her hair, and she was irresistibly drawn down to him. Their mouths met, clung, drew away, met again.

"Anytime ye want, Beau," Dide answered when he at last let her go. He lay back on his pallet, watching as she rose to her feet, knotting up the thick mass of red curls at the base of her neck. "Just as soon as we are at peace."

"If we ever are," she said bitterly.

He smiled up at her, putting his hands behind his head. "Believe me, my Beau, I've never wanted peace more. If I have anything to do with it, we'll win the war tomorrow!"

COMET RISING

ed as blood, the comet pulsed faintly just above the eastern horizon. Already the stars were fading and the serrated outline of mountains was beginning to emerge to the east as the darkness seeped away. It was very quiet.

Isabeau leant her elbows on the parapet and gazed anxiously at the smudge of red in the sky. "It's here," she said to Meghan.

The old sorceress was leaning heavily on her staff, her blue and green checked plaid wrapped closely about her. She squinted up at the sky and said, rather tremulously, "Are ye sure? I canna see it."

Isabeau nodded. "I can see it clearly, I'm afraid."

Meghan clucked her tongue. "My eyes are no' what they used to be, for sure."

"We had best go and tell Lachlan," Isabeau said, turning away. She felt a deep despondency. They had all hoped so much to effect a quick end to the war, but here it was, almost Candlemas, and still they had not found the way to defeat the Fairgean. Lachlan's navy had been reduced to less than thirty ships, and they had lost over five thousand men, a devastating loss. And even though Lachlan raised the Lodestar and stilled the storms again and again, yet another gale would rise the next day and lash them once more.

Despite the foul weather, Lachlan had kept all his men riding up and down the coast, for the Fairgean tried many times to climb the cliffs and attack them from the rear. As a consequence, Isabeau had seen Dide only twice and each time he had been hollow-eyed from exhaustion.

Isabeau closed her eyes and silently called her sister's name. *The Red Wanderer has risen* . . . She knew Iseult would hear her and come.

Soon she heard the sound of boots on the stones and went to open the door onto the battlements. The Rìgh and Banrìgh came out first, Lachlan's general staff close behind as usual.

"Isabeau says she can see the Red Wanderer," Meghan said without preamble, her old face drawn and tired.

Isabeau nodded and pointed to the east. Iseult saw the comet at once, her eyesight as keen as her twin's, though most of the soldiers had to have it pointed out to them. They stared at it, every face grim and worried.

"It is always an evil omen, the Red Wanderer," Duncan Ironfist said.

"The people o' the Spine o' the World call it the Dragon-Star," Iseult said. "It always portends doom, like the shadow o' a dragon falling upon ye."

"Let us hope it portends doom for the Fairgean," Lachlan said, his hand dropping down upon the white glowing sphere he wore always at his belt. The touch of the Lodestar seemed to reassure him. The dark look lifted and he said, "At least the day looks like dawning fair. Happen that priestess-witch has run out o' puff."

Isabeau looked at him quickly. "Lachlan, ye canna mean to set sail again?"

He looked obstinate. "If the winds are right, aye, then I do."

"But Jorge's dream . . ."

"I ken what Jorge dreamed as well as ye, Isabeau," he snapped. "It means we have eight days and eight days only to crush the Fairgean. If we have defeated them, then they canna harness the magic o' the comet and they canna drown us."

"But what if we canna defeat them?" Gwilym the Ugly said grimly. "For six months we've been throwing ourselves against the Fairgean and for six months they've been throwing us off. They can obviously draw upon strong powers indeed. Will Castle Forlorn be high enough if they raise a tidal wave against us?"

"I do no' think so," Lachlan said, just as grimly. "We canna take the chance, either way. My bairns are here, remember! Nay, this is my plan. I have been thinking o' what we must do for weeks now. We have eight days till the comet reaches the zenith o' its power. Ye and the other witches and the healers and the bairns, ye must all retreat back through the forest until ye reach the highlands. Ye must go as high as ye can for, as ye say, we have no idea how high this tidal wave o' theirs will go. Iseult must go too, to look out for the bairns and to show ye the way."

Iseult gave a little protest but he went on, not heeding her, "We'll keep only a skeleton force here, to do what we can to crush the Fairgean before the comet reaches its full powers. I think we have made a mistake in concentrating all our forces on taking back the Tower o' Sea-singers. Isabeau was right when she said they'd fight to the death to hold it."

"I'm glad ye can finally see it," Isabeau said rudely. He ignored her as he had ignored his wife.

"Instead we shall send our force against the priestesses' island itself. If we destroy the blaygird priestess, the Fairgean lose much o' their power. They willna be able to lash us with storms, or raise the tidal wave, or—"

"But Lachlan!" Isabeau and Meghan cried together.

He ignored them both, intent on making his point. "If we fail, then those o' us still alive will flee to the highlands to join ye."

"But, *leannan* . . ." Iseult said in distress. "Such a plan is surely suicide!"

Lachlan turned to her eagerly. "No' if we take them by surprise, and strike hard and fast. We have barrels o' seafire left, no' having been able to use it, thanks to the weather. What if we blasted the entire island with it? Or lured them out in false security and doused them with it then? There must be something we can do! That blaygird Fairge will ken. She was raised at the island. She will tell us how to defeat them."

"But ye canna trust the Ensorcellor, master!" Duncan Ironfist cried. "She will betray us, as sure as the sky is blue."

"No' if we have her daughter," Lachlan replied through his teeth. "If she betrays us, we'll slit her daughter's pretty white throat."

"No!" Isabeau cried. "Bronny is only a lassiekin!"

Lachlan turned on her. "Do ye think I want to do it? She be just the same age as my own lad, and she be my brother's daughter as well. I have no wish to wage war on bairns. I have no choice though, Isabeau. Either we crush the Priestesses o' Jor or we die. Besides, are ye no' the one who keeps reassuring me that Maya hates the Fairgean as much as we do, and the blaygird sisterhood even more? If what ye say is true, she'll be glad to watch them burn!"

He turned on his heel, issuing swift orders to Duncan

and Dide. Isabeau stood, her hands clenched, icy dread filling her. Did she really trust Maya? And what if Maya stayed true to them but somehow failed to give them the help they needed? Would Bronwen still be killed? And what of the Greycloaks? What of Dide? Surely such a mission was suicide.

She looked back up at the comet, its lurid red color already fading as the daylight grew. Soon it would be invisible, but Isabeau would still feel it there, cold, malevolent, tugging away at her mind. An evil omen indeed.

Maya was sitting on their pallet, combing out Bronwen's long black hair, when Lachlan strode in. The Rìgh looked pale and tired, his thick black brows folded tightly over the bridge of his aquiline nose.

"Come, Ensorcellor, it be time for ye to make yourself useful!"

Her hand stilled. She looked up at him, all the color draining from her face so that the odd, scaly shimmer of her skin was more pronounced than ever. "At your service as always, my liege," she said with the ironic inflection she knew flicked him on the raw. "What can I do to be o' service?"

"Ye can tell us what ye ken o' the Priestesses o' Jor. We plan to set sail for their island. We need ye to tell us which one it is and how we can best destroy it."

Maya made an odd sound in her throat. If she had been pale before, she was bloodless now. "Do no' be a fool! Ye canna strike against the Priestesses o' Jor like that! They have such powers at their command, powers about which ye ken nothing."

"So tell me," Lachlan said, watching her closely.

"What powers do they have at their command and how can we defeat them?"

"They are the Priestesses o' Jor! They are Jor's chosen ones. They call upon all the force o' Jor." Her voice was shaking.

"So?"

"Ye do no' understand," she stammered. Her voice took on a strange, chanting quality. "Jor is all. Jor is might. Jor is strength. Jor is power." She took a deep breath, relaxing her fingers on the comb. "He canna be defeated. The priestesses canna be defeated."

Lachlan's wings relaxed a little. He leant against the wall, his arms resting on the Lodestar. The light within the sphere leapt and twisted at his touch. He said, very gently, "We o' the Coven do no' believe in gods and goddesses like ye Fairgean do. We believe there be a single source o' power in the universe, that all o' us are lit by it and linked by it. Your Jor is simply a manifestation o' that power, one o' the many faces o' Eà. He is no' our enemy. And your priestesses are no' invincible. Did I no' shoot Sani the Sinister down out o' the sky with my bow? Ye were trained as a priestess too, were ye no'? Yet I have seen ye bleed and ye are here now, my captive."

Maya said nothing, watching him, her body as tense as a bowstring.

Lachlan went on slowly, "The Coven o' Witches had immense power at their command, they too would have thought themselves invincible, but ye were able to topple and destroy them in a few short days. Nothing in this world is unconquerable, nothing can avoid death in the end. How did ye defeat the witches?"

"I . . . I took them by surprise, struck hard and all at once so that none kent what was happening or were able to organize a defense. I kent it had to be done fast and brutal, for a moment's hesitation—"

"Exactly. That is what we must do to the Priestesses o' Jor."

She shook her head. "Nay, nay, it canna be done."

"It must be done." Lachlan's voice was still gentle but it had the inexorable ring of determination tolling through it. "And ye shall help us do it."

Once again she shook her head. Bronwen gave a little whimper of fear. Lachlan's eyes turned to her. He bent down on one knee. "Do no' be afraid, lassie. Come, ye must go and find your Aunty Beau. It is time for ye to leave the Castle Forlorn, the most rightly named place I've ever been in. Your mother is coming with us, but there is no need to fear. She is going to help us win this war."

"And if I do no'?" Maya asked.

Lachlan said, very harshly, "Och, I think ye will."

At the tone of his voice Bronwen shrank back against her mother, though there was none of the instant understanding of his meaning that there was in Maya's pale eyes. The Fairge held her daughter tightly, staring at Lachlan across the silky black head. Then she ducked down her chin and kissed Bronwen on the crown of her head. "Ye had better get your things together, sweetling. Mama has to go with your *Uncle* Lachlan now."

"No," Bronwen cried, starting up. "Do no' go, Mama. Stay with me!"

"I canna just now, dearling. Aunty Beau will have a care for ye."

"Ye ken ye must do all ye can to help us?" Lachlan warned. Maya nodded.

"Come, then. I have called a council o' war. Time is running out for us and we must make haste. We have only eight days to do what we havena been able to do in six months."

Bronwen did not fully understand all the undercurrents in the room but she was perceptive enough to be very apprehensive. She clung to her mother, weeping. Maya hugged her close, then stood up slowly. She was very white.

Lachlan said gently, "Do no' be so afraid, Maya. Ye have told us something o' what your life with the priestesses was like. It is natural that ye should have a dread o' them and their powers. They are no' gods themselves, though. They are mortal, too. And I have no wish to feel Gearradh's embrace just yet. I love my children and wish to see them grow. If we canna overcome the priestesses, we shall all flee into the highlands, that I promise ye."

"All o' us?"

"Aye, all o' us still living," he said. There was compassion on his face, an expression Maya had never before seen. She nodded, swallowing a constriction in her throat. Bending, she embraced Bronwen once more and then dragged herself free of the little girl's clinging hands.

The council of war had been called in the hall where Lachlan and Iseult normally slept. The pallets had been rolled up hastily and the blankets folded. There was no table but the maps had been flung out on the floor and weighted down with stones. The officers of Lachlan's general staff and the lairds sat on the rolled-up pallets or squatted on their heels.

Reluctantly Maya pointed out a small, isolated island. "But the Isle o' Divine Dread is impregnable," she said. "Like all o' the islands around here, it is an old volcano. Its cliffs rise sheer from the sea on all sides and there is no way in from above the water. The priestesses all live inside the volcano, which is riddled with caves and tunnels."

"But the priestesses must have some way of getting in and out," Dide said in some exasperation.

Maya nodded. "They swim in and out. A few o' the tunnels open up under sea level."

The general staff all looked rather daunted. Few of them could swim, most islanders having a superstitious terror of the sea.

Maya went on. "They are very deep, more than three hundred feet below the sea's surface."

"But that's impossible!" Duncan Ironfist cried. "Can the Fairgean dive so deep?"

"Most canna," Maya replied. "But if one wishes to get out o' the Isle o' Divine Dread, one must learn. Most Fairgean can dive two hundred feet or more. Some as much as three hundred, those who dive for pearls regularly and learn to slow their heart rate."

"So we have no way o' getting in," Lachlan said, clearly disappointed. "Even if we all swam like fish, we could no' dive so deep. What about from above? Surely some o' the tunnels lead to the open air?"

"If they do, I do no' ken where," Maya said calmly. "I do ken I never saw the faintest trace o' light or felt the faintest brush o' fresh air in all the years I was kept in the black depths o' the Isle of Divine Dread."

Many of the men about her gave a shudder. She saw they glanced at her with newly awoken compassion. Maya did not care. Soon they would all be dead, and Maya with them. It was too late for compassion.

"Besides, the cliffs are unclimbable," she said.

"All cliffs can be climbed," Dide said. "They said the Black Tower was impregnable and yet we penetrated that, and rescued Killian the Listener when all thought it was impossible."

"But we took months in the planning o' that and we had Finn the Cat to scale the cliffs," Lachlan said. "That was dangerous enough, that enterprise, but this is far worse. We canna expose a young lass to such danger. Anyway, we do no' have time to be exploring the island and trying to find ways in. No' without alerting the priestesses to what we do."

"Och, the priestesses will ken what ye plan," Maya said. "They have mirrors in which they can see for many miles."

"But they need to ken what to look for, do they no'?"

Maya shrugged.

"Well, if we canna get in, we must lure the priestesses out," Lachlan said, striding back and forth with his usual restless energy. "Maya, there must be some pattern to their movements, there must be! When do they usually come out?"

"The acolytes usually come out at dawn, to catch fish and gather kelp and fish roe. After so much time in the dark, they do no' like the sun and so most will be back inside the island before the day is too far advanced. The high priestesses, I do no' ken. Their habits and purposes are always shrouded in shadow. Those priestesses o' lesser power are usually in service at the court, so they are rarely at the Isle anyway, unless there is a summoning to do, or some other act o' great power."

"So they have circles o' power like we do?" Lachlan asked. "That is good to ken."

"Aye, the Highest Priestess stands alone in the center, her hands on whatever artifact she is using, with six standing around her, and six more in each circle outside, until the last circle has thirty-six o' the weakest priestesses. I have seen them summon gods with their circles o' power." Maya's voice was sick with dread.

"So when they try to raise this tidal wave o' theirs, they will have all the high-priestesses there, even those usually with the King?"

Maya nodded.

"That would be the time to hit them then," Lachlan said.

"But how?" cried the Duke of Killiegarrie.

"And who would do it? When they are all together, trying to raise the tidal wave, is the time it would be most dangerous for any o' us to be here," said Duncan Ironfist.

"Who shall bell the cat?" Lachlan asked, his eyes on Maya. She returned his gaze proudly, her head held high. All the soldiers followed his line of sight, and there was an uneasy shifting and murmuring.

"But she canna be trusted," Duncan implored.

"And how?" said the Duke of Killiegarrie again.

"Think o' the island as a fort we must win," Lachlan said. "We canna scale the walls, we canna undermine them, we have to force the defenders to come out and face us on the field o' war. What would we do?"

"Smoke them out," Iseult replied. It was the first time she had spoken.

Lachlan looked at her triumphantly. "Aye, we'd smoke them out."

"But how are we to do that?" the Duke of Gleneagles asked impatiently. "It's surrounded by ocean!"

"With seafire, o' course," Lachlan answered. "Maya must dive down to the tunnel entrances and plug them with jars o' seafire. Lots o' jars. Then we shall cause the jars to be broken. The fire will run up the tunnels and into the caves. We've all seen how much smoke it creates, and how acrid it is. Many o' the priestesses will die just from breathing it. Meanwhile, we can be bombarding the island from afar with more seafire so it is ringed in flames! If they try to swim out, they will burn to death. If they stay inside, they will choke to death."

"There are a great many caves within," Maya said. Despite herself, her voice shook. "How can ye be sure the smoke will penetrate that far?"

"And what if there are tunnels to the open air?" Khan'gharad asked.

Lachlan said in exasperation, "Must I have all the answers?"

"I could call the dragons," the Khan'cohban answered imperturbably. "I have never claimed their *geas*. I might have, when that Fairge wolf sent her black-hearted soldiers against us, but I was transformed into a horse before I had the chance." He directed a look of the coldest hate towards Maya, who showed no sign of noticing it.

"The dragons," Iseult said slowly. "If they flew around the island, flaming it, that would prevent any o' the priestesses escaping . . ."

"And the smoke and fire o' the dragons' breath would surely penetrate deep into the island too!" Duncan cried.

"No' to mention the likelihood o' many o' the caves collapsing," said the Duke of Killiegarrie with satisfaction. "We could be bombarding the island with our cannons, just to help matters along a wee."

"We still must plug the sea tunnels with the seafire," Lachlan said. "Else they shall all simply swim out to safety."

"How are we to make sure the glass jars break?" Iain asked.

"If the island is being bombarded with cannons and dragon-fire, would no' that be enough to break them?" Lachlan replied. "And happen the priestesses would seek to flee and break the glass in their panic, no' knowing what the result would be."

"What if the Ensorcellor breaks the jars when she's trying to plug the holes?" Iain asked then.

There was a short silence, then Maya said sweetly, "Oh, but o' course I must just try my very best no' to break them, mustn't I?"

No one was able to meet her eyes. She gazed round at them, her nostrils flaring slightly in disdain.

"Well, it is all I can think o'," Lachlan said at last. "In the meantime, we must send messengers out so that everyone everywhere kens to stay on high ground. If we should fail, Eà forbid, we must make sure as many lives as possible are saved."

"After that general warning ye issued afore we came to Carraig, I doubt there's a single fisherman or crab-catcher left anywhere near the seashore now," the Mac-Seinn said. "If we can see the red comet, all o' Eileanan must see it too."

Lachlan sighed. He was frowning heavily, two lines carved deeply between his brows. "If only we kent what to expect," he said. "Yet I ken naught about tidal waves . . ."

"The very fact that ye call them 'tidal waves' shows how little ye ken about them," Maya said with an edge of contempt in her voice. "They have naught to do with the tides."

Lachlan looked up at her swiftly. "What should I be calling them then?"

"The Fairgean call them *ibo*. That means, I suppose, 'quake-wave.' They are usually caused by earthquakes under the sea or even an erupting volcano. The seabed shudders. Part o' it may even be forced up into a new island or undersea mountain. The movement o' the earth under the sea causes the water to ripple up and out. Out in the ocean there is little visible effect, because water always finds its own level, but once the wave rippling out flows over a shallower area, it is forced up into a big wave. The shallower the seabed, the bigger the wave."

"How high can this quake-wave rise?" Gwilym asked swiftly. He had been listening with fascination. Being strongest in the element of water, he was always struggling to learn more since the widespread fear of deep water meant few studied it closely.

Maya shrugged. "I suppose it depends on how forceful the earthquake is, and how close to land. There has no' been one for many years, but I ken the primary wave rose close on a hundred feet then, and was many hundreds o' miles long."

There was a collective gasp. Everyone looked at each other, trying to imagine the consequences of such a wave smashing down upon the coast.

"How can the Fairgean even think o' conjuring such a wave?" Meghan cried, white with anger. "It will kill everything, all the creatures o' the forest, no' just us humans."

"What about the creatures o' the sea?" Gwilym asked. "Surely it will kill them too?"

"What about the Fairgean themselves?" Lachlan asked. "How could they survive a wave o' such height and power?"

Maya shrugged. "I do no' ken the answers. I am no', unfortunately, privy to the King's councils. I imagine they plan to swim in deep sea, however. There the ripple effect is only minor. They will wait there in safety for the waves to subside."

Lachlan's frown had cleared miraculously. "What about

a ship?" he demanded. "Would ships be safe if they were in deep ocean?"

"I suppose so," Maya answered, eyeing him warily.

Lachlan grinned. "Thank Eà, I can save my Ship Tax! If we send the majority o' the fleet out into deep waters, they should be safe."

"Except for sea-serpents and icebergs," Admiral Tobias said gloomily.

Lachlan had leapt to his feet, his wings spreading out. "Come!" he said. "We have much to do before the comet reaches its height. We need to provision the ships and arm them strongly, so they can protect themselves whilst away from the shore. We need to plan an orderly retreat and make sure it has adequate protection from any Fairgean in the river. We need to send out messengers, and consolidate our forces. Then we need to decide who is to stay here with me to try to destroy the priestesses' islands."

"It is for my land that ye have all fought so bravely," the MacSeinn said. "I shall stay."

Lachlan nodded. "Aye, that seems fair. Your son must go, though, so that if we fail there is still a MacSeinn living."

"Thank ye, my liege," the MacSeinn breathed, a white tension leaving his face.

"But *Dai-dein* . . ." Douglas protested.

"No arguments," Lachlan said briskly. "It is your responsibility to your clan to keep yourself safe, and to rebuild your land when we have won it back for ye."

The boy nodded, his face very white.

"I shall stay, o' course," said Duncan Ironfist.

"And I also, master," Dide said.

Isabeau, listening quietly at the back of the room, gripped her hands together tightly.

Lachlan nodded. "O' course. I couldna do without either o' ye."

"I will stay also," said Khan'gharad. "Ye will need me to call the dragons."

"Thank ye," Lachlan said. "I will do my best to bring ye home safely. I ken Iseult and Isabeau would never forgive me otherwise."

He glanced smiling at his wife, who sat beside him. Her face was very stern. "I stay also," she said.

Lachlan's smile died. "Iseult, no! I said—"

"I am coming with ye."

"But *leannan* . . ."

"I am a Scarred Warrior. I will no' be sent to safety like a bairn. I stay also."

Lachlan looked at her helplessly, then slung his arm about her shoulder and drew her close. "If ever there was a more stubborn, disobedient wife in all the world!"

Iseult smiled up at him. "I kent ye'd see reason," she answered.

One by one the other soldiers in the room volunteered their services. Admiral Tobias said he'd better stay and keep his ships safe. Arvin the Just said piously, "Who so sheddeth man's blood, by man shall his blood be shed," which Lachlan took to mean he wished to be part of the action. The Duke of Gleneagles and the Duke of Killiegarrie both decided to stay, as well as all of Lachlan's personal bodyguard, who were sworn to follow the Rìgh into battle. Lachlan's squire Connor also begged to be allowed to stay, but he was gently refused. "I need ye to guard the Keybearer and the other witches," Lachlan said. "Please, Connor, I need a man I can trust."

Despite himself, the boy drew himself up proudly and submitted to his Rìgh's will.

In all, including the thirty crew members of the *Royal*

Stag, only a hundred and fifty men were chosen to stay, among them representatives of every land in Eileanan. Messages were sent to and from Castle Forsaken, with Anghus MacRuraich and thirty of his best men joining the campaign. Everyone else was to retreat through the forest and into the highlands of Carraig. It would be a desperate retreat indeed, with their supplies so low, the snowdrifts so deep, and the roads all overgrown and in disrepair after thirteen years of neglect. Meghan and Isabeau looked at each other in despair.

Duncan Ironfist stood close by Lachlan's elbow, his hands resting easily on his sword belt. By his face, one would have thought they were planning a picnic and not a suicidal mission. Maya stood with them, pointing out and describing the many islands that littered the Carraigean coast, as they endeavored to find a safe place in which to wait out the eight days. Duncan waited until the Fairge was out of earshot, before saying in a low voice, "Master, ye place a great deal o' confidence in the Ensorcellor. How can ye trust her so? Her promises are no' worth a tinker's curse."

"What else can I do?" Lachlan replied in a low voice. "We're grasping at straws now. The Dragon-Star has risen and it chills my blood. Besides, did ye no' see her face? I swear she truly cares for her daughter."

"But it is her Talent, to make ye think she really cares," Duncan said. "Did Jaspar no' believe in her love with all o' his heart, and that was all lies. What about Finlay MacFinlay? She ensorcelled him into trusting her and betraying us. I would no' trust her as far as I could throw a rat. What if she betrays us to the Fairgean?"

Lachlan rubbed his temples wearily. "Then we are all dead," he answered. "Let us hope she is true!"

*   *   *

Isabeau was in the courtyard, busy overseeing the packing of their meager medicinal supplies, when Iseult found her. The Banrìgh was dressed in her battered leather armor, with her hair drawn back tightly from her brow and covered with a leather cap. She wore her weapons belt strapped around her waist as usual.

Isabeau seized her hands. "Oh, Iseult! Canna ye persuade Lachlan to give up this mad plan? Canna ye see it is death to try it?"

Iseult shook her head. "He is determined, Beau. Surely ye ken him well enough by now to ken how stubborn he is? He shall no' give up while there is a chance we can thwart this evil plan o' the Fairgean."

"Must ye go with him?" Isabeau said. "And our *daidein* too? Do ye mean to relieve me o' all my family at once?"

Iseult did not return her sister's smile, as forced as it had been. "Ye must have a care for my bairns," she said deliberately. "I give them into your care, Isabeau."

Isabeau did not misunderstand her. "Ye mean . . ." she faltered. "Oh, Iseult. Ye must come back, both o' ye! It's madness to risk yourselves so."

"Just in case," Iseult answered. "I am no' afraid really. It is a good plan and could work, and if it does no', well, we sail for the open sea just as fast as we can! Do no' weep so, Isabeau. It is no way to say farewell."

Isabeau wiped her eyes and tried to smile, but the cold foreboding of the morning had not faded with the light of the comet. She embraced her sister tightly, wishing they were all safely home at Lucescere, with nothing more to worry about than how to celebrate their upcoming birthday. At last Iseult tore herself away and Isabeau sank down on a pile of sacks, burying her face in her hands.

Someone seized her hands and drew them away. She

looked up and saw Dide. His face was pale, his eyes shadowed. "This is goodbye, my Beau," he said. "The retreat has been sounded. Ye must be gone afore ye lose too much o' the daylight."

"No!" she cried, clinging to his hands. "Oh, Dide . . ."

He kissed her roughly, almost violently. "Have a care for yourself, Beau. Ye must get as far away from the sea as ye can. Promise me ye shall no' dally but will go as quickly as ye can."

"Why must ye stay?" she cried, her arms about his neck. "Canna ye come with us?"

"My master has need o' me," he replied gently. "Ye ken I must go."

She nodded, drawing away. Where she had pressed her face against her jerkin was a damp splotch. She rubbed it with her fingers. "Have a care for yourself too, Dide," she said quietly.

He grinned at her. "Och, I've lived this long, I'm no' going to die now, my Beau. I'm looking forward to peace too much."

She smiled up at him through her tears. He kissed her again, saying thickly, "Och, that be a sight to keep a man alive, I promise ye."

He smiled at her, pinched her chin, then strode swiftly back into the castle. Isabeau sat back down on the sacks, feeling more forlorn than ever before in her life. The MacSeinns had named their castle well, she thought. Suddenly she became aware of Meghan patting her shoulder. "Do no' grieve so, dearling," the old sorceress said. "That one be too full o' wicked charm to be dying so young. I warrant ye'll see him before the week is out."

Isabeau dried her tears. "I'm sorry. I just did no' expect . . ."

"I ken," Meghan replied. "It is hard to send someone

ye love off to war, when all ye want is to hold them tight in your arms and keep them safe."

Isabeau looked up at her. There was something in Meghan's voice that told Isabeau the old sorceress knew exactly how she felt. Meghan smiled at her sadly. "Och, I ken. Because I am auld and grey now, ye think I have always been. I may be four hundred and thirty-five years auld now but I was once as young and bonny as ye are, Beau. I have loved and lost more times than I can count."

Isabeau could not help looking astonished. Meghan laughed grimly. "That is the problem wi' being this auld. Ye live on and on while those ye love grow auld and die, or fall in battle, or waste away with sickness. This is the third war against the Fairgean that I have lived through, and I lost people I loved in every one o' them."

Isabeau hesitated, then could not help asking, "Do ye mean . . . lovers too, Meghan?"

"Aye, lovers too. Though the man I loved more than I thought it was possible to love anyone died o' auld age, peacefully, in my arms. I wanted to die then too, but this auld body o' mine just would no' let go. That was when I gave up the Key and retired to the secret valley. I suppose I would have been in my eighties. I felt very auld then." She chuckled. "Now I think what a sprightly young thing I was. Still, I loved Micheil very much. He was my lover and my friend for almost fifty years, on and off."

"But no' your husband."

"Nay, no' my husband. I was the Keybearer and he was the second son o' a second son and had to make his own way in the world. He served with the MacBrann for a time, I remember. We saw each other often, though. Somehow I was always finding an excuse to visit Ravenshaw." She smiled in reminiscence.

"What about Jorge?" Isabeau asked, having always

wondered about the obvious closeness between Meghan and the old blind seer who had died so tragically.

Meghan laughed. "Isabeau, please! I was about three hundred and fifty when he was born. I do no' think he ever saw me as anything but an ancient crone who used to scold him for dawdling over his lessons. Nay, I loved Jorge dearly but never in that way."

New ideas were beginning to take root in Isabeau's mind. "So when ye were Keybearer, ye still . . . ?"

Meghan looked surprised. "Och, o' course, Beau. Being a witch does no' stop ye being a woman. I do try to discourage young witches from falling in love too soon, because it always wreaks havoc with their studies, but there are no laws against a witch loving. We are no' like the Tìrsoilleirean with all their disgust for the natural relations between women and men, and all their laws and prohibitions. Though I do remember Maya used the witches' so-called promiscuity against us at the time o' the Burning. No' that we were ever truly promiscuous, o' course. All that talk about orgies and so on was pure exaggeration."

She gave a little smile. "Though Tabithas was famous for her many lovers when she was Keybearer. Poor Tabithas. What a shame she died last winter. She was a very auld wolf indeed." She sighed and rubbed Gità's head affectionately. "Come, if we are to ride for the highlands we had best finish packing."

She gave a little motion with her hand and Isabeau got to her feet, wiping away the last of her tears. She helped load the sacks into one of the carts, then made sure her own small bundle was tucked in safely with the books and the chests of tinctures and powders. The courtyard was milling with people, all shouting contrary instructions, while the horses danced about uneasily, sensing the distress in the air. Meghan and Isabeau quietened them with soft whickers of reassurance, then Isabeau helped Meghan up into one of the carts. She swung Olwynne and Owein up, making a soft nest of blankets and straw for them to nestle into, then mounted her own horse, a half-broken colt that had been among the many wild horses they had captured in the forest. Donncan and Bronwen climbed up to the driver's seat, one on either side of Gwilym the Ugly, who was driving.

"Can I take the reins?" Donncan asked eagerly.

The sorcerer nodded and the little prionnsa drove the cart out of the courtyard and onto the road, waving proudly to Lachlan and Iseult, who were standing by the great gates.

"May Eà shine her bright face upon ye," Isabeau said to them both, leaning down from her horse.

"And on ye," Lachlan replied, looking up into her face with a smile. "Do no' fear! All will be well."

"If I do no' see ye afore, happy birthday for Candlemas," Iseult said and Isabeau smiled and nodded, kicking her horse forward. She looked back at the ruined castle and saw, with a little leap of her heart, someone waving a blue cockaded cap from the battlements. She turned in her saddle and waved back wildly until the castle was out of sight.

The road ran down the long headland, curving round towards the stony beach and the mouth of the river. Here the land rolled away in gentle hills into a long, broad valley filled with trees. Through the center of the forest ran the Kilchurn River, a wide, swift river swollen with the melting snows from the mountains. It was by rafting this river that Iseult had been able to bring the MacSeinn and his men to the sea so quickly.

Near where the Kilchurn River met the sea, the large,

sprawling town of Kinnaird had been built on a low hill, surrounded by high fortified walls. Most of the town now lay in ruins. The party retreating from Castle Forlorn gave the old town a wide berth as they made their way into the forest, for all knew that it had once again fallen to the Fairgean. For the same reason they kept well clear of the river, melting snow for themselves and their horses to drink.

By noon they were deep into the forest, following the rutted remains of an old road now so overgrown with brambles it was virtually impassable. Soldiers walked in front with axes, clearing the path and stamping down the snow so it was wide and smooth enough for the carts which carried the witches, the children and the few sacks and barrels remaining to them.

Their progress was further hampered by Meghan's insistence on warning as many of the forest creatures as she could. She sent her donbeag Gitâ scampering through the branches to arouse the tree-dwellers, and called coneys, marmots, hoar-weasels and foxes to her hand, asking them all to spread the word.

"The bears will all be hibernating," she said anxiously. "I hope the other creatures are not all too afraid to wake them. Enit, perhaps you could ask the birds to call the warning?"

So Enit called the birds of the forest to her hand and soon the air was filled with their shrill cries, and the clamor of their wings.

Under the thick, snow-laden branches, dusk fell early. They were forced to make a rough camp, all of them feeling that relentless frustration which comes from having not traveled far enough or fast enough.

The campfires were strung out through the trees as far as the eye could see, for the retreat had been joined by those who had taken shelter at the Castle Forsaken. There were soldiers from every country in Eileanan, plus many of those Carraigean who had come down out of the mountains to help in the war. An air of despondency hung over the entire cavalcade, for all had come to Carraig with high hopes.

The calling of the retreat had effected a reunion of the old League of the Healing Hand. They clustered close about the fire, hearing each other's news and marveling at the changes in one another. Finn the Cat had been sent by her father to help lead the cavalcade to safety, with Aslinn the Piper her devoted servant as always. Jay the Fiddler was accompanying Enit as usual, while Johanna was never far from the healers, and Tòmas and her young brother Connor were never far from her. Only Dillon of the Joyous Sword was not with them, having stayed behind with Lachlan like the other Blue Guards.

With the League of the Healing Hand were their other friends and comrades—Brangaine NicSian, Cailean and his shadow-hound Dobhailen, Brun the cluricaun and Douglas MacSeinn, tense with fear for his father's safety.

"Is it no' peculiar," Finn said, "to think we were all together at Rhyssmadill nine months ago, and now here we are all together again, having been all round the world in the meantime? Have ye all had a great many adventures? I have! They locked me in my room, ye ken, to stop me from coming. I had to climb down, which was a great bother, for it's a drop of three hundred feet and all slimy with spray. And then I had to sort o' trail along at the back o' the army without anyone seeing me, for everyone kens me, o' course, and my *dai-dein* would have had no hesitation in sending me back again. I quite enjoyed that, though. I got to practice my pickpocketing skills, and it was kind o' fun to see everyone realizing their supper or their tobacco had mysteriously gone missing again."

She grinned roguishly. "They blamed the nisses most o' the time, or even goblins, the fools. I was dressed as a lad, o' course, and had cut my hair again but I was almost discovered about ten times. Eventually, though, Goblin and I wriggled into my *dai-dein*'s tent and sat and waited for him on his pallet, for we were getting pretty hungry and sick o' eating everyone's dust. By that time we were on the coast and it was too late to send us back. He was furious, but what could he do? It's been pretty boring since then, though, for he wouldna let me out o' that bloody Castle Forsaken. Flaming dragon-balls! I shall never call Castle Rurach a draughty auld ruin ever again."

"I was never more shocked than when I heard ye were at Castle Forsaken," her cousin Brangaine said. "I kent my uncle would never have permitted ye to ride to war."

"Were ye?" Jay grinned. "I was no' surprised at all."

"It's only because ye can whistle the wind that ye were allowed, muffin-face," Finn retorted. "If I had a Talent with weather, they would no' have tried to make me stay. It's no' bloody fair! And now we all have to retreat, just when things were getting interesting."

"Only ye would say anything so foolish," Brangaine said, shaking her fair head in wonder. "Do ye no' realize how much danger we are all in?"

"Danger? When ye have Finn the Cat to lead ye to safety? Oh, ye o' little faith!"

At the next fire along the witches and the healers sat, all wrapped up well against the bitter cold. Arkening Dreamwalker had suffered the most from the unending snowstorms and she lay in a fevered sleep, her breath rattling in her chest.

"We should have sounded the retreat a month ago," Stout John said, his heavy jowls hanging down like a bulldog's. He was not as stout as he had been six months ago. "It has been futile, all this winter campaign. Utterly futile!"

"All war is futile," Enit replied morosely. She sat hunched and listless, not touching the bowl of thin soup the camp cooks had made. Isabeau knew Enit fretted for Dide's safety as much as she did.

"Come now," Johanna said briskly. "War is no' futile if ye win. The Greycloaks are no' beaten yet. Did no' His Highness raise high the Lodestar and quell the storm? The Rìgh has never yet lost a campaign, and the Bright Wars dragged on far longer than this war has, and with a much higher cost in lives. Ye were no' at Rhyssmadill, where the piles o' dead bodies stretched as far as the eye could see, but I was. Ye canna say that it was no' worthwhile in driving the Bright Soldiers out o' Rionnagan?"

Enit did not reply. Johanna knelt by her side and gently closed the crippled fingers about the spoon. "Eat up, ma'am, else ye'll be falling sick and making more work for me."

Enit smiled briefly and obediently ate a few mouthfuls as Johanna rose and went to quell the argument between Finn and Brangaine. She helped Maura settle the tired, fractious twins to sleep, then distracted Douglas Mac-Seinn from his fears by asking him to help her sort through the bunch of herbs and flowers she had picked that day as they had walked through the forest. Isabeau, watching, wondered what any of them would do without Johanna.

All were tired after the long and strenuous day and so none complained when the fires were banked as soon as the evening meal was eaten, and the lanterns turned down low.

Isabeau was woken from a troubled sleep by a low, hoarse growling. She tensed immediately, sitting up. Cailean's shadow-hound was standing at the edge of the forest, hackles raised, lips drawn back from his fangs, green eyes shining uncannily. The young apprentice witch stood by his side, hand resting on the tall dog's back.

Mist wreathed through the dark trees, writhing along the forest floor and curling around the tree trunks. It smelt dank and evil, like an open grave. Isabeau's throat muscles tightened. She got to her feet and came silently up behind the dog, which turned its sleek head and growled at her.

Peace, she said in its own language. Its hackles sank a little, and the narrow head swung round and stared out into the forest again.

"There is something out there," Cailean said, very softly.

"Mesmerdean," Gwilym the Ugly said. He was sitting near the coals of the fire, well wrapped up against the cold, his staff across his knees.

"No! Here?"

The sorcerer nodded.

"But I thought we had left them behind in Arran," Isabeau said in great distress. "How do they come to find us here, so far away from the swamp?"

"Do no' be a fool, Beau," Meghan said quietly. She was lying still in her blankets but as she spoke she raised herself up on one elbow. "They ken the time o' the rising o' the comet as well as we do. Did ye think we could outrun them?"

"No!" Isabeau cried. She caught up a branch from the

fire and waved it violently, so that its smoldering end burst again into flame. "Go away! Go away!" She ran out into the forest, waving her torch. The mist flowed all over her like ghostly fingers and she fought it, sobbing. Behind her the camp was roused by the sound of her cries.

"Hush, dearling," Meghan said, her feet crunching on the snow as she came up behind Isabeau. "Why do ye waken the whole camp? There is naught that ye or they can do. The Mesmerdean have never been far away from me, no' for all these past months. They just grow eager now and press closer to me."

"No!" Isabeau sobbed.

"Come back to the fire, my silly bairn. Look at ye! Ye're shivering. And your feet bare in all this snow. Ye'll be losing some toes to frostbite if ye are no' careful. Come back to your bed."

The torch trailing from her hand, Isabeau allowed Meghan to lead her back to the campfire. "Is all well?" a few people cried. "What has happened?"

"Naught, naught," Meghan replied soothingly. "Go back to sleep."

She pushed Isabeau down into her pile of blankets and Isabeau huddled them over her numb feet. She felt numb too. The dank miasma of the Mesmerdean hung all around, making her nauseous. Johanna had woken and with her usual practicality had made some hot herbal tea, which Isabeau drank obediently. She did not sleep again, though, lying in her blankets and trying to drive the Mesmerdean away with the strength of her will and desire.

In the morning the mist was gone. The sky was clear and pale, the sun turning all the icicles into sparkling diamonds. "What has happened to all those storms?" Nellwyn asked as she clambered up into the cart. "Does that priestess-witch no longer wish to torment us?"

"Happen she is saving her strength," Gwilym replied glumly.

They forged on into the forest, a long procession of men, women and children, all hoping that Finn's much celebrated sense of direction would not lead them astray. Sometimes the road was so overgrown with saplings that it was impossible to see which way it went. Finn always pointed with great confidence and as she was always right, people soon came to trust her implicitly.

Their progress was slow, nonetheless, and as the days trickled by Isabeau's sense of foreboding only grew worse. She slept little, dreaming of mountains spouting fire, a comet of ice with a fiery tail, a great wave that swept over the land and drowned every living thing. One night she woke with a start, her heart hammering. She had dreamt of a battle, and a Fairge with a cruel face and heavy tusks stabbing Lachlan through the breast. Lachlan had sunk down, down, into dark, fathomless water, sinking out of sight, all the vivid life in his glowing golden eyes snuffed out forever. She lay awake the rest of the night, staring out into the mist, misery weighing down every limb.

At last, just when all were sick with anxiety, the ground began to rise under their feet. Hills shouldered out of the forest, and they drew close to the river again. It ran quickly down through white mounds of snow, ice clogging its edges. Tall evergreen trees thrust into the heavy clouds, their branches weighed down with snow. Here and there the darkness of the forest was broken by the delicate filigree of bare branches.

It grew more and more difficult to clear a path for the carts. Arkening Dreamwalker was gripped with fever, unable even to recognize the faces that hung over her, Enit could not take a step unaided, and the children were not strong enough to walk very far. They had to keep the carts.

Every night the red throbbing of the comet grew more palpable, until not even the most short-sighted needed to have it pointed out to them. It was most visible at dawn and dusk, and that was when Isabeau found her spirits most depressed, when it pulsed in the sky like a clot of blood. The closer the comet came, the closer drew the Mesmerdean, until the forest around their camp was every night thick with mist. It was a shroud that hung over everything, filled with the smell of death, and in its damp, clinging opacity hung the uncanny ghostly figures, watching, waiting.

On the fifth night, Arkening Dreamwalker died in her sleep. The witches were all devastated with grief, for the old sorceress had been a gentle, kind-hearted woman and had suffered much during the cruel reign of Maya the Ensorcellor. Stormy Briant and his young brother Cailean were the most grieved, for they had rescued her from the fire in Siantan eight years earlier and traveled with her all the way to the Tower of Two Moons.

They buried her under stones as best as they could, the ground frozen too hard for digging, and a red-eyed Meghan spoke the death rites over her grave. As soon as the ritual was done, though, everyone hurried on. There was no time for grieving. They had only three days before the comet reached the zenith of its power. Three days to Isabeau and Iseult's twenty-fourth birthday.

On the seventh day they came to a deep pool shadowed by a high, tree-hung cliff. A long waterfall plunged down into its murky waters, icicles hanging from the rock ledges and tree branches. There they stopped in despair, unable to see any way for the horses and carts to go on.

"We had some trouble here," Carrick One-Eye said.

"Our rafts almost went over the edge, taking us with it. Her Highness used her magic to freeze the whole river and the waterfall, and we were stuck in the ice like a fly in cake frosting. We chopped the rafts free and then we carried them down the side of the cliff with us. It was very difficult. Once we were down, she unfroze the river and we rafted safely the rest o' the way."

"What a Talent," Meghan said admiringly. "Och, I wish we could make a sorceress out o' Iseult too! What a shame she married the Rìgh and became a banrìgh."

"It's no' a shame!" Donncan cried indignantly.

Meghan smiled at him indulgently. "Och, I was jesting, my lad. Believe me, no one was happier than I when your mother and father were married."

"We shall have to abandon the carts now," Isabeau said. "There's no help for it. Some of the sturdier ponies will be able to climb this hill. We will mount Enit and Meghan, a twin before them both, and load the others with supplies. Everyone else must climb."

She and Riordan Bowlegs between them coaxed as many of the horses as they could up the steep hill. It was a difficult ascent, in some places seemingly almost vertical, but somehow most of the ponies made it.

Above were open hills and meadows, rising to the steep line of the mountains. Isabeau's heart lifted at the sight of the Spine of the World, towering so high and so white it seemed impossible that they were mountains and not clouds. Higher and higher they climbed, till the shadows were stretching long beside them and the ponies began to stumble. A cliff was above them, a long ridge sloping away behind them. They could climb no more.

The comet was hanging red and ominous in the violet sky. Below the ridge fell the long slopes of the highlands, with an ocean of dark trees beyond. Isabeau could see the shining length of the river winding through, leading the eye inexorably to the sea, almost lost in shadows. "I only hope we have climbed high enough," she said to Johanna. "I wish we could no' see the blaygird sea."

"Och, the sea shall no' rise," Johanna replied comfortably. "His Highness shall stop them from working their evil sorceries."

"How can ye be so sure?" Isabeau burst out.

Johanna paused. "I am no' sure," she answered softly. "But long ago I wished, on the Samhain fire, never to be afraid again. I was always afraid before then, afraid o' being hungry, being alone, being hurt. Finn and Dillon used to call me scaredy-cat, and tease me. So I wished to be free o' fear. What I found was that fear is always with us, there is no escaping it. If we are alive, we must be afraid. Ye have to face up to your fear, though, and get on with things. So that is what I try to do."

Isabeau was ashamed. She took one of Johanna's work-roughened hands, squeezed it, and got to her feet. "Well, I suppose I had best get on with things then," she said.

That evening the mist swirled so close about them it seeped into all their clothes and made the fire almost impossible to keep burning. Everyone shivered in the dampness and huddled close together. The only consolation was that the fog concealed the comet from their view.

During the night it snowed, softly at first, and then with increasing ferocity. The trees were no shelter at all, and the tarpaulins they had rigged up from trunk to branch were ripped away by a rising wind. They huddled together, the Scarred Warriors digging ice caves for the witches and children to shelter in. Isabeau and the healers walked through the encampment, warning people to keep moving their fingers and toes. All the fires had quickly died under the weight of the snow and many people had no more shelter than their coats and a few blankets.

Anger sparked in Isabeau. She remembered how the MacSeinn clan had had to flee through the snowstorm after they had been driven out by the Fairgean. In the morning, the MacSeinn had told, they had found hundreds lying dead, stiff and cold. She could not allow that to happen. Reaching deep inside herself she drew upon all her reserves of power and flung her hand towards an enormous tree trunk that had fallen in a storm many years before. Although it was mounded high with snow, the log burst into flame from its tangle of roots to its shaggy, twiggy head. The flames roared high, the snow all melting with a hiss like a thousand snakes. The refugees gathered close, holding out their benumbed hands, crying aloud with amazement. The healers were able to melt snow in their cauldrons and make nourishing herbal teas for all to drink, and heat stones to put in the beds of the oldest and weakest. Isabeau worked with them through the storm, at last falling asleep with her head on her arms, a long spoon still in her hand from where she had been stirring a cauldron.

She was woken only a few hours later by the sound of her father calling the dragon-queen's name. Like the clamor of a thousand bells it echoed through her skull and all the hidden chambers of her body, resonating and resonating till her teeth shuddered together and her head rang.

Caillec Aillen Airi Telloch Cas! I call thee, Caillec Aillen Airi Telloch Cas. It is time! Come to me, Caillec Aillen Airi Telloch Cas!

All was quiet. Immaculate white snow stretched as far as the eye could see, shrouding bush and tree and stone. Above the sky was clear, delicately tinted with the colors of dawn. Beside Isabeau the fire still leapt and crackled, though most of the log had fallen into cinders. People were crowded around the warmth, sleeping back to back, wherever they could find room. The frosty air hung white before their mouths.

Isabeau saw Meghan's straggly white head rise up from her blankets, Gitâ protesting sleepily beside her. All she could see was the white oval of the old sorceress's face as she turned towards the north.

"Meghan!" she whispered. "Do ye hear it?"

Meghan nodded. "Khan'gharad has called the dragon's name. It has begun."

han'gharad stood alone on the forecastle, staring to the south. Snowflakes fell softly on his horned head, with its long ponytail of coarse white hair.

"What is he doing?" Dide said softly to Lachlan. "I thought he was to call the dragon."

"I imagine he is," Lachlan replied drily. "The dragons speak mind to mind, did ye no' ken?"

"Och, I be naught but a poor jongleur," Dide said with an exaggeratedly rustic accent. "What would I be kenning o' dragons?"

Khan'gharad turned and leapt lightly down to the deck, scorning the stairs. "It is done," he said briefly.

"Thank ye," Lachlan replied.

The Scarred Warrior inclined his head and walked swiftly away to join his comrades, who stood together staring out at the rough waves. Although they fought hard to conceal their emotion, it was clear all the Scarred Warriors were still amazed and disturbed by the sight of so much water.

"What now?" Dide asked.

"We keep on waiting," Lachlan replied. "All we can do is hope the Fairgean think we have fled north into the deep ocean like all the other ships. Under the cover o' darkness, we shall slip out and down the coast to the Isle o' Divine Dread, and attack as planned. We must take them by surprise, else all is lost."

Dide nodded. "And then we can all go home," he said cheerfully. "Och, I tell ye, I canna wait to lie on my back in the warm grass and see blue sky through leaves, and hear birds singing."

"I thought ye'd be wanting a cheery inn with fine whisky and voluptuous barmaids," Lachlan said teasingly.

"Well, I wouldna say 'nay' to that either," the jongleur replied, laughing. "What do ye long for the most?"

Lachlan sobered, looking across at Iseult who stood in silence with the other Scarred Warriors, only the occasional grunt or flicker of fingers to show there was any discourse between them. "Och, I just want to go home," he answered.

The day passed very slowly. Lachlan played chess with the Duke of Killiegarrie, while Dide lounged nearby, strumming his guitar. The others tossed dice or played cards or trictrac, huddled about the table in the smoky galley, occasionally warming their hands at the glowing brazier. Iseult and the Scarred Warriors polished their weapons and practiced *ahdayeh*. Maya sat up in the forecastle, just above the stag figurehead with its spreading antlers. Her arms were about her knees, her long black hair whipping about her face. One wrist was manacled to the railing. Nearby a soldier stood, smoking his pipe morosely and wishing the Fairge had chosen a warmer place to sit out the day. He was the seventh guard assigned to the former Banrìgh and his ears were stuffed with wax, in the hope that would make him impervious to her charms. It had not prevented the previous six from trying to set her free.

The royal fleet had spent the past week harrying the Fairgean, making it seem as if they were flinging themselves in one last desperate attempt to crush the seafaeries. Then they had turned and fled north, chased by fifty sea-serpent riders and their warriors. Iain and Lachlan had together conjured a thick sea mist and the *Royal Stag* had slipped away under its cover. Later, Stormwing, the Rìgh's keen-sighted gyrfalcon, had reported the royal fleet was safe in deep waters, having lost only one more ship to a sea-serpent. The *Royal Stag* had spent the night anchored behind a steep, bare rock, everyone on board trying hard not to show their trepidation.

The sun was sinking low in the sky when a warning was called. "Dragons!" the lookout cried, unable to conceal the terror in his voice. "The dragons come."

Lachlan leapt to his feet, the chessboard flying. His eyes were brilliant with excitement. "They've heeded the call!" he cried. "We canna fail now!"

Everyone clambered up the stairs and onto the deck. It had been a fair, cold day, with the seas the calmest in months. Icicles in the shrouds clinked like little chimes. Icebergs floated about, some towering into huge blue peaks, others flat and broken. High in the sky were seven dragons, flying in a wedge formation, the sun glinting off their bronze backs.

"The seven sons o' the queen-dragon," Khan'gharad said. "The fighting arm."

Straight and swift as an arrow, the wedge of dragons glided down to the ship. As their immense shadows fell upon the men, many dropped to their knees, cowering in instinctive terror.

Three times the dragons circled the ship, then six of them soared away into the sky again. The leader of the wedge, the largest of them all, landed lightly upon the tip of the crag, coiling his long body round and round the rock. His silken scales were dark, metallic bronze on his back and limbs, but pale cream on his throat and belly. His head and neck were crowned with a sharp, serrated crest. The dragon rested his huge angular head upon his claws, the tip of his tail lashing the sea into a white commotion. The *Royal Stag* rocked wildly, the prostrate men sent sliding from one side to another. The ice in the shrouds fell like little translucent daggers, smashing apart once they hit the wood. A few men cried aloud as slivers of ice sliced into their flesh.

So, Khan'gharad, he who calls himself dragon-laird, ye dare to call our name?

Khan'gharad knelt, giving the formal Khan'cohban gesture of deep homage and respect. *Greetings, Great One. I thank thee for answering so swiftly and with such force.*

My mother the queen remembers thee with great affection, the dragon replied. *Now that our little sister has laid her own egg and the perpetuation of the dragons seems assured, she is glad indeed and so feels no anger at your temerity in calling her name.*

I am glad of that, Khan'gharad replied, bowing his head.

Last time our name was called, we took great pleasure in flaming and feasting without restraint. This so-called Pact of Peace that binds the dragons to hunting only in the high mountains and only four-footed creatures irks us greatly. Our diet is bland and without spice or variety. Last time we snacked gladly on human flesh. Is it the flesh of the sea-dwellers that thou now wishest us to taste?

The dragons see both ways along the thread of time, Khan'gharad answered. *It is clear to me that thou knowest what we wish of thee.*

Your thoughts and desires are clear to us indeed, the dragon replied. *Are they clear to yourself?*

I think so.

Ask us then. We shall do whatever thou askest, but thou should take care in the asking.

Khan'gharad nodded. He turned to Lachlan and said, "The dragon says they will help us in whatever way we please but warns us that we had best take care in what we ask for."

Lachlan was staring up at the dragon with mingled awe and trepidation, never having seen one of the great winged creatures before. At Khan'gharad's words he frowned, his wings rustling. "Tell the dragon that we wish to destroy the island o' the Priestesses o' Jor and all that live within," he said carefully. "We wish to free Carraig from the rule o' the Fairgean and win peace in the land. Can the dragons help us in this?"

Khan'gharad turned back to the dragon, who was licking the inside of one wrist with a slender, supple tongue the vivid blue of a summer sky. He raised his immense head and opened wide his topaz-colored eyes. All the men on board stared into them helplessly, hypnotized.

I hear the words of thy winged king, the dragon said and this time everyone on board heard his voice, deep in their minds. *Certainly we can flame the smoking island of those that called themselves Priestesses of Jor. We shall do so with pleasure. The second request is more difficult. We see many possibilities branching forward from this one night. The calling of our name has hewed many branches from this tree of possibilities but new ones sprout forth. All thy destinies and the destiny of the whole land lie in the hands of many. What one does or does not do affects all. Even we the dragons cannot foretell what shall be the consequence. Each moment that passes spins those many strands into one thread and soon the moment when thy destiny can be altered will come and pass . . .*

The dragon slowly shut his eyes and the men stirred and murmured among themselves, the trance broken. They had all moved together to the point nearest the dragon, drawn irresistibly by the charm of his gaze. Now they stepped back, and looked everywhere but at each other or the dragon, shaken by the visions they had seen in the dragon's eyes. Worlds turning, stars spinning, an immense dark emptiness . . .

The shadow of the crag had fallen over the ship. The sun had sunk low in the sky. The waves were bright with the color of the sunset, the icebergs radiant and blue. Lachlan rubbed his eyes, shook out his wings. He found it hard to focus his mind, the echo of the dragon's voice still reverberating through his body, the visions he had seen still dazzling his mind. He thought he had seen his own death, had watched the Lodestar tumble from his hand and sink below the waves, its light quenched. He thought he had seen a blaze of light, a searing pain, as he was reborn.

"The sun is almost gone," Khan'gharad said, affected the least by the dragon's voice. "We must set sail soon."

Lachlan pushed away the troubling mind-images. Looking about him, he saw all the men looked bewildered, as if they had come out of a dark tunnel into glaring light. He seized the captain's shoulder and shook him vigorously. "Let us prepare to sail!"

As the ship sailed out into the ocean, they saw a family of seals basking in the last rays of sun on the side of a huge, flat iceberg. The pups were frisking about and playing, and momentarily Lachlan wished the twins were here to see them. Then he remembered where they sailed and was glad his family were many miles away.

With his hands cupping the Lodestar, he brought mist rising up out of the sea, wreathing the ship's masts and sails and hiding it from view. Maya was crouched against the rail, her face very white, and Lachlan wondered what vision she had seen in the dragon's eye.

Stormwing flew ahead of them, scanning the sea with his far-reaching gaze. As they approached the little island, he flew back to land on Lachlan's wrist. All was quiet, he reported. The seas were empty.

It was growing late when they at last slipped silently up to the Isle of Divine Dread. They dared not drop anchor, for Maya had told them sound traveled much faster and further under water and they knew how acute were the Fairgean's hearing. Instead they furled the mainsails and let the boat drift, keeping her steady with tiller and spritsail alone.

Maya's chains were unfastened and she stood up, her proud face as pale and expressionless as if it had been carved from marble. Lachlan gripped her wrist. "Betray us and your daughter dies," he said harshly.

She raised an eyebrow, her nostrils flaring wide. "Betray ye or no', we shall both die tonight, MacCuinn."

He let go her wrist, breathing heavily, his wings raised high and held stiffly. "No' if ye do your part." His voice was uneasy.

Contemptuously she undid the fastening of her robe and let it fall to the ground, standing naked before them all. Even in the darkness and the mist, her beauty was enough to make every man there catch his breath. Then she turned and dived from the deck. Her body cleaved through the water with barely a splash. For a moment there was silence, and they all peered over the deck anxiously. Suddenly the dark water was broken by the flip of a frilled tail, then Maya rose from the waves in a high leap that took her clear of the sea. For an instant they could see her in all the strangeness of her sea-shape, the graceful curving tail and the flowing fins. Then she had dived back into the water, resurfacing some distance away, her black hair plastered close to her face and shoulders.

Very gently they lowered two glass jars down into the sea, taking care not to bump them against the sides of the ship. Maya seized the ropes that bound them and dived again. For fifteen minutes they waited in silence, all apprehensive, then at last the Fairge's head broke through. Two more jars were lowered, then twenty minutes later, two more. At last all eighteen of the jars had been safely pushed into place and Maya was dragged from the sea, shivering with cold and exhaustion, breathing with such difficulty that all were concerned. She was wrapped up in blankets, then given a steaming cup of herbal tea to drink.

She looked up at Lachlan, her teeth chattering against the cup. "I canna believe it," she said. "I'm still alive. The jars did no' break. I'm still alive."

He nodded. "Ye did well," he said begrudgingly. "I thank ye."

"Kani, hear us, hear us, Kani, Kani, hear us, hear us, Kani, Kani, hear us, hear us, Kani."

On and on the priestesses chanted, their voices echoing all through the dark chamber. Fand stood before the Nightglobe of Naia, swaying slightly as she poured all her strength and her energy into the great sphere of wavering green light before her. She could see the huge bulbous eyes of the two viperfish, their flickering bodies, as they swam back and forth in time to the chanting.

"Hear us, Kani," she said. "Give us the power. Give us the power promised. Hear us, Kani. Give us the power. Give us the power promised. Hear us, Kani. Draw down the comet's power. Draw down the comet's fire. Hear us, Kani. Give us the power. Give us the power promised."

"Come to our call, Kani, goddess of fire, goddess of dust, rise to our bidding, Kani, goddess of volcanoes, goddess of earthquakes, come to our call, Kani, Kani, rise to our bidding, Kani, Kani, come to our call, Kani, Kani . . ."

The mist had drifted away, released from Lachlan's will. He stood on the forecastle, staring at the island before him. Its cliffs rose steeply from the sea, culminating in a sharp peak. A little haze drifted about the peak, but otherwise all was bathed in the light of the two moons which hung fat and bright above the horizon. High overhead the comet soared. Lachlan gripped his hands together to stop

them trembling and nodded at the captain, who shouted
the order. "Fire!"

The cannons all along one side of the *Royal Stag*
boomed. Smoke billowed out. There was a distant crash
and they saw debris fly up as the cannonballs slammed
into the island. The dragons zoomed down, shooting long
plumes of fire. As they passed and rose, the order was
given again. "Fire!"

Again and again the cannons boomed. The dragons
rose and dived in a beautiful, elaborate dance of fire and
smoke. A sudden loud explosion. Green fire shot up out
of the water, raining hissing sparks down onto the tranquil waters. Flames rose and ran out, following the
sparks. Suddenly another explosion, another fountain of
green fire. Soon the island was ringed in flame, immense
boulders crashing down the cliffs as the rock shuddered
under the impact of the explosions. The dragons bugled
triumphantly, swooping down towards the burning sea.
Their scales shone like molten gold.

Upon the *Royal Stag*, Maya stood in the prow of the
ship. The flames danced upon her mother-of-pearl skin,
making it shimmer. There was a look of fierce, brooding
exultation on her face. "So the priestesses die," she said.

"Come to our call, Kani, goddess of fire, goddess of dust,
rise to our bidding, Kani, goddess of volcanoes, goddess
of earthquakes, come to our call, Kani, Kani . . ."

Fand was incandescent with power. She could feel it
racing through her, pouring out of all the pores and ori-
fices of her body, blazing like a river of molten lava. The
name of the goddess echoed in her ears. She screamed it
with fury, with passion, with despair. "Come to our call,
Kani! Give us the power, Kani! Hear us, Kani, Kani,
Kani! Hear us, Kani, Kani, Kani!"

Fire leapt high. She was choking on smoke. Her lungs burnt.

"Kani, Kani, Kani!" she screamed. "Give us the power!"

The power drove down through her hands into the nightglobe, down through her feet into the ground. The earth rocked. The water in the giant Nightglobe of Naia surged from side to side. The viperfish were flung about, tails flopping. Someone screamed. The ground lurched again. Fand was flung to her knees. The nightglobe rocked and then fell from its crystal pedestal, smashing on the ground. Water crept out from the broken shards of glass, met fire and hissed away into steam. The giant viperfish thrashed about on the ground. Crouched down, Fand stared at them. Under her hands and knees the rock was heaving about as if it were a mere crust over an ocean. An ocean of fire. Dimly she became aware of more screaming. She could not move. She was nothing but a husk.

The ship was rocked by waves. From the peak of the island they saw a sudden arc of orange fire, a belch of black smoke. The dragons soared away, bugling. The tail of the comet suddenly flared brightly, a trail of sparks bursting free. As the waves leapt high, Lachlan was flung to his knees.

"What's happening?" he cried.

"The island! The volcano! It's erupting!"

"The spell!" Iseult cried. "They've harnessed the comet magic."

A bitter sense of failure filled Lachlan. He could have lowered his head and wept. Ashes and cinders were showering down upon them, they were all choking in the thick black smoke. Flames danced everywhere. The rocking of the waves was bringing the seafire racing towards them, and through all the smoke they could see the volcano spitting more flame.

"But . . . the priestesses?" he coughed.

Maya was on her knees, white tracks of tears running down her soot-blackened face. "They must have been somewhere else. They must have been at the Isle o' Gods."

Lachlan spread his wings and was upon her in one single fluid movement, seizing her in his strong hands. "Ye mean . . . we . . . bombarded the wrong island!" He could hardly speak for coughing.

"How was I to ken?" she wept, shrinking away from him. His face was dark and terrible. Fire framed him in fierce leaping colors, his wings all gilded with gold and red.

Iseult shouted. The sails were on fire. The boards smoked as falling cinders fell upon them like hail. Men were flailing helplessly from side to side as the ship plunged up and down in the savage waves. Water crashed over the bow, sweeping them all down the deck. Someone was swept overboard, screaming as he fell into the seafire reaching up to devour them all.

"No!" Lachlan shouted. He sprang to his feet. With one swift movement he dragged the Lodestar from his belt. Silver light leapt to life in its heart. They were all flooded with its radiance. For an instant the lurid red of the spouting volcano was blotted out, then suddenly the ship surged forward and up into the sky. Everyone was flung to the deck. One man fell screaming down, down into the sea. Only Lachlan kept his feet, holding the Lodestar high before him. Where he had been outlined in glaring red before, now the clean line of his face, the curls blowing away from his face, the beautiful shape of his wings, all were bathed in pure silver light.

The soaring flight of the ship steadied. Dazed, the men got to their feet. They were high above the world. The ship's charred sails billowed out, the masts outlined in frosty starshine. On either side the dragons flew, their wings translucent in the blazing light of the Lodestar. Below them stretched the sea, the red light of the spouting volcano and the ring of raging seafire reflected for miles.

They saw the waters withdrawing from the land. Slowly the harbor floor was laid bare, fish flopping desperately among the shells and seawrack. Out to sea, the family of seals was swimming desperately in circles, the pups struggling to keep afloat in the drag of the retreating water.

Back and back the sea retreated, sucking itself up into a high wave. From the deck of the flying ship they saw it glistening and heaving, its back stained red with the reflections of the blazing island. It seemed to hover for a moment, a hundred feet tall, then with a shuddering, roaring sound, it swept forward.

The ship soared higher. The crew felt the slap of spray on their faces. There was a dreadful cracking sound. They all hung over the rail of the ship, watching in awed horror as the wave crashed down upon the shore. Kinnaird was engulfed, the raging water funnelled by the two high cliffs into a raging torrent that raced over the shore and forest, drowning it in seconds. On and on the torrent poured, tossing now with uprooted trees.

"How high can it go?" Lachlan cried. "Oh Eà, please let them be high enough."

The flood hit a high ridge and was flung up, surging and tossing. The ship leapt forward, driven by Lachlan's fear. Three hundred feet above the flood, it soared in the tidal wave's wake, while far above the flaming tail of the comet slowly dwindled away.

Isabeau sat at the edge of the ridge, her staff lying against her lap, staring out into the night. It was so clear she could see a long way, fields of soft snow falling away below her. The loch glimmered with moonlight and the night sky above was strangely bright.

It had been another long day. She was weary unto death. They had climbed all day, though the snow was so deep they had not climbed far. Many fell and could not rise again. Those strong enough lifted them and carried them, or they were slung on to the backs of ponies.

As they had walked, the witches had chanted the Candlemas rites, for it was the last day of winter, the beginning of the season of flowers. None had dared take the time to hold the rites as it was usually done, with a circle of power around a fire.

"In the name o' Eà," they chanted, "our mother and our father, thee who is Spinner and Weaver and Cutter o' the Thread; thee who sows the seed, nurtures the crop, and reaps the harvest; by the virtue o' the four elements, wind, stone, flame and rain; by virtue o' clear skies and storm, rainbows and hailstones . . ."

As they chanted, others in the procession took up the incantation until the valley had rung with their voices. *"Oh, Eà, turn your bright face upon us this day."*

At last they had reached a wide valley where a loch stretched out, the Spine of the World reflected perfectly in its smooth, tranquil waters. Although the sun was setting, they had walked round its shores, climbing beyond it in darkness, fighting their way over rocks and through trees until they came to a wide clearing under a high cliff.

They could not go forward and they could not go back, so there they stopped. No one had said much as they had eaten their meager meal. They were either high enough, or they were not.

Now Isabeau waited for the hour of her birth to come and pass, midnight on the eighth day of the comet. As she waited, she prayed.

Suddenly, far away, she saw a huge red flare. All her nerves jangled. She leapt to her feet. "Meghan!"

The far-distant flame leapt and danced. Then Isabeau heard, not with her ears but with her mind, the bugling of dragons. The comet sprouted a fiery tail. She knew, without doubt, that some great act of magic had been done.

"Oh, no!" Meghan cried. "No, no! The comet spell!"

The ground beneath their feet shuddered. The tranquil waters of the loch stirred. They heard the lap, lap of waves. Again the ground heaved, more violently than before. A log fell from the bonfire, scattering sparks. Waves splashed upon the pebbly beach, then surged up towards their camp.

Then they heard, terrifyingly, a distant roar. Everyone sprang to their feet. There were screams and shouts of fear. The roar came closer and closer. People tried to scramble up the cliff or ran into the forest, searching for a way to climb higher. Some swung themselves into trees.

Isabeau leant forward. Moonlight glinted off high, tossing waves. She could not believe how high the water was, or how fast it traveled. Closer and closer the waves surged. They crashed against the cliff where they had left the carts, which were flung high into the air. Huge trees were thrown about like matchsticks. The flood was slowed, but not halted, by the cliff. Raging, it swept up the hill towards them.

Then Isabeau saw a white-sailed ship soaring through

the sky, seven dragons swooping about it. She stared, unable to believe her eyes. It shone like a star, like a ghost ship. She pointed, a hoarse croak the only sound she could make. Other people saw the ship too, crying aloud in amazement.

"It's the *Royal Stag*!" Gwilym cried. "That's the Lodestar that shines so. The Rìgh lives!"

There were cheers of joy. Though some people still ran in panic, most stopped to stare and wonder. The waters of the loch surged up around Isabeau's feet, wetting the hem of her dress, but she paid no attention, her face transfigured.

Slowly the ship floated down until it was resting on the breast of the hill. There it lay askew, the sails drooping as the wind of its magical flight died away. The dragons swooped about, bugling, then soared away, disappearing behind clouds.

Irresistibly Isabeau's eyes swung back to the flood. Still it rushed towards them, gathering itself again into a high black wave, crested with whipping foam. Then Lachlan flew up from the deck of the ship and raised high the Lodestar. Its silver light fell upon the raging floodwaters, dropping a mantle of calmness upon it. Unbelievably, the rearing crest curled over and dropped, drew back, rushed forward, drew back once again.

People were clambering down the side of the ship. Isabeau stared through the misty darkness, the pulse in her throat galloping. "I see Iseult—and Dide! They're alive!" she cried. Feeling a rush of joy and relief that almost undid her, she turned, laughing, to embrace Meghan.

The Keybearer stood in a circle of six Mesmerdean. Mist rose up to her knees and flowed about her white head. The marsh-faeries were leaning over the old sorceress, eagerness on their strange, beautiful faces, their claws stretched out. She was standing calmly, her hand cupping the Key which hung around her neck. On her shoulder Gitâ stood on his hind paws, shrieking in distress.

"No!" Isabeau screamed. "Meghan!"

Meghan turned towards her, holding up her hand. The Mesmerdean swayed away. Isabeau stumbled forward, falling to her knees. "No, Meghan, we need ye! No, please . . ."

Meghan took her hand. Gently she said, "Ye do no' need me, Isabeau. Trust in yourself." She pulled the weeping girl to her and kissed her forehead lovingly, smoothing back the damp red curls. "I have faith in ye. Ye must have faith in yourself too."

"No!" Isabeau wept. She could hear a rushing sound as another wave raced up to engulf them. She heard screams and cries of fear. She took no heed, clinging to Meghan's hand. Spray lashed their bodies, water swirled about Isabeau's body, shockingly cold. Silver light cut through the mist, turning the spray to diamonds. Isabeau buried her head against Meghan's side.

Meghan lifted the Key over her head. She opened Isabeau's left hand and closed her two scarred fingers and thumb over the talisman. Isabeau gave a little cry. Electricity ran up her arm, banishing the icy cold of the water.

"I give ye the Key o' the Coven," Meghan said gravely. "Ye must guard it well and carry it with wisdom and courage and compassion, until it is time for ye to pass it on."

Isabeau stared at her, bewildered. Her head ached, her pulse was thundering.

"Take it," Meghan said.

"But . . . why me?"

"Ye are the one," Meghan answered. "I've known it for a long time."

Isabeau looked down at the Key. Nestled into her palm, the delicate shape of star and circle burnt into her skin like a brand. Very slowly she lifted it and hung it around her neck. The talisman hung between her breasts, at the place where her ribs sprang out, the center of her breathing. She felt her pulse steady and deepen, felt the Key throb slightly as if it too had a heart. She looked back at Meghan.

The sorceress looked very frail. The gusts of spray had plastered her snow-white hair to her skull. Isabeau realized water was washing around their knees. Meghan smiled at her rather tremulously. "Eà, ever-changing life and death, transform us in your sight, open your secrets, open the door."

"In ye we shall be free o' darkness without light, and in ye we shall be free o' light without darkness. For both shadow and radiance are yours, as both life and death are yours." Isabeau took up the chant, though her voice wobbled alarmingly.

Meghan turned and stepped willingly into a Mesmerd's embrace. With her hair whipping about her face, her vision obscured by tears and seaspray, Isabeau saw the Mesmerd bend its alien face over the wild white head of the sorceress. "No!" she screamed.

It was too late. Meghan had crumpled. Isabeau threw herself at the marsh-faery, beating her hands against its hard shell, screaming incoherently. It ignored her, tenderly laying Meghan's limp body down on the ground. The waves washed over her face. Isabeau fell to her knees beside her, dragging Meghan into her arms. The old witch's limbs flopped about like a rag doll's. She was as light as a feather, as if all her bones were hollow, as if she was nothing but withered skin and straggly hair.

With startling suddenness, the Mesmerdean all darted into the air and were gone. Isabeau hardly noticed. She rocked back and forth, keening, stroking the white straggles of hair from Meghan's tranquil face, kissing the thin, limp hand. Meghan's rings cut into her cheek but Isabeau did not notice. "No, no, no," she wept. She kissed Meghan's sunken cheek, then bent her head till it rested on Meghan's body. Though the spray pounded upon her back and water crept ever higher around her, she did not move.

Gitâ crouched on Meghan's throat, his head buried beneath her chin. He keened softly. The sea sucked at Isabeau's strength. She realized she and Meghan were being dragged down the slope. She looked up.

Lachlan was standing waist-deep in water, the Lodestar held high. The sea was threatening to drag him under but Iseult was clinging to him with both hands. It was clear the Rìgh was exhausted. He did not let the Lodestar drop, though, and again its silvery radiance calmed the waves. Slowly the water sank back.

Everywhere people were struggling to climb above the waves. Some had failed and their dead bodies bobbed about in the water. Others were clinging together, helping each other keep their feet, or hanging from the branches of the trees. The *Royal Stag* was almost afloat, water lifting her keel from the ground, then dropping it down again.

"The bairns!" Isabeau suddenly cried. "Oh, Eà!"

A dark figure wading desperately through the water turned at the sound of her voice. "Beau!"

"Dide!"

He caught her up in his arms. "Meghan," she sobbed. "The bairns!"

"The bairns are safe. I lifted them up to the deck o' the ship. What's wrong with Meghan?"

"She's dead. The Mesmerdean killed her, the demons!"

Dide wasted no time on questions. "We must get ye to safety too. The sea retreats, and then surges up again, and what's more the loch has risen high, trapping us on this little ridge. If we are no' careful we could all still drown."

"Meghan . . ."

"I'll bring her body to the ship. Quickly!"

With Dide cradling the sorceress's frail body in his arms, they stumbled through the mud and sea wrack to the ship, hearing a dreadful roar as the sea again began to surge towards them. "I do no' ken how much longer my master can keep the sea away," Dide cried. "Already he has worked much magic tonight."

"The flying ship . . ."

"Aye, is it no' a wonder? Up ye go!"

Dide gave her a strong boost up and Isabeau caught a rope and clambered up the side of the ship. The Key thumped against her breastbone. Hands caught her under the arms and hauled her over the rail and she fell down to the deck. Dide passed up Meghan's limp body, Gitâ clinging tightly to her breast, wet and shivering.

Maya knelt beside Isabeau. "Is that ye, Red?"

"Aye," Isabeau said, trying to catch her breath. She lost it again as Donncan and Bronwen flung themselves upon her, both crying with fear and relief. She hugged them closely, saying sharply, "The babes?"

"They're here," Donncan cried. "Maura is with them."

Isabeau could hardly breathe in her relief. She saw the dark shape of the bogfaery crouched against the mainmast, her arms tight about the twins. Both of the little children had their faces pressed against her skirt in terror.

Isabeau scrambled to her feet. With great clouds pouring in from the north it was hard to see a thing, but she peered over the side anyway. Racing towards them was another great wall of water, curving up and over, spume flinging from its crest. Tree branches tore free, were sucked down again. Then Isabeau saw something that made her shrink back in horror.

"The Fairgean! They come!"

Riding the curve of the wave were a hundred sea-serpents, their heads held high out of the water, a Fairgean warrior astride their necks. Behind them leapt horse-eels, swollen to immense size, their poisonous crests raised. Fairgean warriors swam behind, carried at frightening speed by the force of the wave. All carried spears or tridents.

Just below the ship, Lachlan stood, his wings spread defiantly. The light of the Lodestar shone through the darkness, glinting off scales and jeweled tridents, highlighting the cruel curve of tusk. Behind him Iseult stood, raising high her little crossbow. Isabeau had never seen a more gallant or futile gesture.

The Lodestar sang. Silver radiance spread out from Lachlan's hand. Once again, the fury of the waves was calmed. Though the wave broke down upon the land in a storm of white foam, it fell short of the ridge where Lachlan stood, the last ridge before the cliff below which all his people cowered. The ship rocked as water swept under its lopsided keel. Water swirling up to his armpits, the Rìgh staggered.

The Fairgean fought their way through the tumult of water. One leant down from the neck of his sea-serpent, roaring with rage, as the beast struggled to stay afloat.

"My father!" Maya cried. "Oh, by Jor, it's my father!"

Isabeau was frozen in horror. She saw the jeweled trident flash as the King raised it, and then it was flung across the foaming waters, straight through Lachlan's breast. The Lodestar fell from his hand, its light winking out as it fell into the water. Iseult screamed and flung herself down beside him, but Lachlan's body was dragged away from her, sucked under by the force of the retreating wave. With the loss of the Lodestar, no one could see anything but the spray-swept darkness, but they all heard Iseult's desperate cry. From all across the narrow ridge of land, more cries of horror and despair rang out, then they heard a triumphant ululation as the Fairgean swept forward.

"*Dai-dein!*" Donncan screamed. Before Isabeau could stop him, the little boy launched himself into the air. Isabeau lunged after him, trying to catch him, but he had flown down to the water's edge, his small form disappearing into the darkness. Then she felt a quick movement beside her. Again she was too late. Bronwen had dived after him. Isabeau heard the slight splash as her body cleaved through the retreating water. Then nothing.

"Bronny!" she and Maya screamed together. "No!"

Desperately the soldiers sought to keep the sea-warriors off. Regardless of their background, whether human, Khan'cohban or faery, the soldiers had all been raised with a superstitious fear of the sea, and so not only could none of them swim but they had to overcome their natural terror at the sight of so much water. Iseult was searching frantically through the water, staggering as the waves dragged at her legs. Duncan Ironfist took a blow that was meant for her on the blade of his claymore, striking back with ferocious strength. "My lady!" he cried. "We need ye!"

Tears choking her, Iseult raised her crossbow and sent an arrow whizzing through the breast of a sea-warrior about to strike down the MacSeinn. Again and again she wound on the little bow and fired, taking careful aim despite the clamor of fighting.

The waves came swirling back again, bringing with them sea-serpents that seized soldiers in their mouths and tore them asunder. Duncan Ironfist leapt onto the neck of one and plunged his claymore between its shoulders. It rolled, throwing him high into the air. He landed with a splash in the water and for an instant sank, but managed to regain his feet. Sea-warriors converged upon him and he fought bare-handed until Iseult flew to his side, throwing him her dagger. Back-to-back they fought, the drag of the retreating waves threatening to pull their feet from under them. The night rang with the clash of arms, the cries of rage and pain.

Maya was standing, her hands clenched on the rail, staring into the darkness. Isabeau got to her feet, hunched around herself, a feeling of bitter despair in her heart. Even with her keen eyesight she could see nothing but tossing waves, foam, the swift flash of scale and sword and trident. She sought for her powers, but her staff had been lost with the first wave and she was sick at heart. She did not know what to do. She could not call the Lodestar to her, for none but a MacCuinn could touch it. She could not feel Lachlan's mind in all the surging water. With an enormous effort she thrust away her grief and horror, rolling it all into a great ball of fire which she sent whizzing at the head of one of the sea-serpents. It screamed and dived back into the waves, extinguishing the flame immediately. Darkness fell again.

Suddenly, out of the darkness, a silver light began to glow. It spread and rose, bubbling up out of the water. Isabeau stared, amazed, frightened. Larger and larger it grew, and then Bronwen leapt out of the water, the shining Lodestar held high in her hand. Her scaled body streamed with glittering light, diamond-bright water cascading from her flowing tail. She landed back in the water with a great splash, and then crawled out, transformed back into her land-shape. There, on the very edge of the surging sea, one foot in the water, one foot on the land, she raised high the Lodestar.

Again its magical song rang out. The sea seethed and churned, black branches tossed about. For a moment everyone stood still, staring, wondering. In the bright light, all could see the strain on Bronwen's face. The Lodestar seemed too heavy for her. Her webbed hand shook, the sea surged up around her waist.

Then Donncan flew down, his golden wings luminous. He landed lightly beside her and raised both hands to cup the Lodestar, helping her hold it high. The song swelled out, stronger than ever, and the sea swirled away. Everywhere cheers erupted, and the fighting grew more intense. Slowly, inexorably, the Greycloaks began to push the Fairgean back.

The Fairgean king spun on his webbed foot and began to advance on the two children, his tusked face ferocious with rage and hatred. In one hand he hefted his trident. In the other was a long dagger. He used it to kill one soldier who tried desperately to stop him, and then slashed the throat of another. Bronwen and Donncan saw him looming over them and cowered back, the light of the Lodestar failing. Darkness engulfed them once more.

ide waded through the icy water, the waves up to his waist, his dagger in his hand. Behind him the battle raged but he paid it no mind, calling, "Master? Master?"

Surely Lachlan could not be dead? Surely not? He searched desperately with his mind, but there was no spark of consciousness, nothing of the close link the two men had shared all their lives. Tears ran down his face.

Suddenly he saw, struggling to stay afloat in the deep water, a few white, desperate faces. He splashed towards them, fighting to keep from being dragged under by the swirling sea. There Lachlan floated, his head held out of the water by three pairs of young arms. There was Johanna, barely managing to keep her own head out of the water, Finn, a little black cat clinging desperately to her head and almost pushing her under, and Dillon, his face contorted with the effort. Heart pounding with joy, Dide dogpaddled up to them, sliding his own arm under his master's shoulder.

"Is he alive?"

Johanna nodded, saying tersely, "Just." Her head went under and Finn hauled her up again, letting all of Lachlan's weight sag into Dide's arms to do so. Lachlan was heavy, dressed as he was in leather armor, and with his great wings sodden. Dide went under himself and only managed to come up with a superhuman effort.

He swallowed water. "We . . . have to get him . . . to shore," he gasped.

"The rip is too strong," Finn said despairingly. "We've been trying and trying."

Dide could feel it dragging them back. The shore seemed a long way away. He peered through the darkness, dreading another big wave, but the sea seemed to be slowly withdrawing. There had been light before, but now it was gone again. He could see nothing.

Suddenly the waves surged up and slapped him in the face. Dide felt something silky-scaly brush against his leg. He kicked out frantically. He had dropped his dagger when he had seized Lachlan's shoulders. He was helpless now, unable to even punch out.

Then something rose up right beside him. He felt smooth, scaled arms hold him up, felt the unbearable drag of Lachlan's weight taken from him. For a moment he was giddy with the relief of it, and then he kicked back, desperate with fear. He could hear Johanna crying out, hear splashing and kicking, then he, and Lachlan with him, was being towed at great speed towards the shore.

For a moment Dide continued to fight, then the Fairge locked one arm about his throat, immobilizing him as the oxygen was cut off from his lungs. Dide hung helpless, red lights pulsing in his eyes; then, unbelievably, he was dragged onto the shore, Lachlan limp beside him. In the darkness all he could see was the tusked face of a Fairge close to his, something round and dark hanging down onto its smooth chest. The Fairge made some gesture of reassurance, then plunged back into the sea. In a few moments Johanna and Finn were both towed to safety, coughing and retching.

"What?" Dide said dazedly.

Finn was on all fours beside him, vomiting into the mud. It was bitterly cold. They all shivered as the frosty air penetrated their wet clothes. They were at the far curve of the cliff, well away from the battle that raged around the stranded ship.

Johanna knelt beside Lachlan, feeling his pulse. "I think we've lost him," she sobbed. "Och no, I think we've lost him."

"Tòmas," Finn said. "We need Tòmas." She scrambled to her feet and set off into the darkness at a lurching run. Dide leant over Lachlan, weeping, gripping his slack hand. Johanna began to push down upon the Rìgh's chest, and a great gush of water flooded out of his mouth. Just then the Fairge came staggering out of the water, carrying Dillon in his arms. The sea-faery fell to his knees beside them, and laid Dillon down amidst the wreckage of the flood. Dillon was limp, his eyes closed.

"Oh, no," Johanna cried. "No' Dillon too!"

As the light of the Lodestar failed, both Isabeau and Maya screamed in horror. As Isabeau dropped clumsily over the side of the boat, she saw Maya plunge past her. She reached the two children only a few heartbeats before her father, holding them back against her.

He stood still, his trident raised menacingly, and said something in the lilting language of the sea people.

Maya answered him, defiance and contempt in every line of her body.

The King answered mockingly and waded closer, his trident raised to throw.

Maya clamped her hands over the children's ears, calling, "Cover your ears, Red! Bairns! Do no' listen!"

For an instant Isabeau did not move and then, comprehending, she flung her plaid about her head. There she crouched, she did not know for how long, the freezing water threatening to drag her forward, blind and deaf and terribly afraid.

A hand grasped her, dragged the plaid away. She flung up her hand, conjuring fire, but closed her fingers at the last moment. It was Maya. "Donncan? Bronny?" Isabeau cried. Then she saw the two children, both holding high the Lodestar once again, silver light blazing up in its heart. Their faces were pale, their eyes shadowed. The white lock at their brows blazed unnaturally white. Isabeau could not say a word. She leant her head against theirs, tears overflowing.

"The King?" she managed to say.

Maya made a gesture with her hand. "Dead," she answered.

Isabeau looked. The King lay just beneath the water, the waves flowing back and forth over his face, his hair drifting like seaweed.

After a long moment, Isabeau said, "What was it that ye said to him?"

"He said, 'I should have torn out your tongue like your mother's.' I answered, 'Yes, ye should have.' He said, 'I shall tear it out for ye now.' I answered, 'I sing this song for my mother.' And then I sang the song o' death."

Isabeau could only stare at her. The song of death was the most terrible and potent of all the songs of sorcery, the most dangerous. Even the Yedda had rarely chosen to sing it, choosing instead the more innocuous song of sleep. It took immense power of will and desire to sing such a song, and not have it recoil, or kill the wrong person.

"Yes," Maya said. "And never have I sung so well. It was a shame none but my father could hear me."

* * *

With the last of his strength Jay dragged Enit's body a little bit higher. The water was up to her breast. He had done his best to keep her head above water, but the waves had come with such ferocity they had both been dragged under again and again. He did not know how much longer he could keep her afloat.

"Jay," she whispered.

"Aye?"

"Ye must . . . stop this terrible fighting. This war . . ." She coughed and swallowed water as a wave slapped her in the face. "Too many deaths . . ."

Another wave crashed over them. Enit was almost dragged out of Jay's arms. He clung to her, kicking desperately, managing to lift his head above the water. A log bashed against him. He flung one arm over it, dragging Enit's head free of the water.

She retched, coughing harshly. "Jay, let me go."

"No!"

"Ye canna . . . save us both. The water . . . too strong. Jay, play the song . . . o' love. Play as I taught ye. Stop . . . the dying."

Another wave hit them. He was dragged under, tumbled over and over. He clutched Enit tightly, felt one of her frail old bones break under his fingers. Somehow they both came to the surface, though Jay's lungs were burning and his arms and legs were trembling so much he thought his strength must fail. Enit hung limply in his arms. He lifted her face desperately. "Enit, Enit!"

Her eyes opened. He could see them shining in the silvery light reflected off the water. "Your viola . . . the *viola d' amore*. It was made to play . . . such a song. Let her . . . sing . . . for me." She gave a little sigh and closed her eyes again.

Though Jay tried and tried, he could not rouse her. Her weight, slight as it was, was too much for him to bear. He could find no pulse or feel no breath rising from her slack mouth. The waves dragged them further and further from the ridge. At last, choking with grief, he let her slide out of his arms and under the water. Then he began to struggle back towards the shore.

"Do as I do," Johanna ordered. "Lean on his chest and pump rhythmically. We must get the water out o' his lungs."

Dazedly Dide obeyed, leaning his weight on Lachlan's chest as she had demonstrated. Johanna then moved across to Dillon, leaning her ear against his chest, feeling for a pulse in his limp wrist. "He still lives. He's very cold."

An icy rain had begun to fall, penetrating straight through their sodden clothes. "We all need to get warm," she said, her voice trembling. Dide turned and looked at the broken tree branches and logs that lay scattered all about them, thrown up by the quakewave. They suddenly dragged themselves together into a great pile which spontaneously burst into flame. The Fairge cried aloud in fear and cowered back.

Dide pumped Lachlan's chest until his arms ached and his head swam. The bonfire burnt strongly, defying the wind and the sleet to warm them all. Then Finn came running out of the darkness, dragging Tòmas with her. He was whiter and thinner than ever, his cerulean blue eyes unnaturally large and bright.

Tòmas knelt beside Lachlan, laying his hands upon the great ragged wound in the Rìgh's chest. They all watched him, tense and expectant. Tòmas raised piteous eyes. "His heart has stopped beating."

"Oh, no," Finn breathed. Dide said nothing.

Tòmas moved his hands to Lachlan's head. He touched his temples, the deep lines scored between his brows. "Maybe . . ." he whispered. He closed his eyes.

For a long moment there was no sound but the clash of arms as the battle raged behind them.

"Look at his hands," Johanna whispered.

Tòmas's hands had begun to glow. Brighter and brighter the light grew until it was incandescent as a star. The ragged edges of the wound slowly closed together and healed, leaving only a small red scar. They saw Lachlan's chest heave.

"Ye've done it!" Dide cried. Finn gave a cheer. Tòmas fell back into Johanna's hands, the blazing light in his hands winking out. Johanna clutched the boy to her, leant over him. Frantically she worked on him, pumping his chest, breathing into his mouth. At last she raised her face, ravaged with grief.

"He's dead!" she cried. "Och nay, my wee laddiekin he's dead!"

Once before Tòmas had saved the Rìgh from death, and in the healing of his terrible wounds had come close to death himself. That time Lilanthe of the Forest had given him a flower of the Summer Tree, the sacred tree of the Celestines, to eat. He had been healed himself, his powers returning greater than ever. There was no flower of the Summer Tree this time. Tòmas the Healer was dead.

Johanna, who had been so calm and sensible throughout the long, terrible night, now broke down completely. She grasped the little boy's thin body close to hers, weeping bitterly. None of them could calm her.

"Come," Dide said. "There is naught we can do for

Tòmas now. We have to get my master to safety. Come, Johanna."

He helped the distraught girl to her feet. She would not let Tòmas go, lifting him as easily as if he were only a babe. "Finn, help her. The only place we can shelter is the ship. Dillon, can ye help me support my master?"

Dillon was trembling in every limb but he clambered to his feet and came to help Dide. To their surprise the Fairge, whom they had all forgotten, rose too, coming and lending them his strength. Together they helped Lachlan to his feet. The Rìgh was dazed and confused, but he managed to stumble forward though the torrential rain, all of them slipping in the mud.

"Who are ye?" Dide asked the Fairge. "Why do ye do this?"

The Fairge shook his head, answering in his own strange, musical language. He was tall and slim, with muscles rippling through his chest and arms, and long black hair that hung down his back. Small white tusks curved up on either side of his strange, lipless mouth, and his wrists and ankles were all braceleted with flowing fins. Another fin, long and flat, curved out of his spine. Around his waist he wore a skirt woven of seaweed and jewels.

"Have ye helped us afore?" Dide asked. "Were ye one o' the Fairgean who saved us from the shipwreck?"

The Fairge glanced at him out of pale, almost colorless eyes and said haltingly. "I swore . . . I would not forget. I . . . true."

With his help, they came round the side of the cliff at last. There was the *Royal Stag*, listing over the side of the hill. Her sails were billowing out in the gale, so that it looked as if she still sailed upon the sea. The hillside was a ruin of broken trees and rocks and dead bodies, all thick with leaves and mud. Although the flood had one again subsided, the sleet fell thickly and large puddles of water were reforming in every dip and sag. Lachlan was so weak he could barely keep his footing in all the debris.

Soldiers and Fairgean warriors fought hand to hand on all sides. Most of the Greycloaks had taken up position on or around the ship. The storm lanterns on deck had been lit, so that the scene was illuminated with flickering golden light. Dide saw Isabeau and Iseult fighting side by side, their red hair unmistakable even when covered in mud and leaves and blood. Duncan Ironfist fought wildly beside the MacSeinn, whose face was livid with hatred and rage. On the deck of the ship crouched Maya, her arms around Donncan and Bronwen, her wet hair all over her face.

Meanwhile, the wind had risen sharply. The gale was so fierce that the witches were unable to use their traditional weapons of fire and air. A ball of flame simply sank away under the deluge of water or was snuffed out by the wind, which raged so strongly that broken branches were flung through the air like spears and trees crashed down in the forest. The witches were only able to use their powers to protect their comrades, deflecting flying branches, pushing aside trident thrusts and dragging the wounded to the ship for the healers to tend.

All this Dide saw in an instant. He halted, looking about for a weapon, wishing he had not dropped his dagger in the flood. Then a band of Fairgean warriors saw them and turned to attack. Suddenly the Fairge beside them gave a high piercing whistle. Out of the lashing rain emerged a band of Fairgean warriors, coming up to their rear, all carrying wicked-looking tridents. Dide felt sick. He motioned the others behind him.

Dillon stepped forward, calling in a high, strange voice, "Come to me, *Joyeuse*. Come!"

Out of the stormy darkness flew his sword. Dillon caught it deftly and crouched low in a fighting stance, the sword pointing unwavering at first one group of warriors, then another. His lips were drawn back in a snarl.

The Fairge beside them gave another high whistle and pointed desperately at the group approaching from the ship, making a thrusting gesture. He then pointed to the other group of Fairgean, and folded his hands and bowed his head.

Dillon frowned but he could not defend against both groups at once. He had to trust the Fairge, who had already helped them so much. Shouting, "For the MacCuinn!" he rushed forward to engage with those attacking from the ship. His sword flashed as he thrust and parried, swiftly killing four of the sea-faeries.

The other warriors came up beside them, ringing around the grey-faced, staggering Rìgh and the two frightened girls. Seeing Dide had only a heavy stick he had seized from the ground, one offered him a dagger of sharpened coral, hilt forward. Dide accepted with a curt nod of thanks. Then the Fairgean reached them and battle was joined.

"Lachlan!" Iseult screamed. She kicked down the Fairge seeking to stab her, and flew up into the air. Nimbly she avoided the spears flung to impale her, soaring above the heads of the fighting men to land lightly beside her husband. They embraced passionately; then dashing the tears from her eyes, Iseult turned to join the others in fighting a way through to the ship. Lachlan seized her axe from her weapons belt and joined in the clash, although he was obviously still weak and disoriented. Finn fought too, though Johanna merely clung to Tòmas's dead body, her eyes blank with shock.

There were too many Fairgean, though. Far too many. The Greycloaks were all exhausted after the long day and night, and they had lost hundreds to the surging sea. Despite their desperation, it seemed as if they must all be overwhelmed.

Suddenly a new sound struck through the cacophony. Deep as the throb of the ocean, passionate as the whisper of a lover, tender as a mother's lullaby, warm as the blaze of a winter fire, a viola's contralto voice wove gold and crimson ribbons of music through the storm.

A lull fell over the fighting. Everywhere faces turned to follow the sound. Up on the cliff a slender figure swayed, a viola held under his chin, his hand wielding the bow weaving the most enchanting song they had ever heard.

"It's Jay," Dide cried. "He plays the song o' love. By Eà's green blood, he plays like an angel!"

Swords feel from nerveless fingers, tridents dropped. Faces that had a moment before been twisted with hate now relaxed, intent upon the music, which was filled with such longing, such pathos, such a heartfelt desire for love and peace and redemption that all who listened were touched to the very core of their being. All were exhausted and traumatized by the long and ugly war. There was not one who had not secretly wished for an end to the fighting, for a return to happier days. Centuries of bitter hatred and misunderstanding were ripped away like an infected scab, allowing a yearning for forgiveness and understanding to well up slowly like clean red blood. Entranced, men and Fairgean alike listened.

Up to her knees in mud, Isabeau felt a stab of pure joy. Tears trickled down her filthy face. She looked about the battlefield, amazed. Some men wept. Many slung their arms about the shoulders of their comrades, their faces alight with joy and delight. Then a small bedraggled figure scrambled to his feet beside Jay. Brun the cluricaun, his fur all matted with mud, lifted his flute to his mouth and joined the song. Pure and silvery, the voice of his flute soared up and up in an exquisite refrain. Many among the Fairgean began to whistle and croon in accompaniment, their flat alien faces alight with emotion, their slim scaled bodies swaying in time to the music.

Dide stood straight, his face transfigured, and lifted up his voice to join the song. Others nearby sang too, though none with the strength and beauty of Dide. The soldiers swayed, humming along, only each other's arms keeping their exhausted, mud-caked bodies upright. Nellwyn the Yedda lifted up her golden voice and Lachlan joined her, though his voice was hoarse and cracked from swallowing so much saltwater. Iseult was kneeling beside Lachlan, her arms about him, her face wet with tears. Johanna and Finn clung together, laughing and weeping at the same time. They too began to sing.

Suddenly another voice joined in, a husky contralto that thrummed with power. Isabeau turned quickly, having heard that voice before. It was Maya. She stood on the tilted deck of the ship, holding herself straight and tall as she sang the song of love. A thrill ran all through Isabeau. She felt the hairs on her body rise. Never had she heard a choir of such heavenly beauty. Never had she felt such an upwelling of love for all about her. She seized Dide's hand and sang along with all of her heart.

Fand crouched on a rocky ledge, pressing her body against the cliff behind her. Her long hair was plastered to her face and she shivered, though not from the cold. A sick horror chilled her through and through.

The Isle of the Gods was drowned. Just below her the sea raged, throwing up huge waves all marbled and streaked with spume. She and Nila used to sit on this ledge, looking across the ruins of the Tower of Sea-singers to the shore. There had once been a wide beach there, with a grey town rising behind high walls. There had once been a green swathe of forest, framed by a spectacular curve of sharp-pointed mountains. Now there was nothing but water. No ruin. No forest. No Isle of the Gods. Nothing but water.

The Priestesses of Jor had all been terrified by the force of the magic they had raised. None had expected their own island to explode into fire, nor for the tremors to rock the land quite so powerfully. None had expected the sea to flood through into the deep, hidden chambers of the gods' own island. The attack of the humans upon their island had roused the volcano to greater fury than any had expected.

After the Nightglobe of Naia had smashed upon the floor, Fand had merely crouched, staring about her, not understanding where she was or what was happening. From the red slit of the Fiery Womb, molten lava had lashed out, killing a handful of priestesses immediately. Again and again it had spat out white-hot sprays of fire. Then the water had begun to rise. In her terror and bewilderment, Fand would have drowned if the High Priestess had not grasped her by the hair and slapped her viciously, three times, across the face.

"Wake, useless girl," she had hissed. "You know the way above ground, to where the humans built their useless tower. Show me!"

Fand had stared at her, frozen in shock and horror as

her memory slowly returned. The Highest had slapped her again. "The magic was too strong. We shall all die. Show me the way!"

So Fand had led the priestesses through the Fathomless Caves to the steps the witches had carved out of rock. It was a perilous journey. The hot springs boiled and seethed, throwing up geysers of steam, and behind them raced the icy sea, forcing its way in through every crack and cavern. The priestesses had had to swim through deep water in many passages, fighting the strength of the dragging water. At last they had crawled up the steps to the old ruin, only to find the sea had risen high all around. They had had to climb the peak, while the sea sucked at their feet. Many young priestesses had been dragged into its wild frenzy and lost.

So here they crouched, Fand and the strongest of the priestesses who had worked their sea-magic to hold back the waves long enough to climb to safety. The Highest had in her hands a round mirror, its surface black and shimmering. She hung over it, muttering and cursing. She was a grotesque creature, squat and strong, with pale gleaming eyes, bulbous like a viperfish, and huge, thick scales. It was rumored that she was incredibly old, kept alive by the blood of pretty young slave-boys, but no one knew the truth. Certainly her strength was alarming. She had almost broken Fand's neck with her slaps, and Fand's swollen jaw now throbbed painfully.

Suddenly the Highest gave a roar of fury. "The King! He Who Was Anointed by Jor! He is dead."

There was a flurry of distress among the priestesses. The Highest rocked back and forth, her heavy face distorted with rage. Suddenly she whipped round and seized Fand by the hair again. Fand shrank back, terrified.

"The humans prevail," the Highest hissed. "We cannot

have made such sacrifices only to lose because of the folly of our late, unlamented king. You must work your foul human magic and raise the storm against them once more. You must lash them with ice and lightning and whirlwind until all of them are dead. Do you hear me?"

Fand was sick to the very depths of her being. She wanted no more of their evil brutality. She did not want to kill anymore.

Faltering, she said, "I cannot. The Nightglobe of Naia is broken."

The Highest pressed her face very close to Fand's. "You may use mine. Am I not as powerful as Naia ever was? Am I not alive now when she is long dead? Use my nightglobe, spawn jelly."

She drew out her nightglobe from under her cloak, and at once the hideous green luminance played all over their faces. Fand leant forward and vomited over the Highest's webbed feet. When she looked up, terribly afraid, the Highest had a sharp dagger in her other hand. "Work your magic, spawn jelly, or I will cut your throat and drink your lifeblood. Then shall I have your magic in my stomach and shall work the spell myself. Do it!"

Weeping, her stomach still heaving, Fand put out her shrinking hands and laid them upon the nightglobe.

High in the sky the storm winds began to rise, gaining height and velocity at an incredible rate. The clouds began to gather closer, bulging at the top, spreading out until they formed the shape of a giant blacksmith's anvil. Lightning streaked out, white-hot, cracking into the ground. Thunder boomed. From the top of the immense black cloud, blue jets of fire burst upwards. Red sprites danced, dangling long green tentacles like enormous jelly-fish.

The wind spun and spun, forming a funnel of twisting, rising air. It swayed forward, spinning faster and faster, sucking up the sea into an immense waterspout, dragging up fallen trees and smashed timbers and throwing them high into the air. A sea-serpent was dragged up, screaming, its long body twisted round and round like a wound rope. Lightning spat out continually, illuminating the immensely high, narrow shape of the twister. Hail began to rattle down, lumps of ice as large as pigeons' eggs. Faster and faster the whirlwind swung and waltzed across the ravaged land.

The last haunting chords of the viola lingered in the air. Jay lifted his bow and slowly opened his eyes. He stared down at the crowd, his face transfigured. They all stared back at him, the entrancing power of his music still holding them in thrall. The spell was broken by Finn, who hurled herself across the clearing and up the cliff face, as quick and nimble as any elven cat. She threw herself upon him, laughing and crying at once. He had to hold his viola and bow high on either side of her to keep them from being crushed as she embraced him fervently, sobbing, "Och, Jay, I always kent ye could do it, I always kent ye could! What a song! Look, the battle is over, the battle is won . . ."

He bent his head and kissed her on the mouth, gently folding his arms about her, the viola and bow crossed behind her back. For the first time in her life, Finn the Cat was rendered silent.

Down on the valley floor, everyone was bewildered and disconcerted. No one knew whether to embrace their enemy or again take up their weapons. A few dour old soldiers found they had their arms slung about the necks of Fairgean warriors and scrambled away, astonished and embarrassed.

Then the slim warrior who wore the black pearl about his neck turned and inclined his head towards Lachlan, his hand on his heart. He ululated, a long, clear, warbling call that echoed and echoed from hill to hill.

"My brother offers you his compliments," Maya said drily.

Lachlan stood still for a moment, leaning heavily on Iseult, then he too laid his hand on his heart and inclined his head, in imitation of the Fairge prince. "Please return mine to your brother," he said curtly. "And ask the sea-warriors to lay down their arms."

Maya sang and whistled and crooned, and the Fairgean listened, their flat scaly faces wary and suspicious. Then the Fairge prince replied, at length.

"No' until ye all lay down yours," Maya translated at last.

"We shall lay them down together," Lachlan said, smiling wearily. He jerked his head, and slowly, distrustfully, all the soldiers and warriors laid down their weapons. They stood, unarmed, in the midst of the wreckage and stared at each other, then a few grim faces cracked into smiles, and a ragged cheer arose.

"Who would've believed it possible?" Lachlan said, shaking his head. He offered his hand to the Fairge prince who looked at it in bafflement and then, urged on by Maya, reached out and clasped it. The cheers rose higher.

Suddenly Isabeau felt a brush of electricity along her arms. All the hairs on her body stood up on end. She looked around and lost her breath in a gasp. Racing up the valley behind them was a storm of such ferocity and speed that she could only stare, lost in awe. High in the sky was an immense black cloud, lit from within by constant flares of lightning. Hanging below it was a spinning funnel of cloud, swaying back and forth, its tail lost in another great cloud of water and debris.

She dragged at Dide's hand, trying to speak but able only to point. At last her voice rose in a scream. "Whirlwind . . . comes!"

The cheering faltered. Screams and shouts rang out. People began to run, to look for somewhere to hide. There was nowhere. Within minutes the twister would be upon them.

"Get down!" Lachlan cried. "Find something to hold onto!"

"Caves!" the MacSeinn called. "The saltpetre mines are nearby. If we could just get to the caves . . ."

"Can ye run?" Lachlan shouted. His voice was almost drowned in the booming thunder. "Show everyone the way. Run!"

Everyone took to their heels, scrambling over the wrack flung up by the quake-waves, screaming in terror. There were many who could not run, however, too badly wounded or too exhausted. They shrieked and cowered down upon the ground.

Lachlan's hand fell to his belt but the Lodestar was not there. "No, no, it's lost! I dropped it!"

"The bairns have it," Isabeau cried. "Bronwen saved it from the sea."

The wind was whipping her matted red curls about. Hail peppered them cruelly. Lachlan spun on his heels and reached one despairing hand towards the ship. The Lodestar flew towards him but the wind caught at it, tossing it about. At last it reached Lachlan's hand but even the effort of calling it had been too much for the Rìgh. He sank down to his knees, his face grey. Iseult crouched beside him, supporting him, as lightning stabbed down from the approaching tornado, striking a tree nearby. It crashed down slowly, and all the ground shuddered.

"He doesna have the strength!" Dide cried. "He canna calm the storm."

Isabeau knelt in the mud, looking up at the twisting funnel of air calculatingly. She knew a great deal about the forces of weather after the last six months of fighting it. She knew there was little chance any of them would survive.

"This is no natural storm," she said quietly. "Can ye no' feel it? There is strong sorcery at work here."

"The Priestesses o' Jor," Dide said with conviction. Like her, he made no attempt to run, watching the funnel of storm race ever closer. "They seek to finish what they started."

"I must stop them," Isabeau said. She quickly began to strip off her clothes.

"What are ye doing?" he cried.

"I'm going to change shape," Isabeau said, dragging her rings off her fingers. "Dide, I do no' ken if I can get there in time, though I will try. Get everyone off the ship! It'll be flung into the air for sure. Try to get everyone away from this exposed ridge. On the far side is a wee dip. Get as many as ye can to lie there."

She took off the Key and thrust it into the pocket of her coat, standing naked in the bitter cold. Hail lashed her bare skin, the wind whipped her hair about. She shut her eyes, clenched her fists and concentrated.

Isabeau knew no bird could fly through that storm and survive. She knew of only one creature that had the strength, the power, the sheer immense size to soar through the whirlwind and live. She imagined herself a great, golden, sinuous creature, with wings as translucent as stretched cloth-of-gold and great cruel claws. She imagined herself with hypnotic eyes the color of her dragoneye jewel, and scales as glossy as silk.

The world rocked about her. She felt a painful stretching of her skin and bones and organs, a terrifying stretching of her consciousness. The young woman that was Isabeau shrank to a mere gutter of flame, deep within the shadowy cavernous mind of the dragon.

She opened her eyes. Dide crouched between her claws, staring at her with dread and awe. Isabeau grinned, feeling her tail begin to lash. She tensed her muscles, preparing to spring into the wind. She heard a high, piercing whistle, and turned her huge, crested head.

The Fairge with the black pearl had flung himself at her claws, whistling shrilly. Isabeau understood every word.

"Please, no! It is Fand who conjures this storm. You must not kill her. You do not understand . . ."

Dragons see both ways along the thread of time. Isabeau bent her head. *The one thou callest Fand conjured the quake-wave that has devastated the land for many hundreds of miles. Now she calls up this whirlwind. Why should I not devour her with my flame?*

"She is my love," he cried.

Every creature that has died this night is loved somewhere, by someone. Why should thy love be spared?

He could not answer. The dragon did it for him.

If I kill her, thou shalt hate us; if I spare her, thou shalt be grateful. If I kill her, sorrow will grow from her death. If I spare her, joy shall grow. These are reasons enough. Besides, thy love suffers in this conjuring, as she has suffered in the past. I will have an end to suffering.

Then Isabeau spread wide her magnificent wings and soared up into the turbulent sky.

Never had her strength been tested more sorely. The

force of the wind was overwhelming. It tore at her wings, buffeted her long, sinuous body, stabbed at her with lightning. Isabeau soared on, using the tornado's own velocity to hurl her round the edge of the twister and down towards the sea.

Only the very tip of the Isle of the Gods still rose from the sea, although the flood caused by the quake-waves was slowly receding. A ray of green light shot up from the peak, playing queerly over the undersides of the clouds. Isabeau folded her wings and fell towards it.

She could clearly see the little group of priestesses huddled together on a ledge above the water. Bending over the source of the light was a thin girl, both hands pressed to a glowing green sphere. Standing around her were the priestesses, each with one hand upon her own nightglobe and one hand upon the nightglobe of her neighbor. They were chanting.

Isabeau came so fast they had no warning of her approach. As her shadow fell upon them they glanced up and screamed in terror. Isabeau snatched the girl up with her claws, then spat out a long plume of flame. Again and again she swooped down over the island, incinerating the priestesses with her fiery breath. All the while the girl hung limply in her claws. Isabeau could only hope she had merely fainted from terror.

At last she knew there was none left alive on the island. She gave a loud bugle of triumph, rolled over and over in her joy, then swooped back towards the mountains.

Although lightning still flashed intermittently and the wind still roared, the terrible spinning vortex of cloud and wind had sunk away. Where its swaying tail had touched the ground was a swathe of absolute destruction. Tree trunks had been smashed into splinters, giant rocks had been torn up from the ground and pounded into pebbles. There was nothing left of Kinnaird but a few shattered walls.

Isabeau followed the path of devastation all the way up to the ridge. It stopped perilously close to the *Royal Stag,* which leant a little askew on the hill, every mast and charred sail still proudly raised.

As Isabeau began to circle down to land, seven dragons suddenly soared out of the clouds piled upon the mountains. She saw them with a desperate sinking of her heart. With perilous speed they raced towards her, necks stretched out, tails coiling behind. The huge bronze in the lead opened his jaws and spat out a great gust of fire. For a moment Isabeau saw it belching towards her, felt its intense heat slam into her eyes. She shut her eyelids, waiting to feel all her skin shrivelling and blistering as the flames engulfed her. Then there was nothing but cool rain pattering against her scales. She opened her eyes.

The seven dragons swooped around her, golden-topaz eyes mocking her. *Thou must knowest we could have burnt thy bones to cinders if we had so desirest.*

I know.

We did not desire so. Take our form again and we may not be so merciful.

I know. Isabeau's mind-voice sounded shaky, even to herself.

The dragons laughed and soared away again, and Isabeau circled down to the muddy wasteland of the battlefield, the sound of cheering ringing in her ears.

She landed lightly, laying the unconscious girl down gently before transforming herself back into her own shape. She could not help an intense pang of regret, for the form of a dragon was the most magnificent and wondrous of any she had ever assumed. She felt her consciousness shrinking, all the knowledge and insights of the dragon's mind lost, and tried hard to fix some of what she had learnt into her own mind. It was virtually impossible, however, particularly with the wave of dizziness and weariness that engulfed her.

Dide was the first to reach her. He embraced her fiercely, shouting, "Ye did it, ye did it!"

Lachlan and Iseult reached her next. "Ye saved us all!" the Rìgh cried. "And as a dragon! Who could believe ye could become a dragon?"

Iseult said nothing, just hugged her close, pressing her forehead against Isabeau's.

All round the battlefield men and Fairgean were shouting and cheering. Although a gusty wind still blew, bringing sleet to lash against their faces, the darkness had lifted. It was dawn. The Dragon-Star was sinking.

Isabeau suddenly realized she was naked. As tired as she was, she simply did not have the power to warm herself with her magic and she trembled all over with the cold. "My . . . clothes," she whispered, her teeth chattering together. Her knees suddenly gave way and only Dide's arms saved her from sitting down abruptly. Isabeau saw her pile of clothes a short distance away and held out her hands for them. They were thrust into her arms and Iseult helped her drag them on, wet and muddy as they were.

"Come back to the ship," Iseult said. "There'll be food there and we can make some hot tea. We're all shivering with cold. Gods, what a night!"

Isabeau suddenly stilled, her hand in the pocket of her coat. "The Key!" she cried. "My Key!"

Frantically she threw herself down in the mud, searching through the debris. There was no sign of the magical talisman of the Coven. She tore her clothes apart, crawled about on her hands and knees, weeping as she scrabbled through the fragments of branches, leaves, dead fish and mud. Suddenly Isabeau saw a pair of hairy paws before her. She looked up, dashing away her tears with her hand.

Brun stood before her, his tail twisting about anxiously, his triangular face sheepish.

"What force and strength canna get through,
With a mere touch, I can undo," he said.

Isabeau stared at him. "Yes," she said sharply. "My Key."

He lifted the little jangle of rings and spoons about his neck. The Key hung there among them. "I guard for ye," he said. "It be so marvelous bonny, I did no' want it to be lost."

Isabeau reached up and put her arms about the cluricaun's furry waist, hugging him affectionately. "Thank ye, Brun, thank ye," she said. "I do no' ken what I would do without ye!"

THE LAST
THREAD IS TIED

THE BINDING

T he captain's cabin was full of smoke and
noise. Lachlan, drawn and white-faced, sat at
the table, his wings drooping heavily. Iseult
sat as close to him as she could get. Gathered
around them were the lairds and prionnsachan, all bearing the scars of bloody battle.

Sitting together at the other end of the table were
Maya, her wrist manacled to the arm of her chair, and the
Fairge who had helped rescue Lachlan. His name was
Prince Nila, they had been told, Maya's half-brother and
the only surviving son of the King of the Fairgean. He
stared about him with great arrogance, his slim, muscular
body tense as if the slightest move would cause him to
leap into action. Behind him stood two Fairgean warriors
with the same proud, suspicious stance, holding tridents
whose long handles of smoothed driftwood were embed-
ded with diamonds.

"So ye mean to tell us that ye are willing to make
peace with us?" Lachlan asked incredulously. Maya
translated and the Fairge prince gave a long, melodious
response.

"He says, 'On terms'," Maya replied.

"What terms?"

"The sacred Isle o' the Gods must never be defiled by

the step o' a human again," Maya translated. "The Fairgean must be able to swim the seas and hunt the whale
and the seal unmolested. The beaches and rivers must be
returned to the Fairgean so that their women can give
birth in peace and safety. The humans must no' sail their
ships upon the sea, nor harvest the sea's riches, nor . . ."

"He's mad!"

"This is intolerable!"

"Never sail the seas or fish it or hunt the seals ourselves!"

The prionnsachan all broke into angry refutations but
the Duke of Killiegarrie, seanalair of Blèssem, laughed.
The sound of his genuine merriment cut through the
noise.

"Who would have thought the Fairgean were born negotiators?" he said. "Ye leave this to me, Your Highness."

As Keybearer of the Coven and advisor to the Crown, Isabeau sat through the early part of the negotiations but as
it soon proved that Prince Nila was as shrewd and canny
a bargainer as the Duke of Killiegarrie, she knew the talks
would drag on for many hours, if not weeks. There were
many sick and wounded to attend to and so, telling
Gwilym to send for her should she be needed, Isabeau
went out once more to attend them, Buba perched on her
shoulder as usual. The little owl had taken refuge from
the storm in the forest and had been very happy to be reunited with Isabeau. She sat with her feathers all ruffled
up and her round golden eyes blinking sleepily. Buba
would very much have liked a snooze-hooh.

Isabeau would have liked a snooze-hooh as well, but
there was so much to do after the dreadful events of the
night, and her mind was still all churned up, going over
and over what had happened. The comet spell, Meghan's

death, the rescue of the Lodestar by Bronwen, her own flight through the whirlwind as a dragon. It all seemed so incredible she could hardly believe it had happened. Only the rows and rows of wounded soldiers, and the view of the flattened forest from the deck of the *Royal Stag* convinced her it had not all been some terrible nightmare.

They had buried the dead in the chilly light of the dawn. It had been a long, exhausting task, made no easier by grief and self-recriminations. "If only . . ." people kept saying, Isabeau among them. "If only . . ."

Meghan NicCuinn had been buried at the foot of a great oak tree in the forest. They had time only to build a cairn of rocks over her grave, but Lachlan swore to erect a monument engraved with the magical symbols of the Coven and an account of her remarkable life when things had returned to normal. The donbeag Gitâ had crouched on her dead body all through the tumultuous events of the night and refused to leave her even as the first clods of earth fell down upon her crude wooden coffin. If Isabeau had not lifted him away and held his quivering body closely, he would have been buried with her. Despite all Isabeau's gentle chittering, he would not leave the grave and at last they had walked away, leaving him crouching there, keening softly in his throat.

Enit Silverthroat was buried with just as much ceremony and grief under a rowan tree, where the birds she had loved would gather to eat its berries and sing in its green branches. Jay, Dide and Brun together played a lament of such heartfelt sorrow that even the most hardened soldier was moved to tears. Isabeau, who had been dry-eyed all through Meghan's funeral, wept bitterly. She would have sought comfort in Dide's arms, but Dide had loved his grandmother dearly and more than anyone else there asked himself, "If only . . ." There was no answer to such questions, though, and so he played out his grief and regret through his music.

Among the many hundreds who had died were the Duke of Gleneagles, Admiral Tobias, Stout John, Carrick One-Eye, and of course Tòmas the Healer. The funerals had taken much of the morning but once they were over, everyone felt a lightening of the air, as if the ceremonies had truly marked the end of the war and the beginning of a new era of peace.

Most of the refugees had safely reached the shelter of the saltpetre mines some twenty miles to the north. Enormous limestone caves that ran deep into the rock, the mines would provide shelter as long as it was needed. Those who were strong enough were set to gathering firewood and searching for whatever supplies the valley could offer. Many creatures had fled the quake-waves to the safety of the high country, and the soldiers were confident they could hunt down enough food to eke out the meager supplies.

Those who were too badly injured to walk had been carried to the ship for the healers and witches to work on. Every deck was so thickly lined with rough pallets that it was hard for Isabeau to find room to step. Her ears full of groans of pain, her vision filled with pleading hands and terrible gaping wounds, she found herself missing Meghan and Tòmas more than she would have thought possible. All decisions rested with her now. There was no lad with miraculous healing powers to save those closest to death; no old sorceress with almost four and a half centuries of experience and knowledge to guide her.

Despite all her careful preparations, they were already running low on healing herbs, pain-numbing salves and bandages. Neither she nor the other healers had slept in twenty-seven hours and they were so numb with shock and exhaustion that they sewed up wounds, amputated limbs and measured out medicines by rote. To compound Isabeau's difficulty, her most able healer was sunk in a profound depression. Johanna sat in a corner, staring at the wall. She had not cleaned herself of the night's mud and blood, nor changed her clothes, which had dried stiff upon her.

Isabeau knelt beside her. "Johanna, there's naught ye can do for the laddiekin. He's dead. There are many others who need your help. Canna ye let him go now and come and help me?"

Johanna looked up at her piteously. "He was just a babe, a wee babe. And to die now, when the war is over, when there shall be peace at last. It's just no' fair."

"I ken," Isabeau said, smoothing back the girl's hair, stiff with mud and matted with leaves. "I ken. Life is no' always fair, though. We are born, we die, and it is no' in our power to choose the time or the nature o' our death."

"But he was just a laddiekin. He should've been playing marbles and chase-and-hide with the other lads, he should've been grazing knees and tearing his jerkin for his mam to scold him . . ." Her voice dissolved into sobs.

"But we have been at war," Isabeau said. "All things are wrong in war. These men should no' have their guts torn out by tridents, their eyes gouged out with daggers. Ye should no' be here weeping over a wee lad that ye had loved, but sitting by a fire knitting a cap for your own babe and dreaming o' its birth. I should no' be here . . ." Her own voice broke and she raised her hand and gripped the Key, still hanging around her neck.

"But here we are," she went on, her voice strengthening. "We canna choose what circumstances fate throws at us, but we can choose how we react to them. Ye gave me strength and new resolve when I needed it, Johanna. Remember how ye told me one must just face up to one's fear and get on with it? Well, it is the same with grief. Even a grief that makes ye feel as if your very heart was being torn out."

Johanna looked up at her. "Ye feel like that too?" Isabeau nodded. Johanna sighed. "Well, I suppose I'd best get on with it then," she said gruffly and slowly got to her feet.

Leaving Johanna to oversee the other healers, Isabeau checked on the sleeping children and then went wearily back to the captain's cabin. To her surprise there was an atmosphere of affability in the overcrowded little room, perhaps promoted by the amount of sea-squill wine that had been consumed. The Fairgean had brought a sealskin full of the colorless, odorless stuff and this was now almost empty. One or two of the younger men slept with their heads resting on their arms, and the MacSeinn was weeping as he told once more of his anguish at the death of his family and the loss of his throne. The thirteen years that had passed since had done little to dull his pain.

Nila stood and bowed to the prionnsa. When he spoke, the melodious whistles and warbles were clearly sympathetic.

"My brother says that he too has lost those he loves most in the world. He feels your grief like a trident through his throat. He wishes that the past had been different and that your family still lived, and the ones he loved too. He says he feels great remorse that his family and his people were responsible for such deep, abiding grief," Maya translated, her voice showing a little lift of surprise.

The MacSeinn cleared his throat. "Well, that was very nicely spoken o' your brother, very nicely spoken. No' that it brings back the dead, o' course, but still, very nicely spoken." He had another mouthful of sea-squill wine and then said, very gruffly, "Tell him that I be sorry too, if I was responsible for the death o' any he loved. It was nothing personal, o' course. We were at war. Many things are done in war that one might regret later."

Maya translated and Nila bowed his head in grave acceptance of the prionnsa's apology, as brusque as it had been.

Isabeau slipped into her chair, smiling wanly at Dide, who sat opposite. He smiled back, though he was clearly preoccupied. Isabeau was surprised to see there was already a closely written parchment lying on the table. She took it into her hand and read it swiftly, though it was so marked with crossed-out lines and amendments it was difficult to read. To her pleasure, it showed the beginning of some sort of treaty between human and Fairgean. Although it was clear there were many points still to be argued over and ratified, already the peace council had gone a long way towards creating a lasting truce. Both sides had admitted the wrongs they had done and had accepted their blame, something Isabeau would have thought impossible six months earlier.

All were in desperate need of rest and a period of calm and recovery. The council broke up soon after Isabeau returned to it, both Lachlan and Nila making a formal gesture of acceptance and promising to continue with talks as soon as possible. Only then was the exhausted Rìgh able to seek his bed, Iseult driving the half-drunk lairds out to find a bunk for themselves somewhere else on the overcrowded ship.

Snooze-hooh?

Isabeau smiled and put up one hand to stroke Buba's soft feathers. *Snooze-hooh soon-hooh* . . .

She walked slowly up onto the forecastle, knowing

where she would find Dide. He sat above the bowsprit, his guitar across his lap, looking out over the ruined valley. In the center of all the devastation, the loch lay like a spread of molten gold, reflecting the colors of the sinking sun. Somehow it was too beautiful, as if nothing should be allowed to shine on this terrible day.

Isabeau sat next to Dide, rested her head against his shoulder. He was strumming a sweet and plaintive tune. Isabeau recognized it as one Enit had often sung.

"So ye be the new Keybearer," he said at last.

Isabeau nodded. "I canna think why," she said. "There are so many aulder than me and more knowledgeable. Gwilym for example, or even my mam . . ."

Dide shook his head, though he still did not look at her. "None more powerful. Who else could have turned themselves into a dragon and flown through a tornado? Who else could have overcome the Priestesses o' Jor? None. No one else."

"It was my birthday," Isabeau said. "The power o' the comet was with me. I could no' do it now."

He looked at her then, and grinned. "Liar."

She smiled and shrugged. "Who kens? I do no' feel strong enough to light a candle."

"Ye should get some rest," he said in sudden concern. "Ye're as white as whey."

"It's been a long day," Isabeau agreed. "And a long day afore that. No' to mention the night."

He nodded, swallowing and looking away. "No' to mention the night."

She put up her hand and took his gently. "They have given me a cabin o' my own. I shall have to get used to such consideration. It shall be hard, having been no one for so long."

"Och, ye'll get used to it," Dide said with a ghost of his old smile.

Isabeau smiled in response, then hesitated a moment. "There's nowhere for ye to sleep," she said. "Will ye no' come and share with me?" He looked at her in silence for a moment. To her surprise, Isabeau's eyes filled with tears. "It would be good . . . to hold someone warm . . . and alive," she said, the words coming slowly. "I am so sick o' death . . . and being all alone."

He nodded, and rose to his feet, pulling her up with him. "Lead the way, my bonny Beau. That be an invitation any man'd find hard to refuse."

Isabeau's cabin was small, like all the others, but the bunk was just wide enough for the two of them to lie close. Both had passed beyond exhaustion to a strange floating state where colors seemed too bright, noises too loud, people too confronting. It was dark and quiet in the little cabin, the only sound that of Dide's heart beating against Isabeau's back. She closed her eyes and pressed his hands closer about her, warm and at peace for the first time in many days.

When she woke, it was to the knowledge she was being watched. Isabeau opened her eyes and looked straight into Dide's. Black, unfathomable, they gazed at her intently. Isabeau smiled at him. Dide did not smile back. He shifted his weight a little so she lay below him, all her red ringlets fanning out over his arm. He curled one around his finger.

"So, my Beau, do ye think this be the time and the place now?"

Isabeau smiled. She looked about her. The cabin was very small, the roof pressing close above their heads. It smelt rather unpleasantly of the bilge. Buba slept still, perched on the only chair, her head sunk down into her

wings. She could hear someone snoring nearby. Slowly
she shook her head. Dide's expression did not change,
though he very gently laid her curl back on the pillow.

"Happen it be the time," she whispered, "but definitely
no' the place." She sat up, just avoiding banging her head,
and swung her bare legs over the edge of the bunk. Looking back, she saw his face had changed, grown more intent, the black eyes more brilliant. "Come on," she
whispered, jerking her head.

He laughed then and followed her, catching up his
breeches and dragging them on, tying back his long black
curls into a ponytail with a measure of ribbon. Isabeau
did not bother to tie back her hair. Dressed only in her
white witch's robe, made without buttons, buckles, hooks
or knots, she left all her red curls hanging freely down her
back, simply throwing her plaid about her shoulders and
leading him out into the passage.

They clambered down from the ship and made their
way silently over the rough ground. Before the ship there
was nothing but broken tree trunks and great piles of
twigs and sodden leaves, dead animals and mud, all
churned up into a thick, grey, gluey mess. Behind the ship
the forest rose undamaged, slim white birches swaying,
tall pines soughing, great maples and hemlocks showing
the first unfurling of green leaf at the tips of their
branches. It was just after dawn, and all the valley was
filled with a gentle, silvery light. Birds sang softly and a
breeze riffled the trees.

Deep into the forest they wandered, hand in hand.
They came at last to a copse far from the sight of broken
trees and high cairns of stone. There the bracken grew
vigorously and tall trees cast green shadows over a
smooth stretch of grass and the first few flowers of
spring. There bubbled a spring swollen with melted

snows. Dide cupped his hands for Isabeau to drink and then drank himself. When he slipped one wet hand down the side of her neck, it was shockingly cold.

There, in the sunlit glade, only the song of the wind and the birds to serenade them, Isabeau and Dide slowly, gently, disrobed each other. They did not talk of the future or of the past. There was only this moment. Neither felt any shyness or constraint. All barriers between them had been broken down in other places, at other times. Now there was only the rapture of touch and whisper, the sense of life reaffirmed, death banished, joy rediscovered. Afterwards, Isabeau lay within the cradle of Dide's arms, watching the shadows shift over his lean dark body curled about her soft white one, their fingers entwined, their hair curling together, red and black, fire and darkness.

"I love ye," he whispered.

Isabeau turned her head so she could look into his eyes. "I love ye too," she whispered back. There was no need of other words.

The treaty between the two races was not one to be drawn up in a day, or even a week. It took almost two months. There were a thousand years of hatred to be overcome and many misunderstandings caused by the gaps between the two cultures and ways of thinking.

To complicate matters, there were many among the Fairgean who did not wish to make peace, and many among the humans who still thought the best solution was to totally disempower the sea-faeries, rendering them little more than slaves. Both Lachlan and Nila were determined, however, and the strength of their convictions and of their characters at last prevailed in winning over the dissenters.

After much angry discussion it had at last been agreed that the sea and its shore had always been traditional home of the Fairgean and by rights belonged to them. Many of the northern islands had already been ceded to the Fairgean and most of the safe harbors too. In return, the Fairgean had promised the humans the right to use the safe harbors for their fishing and merchant fleets, as long as a tithe of some sort was paid. Since the Fairgean had no monetary system, this was to be paid in kind.

Already a long list of desirable products had been drawn up. The Fairgean had a great need of grains and fruits, as well as fire-forged weapons and tools. They also had a great admiration of the fine silks and velvets the prionnsachan wore, while the humans coveted the rich furs hanging down the backs of the Fairgean warriors. Pearls had always been very rare among human society and highly prized, while diamonds were much admired by the Fairgean for their clarity and brilliance, yet were found in the sea only infrequently. Perhaps most importantly, the Fairgean prince desired lanterns, candles, tinder and flint, anything to assist in the making of fire. For so long the Priestesses of Jor had been the only ones with any form of illumination, deriving much of their aura of power and mystery from their nightglobes. Prince Nila wanted to make it possible for any Fairge to light his cave and cook fish or seal meat.

For several weeks the only point of contention had been the Isle of the Gods. Even with the new feeling of accord between Prince Nila and Linley MacSeinn, neither would budge on this one point. Finally the MacSeinn had grown so angry he had threatened to leave the peace talks for good. His son Douglas had laid his hand on his father's shoulder. Watching closely, Isabeau noticed at once that the young prionnsa's hand had deep curves of skin running from knuckle to knuckle. His hand was nearly as webbed as Nila's.

"But *Dai-dein*, why do ye want the island?" Douglas said in a low voice. "It has been drowned in the floods and the Tower o' Sea-singers was naught but a ruin anyway, and thick with ghosts, I'd wager. Why would we want such a cold, gloomy, Eà-forsaken place? Canna we build a new castle and a new tower up here, in the mountains? It be so bonny here."

The MacSeinn had stared at his son for a long, tense moment, then suddenly his angry face had relaxed and he had laughed. "Why no'?" he had said. "Eà kens this place has proved lucky for us. We shall call it Bonnyblair, the beautiful field o' war."

And so it was decided. The hallowed Isle of the Gods was given to the Fairgean unconditionally, with no human ever to enter the Fathomless Caves unless expressly invited. With that one concession, the MacSeinn was able to win many compromises from the sea-faeries on fishing rights and harbor fees.

At sunset on the night of the spring equinox, a time of significance for both human and Fairgean, the treaty was signed by Lachlan and the prionnsachan, and by Nila and the most prominent of the Fairgean families. It was signed within the Cave of a Thousand Kings, which had been cleared of sea wrack and restored to its former grandeur. Golden rays of light struck down through the chasm in its high, vaulted ceiling, high-lighting the gleaming colors of the mother-of-pearl walls and striking deep through the vivid aquamarine water.

After the Pact of Peace was signed, Lachlan crowned Nila with the Fairgean King's black pearl coronet and gave him the King's jeweled scepter to hold. The Rìgh had insisted that the Fairgean prince acknowledge his overlordship and swear fealty to him, like all the other peoples of Eileanan. Although the new king of the Fairgean wore a long skirt stiff with diamonds, pearls and opals, and had fastened his magnificent white fur cloak about his shoulders with a jeweled brooch, about his throat he wore nothing but the black pearl hanging on its simple cord.

When the coronation ceremony had concluded, Nila stepped down from his sparkling crystal throne and raised up Fand, who had waited, kneeling, at the base of the throne. She was clothed all in white fur, with a small coronet of white pearls holding back her hair. Nila led Fand up the steps to the throne and stood facing the expectant crowd, speaking for a very long time in the melodic warbling language of the Fairgean.

"What does he say?" Isabeau asked Maya.

"He takes the halfbreed as his wife," Maya answered.

"Aye, I ken that," Isabeau answered impatiently. "I want to ken what he is actually saying." She was eager indeed to learn the language of the sea-faeries, but found it baffling and difficult, particularly since they seemed to take a very long time to say the simplest of things.

"He says, 'I take thee, Fand, as my wife,'" Maya answered mockingly. Isabeau rolled her eyes but had to grin. Even though Maya remained a prisoner of state, she had not lost either her charm or her audacity.

The wedding ceremony was surprisingly brief, given the amount of time the Fairgean spent over most of their rituals. When it was finished, Nila and Fand sat together on the crystal throne, an act which Maya explained was daringly egalitarian, particularly since Fand was the daughter of a human concubine, a half-breed. It was a symbol of the new order, however, where women were no longer mere playthings, to be gambled away at the toss of a sea-stirk's knuckle.

It was growing dark in the Cave of a Thousand Kings. Lanterns were kindled all along the walls, and candles set to bobbing about on the water, a very pretty sight indeed. Now was to come the last of the ceremonies and the one in which Isabeau and Maya were most interested.

It had been decreed, as part of the peace treaties, that the cousins Donncan and Bronwen were to be betrothed. As a part-human was to be queen of the Fairgean, the agreement said, so shall a part-Fairgean in time become queen of the humans.

Although Isabeau had been reluctant to tie the children together when they were still so young and did not know where their hearts would lead them, she knew the betrothal was politically astute. It would silence any lingering opposition to Lachlan's rule, since those who still believed Jaspar's daughter should have inherited the throne would know that in time Bronwen would share it with Donncan, Lachlan's son. It satisfied Nila's concern about the Fairgean swearing fealty to the MacCuinn clan, and showed Lachlan's own clemency towards the seafaeries. And it was a swift and visible way of showing the whole land that the Fairgean were no longer their enemy and that any prejudice towards them was unacceptable.

Donncan was happy and excited about the betrothal, sure that he loved his cousin and that his feelings would not change by the time they were both sixteen, when the marriage was to be consummated. What Bronwen felt was harder to tell. She had learnt to keep her true feelings hidden long ago.

In a long, beautifully carved boat, the two children floated across the water towards the crystal throne, sitting side by side, hand in hand. Donncan was dressed in the

MacCuinn kilt and plaid, but flung over his shoulders was a long cloak of plush white fur like the Fairgean wore. Similarly, Bronwen was dressed as a Fairgean princess, in white fur and pearls, but over her shoulder she wore a drapery of the MacCuinn plaid, crossing her breast and fastened at her waist with a brooch depicting the crowned stag of her father's clan.

It was a striking picture, the boy with golden eyes and curls, his bright wings just showing beneath his cloak, the girl with straight black hair and silvery-blue eyes, both with the white lock of the MacCuinns at their brow. Together they climbed out of the boat and walked up the steps to kneel at Nila's and Fand's feet. The King of the Fairgean crowned them both with delicate little coronets of pearls and diamonds. In the center of Bronwen's coronet was a small black pearl, showing she was acknowledged as Fairgean royalty.

Nila then turned and faced the crowd, holding Bronwen's hand with his right hand and Donncan's with his left. He bowed low to the crowd, then with great ceremony placed the children's hands together, stepping back so they faced the crowd hand in hand. There was much cheering and melodic ululating, then servants began to walk through the crowd, pouring out sea-squill wine and offering little delicacies of raw fish, roe and seaweed.

"Well, I can begin to breathe easier now," Maya said sardonically to Isabeau. "Surely the MacCuinn will no' burn his future daughter-in-law's mother to death?"

There was no doubt Maya the Ensorcellor remained a quandary for the Rìgh. He had been convinced not to demand punishment of Fand, despite her having conjured the spell that had drowned the land. Isabeau had been able to convince him she had been an unwilling tool of the Priestesses of Jor, whom she herself enacted justice upon with her fiery dragon breath.

Maya's case was not so simple. It was not just that she had been Lachlan's arch-enemy for many years now. She was dangerous. So strong and subtle was her charm that the soldiers set to guard her were constantly caught trying to set her free, their loyalties bewildered, their senses befuddled with her beauty. Wherever she went was a little turmoil of trouble and confusion.

Yet she had proved to be one of the linchpins of their victory at Bonnyblair, and Lachlan had to admit peace may not have been won without her. And he knew that peace was still precarious. Maya was King Nila's sister and Bronwen's mother. He would gain little but revenge from ordering her death.

Isabeau was able to provide a solution to one of the problems. Brun the cluricaun was set to be Maya's guard. Cluricauns were impervious to magic and indifferent to human beauty. Brun had suffered greatly from Maya's Decrees Against The Faeries. He would not be swayed by her charm, physical or magical.

Thereafter Maya's tall, slim figure was never to be seen without the little hairy cluricaun, a delicate chain joining them always. A comical sight, yet somehow pitiful. Maya made no attempt to escape, saying huskily, "But I am willing to accept the MacCuinn's justice. I do no' wish to escape." No one knew whether to believe her, not even Isabeau.

A month after the coronation Lachlan and the Greycloaks were ready to return to Lucescere. They had erected monuments to the dead and recovered their strength in the clear mountain air. They had helped the MacSeinn begin building a new town on the shores of Loch Bonnyblair, with a new castle and a new witches' tower, to be called the Tower of Song. There all types of music would be taught and celebrated, not just those that killed Fairgean. All were now eager to return home and pick up the threads of their lives, broken and tangled by the long and bloody war.

"I never thought I would say this, but I must admit I dread the long sea journey home," Lachlan said one night. "Much as I love my ship, I have had enough o' her for quite a long time, I feel."

Everyone agreed fervently. They had been living on the ship for most of the past month while the foundations of Castle Bonnyblair were being built, and cramped and uncomfortable quarters they had been too.

"How are we to get her back to the sea, anyway?" Iseult asked. "Nay, it would be best if we went back over the Bridge To Beyond The Known and crossed the Spine o' the World."

"Either way, it'll take us months," Lachlan said with dissatisfaction. "I just want to get home! I need to see how the rest o' the country has fared in my absence, and how much damage was caused by the quake-wave."

Isabeau was struck by an idea. She said nothing but the next morning she rose early, long before the dawn. With Buba flying before her like a snowflake blown on the night wind, she made her way deep into the forest. She had no need of a light, for she could see nearly as clearly at night as she could by day. It was still a rough scramble, though, through thicket and bush and bramble. She had no prior knowledge of where to go, but her body knew when it came close to a line of power. It thrummed beneath her feet and led her unhesitatingly to a ring of stones raised upon a high, green hill, deep in the secret fastness of the forest.

Her breath was coming fast, for she had hurried,

knowing dawn was near. She waited until the light of the rising sun had struck through the trees and upon the standing stones, then she laid her hand upon one of the symbols engraved deep into the rock. An electric shock ran up her arm and all her nerve ends tingled, but she did not flinch or open her eyes. In her mind's eye she imagined the shadows of clouds racing over fields of wild wheat. The tingling intensified, until her hand felt like it was being stung by a swarm of wasps. She waited until she could bear the pain no longer, then opened her eyes.

A tall, slender figure stood before her, dressed all in shimmering white. Her skin and flowing name of hair were white, and her eyes were as translucent as water. In the center of her forehead, just between her brows, was an intricate knot of wrinkles, though the rest of the Celestine's face was smooth and serene. She lifted her multi-jointed fingers to her brow and bowed, murmuring in her own humming language.

Isabeau returned the ritual greeting, then allowed the Celestine to touch her fingers to her own brow. The bud of wrinkles on the Celestine's forehead slowly unknotted to reveal a third eye, dark as a starless night, that glimmered with liquid reflections.

Greetings, Isabeau Shapechanger. Glad I am to see the Key upon your breast, as sad as I am to know that Meghan of the Beasts is no more. She was always our true friend.

Tears stung Isabeau's eyes. *I miss her horribly. I do no' ken how I shall manage without her.*

But you will, the Celestine replied serenely. *You must.*

Isabeau nodded, swallowing her grief. She did not need to say any more for the Celestine could see clearly into her mind. She stood passively beneath the touch of her fingers and let the Celestine Cloudshadow know all there was to know.

Great grief, great joy. Always they come together, the Celestine said, her mind-voice full of sorrow. *So you wish to travel the Old Ways once more, my friend. And not alone this time, but with many hundreds of strangers, their boots trampling our sacred ways.*

Isabeau nodded.

You know we guard the secret of our roads jealously, the Celestine said. *They would have to walk blindfolded, trusting in me to lead them true.*

Again Isabeau nodded her head.

They will hear the shrieks of banshees and ghosts, and feel the cold clutch of their fingers. They will sense the spite of malevolent spirits, who will whisper doubts into their minds. They will not know if the very next step will lead them astray, to other times and other worlds. Yet none must remove their blindfold. Can you promise me this?

Isabeau hesitated, then mutely shook her head. *I will warn them. I will make sure they all understand.*

Even that proud winged king of yours?

Isabeau twisted her mouth ruefully. *Aye, even Lachlan. Though he will no' like it.*

All to the good, Cloudshadow replied without the faintest inflection of humor. *Very well. Though never before has a Stargazer of the Celestines allowed such a thing. We made our mark upon your king's Pact of Peace, however, and it is true he has tried hard to help the Celestines heal the land. He has sung the summerborne with us many times now and the magic of his voice has made the water run pure and strong. We shall help him go home now in thanks.*

She bowed once more to Isabeau and stepped back through the door of stone, disappearing into empty air.

The date chosen for the Greycloaks' return to Lucescere was Beltane, the first day of May, exactly a year since the Fairgean had taken Rhyssmadill by surprise. In Lucescere, Maya's fate would finally be decided.

Every man, woman and child was securely blindfolded, their hands linked in a long daisy-chain of curiosity and apprehension. One by one they were led through the doorway of stone. Unable to see, the electric shock that ran through them was all the greater. Many jolted to a halt, crying aloud in pain and surprise. They were dragged forward by the hand of the person ahead, in turn dragging on those behind them. It was like trying to run blindfolded through a rough, cold sea full of stinging jellyfish, that swirled about their knees and buffeted them from side to side. Many would have torn off their blindfolds or refused to go on, if they had not been clinging on so tightly to the invisible hand of the person ahead of them.

They seemed to stagger on for hours. The path undulated beneath their feet, and their ears were filled with wailing and whispering, the taunts of a thousand ghosts. Some found it all too hard to bear, and cried out in horror or remorse, begging to be allowed to escape the Celestines' secret way. The daisy-chain of hands held firm, however, and one by one they stepped through another doorway of stone into the garden at the heart of the Tower of Two Moons' maze. The journey which had taken them so many months to complete the year before had taken just a few hours.

In Lucescere the bells rang out in joyous celebration. A great feast was held in honor of the victorious Rìgh, who had done more than any rìgh before him to ensure a lasting peace in Eileanan. For the first time in Eileanan's long and turbulent history, all countries and all peoples were united and sworn to harmony. All their enemies were vanquished, all obstacles overcome.

All enemies except for Maya the Ensorcellor. Her trial was a long and public one. Lachlan was determined that all should see justice be done. Many witnesses were called, and the arguments about her fate were bitter. "Burn her!" many of the witches called. "Let her feel the agony she inflicted on our kindred."

"Let us hang her," advised the judges of the royal court, appointed from both the aristocracy and the merchant classes. "We must show strength against those who plot treason."

"Let her live," said the Keybearer Isabeau NicFaghan. "She has atoned many o' her crimes in the killing o' the Fairgean king and the saving o' Donncan and Bronwen MacCuinn."

"But surely she has no' atoned them all? She should die!"

"Let her live," said Isabeau. "If she dies, we lose all that she kens, o' sea-magic and the power to transform, o' the art o' far-seeing and the culture o' the Fairgean, and much more besides. So much knowledge has been lost already. Let her labor in the libraries, preserving what little knowledge we still have and recording all that she kens."

"But what o' retribution?" the witches asked. "How is that a righteous punishment?"

"But she shall be a servant to the witches that she sought to destroy," Isabeau said. "She shall serve the Coven and work to promote it. The Ensorcellor is a proud woman. She has been the most powerful person in the land, able to decide the life or death o' all about her. What do ye think is a more just punishment? A quick death, or a long humiliation?"

The judges and jurors were silent for a long time. But then Lachlan stood, his face very grim. "She is too dangerous to be allowed to live," he said. "We have all heard o' how she laid her charm upon many hundreds o' people, my own brother Jaspar among them. She is a powerful and subtle sorceress who has no compunction in compelling people against their will. If she was able to ensorcel the MacCuinn himself into raising his hand against the Coven, what could she do to someone o' lesser will and power?

"How are we to ken that ye too have no' fallen under her charm, Keybearer? Ye have spent much time wi' her in the past. I ken ye wish to see no more killing, and fear that the execution o' the Ensorcellor will lead to strife and trouble in the future. Certainly King Nila has asked us most forcibly for clemency and grace in this case. Yet, apart from my own anger and grief at what she has done in the past, I fear what she may do in the future. We have only just won peace. How can we risk it by allowing the Ensorcellor to live?"

The crowd all murmured in agreement. Isabeau nodded. "Your words are just, Your Highness. What if we were to bind her?"

There was a little stir of surprise. "Bind her?" Lachlan asked slowly. "Do ye mean keep her chained as we have done these past months, with a cluricaun to guard her?"

Isabeau shook her head. "Nay, I mean bind her powers. Render her impotent."

They all heard a little gasp of dismay. Maya was leaning forward in the box, all her color drained away. "No!" she cried. "Kill me rather."

The courtroom buzzed. Lachlan waited till the noise

had died away, then said slowly, "But is such a binding possible?"

"If it is a weaving o' the nyx, I believe so," Isabeau answered. "Did they no' weave the cloak o' illusions that kept ye safe in the guise o' a hunchback for so many years? Did they no' weave magical gloves that hid Tòmas the Healer's shining hands? I believe they could find a way to bind her powers."

Lachlan nodded. "Then I think that might be the answer," he said slowly. "If I could only be sure . . ."

"Your son's betrothed would be grateful indeed for the sparing o' her mother's life. It could have only a happy consequence for their future marriage," Isabeau pointed out. "And Bronwen would be able to grow up wi' her mother near her always. Ye ken yourself how much ye have always missed your own mother, who died when ye were so young."

Lachlan nodded, a shadow falling upon his face.

"King Nila would be beholden to ye, and the Coven would no' lose all that the Ensorcellor kens. Believe me when I say the Coven shall be grateful for that. It is time for us to lay to rest the sorrows o' the past and look to building our future."

As she spoke, Isabeau turned to face the council of white-robed witches, a look of intense determination and conviction on her face. Many had found her appointment as Keybearer difficult to accept, for Isabeau was only twenty-four and many among them were older and, they thought, wiser. To her surprise, she saw her words had moved the witches. They were nodding to each other, and one or two were even clapping their hands in approval.

"What say ye, your honors?" Lachlan asked the judges. They had been leaning together and muttering, but now the head judge straightened up, saying with great authority, "If the Ensorcellor can be bound so that she is no longer a danger, and if she submits to laboring at the Coven's behest, well then, I believe we have found a just and merciful solution. So be it!"

So, chained to Brun the cluricaun, Maya the Ensorcellor was led from her prison cell down into the dark and secret caves beneath the ancient city of Lucescere, where no daylight had ever penetrated. There lived Ceit Anna, the oldest and most powerful of the nyx. For forty-two days and forty-two nights the nyx labored, weaving a ribbon from her long mane of wild black hair. Close and intricate she wove her hair, while a circle of witches led by Toireasa the Seamstress chanted spells of binding over the ribbon.

There, in the darkness of the nyx's cave, the ribbon was wound about Maya's throat, the ends woven together so there was no seam that could be unpicked, no knot that could be untied, no button or buckle that could be unfastened. Knife or scissors could not cut it, flame could not burn it or water dissolve it. When Maya was led at last from the underground caves and back to the Tower of Two Moons, blinking and shrinking from the light, it was found she had no voice. And so Maya the Ensorcellor, Maya the Once-Was-Blessed, in the end was known only as Maya the Mute.

"I canna help but wonder if I did the right thing," Isabeau said. "It seems a cruel fate, to be bound speechless and powerless. Happen I should have let them execute her."

"What can any o' us do but wonder if what we do is right?" Dide answered. "Your reasons for pleading for her life were all sound, and ye ken Bronwen is glad, even though her mother can only speak to her with quill and parchment."

"Still, is Maya glad?"

"She's alive at least."

Isabeau smiled. "Aye, there's something in that."

"And so are we, thank Eà." Dide bent his dark head and kissed her lingeringly on the mouth. "Alive and at peace, two things I thought we would never be."

They were in the great library at the Tower of Two Moons, a room which ran the entire length and height of the main building. Six stories high, it was lined with bookshelves from the floor to the domed ceiling, which was painted with scenes from the history of Eileanan. Narrow spiral staircases made of iron lace connected the ground floor to the six galleries, with tall lancet windows looking out upon the central garth where the fountain threw up sparkling arcs of water into the sunlit air.

When Maya's Red Guards had stormed the Tower of Two Moons, they had kindled the Burning with the thousands of books and scrolls that had once lined the great library. Though the room itself had been totally destroyed, it had been rebuilt easily enough with the labor of hundreds of artisans and craftsmen. The knowledge it had once contained was lost forever, though. Most of the bookshelves were empty and apprentices were hard at work all along the length of the room, trying to decipher the charred remnants of those books found in the ruins. Other apprentices were busy copying from texts lent by the Towers of Roses and Thorns and the Tower of Mists, the only witches' towers that had not been burnt to the ground. Among them were Jay and Finn, sitting side by side, whispering and laughing. Finn was meant to be helping Jay in his struggle to learn to read, but by the sound of their low voices, not much work was being achieved.

Maya the Mute also sat at one of the tables, a quill in

her hand, a pile of parchment before her. Like the others quietly working around her, she was dressed in a severe black gown with her hair bound back from her brow. The nyx ribbon was a dark slash about her throat. There was something tragic about her austerity, for Isabeau was used to seeing her resplendent in red velvet and gold embroidery. With her scarred face, greying hair and plain clothing, it was hard to believe she had once been called the most beautiful woman in the land, and even harder to believe she had been the most powerful.

Isabeau turned her attention back to Dide. She knew he had not sought her out merely to talk about Maya. He was hanging over her chair now, toying with her hair, one foot swinging. Though he tried hard to conceal it, he was feeling restless as the days grew longer and warmer.

She smiled up at him. "Finding peace rather dull?"

"Dull as ditch-water," he admitted. "The court seems to do naught but sit around and eat sweetmeats and gossip. Lachlan is busy enough setting up trade routes and overseeing the building o' his new navy, but there's naught for his jongleur to do but sit around and sing love songs."

"I thought there was nothing ye'd rather do," Isabeau teased.

He smiled. "Och, I'll sing to your bright eyes any time o' day or night," he answered. "Ye're always too busy to listen, though."

"I'm sorry," Isabeau answered, seizing his hand. "There's so much to do, though. I canna spare the time to be sitting around with the other court ladies and talking about the latest way to wear a ribbon."

"Aye, I ken. Ye be the Keybearer now. At least I get to see ye at night, in bed, which is where I'd rather have ye anyway."

"Ye need to be doing something during the day, though, else ye'll grow fat from eating too many sweetmeats," Isabeau laughed up at him. "Why do ye no' bide a wee at the Theurgia? Ye could be a strong sorcerer indeed, if ye'd only learn some discipline."

"As long as it were ye disciplining me," he murmured, bending lower to kiss her ear.

She dimpled. "I could probably arrange that. Though I warn ye now, I be a strict taskmaster."

"Promises, promises."

"Dide, I'm serious. We have so few o' any power left. Will ye no' join the Coven?"

"But I hate rules and restrictions, Beau, ye ken that."

"What if we made ye a journeywitch?" she said, laughing up at him. "Ye would no' need to stay here at the Tower, stuck in a classroom, but would learn your craft wherever ye were, from whatever teachers ye found. Ye could bring much wisdom and skill back from the village skeelies and cunning men. Ye could search out children o' Talent for me and bring them back to the Theurgia, and any useful books ye find."

Dide had stilled, looking down into her face with intent black eyes. "Do ye mean it?"

"Aye, o' course. The Coven has been hidebound far too long. No' everyone is suited to the secluded life o' the Towers. I think one o' the major mistakes the Coven made was to shut themselves away from the natural rhythm o' living. They were no longer connected to the way the common people thought and felt, and what their needs and desires were. That's one o' the things I want to change. Sending out journeywitches into the countryside, to help those in need, teach the common people about the Coven and learn the native wisdom o' hedge-witches, seems to me one way o' doing it."

Dide rose to his feet, striding about the table in his excitement. "Ye mean I could be Dide the Juggler again, and travel about in my caravan and write my songs and play the crowds . . ." Suddenly he stopped. He turned back to Isabeau and sat next to her, seizing her hands. "But what about us?"

"What about us?" she asked, smiling at him. "Ye will have to come back regularly to give me reports and bring back the children o' Talent ye've found. And I do no' intend to stay cloistered up here either. There is much for the Coven to do out in the countryside and I intend to be doing it. Ye will be able to tell me where I am most needed, and I will come out and join ye and we can work together to fix it. Do no' forget I can travel where I want, how I want. No need for me to dawdle along in a caravan. I can travel the Old Ways, or turn myself into a golden eagle . . ."

"Or a dragon!"

Isabeau gave a little shiver, remembering the vision of herself burning and blistering in a blast of dragon-fire. "Nay, I think I'll choose a less dangerous shape next time. Maybe a nice plump pigeon."

"Ah, a pretty pigeon for the plucking," Dide said with a leer, pulling her close so he could nuzzle under her ear.

Conscious of the interested gazes of many of the young apprentices, Isabeau pulled away, frowning at him quellingly. "So would ye like that? To join the Coven and be my first journeywitch?"

"Ye ken I must always serve my master first?" Dide said with slight hesitation.

Isabeau nodded. "Aye, o' course. I ken how it is wi' ye."

"There be no reason why I canna serve ye both, though, as long as the tasks do no' conflict. That is why they call me the Juggler, because I be so adept at keeping several balls in the air at once." From somewhere about his clothes Dide pulled out his golden balls and deftly sent them spinning up into the air, before concealing them again, one by one.

"Mind ye, I canna be o' as much use to Himself as I used to be. Too many people now ken that I serve him. I fear my disguise as a mere juggler has worn rather thin."

"Ye will be o' greatest use to him doing as ye've always done, singing your songs and telling your tales, and making him a hero in the eyes o' his people."

Dide nodded, knowing this to be true. They were silent for a moment, then suddenly Dide seized her hand, bending close so he could look straight into her eyes. "Do ye still dream o' him?"

Isabeau smiled up at him. "Nay. I dream only o' ye."

"Liar," he said, his voice husky and warm. "Sweet lies though. Lie to me some more."

"Mmmm," Isabeau said. "Like 'I love ye'?"

"With falsehoods like that ye can lie to me any time."

She kissed him tenderly. "It be no falsehood. I shall miss ye horribly when ye've gone."

"Ye'd better," he answered, drawing her even closer so he could kiss her again. This time Isabeau forgot all about her position as Keybearer of the Coven, and melted willingly into his embrace. Both were rather breathless when they at last drew apart.

"Do ye no' mind?" Dide asked huskily. "That I want to go, I mean?"

Isabeau shook her head, though there was a sheen of tears in her eyes. "I'd no' lock a skylark up in a cage. Why should I wish to lock ye up?"

He toyed with the star and circle talisman hanging

around her neck. "Well, ye do carry a big key," he said with a poor attempt at light-heartedness.

"Aye, but this be a key for setting free, no' for locking up," Isabeau answered. "I ken ye would never be happy, stuck in the one place all the time. Ye were meant to be on the road, traveling free."

"Over the hills and by the burn,

the road unrolls through forest and fern,

taking my feet I know no' where.

happen I'll meet ye at the fair!" Dide sang softly, his eyes alight with happiness.

"Happen I will," Isabeau replied, smiling.

When he had gone, his step now light, his face free of the weariness of spirit that had shadowed it before, Isabeau turned back to her task. On the table before her lay *The Book of Shadows*. She had been writing her account of the Battle of Bonnyblair and all the strange and wondrous things that had happened there. It was a task she had put off for some time, for the sight of the many pages filled with Meghan's spidery handwriting had pierced her with a sword of grief. *The Book of Shadows* was one of the Coven's most precious heirlooms, containing within its pages all the history and lore of the Coven of Witches, all recorded in the many different hands of the Keybearers since the time of the First Crossing. It seemed somehow presumptuous for Isabeau to write in it herself when she had spent so many years gingerly reading its pages under the stern eye of her guardian. Every time she took it down from its shelf and unlocked it with a silver key as long as her finger, she expected to hear Meghan's voice, saying, "Carefully, lassie! Must ye be so clumsy? Och, what a heedless lass ye are!"

At last, though, she had taken it down and let it fall open on the table before her. As she had expected, it opened upon a blank new page at the very back of the book. Upon that virgin white expanse, she had described the attack of the Fairgean upon the Beltane feast, their journey to Carraig and the long struggle for the Isle of the Gods.

She had drawn a picture of the flying ship with its escort of seven great dragons and recounted the signing of the Pact of Peace by the Fairgean. Now she had only to finish the account of Maya the Ensorcellor's trial and her binding by the nyx. She picked up her quill and looked down the room once more.

As if sensing her regard, Maya looked up at her and smiled. For the first time since Isabeau had met her, the Fairge looked to be at peace. Isabeau smiled back and began to write once more.

> *. . . and so there was peace everywhere in the land for the first time in many years, with those of humankind and faerykind living together in harmony and contentment under the benevolent rule of Lachlan MacCuinn and Iseult NicFaghan, my sister. May Eà shine her bright face upon us.*

Isabeau wrote the last word with a flourish and scattered sand over the page. Then she shut the book, laying her hands on the red embossed cover for a long moment. She knew when next she opened it, to write down all that she had learnt and achieved, a fresh white page would be there, waiting for her to write upon.

GLOSSARY

Aedan MacCuinn: the first Rìgh, High Lord of Eileanan. Called Aedan Whitelock, he was directly descended from Cuinn Lionheart (see *First Coven*). In 710 he united the warring lands of Eileanan into one country, all except for Tìrsoilleir and Arran, which remained independent.

Aedan's Pact: Aedan MacCuinn, first Rìgh of Eileanan, drew up a pact between all inhabitants of the island, agreeing to live in harmony and not to interfere in each other's culture, but to work together for peace and prosperity. The Fairgean refused to sign and so were cast out, causing the Second Fairgean Wars.

ahdayeh: the art of fighting.

Ahearn Horse-laird: one of the First Coven of Witches.

Aislinna the Dreamer: one of the First Coven of Witches.

Alasdair MacFaghan: baby son of Khan'gharad Dragon-laird and Ishbel the Winged, twin brother of Heloïse and younger brother of Iseult and Isabeau.

Anghus MacRuraich: Prionnsa of Rurach. He uses clairvoyant talents to search and find.

Arkening the Dreamwalker: sorceress who can travel the dream-roads.

Arran: southeast land of Eileanan, ruled by the MacFóghnan clan.

Aslinn the Piper: piper in the service of Anghus MacRuraich.

Aslinn: deeply forested land ruled by the MacAislin clan.

autumn equinox: when the night reaches the same length as the day.

banprionnsa: princess or duchess.

banrìgh: queen.

Beltane: May Day; the first day of summer.

Berhtfane: sea loch in Clachan.

Berhtilde the Bright Warrior-maid: one of the First Coven of Witches.

berhtildes: the female warriors of Tìrsoilleir, named after the country's founder (see *First Coven*). Cut off left breast to make wielding a bow easier.

blaygird: evil, awful.

Blèssem: The Blessed Fields. Rich farmland lying south of Rionnagan, ruled by the MacThanach clan.

blizzard-owls: giant white owls that inhabit the snowy mountain regions. Sorcha the Murderess had a blizzard-owl as her familiar.

Blue Guards: The Yeomen of the Guard, the Rìgh's own elite company of soldiers. They act as his personal bodyguard, both on the battlefield and in peacetime.

The Book of Shadows: an ancient magical book which contains all the history and lore of the Coven.

Brangaine NicSian: Banprionnsa of Siantan. She can whistle the wind.

Brann the Raven: one of the First Coven of Witches. Known for probing the darker mysteries of magic, and for fascination with machinery and technology.

Bright Soldiers: name for members of the Tìrsoilleirean army.

Bronwen NicCuinn: young daughter of Jaspar Mac-Cuinn, former Rìgh of Eileanan, and Maya the Ensorcellor. Was Banrìgh of Eileanan for one day.

Brun: a cluricaun.

Buba: an elf-owl; Isabeau's familiar.

Candlemas: the end of winter and beginning of spring.

Carraig: Land of the Sea-witches, the northernmost county of Eileanan. Ruled by the MacSeinn clan, descendants of Seinneadair, one of the First Coven of Witches. Clan was driven out by Fairgean, taking refuge in Rionnagan.

Celestines: race of faery creatures, renowned for empathic abilities and knowledge of stars and prophecy.

Circle of Seven: ruling council of dragons, made up of the oldest and wisest female dragons.

Clachan: southernmost land of Eileanan, a province of Rionnagan ruled by the MacCuinn clan.

clàrsach: stringed instrument like a small harp.

claymore: a heavy, two-edged sword, often as tall as a man.

cluricaun: small woodland faery.

coh: Khan'cohban word for the universal life-death energy.

Connor: Lachlan's squire; Johanna the Healer's brother. Was once a beggar-boy in Lucescere and member of the League of the Healing Hand.

corrigan: mountain faery with the power of assuming the look of a boulder. The most powerful can cast other illusions.

craft: applications of the One Power through spells, incantations and magical objects.

Cuinn Lionheart: leader of the First Coven of Witches. Descendants are called MacCuinn.

cunning: applications of the One Power through will and desire.

cunning man: village wise man or warlock.

Cursed Peaks: what the Khan'cohbans call Dragonclaw.

cursehags: wicked faery race, prone to curses and evil spells. Known for their filthy personal habits.

dai-dein: father.

Daillas the Lame: sorcerer and headmaster at the Theurgia.

Day of Betrayal: the day Jaspar the Ensorcelled turned on the witches, exiling or executing them, and burning the Witch Towers.

Deus Vult: war cry of the Bright Soldiers, meaning "God wills."

Didier, Earl of Caerlaverock: the oldest friend of the Rìgh, Lachlan MacCuinn, recently granted the earldom in gratitude for his many years of loyal service. Formerly a jongleur known as Dide the Juggler.

Dillon of the Joyous Sword: Lachlan's bodyguard and a Yeoman of the Guard; formerly a beggar-boy and captain of the League of the Healing Hand.

donbeag: small, brown shrewlike creature that can fly short distances due to the sails of skin between its legs.

Donncan MacCuinn: third son of Parteta the Brave and elder brother of Lachlan the Winged. Was turned into a blackbird by Maya.

Donncan Feargus MacCuinn: eldest son of Iseult and Lachlan. Has wings like a bird and can fly. Was named for Lachlan's two brothers who were transformed into blackbirds by Maya.

doom-eels: sea-dwelling eels with phosphorescent tails that deliver an electric shock if touched.

dragon: large, fire-breathing flying creature with a smooth, scaly skin and claws. Named by the First Coven for a mythical creature from the Other World. They can see both ways along the thread of time.

dragonbane: a rare and deadly poison, distilled from the dragonbane flower and capable of killing a dragon.

Dragonclaw: a tall, sharply pointed mountain in the northwestern range of the Sithiche Mountains. Isabeau and Meghan lived by a small loch at its foot, in a secret valley.

dragon-fear: uncontrollable terror caused by proximity to dragons.

Dragon-Star: comet that comes by every eight years. Also called Red Wanderer.

dram: measure of drink.

Dream-Walkers: name for witches from the Tower of Dreamers in Aslinn. Some can see the future and the past in dreams, others can send dream-messages, or walk the dream-road.

Dughall MacBrann: son of the Prionnsa of Ravenshaw and cousin to the Rìgh.

Duncan Ironfist: the captain of the Yeomen of the Guard.

Dùn Eidean: the capital city of Blèssem.

Dùn Gorm: the city surrounding Rhyssmadill.

Eà: the Great Life Spirit, mother and father of all.

Eileanan: largest island in the archipelago called the Far Islands.

Elemental Powers: the forces of air, earth, fire, water and spirit which together make up the One Power.

Elfrida NicHilde: Banprionnsa of Tìrsoilleir.

elf-owl: the smallest of all the owls, about the size of a sparrow, with a round head and big yellow eyes.

elven cat: small, fierce wildcat that lives in caves and hollow logs.

Enit Silverthroat: a jongleur; grandmother of Dide and Nina.

equinox: when the sun crosses the celestial equator; a time when day and night are of equal length, occurring twice a year.

fain: gladly; willingly.

The Fair Isles: a group of lush tropical islands to the south of Eileanan.

Fairge; Fairgean: faery creatures who need both sea and land to live. The Fairgean were finally cast out of Eileanan in 710 by Aedan Whitelock when they refused to accept his authority. For the next four hundred and twenty years they lived on rafts, rocks jutting up out of the icy seas, and what small islands were still uninhabited. The Fairgean king swore revenge and the winning back of Eileanan's coast.

Fand: slave in the Fairgean king's court.

The Fang: the highest mountain in Eileanan, an extinct volcano called the Skull of the World by the Khan'-cohbans.

Faodhagan the Red: one of the twin sorcerers from the First Coven of Witches. Particularly noted for working in stone; designed and built many of the Witch Towers, as well as the dragons' palace and the Great Stairway.

The Fathomless Caves: the sacred system of caves and grottos that riddle the Isle of the Gods.

Feargus MacCuinn: second son of Parteta the Brave. Was turned into a blackbird by Maya the Ensorcellor.

The Fiery Womb: cave deep within the Isle of the Gods where the Fairgean believe the gods were born.

Finn the Cat: nickname of Fionnghal NicRuraich.

Fionnghal NicRuraich: eldest daughter and heir of Anghus MacRuraich of Rurach; was once a beggar-girl in Lucescere and lieutenant of the League of the Healing Hand. Has strong searching and finding powers.

The Firemaker: hereditary title given to the oldest living female descendant of Faodhagan (see *First Coven*) and a woman of the Khan'cohbans. Able to conjure fire, a power of immense importance on the snow-bound mountain heights, she is considered a gift of the Gods of White to the Khan'cohbans.

First Coven of Witches: thirteen witches who fled persecution in their own land, invoking an ancient spell that folded the fabric of the universe and brought them and all their followers to Eileanan. The eleven great clans of Eileanan are all descended from the First Coven, with the MacCuinn clan being the greatest of the eleven. The thirteen witches were Cuinn Lionheart, his son Owein of the Longbow, Ahearn Horse-laird, Aislinna the Dreamer, Berhtilde the Bright Warrior-maid, Fóghnan the Thistle, Rùraich the Searcher, Seinneadair the Singer, Sian the Storm-rider, Tuathanach the Farmer, Brann the Raven, Faodhagan the Red and his twin sister Sorcha the Bright (now called the Murderess).

Fóghnan the Thistle: one of the First Coven of Witches. Known for her prophetic and clairvoyant abilities, Fóghnan the Thistle was murdered by Balfour MacCuinn, Owein of the Longbow's eldest son.

fraitching: arguing.

frost-giant: huge snow-dwelling faery that lives on the Spine of the World.

geal'teas: long-horned, snow-dwelling creatures which provide Khan'cohbans with food, milk and clothing.

Their very thick white wool is much prized all over Eileanan.

geas: an obligation due to a debt of honor.

General Staff: the group of officers of the Yeomen of the Guard that assists the Rìgh in the formulation and dissemination of his tactics and policies, transmit his orders, and oversee their execution.

gillie: steward to a laird.

Gitâ: a donbeag; Meghan's familiar.

Gladrielle the Blue: the smaller of the two moons, lavender-blue in color.

glen: valley.

Goblin: an elven cat; Finn the Cat's familiar.

The Great Crossing: when Cuinn led the First Coven to Eileanan.

The Great Stairway: the road which climbs Dragonclaw, leading to the palace of the dragons and then down the other side of the mountain to Tìrlethan.

greeting: crying.

Greycloaks: The Rìgh's army, so called because of their camouflaging cloaks.

Gwilym the Ugly: one-legged sorcerer who spent the years of Maya the Ensorcellor's rule in Arran but who escaped the autocratic rule of Margrit NicFóghnan to help Lachlan win the throne. Was rewarded with the position of court sorcerer.

harquebus: a matchlock gun with a long butt, usually fired from a tall stock.

harquebusier: soldier bearing and firing a harquebus.

Haven: large cave where the Pride of the Red Dragon spend their winter.

Heloïse MacFaghan: baby daughter of Khan'gharad Dragon-laird and Ishbel the Winged, twin sister of Alasdair and younger sister of Iseult and Isabeau.

holt: place of refuge.

horse-eel: faery creature of the sea and lochan; tricks people into mounting it and carries them away.

Iain MacFóghnan: Prionnsa of Arran.

Isabeau the Shapechanger: sorceress of the Coven, and twin sister of Iseult. Also called Khan'tinka.

Iseult of the Snows: twin sister of Isabeau, Banrìgh of Eileanan by marriage to Lachlan the Winged. Also called Khan'derin.

Ishbel the Winged: wind witch who can fly. Mother of Iseult and Isabeau.

Isle of Divine Dread: island in the far north of Eileanan; traditional stronghold of the Priestesses of Jor.

Isle of the Gods: island in the far north of Eileanan; traditional home of the Fairgean royalty. It was invaded and occupied by the MacSeinn clan in the early history of the Coven and not regained by the Fairgean until after the Day of Betrayal.

Jaspar MacCuinn: eldest son of Parteta the Brave, former Rìgh of Eileanan, often called Jaspar the Ensorcelled. Was married to Maya the Ensorcellor.

Jay the Fiddler: a minstrel and apprentice to Enit Silverthroat. Was once a beggar-boy in Lucescere and lieutenant of the League of the Healing Hand.

Johanna: head healer. Was once a beggar-girl in Lucescere and a member of the League of the Healing Hand.

jongleur: a traveling minstrel, juggler, conjurer.

Jor: the God of the Shoreless Seas, a major Fairgean deity.

Jorge the Seer: old blind witch who could see the future. Was burnt at the stake by the Bright Soldiers.

Kani: the Mother of the Gods in the Fairgean cosmology, the goddess of fire and earth, volcanoes, earthquakes, phosphorescence and lightning.

The Key: the sacred symbol of the Coven of Witches, a powerful talisman carried by the Keybearer, leader of the Coven.

Khan'cohbans: Children of the Gods of White. A faery race of snow-skimming nomads who live on the Spine of the World. Closely related to the Celestines, but very warlike. Khan'cohbans live in family groups called prides, which range from fifteen to fifty in number.

Khan'fella: twin sister to Khan'lysa, the Firemaker.

Khan'gharad the Dragon-laird: Scarred Warrior of the Fire-Dragon Pride, husband of Ishbel the Winged, father of Isabeau and Iseult.

Khan'katrin: Isabeau and Iseult's second cousin.

Khan'lysa the Firemaker: Isabeau and Iseult's great-grandmother.

Khan'merle: Isabeau and Iseult's aunt, and heir to the Firemaker's position.

Killian the Listener: Tìrsoilleirean prophet who had his ears cut off for heresy.

Lachlan the Winged: youngest son of Parteta the Brave, and Rìgh of Eileanan.

Lammas: first day of autumn; harvest festival.

The League of the Healing Hand: formed by the band of beggar children that fled Lucescere with Jorge the Seer and Tòmas the Healer.

leannan: sweetheart.

Lilanthe of the Forest: a tree-shifter.

Linley MacSeinn: Prionnsa of Carraig.

loch; lochan (pl): lake.

loch-serpent: faery creature that lives in lochan.

Lodestar: the heritage of all the MacCuinns, the Inheritance of Aedan. When they are born their hands are placed upon it and a connection made. Whoever the stone recognizes is the Rìgh or Banrìgh of Eileanan.

Lost Prionnsachan of Eileanan: the three brothers of the Rìgh Jaspar—Feargus, Donncan and Lachlan—who disappeared from their beds one night. Feargus and Donncan were killed but Lachlan escaped and became Rìgh after Jaspar's death.

Lucescere: ancient city built on an island above the Shining Waters. The traditional home of the MacCuinns and the Tower of Two Moons.

Mac: son of.

MacAhern: one of the eleven great clans; descendants of Ahearn the Horse-laird.

MacAislin: one of the eleven great clans; descendants of Aislinna the Dreamer.

MacBrann: one of the eleven great clans; descendants of Brann the Raven.

MacCuinn: one of the eleven great clans; descendants of Cuinn Braveheart.

MacFaghan: one of the eleven great clans; descendants of Faodhagan.

MacFóghnan: one of the eleven great clans; descendants of Fóghnan the Thistle.

MacHamell clan: lairds of Caeryla.

MacHilde: one of the eleven great clans; descended from Berhtilde the Bright Warrior-maid.

MacRuraich: one of the eleven great clans; descendants of Rùraich the Searcher.

MacSeinn: one of the eleven great clans; descendants of Seinneadair the Singer.

MacSian: one of the eleven great clans; descendants of Sian the Storm-rider.

MacThanach: one of the eleven great clans; descendants of Tuathanach the Farmer.

Magnysson the Red: the larger of the two moons, crimson-red in color, commonly thought of as a symbol of war and conflict. Old tales describe him as a thwarted lover, chasing his lost love, Gladrielle, across the sky.

Mairead the Fair: younger daughter of Aedan MacCuinn, first Banrìgh of Eileanan and the second to wield the Lodestar. Meghan's younger sister.

Margrit NicFóghnan: former Banprionnsa of Arran, mother of Iain, the current prionnsa.

Maya the Ensorcellor: former Banrìgh of Eileanan, wife of Jaspar.

Meghan of the Beasts: wood witch and sorceress of eight rings. She can speak to animals. Keybearer of the Coven of Witches before and after banishment of Tabithas.

Melisse NicThanach: Banprionnsa of Blèssem.

Mesmerd; Mesmerdean (pl): faery creature from Arran that hypnotizes its prey with its glance and then kisses away its life.

Midsummer's Eve: summer solstice; time of high magic.

mithuan: a healing liquid designed to quicken the pulse and numb pain.

Morrell the Fire-eater: a jongleur; son of Enit Silver-throat and father of Dide and Nina.

Murkmyre: largest lake in Arran; surrounds the Tower of Mists.

murkwood: a rare herb found only in Arran. Grows on trunks of trees and heals anything.

Neil MacFóghnan: only son and heir of Iain MacFóghnan of Arran and Elfrida NicHilde of Tìrsoilleir. Also called Cuckoo.

Nellwyn the Sea-singer: a Yedda who had been rescued from the Black Tower in Tìrsoilleir.

Nic: daughter of.

Nightglobe of Naia: the most secret and precious relic of the Priestesses of Jor; a globe of immense power.

Nila: Fairgean prince, youngest son of the Fairgean king.

nixie: water-sprite.

nyx: night spirit. Dark and mysterious, with powers of illusion and concealment.

old mother: a Khan'cohban term for wise woman of the pride.

Olwynne NicCuinn: baby daughter of Lachlan MacCuinn and Iseult NicFaghan; twin sister of Owein.

One Power: the life-energy that is contained in all things. Witches draw upon the One Power to perform their acts of magic. The One Power contains all the elemental forces of air, earth, water, fire and spirit, and witches are usually more powerful in one force than others.

Owein MacCuinn: second son of Lachlan MacCuinn and Iseult NicFaghan; twin brother of Olwynne. Has wings like a bird.

Parteta the Brave: former Rìgh of Eileanan; the father of Jaspar, Feargus, Donncan and Lachlan MacCuinn. He was killed by the Fairgean at the Battle of the Strand in 1106, ending the Third Fairgean Wars.

pilliwinkes: instrument of torture similar to thumb-screws.

prides: the social unit of the Khan'cohbans, who live in nomadic family groups. Seven prides in all, called the Pride of the Fire-Dragon, the Pride of the Snow-Lion, the Pride of the Sabre-Leopard, the Pride of the Frost-Giant, the Pride of the Grey Wolf, the Pride of the Fighting Cat, the Pride of the Woolly Bear.

prionnsa; prionnsachan (pl): prince, duke.

Ravenshaw: deeply forested land west of Rionnagan, ruled by the MacBrann clan, descendants of Brann, one of the First Coven of Witches.

Red Wanderer: comet that comes by every eight years. Also called Dragon-Star.

reil: eight-pointed, star-shaped weapon carried by Scarred Warriors.

Rhyllster: the main river in Rionnagan.

Rhyssmadill: the Rìgh's castle by the sea.

rìgh; rìghrean (pl): king.

Rionnagan: together with Clachan and Blèssem, the richest lands in Eileanan. Ruled by MacCuinns, descendants of Cuinn Lionheart, leader of the First Coven of Witches.

Rurach: wild mountainous land, lying between Tìreich and Siantan. Ruled by MacRuraich clan.

Rùraich the Searcher: one of the First Coven of Witches. Known for searching and finding Talent. Located the world of Eileanan on the star-map, allowing Cuinn to set a course for the Great Crossing.

sabre-leopard: savage feline with curved fangs that lives in the remote mountain areas.

sacred woods: ash, hazel, oak, blackthorn, fir, hawthorn, and yew.

Samhain: first day of winter; festival for the souls of the dead. Best time of year to see the future.

satyricorn: a race of fierce horned faeries.

Scarred Warriors: Khan'cohban warriors who are scarred as a mark of achievement. A warrior who receives all seven scars has attained the highest degree of skill.

Scruffy: a nickname for Dillon of the Joyous Sword.

scrying: to perceive through crystal gazing or other focus. Most witches can scry if the object to be perceived is well known to them.

seanalair: general of the army.

sea-stirks: milk-bearing aquatic creatures, looking rather like elephant seals.

Seinneadair the Singer: one of the First Coven of Witches, known for her ability to enchant with song.

sennachie: genealogist of the clan chief's house. It was his duty to keep the clan register, its records, genealogies and family history; to pronounce the addresses of ceremony at clan assemblies; to deliver the chief's inauguration, birthday and funeral orations and to invest the new chief on succession.

Sgàilean Mountains: northwestern range of mountains dividing Siantan and Rurach. Name means "Shadowy Mountains."

sgian dubh: small knife worn in boot.

shadow-hounds: very large black dogs that move and hunt as a single entity. Are highly intelligent and have very sharp senses.

The Shining Waters: the great waterfall that pours over the cliff into Lucescere Loch.

Sian the Storm-rider: one of the First Coven of Witches. A famous weather witch, renowned for whistling up hurricanes.

Siantan: northwest land of Eileanan, famous for its weather witches. Ruled by MacSian clan, descendants of Sian the Storm-rider.

Sithiche Mountains: northernmost mountains of Rionnagan, peaking at Dragonclaw. Name means "Fairy Mountains."

skeelie: a village witch or wise woman.

Skill: a common application of magic, such as lighting a candle or dowsing for water.

Skull of the World: the highest mountain in Eileanan, an extinct volcano which plays an important role in the Khan'cohbans' mythology and culture. Called "the Fang" by Eileanans.

solstice: either of the times when the sun is the farthest distance from the earth.

Sorcha the Red: one of the twin sorcerers from the First Coven of Witches. Also called Sorcha the Murderess, following her bloodthirsty attack on the people of the Towers of Roses and Thorns after the discovery of her brother's love affair with a Khan'cohban woman.

The Spine of the World: a Khan'cohban term for range of mountains that run down the center of Eileanan, in Tìrlethan.

Spinners: goddesses of fate. Include the spinner Sniomhar, the goddess of birth; the weaver Breabadair, goddess of life; and she who cuts the thread, Gearradh, goddess of death.

spring equinox: when the day reaches the same length as the night.

Stargazers: another name for the Celestines.

Stormwing: Lachlan's gyrfalcon.

summer solstice: the time when the sun is farthest north from the equator; Midsummer's Eve.

syne: since.

Talent: witches often combine their strengths in the different forces to one powerful Talent; e.g. the ability to charm animals like Meghan, the ability to fly like Ishbel, the ability to see into the future like Jorge.

Tears of the Gods: a waterfall at the Skull of the World.

Test of Elements: once a witch is fully accepted into the coven at the age of twenty-four, they learn Skills in the element in which they are strongest, i.e., air, earth, fire, water, or spirit. The First Test of any element wins them a ring which is worn on the right hand. If they pass the Third Test in any one element, the witch is called a sorcerer or sorceress, and wears a ring on their left hand. It is very rare for any witch to win a sorceress-ring in more than one element.

Test of Powers: a witch is first tested on his or her eighth birthday, and if any magical powers are detected, he or she becomes an acolyte. On their sixteenth birthday, witches are tested again and, if they pass, permitted to become an apprentice. The Third Tests take place on their twenty-fourth birthday, and if successfully completed, the apprentice is admitted into the Coven of Witches.

Theurgia: a school for acolytes and apprentices.

Tìreich: land of the horse-lairds. Most westerly country of Eileanan, ruled by the MacAhern clan.

Tìrlethan: Land of the Twins; ruled by MacFaghan clan.

Tìrsoilleir: The Bright Land or the Forbidden Land. Northeast land of Eileanan, ruled by the MacHilde clan.

Tòmas the Healer: boy with healing powers, formerly apprentice to Jorge the Seer.

The Towers of the Witches: thirteen towers built as centers of learning and witchcraft in the twelve lands of Eileanan. The Towers are:

Tùr de Aisling in Aslinn (Tower of Dreamers)

Tùr na cheud Ruigsinn in Clachan (Tower of First Landing; Cuinn's Tower)

Tùr de Ceò in Arran (Tower of Mists)

Tùr na Fitheach in Ravenshaw (Tower of Ravens)

Tùr na Gealaich dhà in Rionnagan (Tower of Two Moons)

Tùr na Raoin Beannachadh in Blèssem (Tower of the Blessed Fields)

Tùr na Rùraich in Rurach (Tower of Searchers)

Tùir de Ròsan is Snathad in Tìrlethan (Towers of Roses and Thorns)

Tùr na Sabaidean in Tìrsoilleir (Tower of the Warriors)

Tùr na Seinnadairean Mhuir in Carraig (Tower of the Sea-singers)

Tùr de Stoirmean in Siantan (Tower of Storm)

Tùr na Thigearnean in Tìreich (Tower of the Horse-lairds)

tree-changer: woodland faery. Can shift shape from tree to humanlike creature. A halfbreed is called a *tree-shifter* and can sometimes look almost human.

Triath nan Eileanan Fada: Laird of the Far Isles—one of the Rìgh's many titles.

trictrac: a form of backgammon.

Tuathanach the Farmer: one of the First Coven of Witches.

two moons: Magnysson and Gladrielle.

uile-bheist; uile-bheistean (pl): monster.

The White Gods: nameless, shapeless gods of the Khan'-cohbans, and greatly feared and revered by them.

Whitelock Mountains: a range of mountains in Rionnagan named for the white lock of hair all MacCuinns have.

winter solstice: the time when the sun is at the southernmost point from the equator; Midwinter's Eve.

Yedda: sea-witches.

Yeomen of the Guard: the Rìgh's own personal bodyguard, responsible for his safety on journeys at home or abroad, and on the battlefield. Within the precincts of the palace, they guard the entrances and taste the Rìgh's food. Also known as the Blue Guards.

KATE FORSYTH was born in Sydney, Australia, in 1966, and wanted to be a writer from the time she first learned to read. She has worked as a journalist and magazine editor, and is an internationally published poet. To help support herself while writing full-time, she works as a freelance journalist. She lives in Sydney with her best friend, who also happens to be her husband, and their two children. Ms. Forsyth also has a little black cat and far too many books.